P9-BYK-759

GWYNNE FORSTER

Obsession

ARABESQUE®

OBSESSION

An Arabesque novel published by Kimani Press/June 2008

First published by Kensington Publishing Corp. in 1998

ISBN-13: 978-0-373-83103-6
ISBN-10:   0-373-83103-X

www.kimanipress.com

Printed in U.S.A.

Acknowledgment

To my dear friends, Dr. Melissa M. Freeman,
Carole A. Kennedy and Carol Joy Smith,
whose numerous gestures of love
and friendship I have enjoyed over
the years, and to my husband,
whose love and support sustain me.

My thanks to Joanne Harris for her inspired
editorial guidance of *American Visions,* the
magazine that continuously feeds my hunger
for uplifting information about Black America
and from whose pages I've learned much
about the African-American artists often
mentioned in my books.

Prologue

Selena Sutton strode out of New York's Civil Court, casting a reproachful eye at Judge Lydia Jacobs as she left. She had lost her case, and Jonathan Hilliard III, chief executive officer of Hilliard and Matting, and his partners would not pay for their blatant disregard of the law. For the past six years, she had been a stockbroker with the firm, one of Wall Street's most prestigious. Her climb from entrance level to executive stockbroker by age thirty with entitlement to partnership was the talk of the Street. But when she'd solicited the necessary votes for promotion to partnership from the three senior partners, men who extolled her virtues as a financial expert, none had been willing to have her as an equal. One wanted intimate favors in exchange for his vote. Her regular luncheon pal said he knew she deserved partnership, but was certain that a woman partner would lower the firm's prestige. She'd gone to Patrick McHenry, who had engineered her promotion to executive broker, but he had smiled diffidently and told her he didn't think she'd want to be the only woman or the only person of her color at their high-powered board meetings and that she might feel uncomfortable at some of their corporate client luncheons. After giving him a piece of her mind, she'd stormed out of his office, certain that she was being blackballed. They'd gotten together on it, because they'd known she would approach them. Affronted, she had appealed to the CEO, but he had withheld his support, and she'd filed a civil suit against the firm and named the four as corespondents.

Devastated by the Civil Court's judgment against her and the unfavorable discourse among her peers that her civil suit had generated, she'd instructed her lawyer to take her suit to the Court of Appeals, but he'd warned her that, without a witness to either offense, she didn't stand a chance of winning. When the Court of Appeals proved him right, she knew she had to make a change. She didn't fool herself; few, if any, top-level firms would knowingly take on a female partner who had battled the system.

She packed a suitcase and drove to Prospect Harbor, Maine, on the Atlantic Ocean, hoping to get perspective on her life and plan her future. In six years, she had not taken a vacation; work had been enough, stimulating and recharging her. She had endured around-the-clock stress, had of necessity associated with people for whom she had little or no respect, had sacrificed friendships and, most of all, had denied herself the children and family that she desired so desperately. At times, she had even compromised her integrity, as when she'd agreed with corporate decisions and actions of which she did not approve because that was expected of her. And for what? What had it done for her?

She'd had an enviable work record but for that final promotion, that coveted partnership, her achievements counted for nothing. She sat on the beach at the edge of the ocean, where she heard only the slashing water, and the stars shooting across the horizon were all that she could see. Peace. She'd forgotten what it was like if, indeed, she had ever truly known. But she would find it, and she would find herself again. Thanks to sensible investments, she had acquired wealth, and she had the freedom to seek a stress-free life among genuine people, preferably in a small town. A place where men were gentlemen, tipped their hats, addressed women as ma'am and didn't need a "happy hour" to fortify themselves with liquor before going home to their wives.

Selena had gotten her undergraduate degree in psychology and owed much of her success as a stockbroker to her understanding of people. That degree qualified her for a job as a counselor. With the help of an agent, she found one in Waverly, Texas, the kind of small town in which she thought she'd like to live. She took a suite of rooms in the Waverly Inn, began a new career as a psychological counselor and relegated New York City to her past.

Chapter 1

Selena pushed herself up in bed and tried to make sense of the scene before her. Gradually, she brought into focus the man who sat a few paces from her hospital bed, and began to fit together the scenes she'd glimpsed over the past weeks as she'd journeyed in and out of consciousness. Each time she'd become aware of herself, he'd been there.

Sunlight streamed in the uncurtained window, and she closed her eyes for a moment, getting her bearings, so that she could deal with him.

"Why are you here? Did you come to protect your family name?" she asked him.

Magnus Cooper tipped back his chair, spread his long legs and stuck his hands in his pants pockets. "I'm here because you need me," he told her. She wasn't so sick that she'd let herself be fooled by another Cooper, even if the population of Waverly, Texas, thought this one propelled himself with wings.

She could see in his bearing that he was accustomed to

wielding authority; even his deep, soothing voice carried a command, though she didn't detect in him any arrogance or self-satisfaction. Still, she didn't know why he'd come, so she'd best be on her guard. Strange pinions of excitement shot through her as his gaze captured hers.

"I came here to help you," he repeated, smiling and leaning toward her as though to appear less threatening.

"You want me to believe you're *that* different from your brother?"

His whole visage darkened in an expression of pain. "I love my brother, Selena, I won't deny that. He is my flesh and blood. But I have never countenanced his wrongdoings, and I won't defend him when he's wrong. I know what he is, and there are times when I wonder that we have the same genes. He's without morals where women are concerned, but I don't suppose I'll ever give up hope that he'll change. I know what he's capable of. That's why I'm here. How do you feel?"

She didn't know whether to believe him, whether she could trust him. "Please go away and leave me alone." She tapped the bell that rested on the table beside her bed.

"I can't leave you alone," he said, his tone low and soothing. "You need me."

Selena tugged the rough sheet up close to her neck, hating the feel of its irritating texture against her skin. "How do you know what I need?" And what did he know about it? She wouldn't be lulled into a trap, especially not one shrouded in what seemed to be trustworthy manliness.

A nurse rushed through the door and saved Magnus a reply to Selena's question. "We have to check you out today, Miss Sutton. Hospital policy, you know. After six weeks here, we recommend a convalescent home. I can give you the name of one in San Antonio, since we don't have one here in Waverly."

"Six weeks? I've been here six weeks?" She sniffed and covered her nose against the odor of alcohol and disinfectant. She'd made an awful mistake uprooting her life and moving south to Waverly in search of a stress-free existence and the company of genteel men; so far, not so good. And what she wanted most, a child of her own before she got to be thirty-five, now seemed like a pipe dream, because she hadn't been out with one eligible man in the seven months she'd lived in Waverly. She glanced at the handsome one who sat inches from her bed. A smooth brown face with wonderful hazel eyes and, if ever she'd seen an invitation to a wild romp and unrestrained hedonism, he was it. Well, one man didn't make it Sadie Hawkins Day in Waverly, Texas.

The nurse favored her with a professional smile. "Six weeks, dear. You don't get over pneumonia and fevers overnight, and especially if you've got three broken ribs. Mr. Cooper here has been to see you every day of those six weeks. Don't find men like him often. Mr. Cooper's checking you out this morning. You take good care and see your doctor in three weeks for your checkup," the nurse admonished as she swished out of the room.

"He's doing… *What is this?*"

"I'd better get back to my station. Mr. Cooper will tell you all you want to know," the nurse said from the door. Selena sensed that the two were in cahoots, but didn't air her thoughts. The effort required to sit up in bed had exhausted her, and she lay down and turned her back to Magnus Cooper.

"Selena, listen to me. I'm not your enemy. You can't go back to your rooms at the Waverly Inn, because they've been rented. Besides, you're not strong enough to take care of yourself. And even if you were, you'd be vulnerable to whatever vengeful trick Prince decided to pull."

Anger sufficed for strength, and Selena flipped over and sat up. "What the devil has *he* got to be vengeful about? I didn't do anything to him. It was the other way around. How can you suggest…"

"If what you've accused him of occurred, and I have no reason to disbelieve you, he doesn't deserve defense, and he isn't getting that. Please hear me out."

His quiet, soothing way of speaking comforted her and

invited her trust. "Selena, I know my brother, and I am aware that, where women are concerned, he can be mean, ruthless and abusive. Will you tell me what happened?"

After her bitter experience with his brother, she wasn't going to be taken in by Magnus Cooper's smoothly persuasive manners.

"Selena," he insisted, "you're going to have to trust someone, and you're safer trusting me, because I haven't judged you. What happened? I know what the gossips say, but I need to hear it from you."

Selena gazed at him, judging him as best she could. A smile flickered at the side of his mouth as he waited for her answer, and she knew he not only understood her hesitance, but appreciated it. She would trust him a little. But not blindly and not completely.

"Your brother gave me an ultimatum," she began, gauging his reaction. "I quit my six-figure-a-year job as a Wall Street broker because I refused to be victimized. A full partnership in a prestigious firm, a hot stock portfolio and a fat salary were not worth my integrity.

"After I sued and lost my case in the appeals court, I moved down here in the hopes of living among kinder and friendlier people. Not your brother. He offered me a ride home during a heavy downpour. Four short blocks. But instead of taking me home, he drove up on Whisper Hill, parked and began pawing over me. He swore that if I hadn't wanted his attention, I wouldn't have gotten in the car. The fact is, I'd always smiled and ignored his passes, and he couldn't have expected me to accept his advances. Alone on that deserted hill, he had the advantage. I resisted him until he became angry, tore my dress and attempted to force me. I realized that he was out of control and that, if I didn't escape, he'd have his way. I told him I'd sue him in court if he touched me again.

"Let's see. His exact words were, 'Give it up or get out.' I'd never been on Whisper Hill, didn't know it existed. But pitch-dark, a torrential rainstorm and that rocky, snake-infested ridge looked better to me than he did, so I got out. But I tripped over a rock bed and fell. My side hurt so badly that I had to crawl part of the way. By the time I got to the highway, I'd lost a shoe, my clothes were torn and soaked by that rain and I was freezing. I flagged the first car that passed. I think it was Cora Moore, though I sure hope it wasn't. That's about as much as I remember."

A muscle jumped at the side of Magnus's jaw. "It was Cora, all right. Of course, her version doesn't match yours."

It hurt, but she hid it. "I wouldn't expect it to."

He leaned forward. "Selena, will you tell me why you got in that car with Prince? I have never associated you with him, and learning you'd been with him shocked me. Had you been seeing him?"

"No, indeed. He's asked me numerous times to go out with him, but Prince is not the type of man whose company I'd choose. That evening, a group of us were standing in front of the Center after work waiting for the rain to slacken. Prince drove by and offered Eloise and me a ride home. He let her out first, but he didn't take me home to the inn as he'd promised."

Magnus stood and rubbed the back of his neck, as though frustrated. "Typical. He's devious. You can't go back to the inn, because they've rented your rooms. People around here will desert you in a hurry, if they think they'll lose a dollar. You're better off at my ranch."

"What? So I'll be easy pickings for your brother?" She glared at him. "And maybe you, too?"

Magnus raised himself to his full six feet, three inches, walked over to her bed and lifted her hand. "My home is the one place in or near Waverly where I know you'll be safe from Prince. You rejected him. He'll stay after you 'til he gets you—one way or another. He left town the morning after he abused you, but he'll come back here, as he always does after the 'tumult and the shouting' die. Prince is not used to having women ignore him or turn him down, and you can bet his ego needs a shot of retribution. But this time, I'm not going to let him hide behind our mother's social status to escape punishment."

She folded her arms across her chest, but she missed the feeling of safety and the warmth that had begun flowing through her the second he grasped her hand. "I'm not going to jump out of the frying pan into the fire."

"I'm trying to help, Selena." A muscle twitched involuntarily beneath his right eye. "If you're afraid to be around me, I'll lock your room door and give you both keys."

"Afraid? I wasn't scared when I stepped out of Prince's car on that hill full of snakes and cacti in a drenching rain. Why should I…" She paused when she saw him flinch as though in pain.

"Don't," he said. "I'll never forgive him for that."

"*You* won't forgive him. He hasn't heard the last from me. Believe it."

"Come home with me, Selena. The ranch is sprawling, and my home is spacious. You may have the guest apartment, and you won't have to see me, if you'd prefer not to. My housekeeper is there, and she'd love to have company. Selena, I know you're capable of taking care of yourself, but you don't know Prince. Come with me and stay until you've fully recovered. I give you my word you'll be safe."

If she had to bet, she'd wager that he was a man of honor. Still, nobody was quite as they seemed. "What choice do I have?"

He slanted his head to the side and narrowed one eye. "Several, I'd say—all of them unacceptable."

She couldn't help smiling. He didn't attempt to paint it good or bad, but told it as he saw it. "All right. I'll go with you." She knew she wasn't taking a chance. Magnus Cooper had an enviable reputation and was much admired as a community leader—everything that his younger brother was not.

Selena looked up at the massive replica of a longhorn steer's head that guarded the gate to Cooper Ranch. White wooden fences that reached beyond her field of vision corralled spotted red longhorns and, at the end of the long roadway, there loomed before her a sprawling white Georgian-type mansion, its windows shuttered in dark green. Great pecan trees lined the roadway and shaded the house, and several willows swayed in what seemed to be a garden. The abode of a rich man. The silent invitation of the slowly opening front door unsettled her momentarily, and she let herself lean on Magnus's strong arm.

"I thought y'all would never get here. Come on in." Magnus hadn't mentioned his mother, and Selena wondered if the short and slender dark woman who rushed to her with a broad smile and open arms could be her. Somehow, she sensed that this stranger loved Magnus, but was not the woman who had given him birth. At five feet, eight inches tall, Selena could barely return the hug, because bending to the petite woman's level proved uncomfortable.

"Selena, this is Tessie Jenkins, my housekeeper and dearest friend."

"Magnus didn't tell me that I could expect such a warm greeting, Tessie. I'm happy to meet you." And indeed she was, for the friendly, motherly woman's manner eased her concerns about staying in Magnus's home.

"Me, too. Now, maybe I'll get to see Magnus once in a while. Between work and that hospital, I've barely glimpsed him for weeks."

Inside, Selena looked up at the staircase and groaned, as Magnus steered her toward it.

"I'm not sure I can take those stairs," she said and immediately felt herself heaved up into Magnus's arms.

"Look, I didn't mean to… I wasn't asking you to…" What had come over her? She didn't sputter, but neither had she been in this man's strong and strangely comforting arms.

"'Course you were," he said, surprising her with the teasing. "And I'm settling you upstairs, so I can carry you up there. Gives me a chance to get you in my arms."

"What?" She closed her eyes and looked away. It had to be the shock of feeling his arms around her that had caused her to react that way. They were only hands that held her, she reminded herself, but they made her want to hold on to him. Stupid. What was the matter with her?

"Magnus, don't tease. You'll make her uneasy," Tessie scolded. "You'll be comfortable here, Miss Selena, and safe, too."

Selena smiled at the woman, glad for her presence. "Call me Selena, Tessie."

She sensed a special relationship between Tessie and Magnus, and, after Magnus left them, the housekeeper confirmed it.

"You are more to Magnus than his housekeeper, aren't you?" she asked Tessie.

"Yes. I went to work for his family when his mother was carrying him. When he came back home here and built this house, I left Miss Anna—that's his mother—and joined him. Magnus is like a son to me. His father was a wonderful human being, and Magnus is like him—dependable, kind and gentle, but you can't bend him. Magnus is a strong man."

"And Prince? Is he also like a son to you?" She watched Tessie brace her sides with the backs of her hands and stand akimbo and wondered if she'd raised the wrong topic.

"Prince?" Tessie asked. "Only a mother could love Prince, and she don't love him in the right way. Catering to your child's every single whim ain't love, it's indulgence. No, indeed. Can I bring you some iced tea or something?" End of conversation. Selena had irritated a bruise. Tessie Jenkins was not enamored of Prince.

Magnus hooked the strap under Cougar's belly, patted his haunch and mounted the big bay stallion's back. He needed fresh air and to think. Selena Sutton was in his home and under his care. She'd been in his arms, too, and he'd sensed that she felt comfortable there, but the happiness he should have felt eluded him. Of all the women Prince could have chosen to molest, why had his brother picked the woman of his heart? Selena didn't know how he felt, and she never would. The first time he saw her, he'd reacted as though his blood had suddenly begun flowing backward. He'd wondered if the moon, stars and every planet had landed on him. Never had he experienced a trauma of such power and intensity. Tall with smooth, dark skin, large long-lashed eyes and a made-for-loving pouting mouth, she'd stopped him dead in his tracks. A regal beauty. She had his mother's cool, delicate, almost flawless good looks, walked with head high and a kind of careless disdain for all around her. In those first minutes, he had burned for her. But he'd had thirty-seven years in which to learn that such beauty didn't mean gentleness, tenderness and caring, that its possessor could be mean, unfair and miserly with affection. He smiled at the memory of her beguiling grin when she looked up and saw him. She'd gotten out of a taxi just as he drove up to the inn....

"Help you with those bags, ma'am?" She'd looked up at him, and a smile eclipsed her face—and changed his life.

"Would you? Where I come from, I'd be afraid to let a stranger help me with my luggage."

He'd never seen such a vibrant smile, such dark, flashing eyes. "And where's that, ma'am?" he asked, putting a suitcase under each arm and two others in his hands.

"New York. I can see already that it's different down here, and that I'm going to like it."

He couldn't take his eyes from her. "Staying long?" He hadn't known what he wanted her answer to be, because he wasn't sure he enjoyed being poleaxed by a strange female. That breathtaking smile again. "I'm moving here. My name's Selena Sutton."

His heart kicked into a trot, and he had an unfamiliar sensation, like flying through the air. Her gaze, light and friendly, gave him a sense of being suspended in time, and he couldn't help being glad that he carried those suitcases; if he'd touched her to shake hands, he'd have hugged her.

"I'm Magnus Cooper. We'll no doubt be seeing more of each other."

Her smile dazzled him. "I hope so." He put her bags down beside the registration desk and, though he prayed she wouldn't, she held out her hand.

"Thank you so much, Mr. Cooper. I can't imagine how I would have managed alone."

He knocked his Stetson to the back of his head with his thumb and forefinger, decided to take it off and accepted her handshake only to have his entire arm tingle from the touch of her small but surprisingly strong hand. He held it for a second, put his hat on, tipped it and got out of there while he still had his wits....

Little had changed in that regard, he admitted, as he brought his mind back to the present. In the ensuing months, he'd been tempted to go after her in spite of his wariness, but he'd discovered that she could follow an act of compassion with one of icy haughtiness. He remembered seeing her leave her date to help a woman who struggled with two children in a blinding rain, soaking herself and infuriating her date. The man reprimanded her and, without a word, she hailed a taxi and left him standing there. Seeing the caring side of her had increased his vulnerability to her, but his glimpses of her in Waverly walking head up, as though she communed only with God, would remind him again of his mother, gliding through life oblivious to other beings.

Like Selena, his mother always dressed impeccably. If his father attempted to caress her, she would push him away claiming that he crushed her dress. And his father's kisses were refused, because they'd ruin her lipstick. Her hair was not to be touched, lest a strand stray from its lacquered place. The memory of it sickened him. He didn't want that kind of woman. He didn't believe his mother was evil, but he'd never understood her values.

He hadn't been willing to take a chance with Selena, and he
had never approached her, because he didn't want to learn a
second time the lesson his mother's coldness had taught him.
He'd go to any lengths to protect Selena, but he didn't want to
be involved. He gave Cougar his head and, for a few minutes,
they ran with the wind.

After supper, he went to the kitchen to give his housekeeper a chance to speak her piece about Selena. "Tess, how
is Selena?"

Tessie poured out the gossip. "The snobbery and hypocrisy
of the people in this town would wear on a saint. Lettie claims
Selena is her best friend, but she just called and told Selena she
couldn't be her maid of honor considering the talk about her and
Prince up there on Whisper Hill. She said everybody knows
what kind of girls go with Prince. Something about what people
are saying. And another thing. Old man Lightner's got no
business being chairman of the Community Center's board.
Claims Selena's immoral and wants to fire her from her job as
counselor at the Center. A bunch of phonies. I wonder how the
babies get here, since nobody approves of sex."

He mounted the stairs two steps at a time. "Selena, I want to
speak with you." When she didn't answer, he called out,
"Selena, are you all right?"

"I'd rather not have a guest, Magnus."

"I'm not company, and we can speak through the door.
Gossip is what keeps this town going. Tomorrow or the day
after, the gossipers will find another victim. Ignore it." The
door opened, and he sucked in his breath at the sight of her,
wan and lovely in a bright red jumpsuit. "Just concentrate on
regaining your strength, and don't forget, you may stay here
as long as you want to."

"I appreciate your generosity, Magnus, but I won't accept
charity from you."

He hadn't expected that she'd assert herself so soon. "I'm not
offering charity."

"I know. You'd invite any old stranger to loll around in this palatial suite? I don't think so, and if I stay here, I pay."

So she had a sharp tongue. He caught himself rubbing his right thumb and forefinger together and steadied his mind. No point in letting her vex him. "I don't sublet parts of my home, Selena."

"Then I'm moving out right now."

How could she possibly believe he'd take her money? He scrutinized her carefully and, from her stance, figured he might as well give in right then and save time. He ran his fingers over his hair and resisted pacing. "All right, if you want it that way. Twelve hundred a month." That ought to straighten her out. "Can you handle it?" He couldn't believe it; she didn't even blink.

"I can handle it."

"Forget it. I only meant to challenge you. I won't accept your money."

Her pursed lips and narrowed right eye were enough of an answer, but she told him anyway. "You will, and you'll cash the check. Or I move."

He paced the hallway, walked back and asked her, "Where will you go?" He paused in front of her.

"Waverly, Texas, is not the end of the world."

He stuck his hands in the back pockets of his jeans where they'd be less likely to yield to the temptation of shaking her, and spoke in an authoritative manner that he hoped would convince her.

"You can't maneuver three city blocks, Selena. We'll talk about this some other time."

"You give me your word, or I'm leaving. Now."

So much for that effort. "You can pay."

"And you'll cash the checks." When he didn't reply, her chin poked out and her right eye narrowed.

"Selena, please try not to be difficult." What had he said now? Her hands went to her hips; she sucked her teeth; she looked up to heaven.

"Don't be dense, Magnus. I can afford to pay you, and I will. I'll…say good night, now." Both her tone and her facial expression amounted to a royal dismissal. He couldn't help laughing.

"What's funny?"

"I'm trying to remember whether anybody ever looked down their nose at me. I don't think so." He deliberately stopped smiling. "It's interesting, Selena, but do your best to avoid it with me."

"You hadn't impressed me as a dictator."

If she wanted to change the subject, all right with him, so long as she remembered what he'd said. "Probably because I'm not one. But I *am* an egalitarian, thanks to the lesson I learned from my mother's class-conscious snobbery. So, if you feel superior, stretch yourself a little and don't show it." Her mouth formed a large round *O,* but she didn't give him the snappy retort he'd expected.

Magnus walked back down the stairs, giving each step its due, went into the den and, for the first time in a long while, he needed his father's advice and comfort. What would that wise, gentle man, whose strength had been his childhood cushion, have said about his feelings for Selena and the way in which he had inveigled her into living in this home? He answered the hall phone and, preoccupied with his own feelings, gave no thought to the silence on the other end until a noise like the rattling of papers startled him.

"Hello," he repeated again and again. "Hello." He replaced the receiver in its cradle and dropped his body into the nearest chair. Prince. Anonymous phone calls were some of his brother's favorite nuisance games. If a man could act so callously with his own brother, no sane person would expect him to be more charitable with a relative stranger. He knew he'd have his hands full looking after Selena.

Magnus operated his real estate business out of his Houston office, and he needed to spend more time there. But Selena's vulnerability to Prince gave him no choice but to remain close to the ranch and work out of his home office. He phoned his Houston office.

"Oh, Magnus, we're so disappointed. You've been scarce as hen's teeth around here lately, and we're feeling rudderless. Want our captain back, you know."

"Thanks, Madeline," he said, settling into his chair. "I expect you're going to see less of me for at least a couple of weeks."

"Any problem or anything I can help you with? We're here for you, you know." His only complaints about his secretary were her habits of adding "you know" on the end of her sentences and referring to herself as "we." Madeline was his right hand, and he'd bet his ranch on her loyalty. He gave her instructions, including orders for building materials.

"Fax those contracts for my signature. I'll call you every morning at ten, so try to be at your desk then."

"Of course, Magnus. We're here for you day and night." He ignored Madeline's idiosyncratic ways. She'd been with him nearly a decade, and he couldn't remember finding fault with her work. Still, he sometimes wished she'd leave her halo at home.

Perplexed and uncomfortable about her deepening attachment to Magnus, Selena longed to talk with her godmother, Irene Perkins, the woman who had cared for her since she'd been orphaned at the age of seven, sacrificing her youth for a child she hadn't borne.

"You always call when I'm thinking about you. They told me at the inn that you'd moved, something about you going to live with a man. I told them they were lying and hung up."

Selena had to laugh. Irene's bluntness was what her detractors needed. Selena gave her an edited report.

"Honey, you ignore those hypocrites. Those kind of people sprout up like weeds all over the country, so forget about them and think about that man. He sounds wonderful to me."

"There's nothing between us, Reenie. He's just making up for what his brother did."

"Do tell. He could've done that with money—ever hear of bodyguards? Uh-uh. There's more to him than he's showing."

Selena didn't ask herself why hearing those words from her godmother made her feel so good. "How's Roe?" She had a deep affection for Roosevelt Perkins. He had waited for years for Irene, who had refused to marry him until Selena got her first job and was able to support herself.

"Roe's fair. Getting out of the house at six o'clock in the morning this winter didn't do his arthritis much good, and he feels it. You take care, and pay attention to that man," she added, as they hung up.

For the next several hours, Magnus alternately paced the floor in the den, gazed unseeing out its twelve-foot windows and played darts, missing the bull's eye every time. The realization bore heavily on him that, unless Prince was dead, he would come back to finish what he'd started. He'd never understood his brother's seemingly psychotic need to have every woman desire him and, at his bidding, surrender to him. It bordered on being a dangerous illness. He headed for the second floor…and Selena. Tessie caught him and tugged at his arm.

"I'd leave her alone right now, if I were you," she said. "I transferred another call to her from old man Lightner. Imagine him saying she wasn't a moral person. No matter how awful a man acts, in his mind, it's the woman who's responsible. How do you like that?" Her hands braced her hips. "Why, that old coot's been tailing after me for the last twenty years. And him a married man. He's out to ruin Selena."

Magnus clutched Tessie's shoulders, his patience shot and his temper rearing for release. "Tell me I didn't hear you right, or I'll pull the rug out from under that man. I'll…" Her compassionate expression told him that his face mirrored his feelings.

"You care for that girl, don't you? Yes, you do, but… Well, I declare. You can't run her life like you run your business just 'cause you want her. You try that, and she'll leave here in a minute. Besides, if you kick Deacon Lightner off the Center's board, he'll die. It's his life."

He let go of a long, deep breath. "Why do you and Selena think I can twiddle my thumbs while the local saints persecute her? Forget it. I won't stand for it."

"Magnus, your heart ain't never been involved since your daddy passed on, but you'd better look out now. This woman is different."

If he knew anything, he knew that. "Tell me about it. She stands out like a rose in a field of bluebonnets."

"And if you get overprotective, she'll be gone faster than a jackrabbit in hunting season. I ain't saying no more."

Magnus grabbed the phone after its first ring. "Cooper." His face must have registered astonishment, for he felt Tessie's grip on his arm, sensed her anxiety and saw her deeply furrowed forehead. He covered the mouthpiece. "It's all right, Tess."

He wanted to rip the telephone cord from the wall. "Listen to me, Lightner. You're supposed to be a leader in this town, but you're peddling gossip. Since when did a staunch Christian like you judge a person on the basis of gossip and persecute her? You'd better watch your step." He hung up.

"If I can't yell in this house," Tessie needled, "you can't slam down the phone."

"Thanks for reminding me. If Lightner calls Selena again, let me know," he threw over his shoulder as he hastened out the side door, away from people and phones, to deal with his dilemma.

Chapter 2

The knock on her door sent little tremors shooting through Selena. She hoped Magnus wouldn't support Lightner. She opened the door, looked up at him and sighed in anticipation of the worst.

"Don't you need some fresh air?" Magnus asked her. "How about a ride around the ranch with me?"

Her heartbeat slowed down to normal, then kicked into a fast trot. His smile and a quick flick of his brow told her he knew he'd put her off balance. She'd noticed that he rationed his smiles, and she enjoyed the tilt of his bottom lip as its corners curved. Resist this man and his smile, she cautioned herself.

"I think I should leave here," she said, though honesty forced her to acknowledge the untruth of it. "I appreciate your help, Magnus," she went on, "but I have to put an end to this gossip."

The steady gaze of those strange, hazel eyes unnerved her, but his words had a calming effect. "I won't try to hold you if you want to leave, but where will you go?"

Where indeed? "Don't worry. I can stay with Eloise."

"In a one-room apartment?"

"How do you know how big her apartment is?" she asked him and could have bitten her tongue.

"It's my building. I don't know how you've been spending your days, but surely you'd like a ride around the ranch. Come on. Take a ride with me, or do you ride?"

She'd noticed before that when he wanted to persuade her to do something, his voice became soft, mellifluous. And it worked, too. Furthermore, he knew it. "I love to ride. I used to spend my Saturday mornings cantering in Central Park with members of my riding club." It pleased her to tell him about it, for she wanted him to know she hadn't left New York as a failed person, but one who'd had a life that many envied, that she'd left to find a quieter, more fulfilling and peaceful existence.

"Then come ride with me," he drawled in his deep, lilting tones. "Riding club, huh?" He winked, and something hot flitted through her. This won't do, she told herself. She'd have to get used to his way of speaking, too. Sexy. Beguiling. And in his face a childlike hope that she'd go with him.

"I know you don't have much energy," he said, "so we won't go far. I want to show you around my place."

"I'm not sure I can sit on a horse."

His slow grin would have enticed a saint. "I've trained my horses to treat women as I do, firm but gentle. If you tell him to stop, he stops. If you'd like a faster ride, just tighten your legs on him. If you want to gallop, lean forward and caress his neck. If you want to go slow and easy, just relax, and give him a gentle pat on his haunches and leave it to him. Not to worry." His hazel eyes seemed to heat up as he said it, and his gaze weakened her knees, but he'd never know it.

"I've been riding since I was eleven, and I know that any horse worth his hay would throw me a mile if I tried that."

"You really thought I was talking about a horse? I thought you'd stretch your imagination." He grinned at her. "You need training." She nearly lost her breath. Get away from here, her mind told her.

"When do the classes start?"

He gazed at her as though transfixed. Her body tingled, and shivers raced through her when his face lost its wicked air. She'd never seen him more serious.

"Now we're getting somewhere," he said, dampening his lips. "Get dressed, and hurry down. I'll take care of you." She raised an eyebrow, but she would use a different opportunity to tell him how capable she was of taking care of herself.

Magnus helped her onto a gray quarter horse, checked her saddle and mounted Cougar. He headed them toward the lake, their horses abreast.

"I have to stick close to you," he explained. "Minerva is gentle, but she's still a horse, and you haven't fully recovered your strength. I want to be able to grab those reins if I have to."

She looked over at him. "You can do something with the reins to my horse that I can't do?" Maybe it was his unruffled, laid-back stance that begged her to challenge him; she didn't know and hadn't tried to figure it out.

"Plenty. Just hope we don't have to find out," he drawled.

His sensuous voice washed over her, and the thought occurred to her that Magnus would be a wonderful lover. If you wanted a man's undivided attention, you could get it from Magnus Cooper. She patted her hair and wished she'd controlled the urge to do so, but his gaze traveled over her slowly, as though memorizing every inch of her, discombobulating her. When he looked at you, you'd been seen.

Hoping to distract him, she said, "I wouldn't have thought that riding in the moonlight could be so pleasant. Is this something you do regularly?"

"Selena, horseback riding with you on this flawless spring night is more than a pleasant experience. Doing the same thing alone would be a bummer. Want to get down and walk a bit?"

She didn't, but it wasn't a night for logic. "All right, if you like." His strong fingers gripped her waist as he lifted her from the big mare, and entwined her fingers with his own as they strolled over to the lake and looked down at their reflection in the water. Magnus Cooper could grow on a woman.

"How'd you get into ranching?" she asked. "It's not common among African-Americans, is it?"

He shrugged and looked into the distance. "Only a small percentage of Texans, black or white, own a ranch, but an awful lot of us are in the ranching business. African-Americans worked as cowboys during slavery. After Emancipation, the number increased, and quite a few bought land and began ranching. Around 1850 and for sometime thereafter, a man named Aaron Ashford—a black man—owned the biggest herd of cattle in what became Jefferson and Orange Counties. And the Taylor-Stevens Ranch over in Houston dates to 1875. Oh, yes. We have around thirty African-American-owned ranches in a hundred-mile radius of Houston. Tell you what—when you're up to it, we can run over to San Antonio and visit the Carver Community Cultural Center and see what they've got on black ranchers."

"I had no idea." If she planned to make her home in Texas, she'd better learn about it. "How'd you start ranching?"

"I always wanted a ranch, and I like working outside, though I don't often get a chance. I got a bachelor's degree in animal husbandry at Texas A&M, but ranching is a business, so I took a master's in business administration.

"My grandfather willed me a small plot that had been Cooper land for at least a century. It's not far from the house. I liked the site and, as soon as I got out of school and got a job, I began buying up adjacent property. It wasn't expensive in the beginning—a few run-down shacks, thistles and weeds on untended land. But as I developed it, the price climbed. I bought in spite of that and kept adding until I got the size holding I wanted. By then, I was land rich and cash poor, so I couldn't buy livestock or build a house. I sold a plot near Whisper Hill and went into the building business one house at a time. Within two years, I was able to begin ranching, and I've raised longhorn breeding cattle for the last five. My building business mushroomed after I built houses for two famous people."

"But you're not an architect. How do you manage it?"

"Good question. I fund the package and hire an architect and engineer to do the job, the way a producer decides to make a movie and engages a cast and a director. After I hired an engineer named Wade Malloy, I began building in developing countries. My presence wasn't necessary, because he's honest to a fault and a genius with building plans. We've since become partners."

She told herself to move when she realized she leaned on him, but he stilled her when she would have stepped away from him, and she gave in to her need for a man's comfort and relaxed against him. His breathing quickened, just as hers did and, because she didn't want to mislead him, she squeezed his arm and moved away. He didn't protest.

"Could we go back now?" Her heartbeat accelerated, and she had to steel herself against the fear. This was the test, because she still didn't have the strength to mount that horse without his help; at his mercy, she would know him. She hadn't thought of danger when she left the house with him, because Magnus inspired confidence. If he had none of Prince's nastiness, as he claimed, she'd soon find out.

"Of course. I shouldn't have kept you so long," he said and whistled for the horses, "but I began reliving those difficult days when I was getting started, and talking with you was balm for those last old wounds."

She knew the night obscured from him her inquiring look. "Wounds? Why do you have wounds?"

"My father had passed on, and my mother didn't show any interest in the ranch. Whenever I got money in the clear, Prince would manage to get into trouble, and I'd have to bail him out.

When he wasn't in trouble, he was asking for a loan, which he never repaid. And he drove wedge after wedge between us. Wounds? I only have one brother, Selena." He settled her on the horse, checked that her feet were secure in the stirrups, handed her the reins and asked if she was comfortable. The fullness in her chest trapped her words, and she could only nod and try to smile. He mounted the stallion and hummed softly while the horses took them home.

"Let's sit in here for a bit," he suggested, as he led her into the den. "I'll put some logs on the fire and make us some coffee. Chilly?" She inclined her head. "Good." He stoked the fire and added a few logs. "I'll be right back."

I'm not going to fall for him, she told herself, admitting that he was a decent, honorable man, that his behavior bore out the rumors of his kindness. He was nice tonight, she told herself, but blood was thicker than water, and if Prince came back, she didn't want to test that theory. He returned with a tray bearing their coffee and two slices of Tessie's chocolate cake, placed it on the silver-inlaid, brass coffee table and sat beside her on the sofa.

His gaze roamed over her. Slowly. A laser penetrating her being. The ends of her nerves burned. "Selena, I have to ask you why you went with Prince. You must have heard about him. He's the talk of Waverly."

She explained, for the last time, she hoped, that she wasn't "with" Prince, but had accepted his offer of a ride home in the midst of a downpour.

"I know. But you said he'd asked you frequently for dates, so you knew he had an interest in you."

She didn't like being questioned in that manner. "What are you after? Nothing justifies what he did. Even if I had been seeing him on a steady basis for years, he'd have been out of line. I didn't want him, and I told him so."

"Then you're one of the few women around who hasn't fallen for Prince's pretty face."

"Where I come from, good-looking men are ten cents a dozen. It takes more than a face to turn my head."

He was persistent, she learned. "You're saying he's never interested you? That you aren't and never have been attracted to him?"

She suppressed the anger. "I might have been, if he hadn't always acted so crudely."

"So you admit he attracts you." She heard the disappointment and resignation that tinged his words.

"I didn't say that. I am not attracted to crude men."

"Then why did you get in his car? It always stops raining sooner or later."

"How many times do I have to tell you?" She bristled, setting her cup aside. "It was a four-block ride. Half a dozen people saw Eloise and me get in. I didn't expect him to pull a trick like taking me up on that hill and demanding sex."

He raised his hand, palm out, as though asking for silence. "All right. All right. I don't want to hear about that again."

"If I ever see him, you will definitely hear about *that*."

"That may be months from now. He usually leaves town after he's run afoul of the law, and comes back when the furor subsides. I'll be waiting for him."

"So will I," she promised.

He looked steadily at her and spoke in his slow drawl, seeming to measure his words. "Be certain of your motive. If you're susceptible to him, stay out of his way."

She sucked her teeth in disgust. "If his head is as hard as yours, I'll be smart to avoid him. Thanks for the ride, Magnus. And, in spite of your giving me the third degree, I enjoyed sitting here and talking with you. I'd better turn in now, so please excuse me." She grasped the intricately carved wrought-iron banister at the bottom of the stairs and started up the steps.

"Let me give you a hand," he said.

"Thanks, but I'm fine. I don't need any help." While he watched from below, she took a few steps up and had to stop.

His strong hand supported her waist. "You do need me, Selena. You don't know how much."

"What I need is peace of mind. What I'm in is turmoil. I'm tired of it and, if I stay here with you, it will only get worse."

His words reached her as a plea. "Selena, can't you trust me? If you leave the ranch, you will regret it. Prince may be in Waverly right now, waiting to surprise you. Please don't leave here."

She wondered why he cared. If she meant anything to him, why didn't he tell her? She climbed the steep, winding stairs with his help and told him good-night at her door. He stood there for a moment as though pondering unfinished business, squeezed her hand and loped on down the stairs. Was he planning to collect? A patient man would bide his time, and she'd discovered that Magnus was, if anything, patient.

Several mornings later, Magnus prowled the office that he'd built near the house, slapping his right fist into his left palm, frustrated. He had to find a solution for Selena. She was vulnerable to Prince, she needed a safe place to stay and the gossip was wearing on her. But the solution that repeatedly surfaced in his mind stunned him. It would solve their problems or, at least, his, but would it be good for her?

His mother's call interrupted his musings. "Get that awful woman out of your house, Magnus. She's slandered your brother, and you shouldn't be protecting her. I want her out of Waverly."

Patience. "Mother, if you don't have any compassion for a woman who could have died because of your son's cruelty, I'm sorry for you. She stays here as long as it suits her, and I won't tolerate any interference from Prince."

"How could you?"

"That's the way it is, Mother. Goodbye." He hung up. Prince would never be a man as long as their mother coddled and protected him.

Tessie stopped him as he entered the kitchen. "Somebody left a newborn baby on the steps of the Community Center last night. The whole town's in an uproar, and Miss Anna swears the baby is Selena's. I gave her a few pieces of my mind about that."

"She wants Selena's blood." He walked back outside and let his gaze roam over his vast holdings. He looked at years of struggle, all by himself, from morning until night. And for what? For himself, he would have been satisfied with far less. He needed children to ride the young colts and swim in the lake; a wife to roam the pastures with him, join him for walks through the gardens on summer evenings, to share his life. He needed a woman's love to fill the awful void inside him, to banish his loneliness.

He loved Selena, but he wasn't convinced that their lives should be permanently linked. Yet, as days passed, her gentleness, strength, compassion and courage deepened her endearment to him, and the more he saw of her, the more he wanted her.

Selena looked up from her work on a magazine article that she had agreed to write for *Wall Street World* to find Magnus peeping over her shoulder. She used the office that would have been his secretary's, if he'd hired one.

Butterflies fluttered dizzily in her stomach when she heard his low, seductive tones. "Have dinner with me tonight. You eat too late. How about it? Seven okay?"

She patted his hand. "Okay. Seven. Now beat it."

She didn't ask herself why she dressed in a Dior blue silk miniskirted sheath for dinner with Magnus, or why she added a rope of pearls and navy-blue spike heels and dabbed Fendi perfume in strategic places. But she felt good doing it.

Magnus left the office, and went to find Tessie. "Tess, Selena's having dinner with me tonight, so have something nice."

She half turned and looked at him over her shoulder. "'*Have something nice.*' Like I don't always have something nice. If you ain't satisfied with my cooking…"

Magnus let a full-throated laugh float out of him. "You always say that, and you never finish the statement. I'm not worried, Tess." He reached toward a pot to lift its lid, and got a smack on his wrist.

"Don't you dare. You'll find out what you're eating when I put it on the table."

Seven o'clock was a long time coming. "I see you dressed for her," Tessie said, when he peeped into the kitchen. "She's a fine one, Magnus, a real fine one, and I hope you ain't blind." Tessie's concern could deteriorate into meddlesomeness, so he winked at her and left the room. If she'd forgotten that he'd passed his thirty-seventh birthday, he hadn't. He stepped to the bottom of the stairs, and watched Selena glide down, a feast for his eyes. Cool, yes, but he'd begun to see beyond that veneer to her warmth and compassion. They entered the dining room to a table that might well have been set for royalty and, for the first time, he believed he could risk anything to keep the woman at his side with him forever.

Tessie hadn't been subtle, and Selena knew at once that the woman was aiming for a love match between Magnus and herself, but Magnus hadn't suggested any such thing to her.

"Walk down to the gate with me?" he asked her after dinner.

She looked at him and quickly shifted her glance. He dazzled her. "I'd like that."

If the gentle spring breeze, heady aroma of the spring flowers, a seductive moon and scattered stars weren't seduction enough, the man beside her took her breath away.

"Do you feel like walking a few more steps? Are you too cool? Are you enjoying our walk?" A finger to her elbow, a hand splayed briefly at her back. All that without letting her feel suffocated. She felt as though he cared. He touched her heart.

I'm in danger here, she warned herself.

"Magnus, you've been wonderful to me, but I have to find my own place," she said to him.

He stopped walking and took her hand. "I know you're sick of the gossip and that you're used to being independent, but the ranch is the best place for you right now. Don't leave, Selena."

She looked into the distance. Don't leave, or don't leave *him?* If only she knew. Raindrops preceded the advent of a sudden rainstorm, and he lifted her into his arms and sped through the downpour. He held her close to his heart as though she was precious to him. She didn't care how much it rained.

As she prepared for bed that evening, she answered the phone and listened in horror to Prince's promise to get her as soon as he got back to Waverly.

Stunned, she asked him, "Where are you?" as sweat dripped from every pore of her body.

"Doesn't matter, baby. You're mine, you want me, and I'll get you. Rich boy can forget it." He hung up.

She wouldn't have mentioned it to Magnus if Tessie, who'd transferred the call the night before, hadn't said she'd tell him. Selena walked out into the early morning air to look for him. He erupted into anger, and demanded again that she explain her relationship with Prince. She winced at his interrogation.

"Talk to me, Selena," he demanded. She related Prince's conversation and added that she hadn't told him earlier because she hadn't wanted to spoil his day or to cause problems between brothers.

"If I had let him, Prince would have spoiled my whole life. Do you want to see him?"

His hands grasped her shoulders, and she twisted away from him. "Magnus, don't let me have to tell you this again, because if I do, I'll leave here as soon as I can pack. I don't care where Prince is or what kind of trick he tries. Do you hear me? Do you? *I do not, repeat, do not want your brother. I never have and never will.*" She swung away and rushed into the house.

* * *

Tessie knew she'd done the right thing in insisting that Magnus know about Prince's pursuit of Selena. He'd called her twice, and she knew that was only the beginning. She busied herself in what she regarded as the best time of the day and hummed happily as Jackson Griffith, the ranch manager, entered the kitchen for his breakfast.

"I suppose you're wanting your coffee, Jackson, but you'll have to wait for Magnus." She hid her delight in his company with as crusty an attitude as she could muster.

"Well, if you can't fill my belly, Tessie, I can at least feast my eyes on you, though the smell of that good coffee of yours is sure making my mouth water."

"Oh, you go 'way from here," she demurred. "Always talking foolishness."

"Nothing foolish 'bout what I said, Tessie. You're nice to look at. Smoothest brown skin I ever did see."

"Aw, shucks. You just trying to wangle that coffee out of me." She didn't want him to know how pleased she was; a woman half of her fifty-five years couldn't get a nicer compliment.

Impatient with her attitude, Jackson released a long breath. "I never could figure it out. You lie to a woman, and she believes every word. Tell her the truth, and she swears you're lying." He shook his head. "It's an amazement to me."

She began setting the table. "Your tongue gets bolder every day, Jackson. I ain't lived this long without recognizing a snow job when I hear one."

She eyed Jackson from beneath her lashes as he threw up his hands in exasperation. "Now, Tessie, have I done something to give you the impression that my word's good for nothing?"

She tossed her head. "You wear pants," she said and glanced around as she heard Magnus's footsteps.

"Tess, are you giving Jackson a hard time?" he teased, taking his seat at the table.

"Worse than that," Jackson told him. "She as much as said you can't trust the word of anybody who wears pants."

Why did he pick that time to waltz in here? Tessie mumbled to herself. "You misunderstood me," she said aloud. "Jackson, you have to learn to treat a woman nice—like Magnus here treats Selena."

"I don't need to learn nothing about women, Tessie, and if you want references, I got a slew of them. Now, there's Emma over in…"

"That's enough. I won't have you scandalizing my kitchen."

She whirled around and glared at Magnus when he laughed aloud. Men claimed they loved women, but they always ganged up on them. "I didn't say every pair of pants," she protested. "There are a few exceptions."

"Glad to hear it," Magnus said, grinning. She gave him a cup of coffee and made a ceremony of pouring a cup for Jackson. But when she saw Magnus's raised eyebrow, she knew he was onto her secret: a mere glimpse of Jackson Griffith made her day.

Jackson looked at his empty cup and held it out to Tessie for a refill. When she took her time doing it, he complained. "You talk about how Magnus treats Selena. Well, it wouldn't hurt you none to watch how Selena treats Magnus. I got yet to see her glaring at him with a hand on each hip and her chin poked out. Pretty gets as pretty does."

"That's 'cause she knows how Magnus feels about her."

Jackson stood up. "Where've you been, woman?" he growled. "I can make coffee as well as the next person, and my biscuits would make yours cry."

"Why you… Then go home and eat your breakfast there."

"You two stop fighting, and don't talk about me as if I'm not here," Magnus said. "Tess, how do you know what I feel for Selena? Did I tell you?"

"You didn't have to. I got eyes, and I've know you since you was born. I know you better than your own mother does, and if I say she's tied you in a knot, you're tied."

Magnus looked steadily at her, drained his cup, stood and spoke to Jackson. "I'll be in my office all morning. Come in around eleven. I want to check a few things with you." He paused at the door. "You're the one given to old sayings, Tess, so you should know that more flies are trapped with honey than with vinegar." He was out the door before she could answer him. She looked at Jackson briefly and dropped her head in embarrassment.

"Don't pay it no mind, Tessie," he soothed. "You're straight with me." His big hand grazed her shoulder in a fleeting caress as he passed her on his way out. She had to lean against the counter. He hadn't touched her before, and never before had a thousand kettle drums pounded in her chest.

"Going somewhere?" Magnus asked Selena two mornings later when he met her on the stairs.

"I have to go for my checkup. Tessie loaned me her car."

He couldn't go with her unless she asked, but he hated that Prince might find her. "Be careful. Prince is devious, and he could be anywhere."

"Thanks. I will."

His nerves stood on end as he watched her drive off. He couldn't tie her to him, but he had to protect her, and not only for her sake. With each day that passed, she buried herself more deeply in his heart. He had to give it a shot.

For safety's sake, Selena parked in front of the doctor's office. Thoughts of Magnus swirled in her head. He'd said, "Be careful." His piercing gaze had held more than indifferent concern, and the sparks flying from him had ignited every molecule of her body. If only he'd tell her what he wanted or what he felt.

She didn't like her doctor's cautious words. "Do I have a problem, Dr. Barnes?"

"Let's not cross that bridge yet. I have to take a few more tests before I'm certain of my findings. But don't worry. We'll take care of it."

She left him and stopped by the Center to see Eloise, director of the Community Center where she worked as youth counselor. "Hey, girl," Eloise welcomed her, "I was wondering when you'd come by."

Selena had become fond of Eloise. "And I was wondering why you didn't call," she chided. "Everybody in town knew where I was."

"That was the problem. If *everybody* knows it in this town, you can usually discount it."

"This time *everybody* had it right. I've been at Magnus Cooper's ranch."

"Not after what happened with his pig of a brother, you haven't."

"Yes, I have. Magnus has been an angel."

Eloise swung around in her swivel chair and gaped. "Well, I know he's not like Prince, but aren't you scared Prince might show up there? He's the devil untied, you know."

"Magnus told me I'd be safe."

"Well, if he said so, but you'd better watch out. Prince isn't the only looker in this town. There aren't any flies on Magnus, either, and I hope you know he leaves the local women alone. You take care. A man like Magnus has a woman somewhere."

Selena didn't question Magnus's attentiveness. He took her for walks around the ranch and horseback riding through his pastures, proudly showing her who he was. He introduced her to the countryside in nearby towns famous for their scenic beauty. In San Antonio, they strolled the streets holding hands and, seduced by his powerful personality and gentle manners, she let him bait her into the riding the roller coaster in Six Flags Fiesta. Tremors shook her body when the steep climbs and sharp dips petrified her, and she clutched him as though her life was at stake.

"You're afraid," he said.

"N…n… A…uh…a little bit."

"It will soon be over. Try to relax." He took her as fully into his arms as their straps would allow. Lord, but it was so good to have her so close, clinging to him, *needing him*. Her shudders subsided, and he could feel the tension leaving her. He wanted to keep her in his embrace, to taste her openmouthed kiss, but he controlled the urge. Did she realize how intimate they were? If she did, he'd like to know how she felt about it. The roller coaster slowed and came to a halt, and still she held him. The other riders disembarked, but she didn't budge. He relaxed his arms, and she raised her face to him. A spasm of pleasure rippled through him as he saw recognition in her eyes, an awareness of him as a man, and heat pooled in his loins, hardening him. Stunned, he forced himself to break the trance and shift his gaze.

They got back to his Town Car to find five teenagers sprawled over the hood who became belligerent when Magnus asserted ownership. Seeing the potential for danger, Selena approached the oldest one and introduced herself.

"My name is Russ," the boy replied, his status having been acknowledged. "Okay, guys, Selena's ready to split." He held out his hand to her, offering to shake. "You need anything next time you 'round, Selena, like protection for your car, look me up. No charge."

Hours passed before she could defuse Magnus's anger over her intervention. "But he'll look out for your car," she said in her defense.

"Just what I need, protection from that little ruffian."

When he parked in front of the house, she jumped out of the car, and he sat there smarting. Angry at himself for ruining a magical day and killing a chance at what would have been the sweetest kiss he'd ever tasted.

She'd said Prince meant nothing to her and never had. He recalled the expression of joy on Selena's face when a little Mexican child had hugged and kissed her after she gave money to her mother, a beggar woman with three children. And her compassion had touched him right after she'd arrived in Waverly, when she'd braved the traffic to help an old woman who stood stranded in the midst of a busy intersection afraid to move. She'd lived in his home for five weeks, and had shown only gracious, gentle manners. No, she wasn't the prima donna she'd at first seemed. Such a woman wouldn't have gotten her silk dress and her hair soaking wet in a torrential rain in order to rescue a newborn puppy as Selena had. She'd taken the little animal to her suite, and nursed it to good health. His heart galloped in his chest with the thought that she could be what he needed.

He put the car in the garage and went in the kitchen for some juice.

"Have a good time?"

He'd as soon not have any of Tessie's good sense. "Why?"

"'Cause I hope you ain't planning to let this girl slip away from you. Selena don't come in pairs, and don't tell me she's like Miss Anna. Your mama ain't seen the day she had a heart like Selena's."

Didn't he know it. He sipped the juice. "Want some?" She nodded her thanks, and he got it for her.

"Mother saves her warmth and compassion for Prince."

Tessie took a long sip. "Well, be generous, honey. Your mother ain't never had much warmth to give. I pity her."

"She's going to need pity, if she encourages Prince to take revenge against Selena. She was an innocent person, and he victimized her, but if he harms her again, if he touches her, I'll be merciless. Believe me, if I have to put my hands on Prince, he won't recognize me."

Chapter 3

She climbed the stairs, fighting the tears. He had held her so protectively and tenderly while she'd shivered with fright on that roller coaster that she'd stopped being afraid and luxuriated in the haven of his arms. The ride ended, but she hadn't known when. All of her senses had been centered on Magnus, and she had wanted to feel that way forever. But he'd gotten uptight about Russ, spoiling the closeness between them, and then he'd burst the balloon completely by interrogating her about Prince. The tears that brimmed in her eyes dried up; whenever she got soft on Magnus, she'd better remember that night on Whisper Hill.

Eleven-thirty was late for a call on her private line. She let the phone ring until she tired of the persistent noise and snatched the receiver from its cradle.

"Hello."

"If you're as smart as everybody says you are," the voice began, "you'll get off Cooper Ranch."

"Cowards don't frighten me," she shot back at Prince. "Where are you?"

"You don't need to know. It's where I'll be that you have to worry about. He can try to lock you up, but trust me, baby, I'll get you. And once you get a taste of me, you'll be on your knees begging." She hung up, turned off the phone, ran a bubble bath and got in the tub. If he didn't leave her alone, she'd silence him with a court order.

"You down early," Tessie said to Selena the next morning.

"Morning, Tessie. Can I help you with something?"

"'Course not. What's troubling you?"

There was so much that she didn't understand about Magnus. Like her suite, for example. "Tessie, has Magnus been married?"

"*Married?* Far as I know, he ain't even thought about it. Why?"

Selena breathed. There was no other woman in his life. "Who uses my suite? His mother?"

"Miss Anna? If she ever spent the night here, I don't know it. That was always the guest suite."

"Decorated like that? Where do you put the male guests?" Selena persisted.

Tessie leaned her slight body against the counter and waved the spoon that she was using to stir grits. "I'll tell you, but you won't put what I say to no good use. Magnus redecorated that suite the week before you came here. He asked me what colors a woman born in October would like, and I looked it up and I told the decorator."

"How did he know when I was born?"

"Miss Eloise told him. You like how it looks?"

Her amazement must have been obvious, because Tessie lifted an eyebrow and grinned. "Don't looked so shocked, honey. Magnus don't half-do nothing."

"The rooms are beautiful. I wish I knew why he did that."

Tessie turned back to the stove and stirred her grits. "Well, if he'd done it for me, and I was in your place, I wouldn't have to ask. But, then, ain't no two people alike."

Be careful, Selena warned herself, he's too good to be real. "I'm going for a walk," she told Tessie, neglecting to say she hoped to intercept Magnus as he came in from his morning rounds.

"Twenty minutes," Tessie called.

Selena walked swiftly to the stable, leaned against the old pine tree that faced the door and watched him approach. Magnus on a horse was something to behold, a man whose potent masculinity stood out even from that distance. More than a city block away, she could feel his presence, the pull of his power. She didn't want to be affected by his magnetism, because he didn't trust her, and he was Prince's brother. He stopped Cougar nearby, dismounted and walked to her holding the horse's reins. With the tree at her back, she couldn't move away to get the space she wanted, so she had to stand there while his heat curled around her, and she inhaled the smell of musk and hot man into her nostrils. His wet shirt, clinging to his chest, outlined his prominent pectorals, and she stared at them while water accumulated in her mouth. She made herself glance up, intending to greet him, and jolts of electricity whistled through her veins when she saw the torrid desire mirrored in his eyes. She'd never seen such want in a man, and her shock that a heat of her own answered his must have been reflected in what she knew was her stunned expression. His nostrils flared and, in seconds, he closed the space between them. Panic threatened, and she blurted out the one cooling agent at her disposal.

"Prince called me again last night after I left you," she said, as his hands circled her body.

The lights in his eyes dimmed, and he stepped away, tipped his hat to the back of his head and pinned her with a frosty stare. Then, without a word, he turned and led Cougar to his stall.

She walked back to the house with less spirit than when she'd left it. Their sexual fencing had begun to wear on her.

"I'll just take a cup of coffee up to my rooms," she told Tessie. "Where's Magnus?"

"He's coming."

Tessie poured a cup of coffee and handed it to her. "Didn't I tell you it wouldn't do you no good to know who Magnus fixed up that suite for?"

"Right," Selena answered and rushed to get out of the kitchen before Magnus walked in. She'd call her New York real estate agent and ask her to find a place close to Waverly, where she could stay until she built a house.

Magnus didn't want food, he wanted Selena Sutton, and he pushed away the plate that Tessie set before him. In that moment, he'd almost broken his pledge to himself and let her know how he felt. Tongues of fire had licked his guts when she'd looked at him with the eyes of a woman who needed completion.

"You and Selena have a fight?"

"Prince called her again last night. He's either somewhere around here or he has information about our movements. We got back from San Antonio at about eleven, and he called her at half past."

"Is that any reason for the two of you to act stupid? Selena don't want Prince."

He wanted to believe it, to think her that different from the other women her age. "That's what she says, and after what he did, I'm sure she doesn't want him *now*. But my question is, did she ever? I'm not getting involved with a woman who was even slightly mixed up with Prince." In spite of all that had passed between them, he loved his brother and longed for his rehabilitation, his development into a man of whom he could be proud and with whom he could share jokes, laughter and tears. But he wouldn't allow Prince to continue filling his life with unpleasantness.

Tessie pushed his plate back in front of him and sat down. "You're already involved with Selena. You know, Magnus, all that talk about women wanting Prince is just that—talk. Prince got a warped mind. Sometimes I think he ain't even hooked up right. He believes every woman is after him, 'cause Miss Anna gives him the impression he's the best thing in breeches. The Archangel Gabriel in a Brooks Brothers suit. Prince don't think he's evil. He's so in love with himself, he don't think about nothing but Prince, and I tell you a man that wrapped up in himself makes a real small package. If Selena wanted Prince, would she've taken that big risk? You know how dangerous Whisper Hill is. It's the mercy of the Lord a copperhead or rattler didn't get her. Here. Drink your coffee and eat some of this."

He sipped the coffee but, in his reflective mood, he couldn't use Tessie's good sense. He hadn't overreacted. "I ought to be in Houston, not to mention Sierra Leone, but I can't leave here not knowing where Prince is. See you later."

He met Selena in the hallway. "Going out?" He noticed that she'd dressed for a trip into Waverly.

"I'm going in to pick up my new Ford Taurus. Jackson said he'd give me a ride."

Annoyed that she hadn't asked him to take her, and not caring if she knew it, he told her, "Jackson's busy. I'll take you. Give me a minute to get dressed." She'd protest, but he didn't care. He wouldn't let events take over his life and, if she planned to leave the ranch, he'd do everything within his power short of force or chicanery to stop her.

"But I also have to get my checkup."

"I'll wait for you."

"You're busy, and I don't—"

He interrupted. "Selena, I am not in the habit of volunteering to do something I don't want to do, so if I say I'm prepared to take you, it will be my pleasure to do so. Wait here."

"You say your periods are lasting too long?" Dr. Barnes asked her. "That certainly doesn't come from pneumonia. I'd better give you a pelvic exam."

The doctor finished the tests, and Selena dressed and went into the waiting room, where Magnus paced the floor. Warmth enveloped her when he grasped her arm, his face etched with concern. She'd better watch her reactions to this man.

"Are you all right?" She nodded, and she could see his face lose its tension. "Want to go to Sea World?"

She hated to disappoint him, but she didn't want to see any fish. "Magnus, I know you don't want to hear this, but I've engaged an agent to find a place for me until I can build a house. If I'm going to stay in Waverly, I'll need more than the small apartments available here." She didn't want to leave him, but she couldn't justify remaining in his home.

He shrugged. "I suppose it was inevitable that you'd want a place of your own. You've been independent for a long time. Look, if you don't want to go to Sea World, how about La Villita? It's San Antonio's original settlement. It has a church that could sit in my living room, artisans' workshop, charming little adobe houses, narrow streets—you're back in another century. Come with me." His mouth gave way to a smile, lights danced in his hazel eyes, and she wanted to please him.

"When will we get my car?"

"I'll phone Juardo and tell him we'll be there before he closes." He called on his cellular phone. "Your car's not in yet."

They ambled through La Villita, ate Mexican food and merged with the tourists in the shops and galleries. They strolled along the River Walk and got a ten-cent trolley ride to the Mexican Market. Selena bought several carved Mexican and Native American dolls and confided that she owned at least two hundred of them, six inches or less in height.

"Do you like kids? Is that why you have all those dolls?"

"Yes, I love them." She looked at the passing taxi, at the banner proclaiming Texas as the end of the world, and at the revelers along the bricked shore, but not a Magnus. His question touched her hidden pain. That raw, vulnerable spot inside her that she guarded with such care. He tipped her chin with his forefinger and nudged her face so that he could see her eyes.

She forced herself not to close them, looked at him and saw that his own glowed with an expression she hadn't witnessed in him, but he said nothing, and she finally let herself breathe.

"The annual spring fiesta begins next week. If I get tickets to some events, will you go with me?" She told him she would.

When they got back to the ranch, she thanked him for the excursion and rushed off to her suite, fearing that if she stayed with him one minute longer he'd sense her vulnerability to him. Her answering machine was flashing red when she walked into her bedroom. She punched the play button but quickly slammed down the receiver, her heart galloping in her chest and cold chills snaking down her spine. Prince, bold and cunning, had left that message and, with it, the impression that he had nothing to hide in his pursuit of her. She wanted to scream.

Right after sunrise the next morning the phone rang. Selena rolled over and stretched languorously.

"Hello."

"Did I awaken you, Selena?"

Abruptly, she sat up. Her dream had merged with reality, except that she wasn't in Magnus's arms on the grass beside the lake, but in her bed, holding the phone.

"I think so." A burning sensation stung her face.

"I have to choose a colt as a gift for a friend. Come help me select him."

"Okay. Half an hour."

She jogged to the stables where Magnus waited with three young colts. "Who's he for?"

"I promised a friend that, when her first child was born, I'd send it a thoroughbred colt. She had a boy about six weeks ago, and it's time I sent him. Which one do you like?"

"Some friend. What happened? Did you lose out to another guy?" If he had, she'd give her eye teeth to see that other man.

His smile wound its way over his face. "Not really. Seems she flipped backward the minute she saw him, so when I met her, she wasn't available."

"Mind telling me her name?"

"Melissa Grant Roundtree."

"Say, wait a minute. Roundtree's a hot name on Wall Street. Any connection?"

"One and the same. She's married to Adam Roundtree."

"Well, I'll be... Do you like him?"

His shoulders bunched in an elaborate shrug. "I can take him or leave him, but since it wouldn't matter a hoot to him one way or the other, we're on good terms." He looked down at the colts. "Which one do you like?"

The white-nosed, long-legged bay nuzzled her and refused to move when she told him to. "He's friendly. I like him," she said, and watched another smile amble over his face until it lit his hazel eyes.

"He was my choice, too. I'll register him as Morris Hayes I after the boy's great-grandfathers."

"I'll finish up in my office at about one, Selena." He paused and his voice lowered, kindling inside her sensations that were becoming familiar. "There're so many more things I want to show you, right around here." His hand swept the horizon. "Come with me this afternoon." She thought about the magazine article she had to write and the deadline that she faced, but he smiled, and she went with him.

Selena had to admit that Magnus was filling her head with himself, giving her little time to think of anything else. Over the next week, he seemed intent on immersing her in the joys of ranching. He took her riding, fishing in the lake and the brooks, and on his morning rounds. And in it all, he seemed to be saying, *Can you leave this?* She almost hoped the real estate agent wouldn't find her a place. Joy suffused her when he sat her in a field of bluebonnets and pink phlox and snapped her picture.

She picked a flower, handed it to him and watched his eyes darken with passion.

"Is this flower symbolic of anything?"

Heat burned her face. "I'm an innocent. Is it supposed to be?"

He stared at her. "You want to make your meanings real clear, good and plain when you talk to me, Selena. I'll take you at your word."

"That's what you're supposed to do."

Magnus studied Selena's face. He wouldn't press the question. She had many sides. He didn't know when anything had moved him as deeply as the tentative way in which she'd handed him the little blossom. Had this fragile, sensitive nature always been a part of her? She still walked with head high and shoulders back, still had the look of a porcelain princess every time he saw her, still a perfect beauty. She still had that royal air that left you with the impression she could snap her finger and change the color of the sky, but now, he knew her, knew that the facade he disliked camouflaged tenderness, warmth and compassion. Could he risk it?

He might as well admit that it wasn't desire that bound him to her, but a love he knew would never change. The business with Prince had to be cleared up to his satisfaction before he'd take a chance—if he ever did—and let Selena know his weakness for her and the strength with which it had grown since the first time he'd glimpsed her. Yes, she was part of him and, if she thought he'd let her leave him, she'd never been more wrong. She'd be his biggest challenge, but also his greatest prize. In his mind's eye, he could see her as she'd been that rainy night with the little puppy, the way she still cared for it and loved it, and he promised himself that, one day, he'd see her hugging his child with that same expression of love on her face.

Selena was about to embark on a campaign of her own. "Eloise," she began, when her friend answered the telephone. "Eloise, I'm going to the Kappa's Fiesta dance in San Antonio. How do they dress?"

"You go, girl," Eloise shouted. "Everybody who is anybody will be there from miles around. It's the shindig of the Fiesta. Don't worry about what to wear. You just go for broke, and let it all hang out, because the gals will have their year's salary on their backs."

Taken aback, Selena asked, "In San Antonio?"

"You betcha, honey. This is Texas."

Later she was glad she'd chosen an intricately beaded red sheath that was strapless except for a string of rhinestones on one shoulder. Magnus's whistle split the air as she reached the bottom step.

If she'd known how, she would have returned the compliment, because Magnus in a tuxedo was magnificent in his manliness. She had to stop right there and feast her eyes on him. He misunderstood, however, stepped quickly to her side and held out his hand as though to support her.

"Are you okay?" he asked.

"I'll get over it." She had to suppress a grin.

"If you don't feel up to it…" His voice trailed off before he added, "Still, I'd hate to pass up the chance to show those guys what kind of woman I've got. You are so beautiful." Awe colored his voice.

Her eyes widened in astonishment and, for a few seconds, she let herself enjoy the pleasure of being a woman.

She hadn't thought about what it would be like to dance with Magnus, and when he pulled her into his arms for their first dance, she missed a step. His grip claimed her, and his cologne teased her, demanding submission. For the first time in her life, her feminine self welcomed a man's proprietary manner. What had happened to the casual man she thought she knew? She had never had a man's personality and will overpower her own as his did. Effortlessly. He moved them around as much with his torso as with his feet. Swivel-hipped and sure-footed, he twirled to the sensuous Creole rhythms, commanding her to follow. His gaze heated her body until pictures of other joys flooded her brain, and his strong fingers on her bare flesh left their mark on her senses, toying with her nerves and triggering lustful thoughts in her head. His every move and gesture proclaimed that this was the real Magnus, *the man,* as he revealed himself to women. His pelvis tilted toward hers and, without thought, her body went to meet it. But his strong arm held her inches from her goal. She fastened her gaze on his lapel, prayed for sanity, and wondered what attributes he hid behind that laid-back facade.

"Look at me, Selena. One of the joys of having a tall woman for company is being able to look into her eyes without breaking my back." His husky, deep drawl caressed her lovingly, washed over her, and she didn't want to open her eyes and destroy the magic. "Look at me," he asked her again.

The touch of his finger, strong and callused, beneath her chin urged her compliance, and she made herself look into his fiery gaze. She'd always thought his eyes beautiful, but what she saw in them now was beauty and more—a fierceness, a bold command to give herself to him. Charmed, mesmerized, she didn't divert her gaze as his eyes delivered his erotic message. Magnus Cooper was many men in one body. Though the music had ended, he held her without touching her. What a man!

"I wouldn't have dreamed that you'd be such a dancer," she managed, wanting to dispel the charged atmosphere. "Anytime you need a partner, look me up."

"Small talk can get you into trouble, Selena. Better make plain what kind of partner you have in mind."

She focused her gaze on the far corner of the room. "I meant your dancing partner, and you know it."

"A partnership is a union and, like dancing, if it isn't smooth, a perfect synchronization, it isn't worth much. And you get perfect union by frequent practice and intimate knowledge that lets you anticipate each other's moves."

His eyes darkened as he spoke, and the suggestive tenor of his speech made her face burn.

"You still with me?" It was more a tease than a serious question.

"I take it you're still talking about dancing."

He splayed his fingers on her back and guided her to their table. "At times, Selena, you're amazing. I'd forgotten the business about your being my dancing partner. But I suspect you knew that."

Throughout the evening, Magnus besieged her with un- spoken messages, and she got the meaning of every one: *I want you.* But she intended to hold out for mutual love. Otherwise, she'd never get what she wanted and needed most: a home and family of her own. The trouble was that her blood raced when she looked into this man's face.

At home after the dance, Magnus walked with Selena into his house and guided her into the living room. Beside the big, silk- tufted sofa on a Duncan Phyfe table rested a service for two and a bottle of Moet and Chandon in a bucket of ice; a silver tray held long-stemmed champagne glasses, toast points and an iced dish of Beluga caviar garnished with chopped eggs and slices of lemon.

"You look good sitting there," he observed, eyeing her glit- tering red dress against the antique gold silk of the sofa.

"Thanks." She looked around, and he knew she assessed the trappings of wealth, before glancing at its possessor. He didn't apologize for what he had, because he'd earned it, had sacrificed for it. When she sucked in a deep breath, he knew that what she would tell him wouldn't fall easily from her tongue, and he braced himself for the worst.

"Don't tell me you've found a place and you're leaving. I don't want to hear it," he said and sat across from her in a wing chair.

"Eventually, I would have to. So why postpone the inevitable? Whenever I have to face the music, I say, let it play. My agent has two houses over in Ashville that seem perfect for me."

Apprehension knotted his insides. "You don't have to leave."

Her look of surprise seemed genuine, and he could hardly believe that she hadn't an inkling of his feelings. "You're not suggesting that I stay here indefinitely?"

He leaned forward, his hands cupping his knees. "No. Not indefinitely. Permanently."

Her body stiffened, and her eyes flashed in annoyance. "Now, you wait a minute. I had just about decided you had redeemed men for me, and now you…"

"Marry me, Selena." He hated the stunned expression that clouded her face. "Yes. I'm asking you to marry me."

Air hissed out of her lungs. She leaned back against the sofa, folded her arms beneath her bosom and shook her head.

He waited for her words, hardly daring to breathe. Imported silks covered the chair on which he sat. Precious Persian carpets rested beneath his feet, and hand-blown Italian Murano glass enclosed the bulbs that lit the room. He looked around at all of it. It meant nothing; he wouldn't experience one pain if he never saw any of it again. But if she turned him down, he doubted anything would ever again have importance and meaning for him.

After what seemed like hours, she spoke. "Magnus, what about love? I don't think I can… Well, without love, what kind of marriage would that be?"

He got up, sat beside her and took her hand. "We've got more going for us than most couples who've sworn eternal love. Don't answer now. Think it over." For his part, love existed in abundance; one look at her was all he'd needed. He opened the bottle of champagne, filled their glasses and gave one to her, but his heart sank when she placed it on the cocktail table.

"But, Magnus, shouldn't a woman love a man and know he loves her before she consents to that kind of intimacy? Otherwise, she could be asking for disillusionment and misery, couldn't she?"

He placed her glass in her hand. "I'll wait for your invitation. You won't be sorry. I swear it. Think it over." His heart-beat accelerated, and heat spiraled through him when she lifted the glass to her lips and sipped.

"You seem confident that I'll extend that invitation."

"I am, and it's the reason why I can be patient."

"All right, I'll think about it." Her words were a love song to his ears. He wanted to take her to him and love her, but he'd promised, and he'd keep that pledge.

Selena crawled into bed, more weary than she could ever remember having been. Magnus's proposal had drained her. If she'd thought he loved her, she would have charged into his arms like a rocket, but he hadn't professed love. He wanted her and had the sense to know that, in view of her experience with Prince, he was unlikely to get her on any other terms. But wanting her was not enough; desire was not love. She cared for him…no, she loved him, but going to his—or any man's—bed knowing that he didn't love her held no appeal. She had to leave.

Several days later, she rode into town with Jackson, picked up her car and drove to her doctor's office.

"The news isn't good, but it isn't all bad," the doctor told her. Asked what that meant, he replied, "Your extended periods are due to fibroid tumors, but they're benign, and they haven't started to cause enough blood loss to be considered dangerous. They're also tiny, and you can still have children, but if they grow, I may have to remove them or the uterus itself. If you're planning to have a baby, I'd say hop to it. There you have it."

When she could speak, she asked, "Do they usually grow rapidly?" He'd dealt her a lethal blow, but she looked him in the eye. If he had the courage to tell a woman that, she had the guts to take it.

He didn't spare her. "If you want a child, my advice is to get to work on it right now."

* * *

If she wanted a child. *If she wanted a child.* She had walked five of Waverly's longest blocks before she remembered that she had a car, and she didn't realize that she'd driven back to the ranch until she parked her car in front of the garage. She walked into the house through the side door, hoping to avoid meeting Tessie or Magnus.

"Be careful," Tessie cautioned. "I just put fresh wax down and I ain't polished it yet. You'll… What's the matter with you, honey? Come on back here and sit down."

Selena brushed away the tears that had threatened since she'd gotten the doctor's report. "I'm…I'm all right, Tessie."

"You been down to the Center? Magnus told me to let him know if Lightner bothered you."

Selena shook her head. She didn't want to talk, but she welcomed the iced tea that Tessie gave her. "I got a little surprise, but I'll be all right."

"Seems to me like you ought to be skipping and jumping with that brand-new car Jackson told me you got. Well, don't let me trouble you. If you need something, I'm here."

Selena made her way to her rooms and closed the door. Waverly didn't boast of one eligible man. Not a single… *What was wrong with her?* There was one, and he had asked her to marry him. She smiled at her good fortune, but her euphoria disappeared as quickly as it had arrived. She could not live in a loveless marriage, and if only one of the principals loved, the marriage wasn't a marriage.

She telephoned her godmother. "Do you think he would learn to love you?" Irene asked. "With men, desire usually comes before love. Seems to me he's too precious to throw away. And it isn't for nothing that he asked you to marry him."

"I finally figured out that he wants to protect me, because he thinks Prince is somewhere around."

"Pshaw, child. That man can see that the bag lady needs protection, too, but you won't catch him proposing to *her.* What do you have all those degrees for? Use your head."

"I don't know, Reenie. He's been so nice. I...don't want to cheat him."

"How can you cheat him, when he hasn't asked for more than marriage? Maybe he needs somebody to go places with him. Don't let that man get away and make the biggest mistake of your life."

Selena hung up. No help there. She didn't know whether she could teach him to love her, because he marched to his own tune. She'd have to tell him no. But as though he conspired against her, she found a box of one dozen long-stemmed roses beside her door when she opened it to go downstairs. A note inside read, "Come live with me and be my bride...and we will all the pleasures prove. With apologies to Marlowe. Yours faithfully, Magnus."

She put the flowers in a vase and laid the note beside them. He was romantic, and she loved that about him. He's pouring it on, she mused, when she found a sprig of lavender beside her plate at dinner that evening.

"Did you put this lavender here?" she asked Tessie.

"Me? I don't give women no flowers," Tessie had her understand. She looked at Magnus for confirmation, but though he said nothing, his darkening eyes spoke more powerfully than words.

"Walk out to the road with me," he suggested after dinner.

Their idyllic stroll enlivened her senses. She hadn't noticed that the flowers on the trees had given way to tiny green nuts, nor had she taken time to look at the bluebonnets that had sprung up everywhere. And as they neared the end of the road, the fragrance of hundreds of roses teased her nostrils, while the pecan trees around them swayed gently in the breeze. She could taste the night's freshness. He took her hand.

"I want to kiss you."

She gasped. Wordless. Motionless. Her heart hammered wildly as anticipation rocked her. She hadn't let herself think of what it would be like in his arms and, as she welcomed it, heat flooded her body, her scalp tingled and her every nerve stood at attention.

"Kiss me," he whispered, though he didn't touch her, and he wouldn't, she realized. It was her move.

She rimmed her lower lip with her tongue as his gaze followed the movement. She wanted to. Oh, how she wanted to be in his arms. But he stood motionless as the last light of day frolicked in his eyes.

"Selena."

With trembling fingers, she touched his cheek, and that was all he needed. He had her in his arms. His hands held her head while he gazed into her face, seeking...she didn't know what. Unable to bear the tension, she grasped the back of his neck.

"Magnus...Magnus." His lips pressed into hers in a feverish demand, and his tongue flicked against her mouth, seeking entrance. Joyously, she parted her lips and took him into her body. He claimed every crevice, simulating the act of love as he drove her to a state of mindlessness. She let her twisting hips have their way and moved them to him with every ounce of strength she possessed. Wanting more, she sucked his tongue deeply into her mouth and, when he slacked the kiss, she clutched his hips and held him to her. His moan of passion, long and intense, sent tremors through her, and she pulled him closer, her only thought being to give him the loving he needed. His kisses then covered her face, while his fingers danced against her nipple, and she cried out from the sweet torture of it. His other hand pressed her buttocks to him until the boiling heat of desire dampened her, and she felt him rise hard against her.

She attempted to move away from him then, and he released his hold on her at once. But the hot passion he had aroused wouldn't let her go, and she had to lean against him, though she didn't dare look at him, lest she betray all that she felt. He had the advantage, and she didn't think his knowing it would bode well for them. Made vulnerable and exposed by the passion he'd unleashed in her, feelings such as she had never before experienced, she locked her arms tightly around her middle and tried to steady herself.

Magnus wanted to halt the beating pulses in his temple, the wild trotting of blood through his veins. He'd started that explosion to test the water, because he knew that, having made up his mind, he'd persist until she married him. And if he was going to give it all he had, he needed to know whether she had fire in her. Satisfied that he could unravel her cool facade and kindle in her a furnace of desire that matched his own, he pressed a kiss to her forehead, took her hand and started back to the house.

Selena didn't delude herself that living with a man who wanted her and whom she loved while failing to consummate their feelings would be easy. She wanted to be his wife in every sense, but not until she knew he loved her. She regarded his profile, pensive and thoughtful, then she looked up at the sky that was lit by the moon when, less than an hour earlier, the sun had been its source of light. Time wouldn't wait for her, either. If she wanted a child, she had to get started. And could any woman find for her children a more wonderful father than Magnus? She would take that step, and she would do everything a woman could to teach him to love her.

"Magnus, I can't… I don't believe in lovemaking without mutual love. I believe we could make a go of it, if…if we let ourselves learn each other. You know what I mean. It's hard to explain."

He stopped walking and looked at her, his face grim with disappointment. "I understand, and I can appreciate it. If the time comes when you feel you…love me, will you accept me?"

She thought her heart would break. What a conversation to have with the man you loved. "I'll be honest with you about everything, and especially about this." Lord, she hoped she wasn't making a mistake. "Why, Magnus? Why would you consider this arrangement?" She wasn't about to ask him if he loved her. He acted like a man who cared, but so far he hadn't seen fit to articulate it.

His half smile held no joy. "I have my reasons and they are all honorable ones." Her body tingled when his fingers tightened around hers. "Deal?"

Her gaze swept over his face. "And will you be honest about your feelings?" She thought he hesitated before saying that he would. She squeezed his hand. "All right. Deal."

Not even the clouds that raced over the moon obscured the glints that danced in his eyes. "You'll marry me?"

"People say you're a man who honors his word. Yes."

His arm encircled her waist and, as quickly, he dropped his hand. Regretfully, she thought.

"Selena, the church is important to me, and I want us to get married in one. I also want my buddy to stand up with me."

Startled, but pleased that he should express that sentiment, considering the nature of their marriage, she gaped at him. "Uh, anyone around here?"

"Wade Malloy up in Accord, New York. My business partner."

Now was the time for demands, she realized. "Magnus," she said, sliding her hand along his forearm, "I want us to marry in a church, too, and I want to wear a wedding gown."

His grin showed his delight in her suggestion, and his arm circled her waist in a quick hug. "Of course. You'll be a beautiful bride."

They walked arm in arm to the house. Inside, she stood by as Magnus banged on Tessie's door.

"Don't tell me the house is on fire," Tessie called out just before she cracked the door and looked at their locked hands. "Saints preserve us, you're getting married." She flung open the door and grabbed Magnus in a hug before bestowing her blessing on Selena.

"We are," he confirmed, "but how did you know it?"

"From the looks on your faces," she said, "and besides, I been expecting it."

Selena glanced at him, and thought her heart would burst.

He might well have been the only peacock in a barnyard filled with peahens, or the man who'd just topped Mount Everest. Yes, she could teach him to love her, and she would.

Three weeks later, in the presence of Wade, Nadine and Christopher Malloy, Tessie, Jackson, Eloise and the members of St. Matthew Episcopal Church, Selena Sutton became Selena Sutton-Cooper. Gowned in a floor-length ivory satin dress, she gazed unflinchingly into his eyes. He lifted her white lace bridal veil and pressed a quick kiss to her lips as tears dropped down her cheeks.

Icy apprehension gripped him when he remembered how her lips had quivered when she said, "I do."

"Are you sorry?" he whispered.

"Never." Her tremulous smile tore into his heart. He had restored her reputation; now he could protect her from Prince. She was his and, God help him, he would love her forever.

Chapter 4

Selena sat beside Magnus at her wedding supper, with her gaze locked on Nadine and Wade Malloy, their love swirling around them, palpable in its intensity. Nadine's open adoration for her husband reflected what could only have been hours of contentment, happiness and earth-shattering fulfillment in her husband's arms. Selena couldn't help envying her. When Magnus caressed her hand in a gentle, fleeting touch, she shifted her gaze to him and, when she would have looked away, he touched her chin with his free hand, stared into her eyes and let her read in them his desire and frustration. He wanted her, and she gloried in that knowledge, but what she needed was his love and himself, all of him. She wanted that blanket of love around her that she knew Nadine Malloy received from Wade.

"Nothing is perfect, Selena," Magnus whispered. "I'm sure Nadine and Wade had their ups and downs before they got where they are now. If we work at it, we can find what they have...." His voice trailed off. "That and more. And I aim to do my part. What about you?"

She hadn't realized that her reaction to the couple was obvious to him, but she wished from the pit of her soul that, when they left their guests, she would go to Magnus Cooper as his bride. "I'm in this for the long haul, Magnus, and I'm not afraid to reach for the stars."

He gazed into her eyes. Searching. Always seeming to look for something deep in her. Then he smiled. "In that case, we can't lose."

Magnus stood, raised a glass of champagne to their friends, kissed his bride and thanked everyone for their presence at his wedding. "It's time we left," he told them. "Enjoy yourselves."

Selena knew she'd better deal with her attitude when she walked with her husband of five hours into the living room, where bouquets of red roses and bluebonnets, a magnum of fine Dom Perignon champagne and a tray of petit fours awaited them. She took it all in; the day had been all that a bride could have desired, except for the absence of that most precious of gifts, the love of her groom.

"Magnus, I appreciate your going to so much trouble to make this day memorable, and maybe I'll someday see all this in a different light, but I can't handle any more. I...I want to go to my suite."

He turned his head only slightly and continued pouring the champagne. "We promised to give this marriage every chance, and I intend to keep my word, starting now. I remember—dammit, I can't forget—that consummation isn't part of our deal, at least not for now, but that doesn't preclude a loving relationship."

Shame poured over her; she had released her frustration on him. She took the steps that brought her to his side and laid her left hand lightly on his arm, glancing first at the blinding fire of his diamond on her finger and then to his face.

"I'm sorry. You didn't deserve that. It's just that…" Her search for the words proved futile.

His grim smile told his own tale. "Neither of us is getting what we need right now, but we entered this with open eyes. I'm frustrated, and I know you are. If I did what I want to, I'd have that dress off you in seconds, and if I started it, you'd go all the way with me. And tomorrow morning, we'd be further apart than the day we met. Sit here with me for a few minutes, will you? I'm not ready to end this day." He took her hand and sat with her on the sofa and, with the fingers of his right hand still entwined with hers, he passed her a glass of champagne and the tray of little cakes.

"Selena, we can look forward to years of happiness or days of misery—it's up to us. Whatever we bring to this marriage is what we'll get. I hope to be married to you until the day I die, even if that's seventy-five years from now, but it can end tomorrow morning if you can't handle it. I hope you'll give us a chance."

Her heart stilled and then kicked into a somersault that left her winded. It was what she wanted, a real marriage with him, but he'd said nothing of love and, if he said it now, would she believe him?

She edged closer to him, partly out of guilt and also because she needed to feel his strength. "If we just act natural, I guess it'll all work out."

His robust laughter startled her.

"I'd give a lot to see the fun in this situation," she told him, with no small amount of testiness.

His grin widened. "If we acted natural right now, honey, we'd have one hell of a romp."

"Oh, *you*," she protested, poking him in his belly, and releasing a peal of laughter of such superficiality that a stranger would have detected it.

Magnus turned fully to her, and the playful pat she aimed at his thigh missed its target. She tried to jerk back her hand, but he grabbed it and held.

"*Magnus*. I…I'm sorry. I…I didn't mean to…"

"Come here," he growled. "Sweetheart. *Baby, come here to me.*"

She shifted slightly away from him, but his plea rang in her heart and she opened her arms. "Magnus, this will be a mistake. More than you know, but I…"

She tasted his open mouth, and heat spiraled through her, churning in her belly and settling between her thighs. She moaned in passion as his tongue possessed every centimeter of her mouth, and he pulled her onto his lap and pressed her to him. She wanted to think, to tell him they should stop, but instead she grabbed his hand and pressed it against her hard nipple. Fire raged in her as he stroked it, pinched it and, with his flat palm, teased it in a circling motion until she cried out.

"I can't stand this, Magnus." She heard her whimpers of desire, and, when he moaned, she knew he answered her passion. She should stop it, but he drained her of her will; his every touch torched her body with the fever of desire. Frantic, she parted her legs and rocked against him.

"Easy, sweetheart," he cautioned. "Let's not let this get out of hand." But she crossed her knees and shifted her weight, and he stood abruptly, putting her away from him.

She caught her breath. "It…sneaked up on me."

Holding her at arm's length, he said, "Me, too. But it caught us. If you go to my bed tonight, you sleep there from now on. I won't have an on-again, off-again marriage. I don't think you're ready for it, though it may be what we need right now, but any more of this, and I may be out of control."

She turned from him in embarrassment but, with gentle hands on her shoulders, he brought her to face him and soothed her with the gentle lilt of his voice.

"Neither of us has cause for shame or regret, because we learned something here. If we give ourselves a chance, we'll make it."

When she didn't look at him, she felt the back of his hand

smooth her cheek. More than anything she'd ever desired, she wanted the sweet, intoxicating haven of his arms around her.

"Selena, you're the only one I've...I've truly...wanted. You'll come to me. I'm not worried about that." He took her hand. "I'd better see you to your rooms."

She stopped and looked straight at him. "How can you be so sure I'll go to you, when I don't know that myself?"

He didn't smile, but he didn't appear sad, either. "If we stay together, and I don't doubt that we will, we'll consummate this union. I'd bet the ranch on it."

They climbed the stairs, and she let him hold her hand until they reached her door. Then he took her in his arms and hugged her, almost as he would a sister, and she knew he wouldn't risk another kiss.

"I'm no angel, Selena, but right now, I sure as hell feel like one. Sleep well." She watched him as he loped down the steps. Then, she went into her living room, closed the door behind her and let her tears crawl mercilessly down her wedding dress.

She hadn't expected this longing for him, but it was she who had laid out the rules, and she had to abide by them. That meant treating him fairly and avoiding such hot sessions, unless she intended to go all the way. But when he'd reached for her, his beautiful eyes a sea of pain, she'd forgotten her vow to wait until he reciprocated her love. If he had wanted her half as badly as she'd desired him, she mused, he had to be miserable right then. She had to be more careful.

Selena looked at her bed, went back into her living room, got out of her dress and shoes and curled up on the sofa. She was doggoned if she'd sleep in a bed alone on her wedding night.

Downstairs, Magnus, too, was discombobulated. He went into the living room to clear it of the remains of his wedding day, sat down and stared at his hands. He'd never come so close to losing his power over himself as he had minutes earlier. Why hadn't she come to him? The strength of her passion should have told her that she was ready for him, unless... He discarded the thought; a thirty-year-old woman had to understand her own sexuality. And he didn't see how in the name of kings a woman her age couldn't see what he felt for her. He sat upright. A woman didn't go at a man the way Selena had gone at him unless she needed him; sex alone wasn't cause for a woman with her personality and outlook to drop every defense, shed her protective shield. Unless she'd been acting, and he couldn't believe that. Of course, she could have meant to befuddle him, to take his mind off her and Prince, but he couldn't believe that, either.

He hadn't a right to be disappointed and, in fact, he wasn't, because he'd gotten more than he had hoped for. If Prince or any other man thought he had a claim on Selena, tough luck. She'd sent him the message that he could have her and, as soon as he could satisfy himself that he wasn't competing with his brother, he'd go after her and get her. She wanted a mutual love? Well, he already loved her and, if he did nothing else for the rest of his life, he'd teach her to love him.

Selena didn't want to meet Tessie's all-knowing eyes that morning, but there was no escaping it. "You don't tell, and I don't ask," Tessie said by way of greeting. "All the same, I never thought brides left the marriage bed at six-thirty in the morning. But then, ain't nobody give me a blow-by-blow account of what happens on these occasions. Here's your coffee." She passed a mugful to Selena, braced one hip and waited to see what reaction she'd get to her comments.

"Right," Selena replied, "and this body won't be the first to do it."

"Well, I knew all the time that you two needed a little more seasoning, but that'll come, so I ain't worried. But I want you to know, Selena, that I'd give Magnus my right arm if he needed it. You follow me?"

Selena managed a smile. "What would he do with three right arms—his, yours and mine? I'm going to the Center for a few minutes this morning, but I'm expecting some personal things from New York. Will you be here?"

"Sure will." Tessie laughed. "You can say 'butt out' sweeter than anybody I ever knew. Just tell me this. You gonna stick with Magnus?"

Selena drained her cup, walked over to Tessie and draped an arm around her shoulders. "'Til death do us part. Now, stop worrying."

"Praise the Lord. You take care driving to town now, you hear?"

She turned into the hallway and stopped when Magnus walked out of his suite, looked up and saw her. What was she supposed to say, and how should she act? He walked arrow-straight to her with his lazy, loose-hipped gait, and she thought his smile had never seemed so brilliant nor his whole self so inviting. He stopped in front of her, so close that his shirt grazed her dress, she could see his pores and inhale his breath.

"Good morning, Mrs. Cooper."

"Good morning, Mr. Cooper." What else could she say? *I feel strange, because I don't know how to act with you anymore?* He stared into her eyes, boldly, salaciously, his message clear. She took a step backward; he took one forward, held her face with his hands and let his marauding lips fire up her mouth. Then he stepped back and grinned.

"I don't have to get permission to do that anymore."

She recovered from the jolt he'd given her. "Who said so?"

"I got it in black and white. Yesterday. Read the contract."

"What contract? I didn't sign any... Oh, you mean..."

He nodded. "That's right. We signed what amounts to a marriage contract, and that piece of paper, that marriage certificate, gives me rights."

"Now look-a-here. You promised me..."

"Of course I did, and you also promised me. What's the problem?"

"Make sense, Magnus. We're supposed to be working up to...well, you know..."

"No, I don't. Come on, kiss your husband. I've got to get started on my rounds." Before she could say another word, he pinned her to the wall, ravaged her mouth with his tongue and let his hands plunder every inch of her body from her shoulders to her knees. Numbing her senses. Moisture beaded her skin.

"See you later," he drawled.

She stared at him for a second as he strolled off. Then she grabbed the wooden Nigerian Kweepee doll from the table beside her and sent it zinging after him with such aim that it crashed against the doorjamb right beside his head. Only momentarily stunned, he grinned, treated her to a mock salute and let the door close behind him. So he likes to play, does he? she fumed. Well, she could promise him the best of entertainment; when it came to games, she hadn't met her better.

Magnus rode Cougar out to the grazing field to check on the new fencing. He dismounted and walked along the barbed wire, testing its strength and examining the posts. He had to laugh when he thought of the scene that might have taken place if the Kweepee doll had struck his head. He doubted that she would have enjoyed seeing him in pain, and he'd have milked it for all it was worth. Selena's compassionate nature would have brought her to her knees. Contrite. He grinned at the thought of himself moaning in pretended pain while she hovered over him, soothing and loving him. He leaned against a post. Maybe not. After all, she'd been furious with him for deliberately heating her up. Well, she could expect a lot more of what she got that morning. He meant to lay the loving on her until she craved him day and night, until she had to have him. He'd have to be careful, though, because his wife had a hot, unpredictable temper.

Selena drove into the Center's parking lot and parked her car, but intuition wouldn't let her relax until she was in her office with the door locked. Inexplicably uneasy, she telephoned Magnus.

"Cooper."

"Magnus, it's me, Selena. I'm at the Center for a while this morning."

"I see."

"Magnus?"

"I... You got there without incident?"

"Yes. Except for this feeling that I should be careful."

"How long will you be there?"

"Another hour." She waited during an extended silence.

"I don't think you want to hear this, Selena, but I'd like you to wait 'til I get there. I'll drive you home or wherever you want to go."

"Magnus, I don't need this."

"I know that, Selena, but I do. I have to know you're safe. Will you wait?" She told him she would. An hour later, she walked out of the Center with her husband, just as Prince Cooper jumped off the hood of her car, and she couldn't help being glad that Magnus was with her. She took her car keys out of her bag.

Magnus held out his hand for them. "I'll drive us. Jackson came along to take my car back."

She waited out his silence during their ride to the ranch. It was his move. He parked in front of the house and turned to her.

"Thanks for picking me up," she sang in as merry a voice as would a Broadway chanteuse. "I was expecting a shipment of personal effects from New York today. Did..."

"It came a couple of hours ago."

She opened the door, but his arm moved past her in lightning speed and held the knob. "How did Prince know you'd be at the Center this morning?"

Anger boiled up in her. "He's probably got some supernatural powers that he didn't tell you about. Now, would you please let me out of here?"

He ran his fingers over his hair and fell back against the seat. "I'm sorry. I know you didn't plan it. It's... The idea of having to tangle with my brother over my wife is…is sickening. I wish he'd grow up."

She supposed it was too much to hope that Magnus hadn't seen Prince. She laid her hand on her husband's arm. "Magnus, Prince won't be a problem for us unless you let him. If we ignore him, he won't enjoy his meanness."

"I wish I thought it. He'll only invent other ways of getting to me, to us, and one day he'll go too far. I've tried to understand him, to help him, to turn him around, even to love him, but he's oblivious to common decency. He won't change, and I can't erase the fact that he's my brother, and that I care about him."

She moved closer, opened her arms and held him. She had no words to give him; he had to believe. Her heart soared when he kissed her throat and squeezed her to him before getting out of the car.

Magnus walked rapidly around the house to the small building facing the garden that housed his office. Minutes after he sat down to his desk, he heard a knock. Jackson. He stiffened. It could also be Prince. Relief, palpable and heady, spread through him when he opened the door to his ranch manager.

"Sorry to bother you, Magnus, but I'd swear I saw Prince hightailing it out of that parking lot."

"I saw him. He intends to be a thorn in my flesh, but if he goes too far, I'll stop him."

"He can't be crazy enough to…" Jackson shook his head. "I've never seen the beat of that fellow. Just thought I'd tell you. Oh, by the way, we need to switch B herd to the northern pasture. The old heifers have been grazing too heavily in the eastern fields. What do you think?"

"We can start whenever you get two other men free. Let me know when you begin." He began checking the payrolls. He trusted his accountant but he didn't expect anybody to protect his business for him; that was his job. He signed the checks for the ranch's employees, threw his hands up, locked his desk and left his office. *He had to stop thinking of Selena in relation to Prince.*

Several days later, Selena unpacked the last box of dolls, her most prized ones, and arrayed them on the mantel in her living room. She hoped Magnus wouldn't mind if she put some of them in the foyer. Just as she thought to call him and ask what he thought of it, the telephone rang.

"Hello."

"Hello. Who's this?" She thought she detected a falsetto note, but discounted it.

"Mrs. Sutton-Cooper."

"Well," the strange voice continued. "Well, well. This is Edwin, your brother-in-law. I just called to say I'm on my way out. See you shortly."

"You're Magnus's brother? How nice. I was under the impression that he had only one brother."

"You're kidding. That shows you shouldn't be guided by your impressions. I'm looking forward to seeing you, Selena."

"I'm sure Magnus will be happy to have you visit us, Edwin."

She wondered why he seemed anxious to terminate the conversation. Wait a blessed minute. Magnus definitely said he only had one brother. And she hadn't given the man her name. A reporter, maybe. She dashed downstairs to find Tessie.

"Magnus got one brother," Tessie confirmed for her. "Edwin and Prince is one and the same. Miss Anna thought he was so cute, she nicknamed him Prince and it stuck. If he's coming here, you'd better go tell Magnus."

Magnus was a bull seeing red when it came to Prince and her, and she'd as soon not be the one to tell him about his brother's latest stunt, but it couldn't be avoided. She checked her stride as she neared the office. Luck wasn't with her; he was yards away at the stable door, when she saw him mount Cougar and gallop off.

"He and Cougar went toward the lake," she told Tessie and could only gape as the woman used the sides of her skirt to clean the biscuit dough from her hands. She'd never known Tessie to be disconcerted. "Where're you going?"

"To lock all the doors. I wouldn't put it past him to stroll right in here uninvited and make a nuisance of himself 'til Magnus gets back here and throws him out." Air swished out of her, and she dropped into one of the kitchen chairs. What had she gotten into?

"You stay right in here with me," Tessie ordered when she got back in the kitchen. "Prince never did know nothing about the truth, and if you're here with me, it won't matter what kind of lie he tells nor how many. I declare that boy's gonna find himself in trouble come Judgment Day."

Magnus left Cougar with the groom and walked rapidly to the house. He reached for the door to the screened side porch and stopped.

"To what do I owe this honor?" he asked Prince, his temper rising at the arrogant smirk on his brother's face.

"Since I couldn't make it to the wedding, I came to kiss the bride. You wouldn't begrudge me that little consolation prize, would you?"

Magnus knocked his Stetson to the back of his head and propped his booted foot on the step. "Did you expect me to insult my bride by inviting you to her wedding after your brutal treatment of her? And how do you get the temerity to come here to my home after my wife?"

"Your lovely bride invited me. She said you'd be glad to see me."

Magnus straightened to his full height. Bold. Intimidating. "You're lying." Cool off, he told himself when he began rubbing his thumbs and forefingers together, a sure sign that his temper was ready to fly. He had the satisfaction of seeing Prince take a few steps away from him.

"Ask her. Don't tell me she isn't allowed to see her friends."

Magnus laughed, if the feral sneer that left his lips could be called that. "You were never anybody's friend. Grow up and learn basic decency before you get yourself into a mess that you can't get out of."

"You wouldn't let your little brother suffer just because you're jealous, would you?"

Prince's eyes widened as Magnus walked toward him, and he would have laughed at the look of apprehension in his brother's eyes, but for the pain that pummeled his chest. "If you come here again without a personal invitation from me, I won't be responsible."

"My, my." Prince sneered back, "I didn't know you cared. Selena wants to see me, and I want to see her. You can't stop the river from flowing to the ocean, brother, and believe me, this ocean will be there to drink it in. You married her to get her away from me, but forget it. She's mine, and I'll get her."

Magnus grabbed Prince's shirt, pulled the man close and spoke in his face. "Touch my wife, and you'll remember the consequences as long as you live."

Prince jerked away. "Well I'll be damned. You're in love with her. Call her right now and ask her if she invited me to come here. Ask her," he taunted. "You think she's different from all the other women in this town? We just had a lovers' spat. She wanted me, and she still does."

Magnus's face twisted in anger. "From the day you were born, you only wanted what belonged to someone else, and especially to me. You've stolen, cheated, mistreated people, and abused women and done so with impunity, because you had Mother and me to bail you out of every scrape you got into. From now on, you're on your own, Prince. If Mother goes to bat for you, I have the power to reverse whatever she does. And I will. I've had it with you. It's time you paid for your misdeeds."

Prince grinned. "That won't keep your wife home. Think about that."

Magnus had a vision of Iago planting the seeds of murder in Othello's head with his lying indictment of Desdemona. "You'd lie on your deathbed," he bit out, shortening the distance between them. "You move your ass off my property. And you do it *now*." Magnus whirled around, walked back to the screen door and reached for the knob. Anger seethed in him. He went inside to his office and sat there until the noise from the motor of Prince's car died away. Interrogating Selena about her relationship with Prince would wipe out what headway he'd made with her. And if he did it in Prince's presence, she'd never forgive him. She'd said nothing existed between his brother and her and that nothing ever had. He believed her. He had to.

"Where's Selena?" he asked Tessie when he walked into the dining room. "She doesn't answer her phone."

Tessie laid the plate of pickled mushrooms on the sideboard and walked around to where he stood. "Did Prince come here not long ago?"

He wasn't in a mood to fence with Tessie, and he didn't want her meddlesomeness. "You might answer my question before asking one."

"Selena's setting her hair, and with the noise from that hair dryer, she probably couldn't hear the phone."

"Yes. Prince came here, but I sent him packing."

Tessie took a few steps away from him. "Selena made me listen in on the…"

Cold darts shot down his spine, numbing him. "He said he talked with her, that she invited him here."

Her hands went to her hips. "Magnus, Prince identified himself as Edwin and said he was your brother. Led her to think you had two brothers. You know how he is, and you know he can change his voice to suit the occasion. You ain't gonna let him get between you and Selena, are you?"

He smiled. "Not on your life, Tess, but there's no telling how far he'll try to push me. I don't want to be alienated from my only brother, but if he tries to get between me and my wife, though, something will give. The awful thing is that he's so sure of himself where she's concerned. He believes what he's saying. I don't want to have to…"

"I hope you ain't gonna talk yourself into taking what he says seriously."

"No, but I can't figure out how he knew Selena would be at the Center the other morning. She's only been there twice since she came to the ranch."

"Son, he could have been hanging around here every day, waiting for her to go out by herself."

He ran his hand over his hair in frustration. "Yeah. He'd do that."

You could carve the silence in here, Selena thought, as they finished dinner that evening. What she had to say wouldn't warm things up, either, but she wouldn't let that stop her. "I'm going back to work. I've indicted Lightner for breaking my contract, and I expect him to retract the dismissal order. While he's getting around to doing it, I'll be back at work."

"If y'all don't want anything else," Tessie said, getting up from the table, "I'll just straighten up my kitchen."

"What're you talking about?" Magnus asked when they were alone. "If you go back there, Prince will assume it's for his convenience. I don't like it."

She gazed at him, her dessert spoon suspended between her plate and her mouth. "Magnus, are you suggesting I quit work? I enjoy my work, so why should I give it up? I won't be Prince's victim any more than I'll let Lightner walk over me. I have a job, I'm well enough to work and I intend to fulfill the terms of my contract."

A muscle twitched in his jaw. "I know you're right," he said, his apprehension obvious, "but you don't need to work."

"I don't need to knit, either."

He wanted her happiness more than his own, but he didn't trust his brother.

His tone softened, as he reached across the table and grasped her fingers. "You're too vulnerable over there in Waverly, where I can't help you if you need me."

She squeezed his fingers lovingly, and decided to try to placate him. "If I got a cellular phone that I could use in the car and wherever I went, would you be less worried?"

He got up, walked around the table and hunkered down beside her. "All right, but I want to program it so that you only have to push one button, and you'll get me."

"You'd have to keep your phone with you all the time."

"I don't care what I have to do. I want you safe."

"I'll be careful." He rested his head in her lap and prayed she'd put her arm around him. Her fingers began to stroke his back, easing his tension, and he pressed his lips to her belly.

When he gazed up at her, she let her fingers caress his brow. "Maybe I'll restart my brokerage business. I can do that from the ranch. I'll be happy, and you won't be nervous every time I go to work."

He hugged her waist. "It's a good idea, anyway. It's your profession, you like it and you're good at it."

Selena hooked the cellular phone to her belt and headed for Eloise's office to announce her return to work.

"Hey, girl," Eloise exclaimed, leaving no doubt as to her joy at having her friend back on the job. "Girl, am I glad to see you."

Selena got down to work, and lunchtime arrived quickly. She started across the street for lunch at the Waverly Inn and, to her amazement, Magnus stood at the curb talking with the sheriff.

"Magnus! What a surprise."

"Hi. Somebody took off with five of my heifers, but they're already back at the ranch. That's a great thing about longhorns, honey. Unless the river they have to cross is too deep, their homing instinct takes them back home."

She found his hand with her own. "Will they try it again?"

His gaze darkened. "Yeah, but don't let that bother you."

Her heartbeat accelerated at the tenderness she saw in his smile. "I care about everything that happens to you."

"You're telling me we're a team?"

She could only nod her agreement, lest her heart betray her. He opened the truck door, and pulled her inside and into his arms.

"Honey, I need some sugar," he said, his eyes gleaming with merriment. A kind of devilry she hadn't seen in him. "This whole business has just about zapped my adrenaline." He pulled her closer. "Stop laughing at me. I'm a man without defenses, and my wife thinks I'm a joke...." when she sucked in her breath and didn't remember to mask her reaction, his voice trailed off. In a flash, his body quickened, and she knew he wanted her.

"Baby, I..." She pulled him to her, held his head and loved his eager lips. Why couldn't he love her? She needed for him to love her.

She eased away from him. "How's your adrenaline, right now?"

He grinned, brazen and wicked, and shivers of awareness rippled through her. "I could throw a bull."

Selena looked first at Magnus and then at the street. Bad timing; one day she'd call him on his sexy behavior. "Anytime you run low on adrenaline, I'll be glad to help you get it flowing again."

"You're doing an awful lot of talking this morning," he said, his drawl soft and low. "For reasons you don't know, I'll let you push me—up to a point. But no further."

She had a feeling that Magnus could be wild, that he could shed that cool, genteel facade and get down to earth. She closed her right eye in a slow wink. "You haven't been too quiet. And you haven't kept your hands to yourself, either. You want me to tap dance to your tune, beat it out to—"

He grabbed her shoulders. "I want you to dance to my rhythm, and you know it."

She gazed into pools of naked desire and had to grasp his forearm to steady herself.

"Give me time, Magnus."

Magnus shook his head. "I know, but waiting for you seems like…like *Waiting for Godot*." He dusted her cheek with his index finger. "I'd better let you eat lunch and get back to work."

Seconds after she got back to her office, the phone rang. "When can we get together, baby? I'm getting sick of hanging around waiting for you to ditch your rich husband. Can I meet you after work?" She slammed down the receiver and slumped in her chair. If she had to get a court order to make him leave her alone, she'd do it. She was doggoned if she'd complain to Magnus every time Prince decided to make a nuisance of himself. But what if he decided to hang around the Center? That would be all the local gossipmongers needed for a field day at her expense.

Magnus parked his pickup in front of Jackson's bungalow, hopped out and raced up the steps. "Man, the thief who tried to steal those heifers didn't leave a trail. What do you think?"

"Can't say. But by nightfall, this ranch will be cattle-thief proof," Jackson promised. "We've finished the fences, and the men are stringing electric sensors around the edges. The livestock won't go near it unless they're forced, and the person who tries that will regret it."

"Good job," Magnus said, sticking his hands in the back pockets of his jeans and pacing the short hallway. "Got any hunches about the culprit?"

Jackson frowned and puckered his lips. "Not a clue. I've thought of nothing else since this happened, and I can't imagine who'd do it."

Magnus looked him in the eye. "Not even Prince?"

Jackson laughed. "Least of all. Prince wouldn't think of doing anything involving that much labor. Herding cattle into a truck is work, and he's too clever to incriminate himself by trusting an accomplice."

Magnus nodded, relieved. He didn't want to give up on his brother.

He put the truck in the garage and entered the house to hear Tessie say, "Here he is, Miss Anna. You take care, now. You hear?" Tessie handed Magnus the phone.

"Hello, Mother." She had refused his invitation to his wedding, and it was typical of her to wait ten days for her temper to boil over so she could vent her displeasure with as much passion as possible.

"I'm so disappointed in you, Magnus. You rushed off and married that woman when you knew I didn't approve. Poor Mavis is devastated. How could you do that to her?"

He laughed. "Mother, you're a riot. What man ever married a woman because she hung out with his mother? I've been careful to avoid even the semblance of intimacy with Mavis, because she isn't my type. That woman would stoop to just about anything to avoid getting a job. You bet I wasn't going to be her meal ticket."

She sniffled, warming up to her act. "But a nobody. How could you bring a nobody into our little family?"

"Be careful. Water seeks its level—if my wife is a nobody, so am I."

"Is she pregnant?"

He resisted hanging up. "You're overstepping your bounds, Mother. This isn't your business."

"Yes, it is. I have a right to know which one of my sons is the father of my grandchild. Do you at least know?"

He stiffened. "If you want any future contact with me, you'll kindly watch your tongue and respect my wife. I plan to be married to Selena Sutton-Cooper as long as I live, and you and everybody else will accept that and respect her."

"But Prince said you married her just to get her away from him."

Scalding fury threatened to suffocate him, and he had to breathe deeply before he could speak. "You've had plenty of occasions to learn that Prince isn't truthful, Mother. He's thirty-two years old. Why don't you let him go, and give him a chance to be a man? As long as you coddle him, run under him every time he gets in trouble and uphold him no matter what he does, he'll be a rotten excuse for a man. I've finished being his Santa Claus, and if he interferes with my wife, I'll treat him exactly as I would any other man who had the temerity to do that. So don't encourage him." He hung up, slapped his fist into his palm and stared at it. God forbid he should ever strike his brother.

The thought chilled him, and he went in search of Selena, seeking her smile and her warmth as balm for the ache inside him.

Selena sat at the computer in Magnus's office, searching the Internet for information on black women in money management occupations, particularly on Wall Street, when a direct message to Magnus flashed on the screen.

"We'd love to know when you'll be back with us in the office here, sir. We're looking after things, as we always do, but all of us miss you, M."

An employee, no doubt. She filed the message and put a note about it on Magnus's desk.

Warm fingers closed over her eyes. "Got a minute? I want to show you something special." When she turned to him, his smile caressed her. Every time she saw him, he drew her closer, and she longed for greater intimacy with him.

"Come with me?" he asked in a voice that wrapped her in warm contentment.

Wordlessly, she rose, held out her hand, and his smile broadened.

It could be so wonderful, if he'd learn to love her. He took her to the rose garden, placed his fingers against his lips and whispered, "Over there." She followed his gaze to a nest of brightly speckled bird's eggs.

"Where's the hen?" she whispered.

"She isn't setting yet."

Selena watched as the bird flew to the nest and perched beside it. Minutes later, her mate arrived carrying bits of straw in his beak, added it to the nest, and joined her. Selena looked up at the man who reached for her hand as though to suggest that they shared something special, and tremors plowed through her when her gaze settled on the unshielded adoration in his eyes. Could she hope that he envisioned them as a family, nesting, caring for their young, as his wordless message implied? She feared naming what her eyes beheld, scared that her imagination and desires had obfuscated reality.

"It's here," he said, bringing her back to him. "It's all around us and, if we're honest with ourselves and with each other, we can't miss."

She leaned against him, not for strength, but for his loving warmth. "You're not discouraged?" she asked him, wondering at his patience and self-control.

His arms encircled her. "I don't have a reason to be disheartened, Selena. Most people do their courting before they marry. That's what we're doing now, getting to know each other. And, honey, we have a lot to work with."

Impulsively, she turned in his arms and hugged him. "If you hadn't pressured me into coming here to recuperate for a few days, I'm sure I would never have gotten to know you. What a dreadful thought."

"Yeah. A backhanded gift from Prince." He stared deeply into her eyes, and she supposed he searched for reassurance. "You're not sorry you married me?"

She wouldn't have expected him to ask her that question at this stage of their relationship. Couldn't he see how she felt about him? "Sorry? Never."

He probed on, but she didn't resent it; that, she'd learned, was his way. "With my brother and mother like albatrosses around your neck, you're still glad we married?"

She shrugged. "I'd be happier if they weren't against us, but they don't figure in my dreams."

He grinned. "Who does?"

She tweaked his nose. "Depends on whether I'm smiling or in a nightmare."

"That so? And when you dream about me?" he persisted.

"Smiles all the way." Anna Cooper might not figure in her dreams, but she was about to learn precisely where she stood with Magnus's mother.

Chapter 5

What on earth does she want with me? Selena asked herself as she rushed to her desk.

"Thanks, Eloise." She took the phone.

"This is Selena Sutton-Cooper," she informed her mother-in-law. "What a surprise. How are you, Mrs. Cooper, and how may I help you?"

Magnus's mother didn't bite her tongue. "How may you help me indeed. If Magnus won't arrange for us to meet, then it's up to me."

Selena didn't like the way the conversation seemed headed, because she had no intention of letting the woman trap her into disloyalty to her husband. "Did you ask him to introduce us?"

"Of course not. Why should I? I'm his mother, and if he married somebody, I ought to know who she is. You'll admit that, won't you?"

Selena bristled at the woman's sharp manner and repeated in a slow, even tone, "What did you have in mind?"

"Well, I thought we might have lunch today, since I'll be in town around noon. Twelve-thirty's best for me. I'll be at El Prado. Not that I prefer Spanish food, I don't. I go there because the place is civilized. The waiters wear a tux as they should, and the white linen tablecloths are always spotless."

Selena heaved a deep sigh and prayed that, since coming to Waverly, she'd changed to the point where she could show some tolerance for her mother-in-law. She tapped her foot for a second or two and told herself that, if she was fortunate enough to have children, she'd have to tolerate the woman. Might as well start now. She'd give a little, but Anna wasn't going to walk on her.

"I'll see you there, but I won't be free for lunch until one. If you can manage…" She let it drift off. That or nothing.

"Yes. Yes. All right."

Selena looked at the receiver as the dial tone hummed. How could such a person have raised Magnus Cooper? If she had deigned to attend the wedding of her firstborn son, she would have met his bride at the ceremony, if not earlier. Selena imagined a full-chested dowager who didn't have a strand of hair out of place, and wrinkled her nose in distaste.

Anna Cooper did not disappoint her. Selena would have picked her out of a crowd, though neither of her sons resembled her. The woman studied her menu with a look of bored distaste, sipped her iced tea and glanced at her watch, though not toward the door. Her beige linen suit and blouse were in impeccable taste, as were her pearl earrings. She did not stand when Selena arrived at the table, and she seemed to prefer not to accept her daughter-in-law's outstretched hand. However, Selena stood her ground, hand extended, and won the first round. Anna Cooper shook her hand.

"Sit down, please, Selena." She glanced at her watch. Exactly one o'clock. "I'm ready to order."

Selena smiled inwardly; Magnus's mother was a tough cookie. "Give me a minute to read the menu."

Anna laid her own menu aside, while she waited for Selena to decide what she'd have. "What does your father do?"

Selena glanced up at Anna, her eyes wide. "My father? Nothing. He's dead." She had the pleasure of seeing the woman lose her composure.

"Well!" was all Anna could utter, and Selena thought of the old Jack Benny movies and sitcoms that she loved to watch on late-night TV. They ordered and immediately the waiter brought the first course, half a grapefruit for Selena and consommé for Anna. When a smile bloomed on Anna's face, Selena followed her gaze and stared horrified as Prince Cooper walked toward them.

"What is this?" she asked Anna. "How dare you arrange lunch with me as a convenience for Prince? I would have thought such behavior beneath my husband's mother." She stood as Prince reached them and leaned toward her as though to kiss her. Her hand shot out, palm forward, and would have landed in his face if he hadn't ducked.

"Why, Selena, honey, you don't have to act like this just because Mother's here. She knows how things are with us."

"You swine. You detestable swine." She walked rapidly out of El Prado aware that every one of the diners had caught the show. The tongues would wag. Oh, they'd have one gossiping good time, but she didn't intend to let it touch her.

She wouldn't tell Magnus. His family had given him enough pain, enough trouble. She didn't want him to know that his own mother had conspired with Prince to gain his wife's disloyalty to him. Anna Cooper probably had some form of psychological dysfunction, but she couldn't tell Magnus that, either. One of the local gossipmongers took care of it.

For the first time in three years, Magnus went voluntarily to see his mother. He walked into the four-bedroom ranch-style home in which he'd grown up. The same Kashan Persian carpet covered the hallway, the floor-length mirror with its ornately carved wooden frame still hung beside the living room door and the bells that an Egyptian belly dancer gave him after she sat on his lap in a Cairo nightclub collected dust on the edge of the mantelpiece. He'd given the bells to Prince, who had wanted them but had thrown them aside as soon as he could claim them as his own.

"I don't like what I just heard, Mother, and I won't stand for this game you and Prince have started." He scrutinized the impeccable woman who'd given him birth. What an actress, he mused in admiration at the look of innocence on her face.

"What could you possibly be talking about?" she asked.

"I've taken a lot from Prince, beginning with the day of his birth, and you're entirely responsible for that. You'd better stop this dangerous game. You don't know me, Mother, but if you and Prince keep this up, you will, and you won't like what you find."

"Oh, please. Selena left in a huff because of a lovers' spat. I don't see why you're making so much of it."

He glared at her, wondering if he knew her at all. "My wife had a lovers' spat with my brother in *your presence?*"

"Lower your voice, please. It's no secret. The whole town saw us."

"Of course. That's why you staged it at El Prado. You'll convince me Selena voluntarily agreed to meet Prince about as quickly as a broomstick will take you to Mars." If he'd implied she was a witch, he was too angry to care.

"You're being mean. Sit down, and let's discuss this in a civilized manner the way I raised you."

She couldn't be serious. "Thanks for letting me know you raised me," he retorted, his tongue heavy with sarcasm. "I always thought Tessie did that, but if you say so..."

"Don't be rude, son. Surely you don't believe I would abet anything unseemly. Prince wanted me to join them so he could set things straight with her, but it degenerated into a lovers' quarrel because of her senseless accusations."

His eyebrows arched, and he would have laughed if he hadn't been so mad. "*Son, eh?* If there's anything that makes me nervous, it's one of your late-life motherly gestures. You pushed me aside and spent your time taking Lamaze classes, visiting your exercise teacher, doing your mother-in-waiting yoga, and I don't know what else while you carried Prince. I wasn't quite five years old, but I remember my father trying to explain you to me. But after Prince was born, you spent all of your time with him, indulged him, spoiled him, gave him anything he wanted, even if it was mine. Now, he's a lousy excuse for a man, and you want me to countenance that. *No more!* If he touches my wife, the result when I find out will be worthy of a CNN special report. Trust me."

She bounced forward in her chair. "You won't hurt him. You won't." But for her unassailable dignity, he would have pitied her.

When she shrunk back, he knew his grin was as feral as he'd intended it to be. "My fingers are itching for him. You can't even guess how badly I want a piece of that man." He walked out and closed the door behind him. Anger boiled up in him, and he spun around.

"Where are you going," his mother called out, as he raced down the hallway. Knowing that her interest was in protecting Prince only exacerbated his fury. Ignoring her, he banged on his brother's bedroom door.

"Don't break the door down. I'm coming." The door swung open, and Prince's face creased into a grin. "What brought you here?"

Magnus stared at him. Prince was unprincipled; he had no morals, didn't understand the concept. A thirty-two-year-old man with no thought of ethical behavior. "I wanted to smash your face," he told Prince, "to rearrange it so thoroughly that people would turn their heads in disgust rather than look at you. I wanted to make it impossible for you to use your looks to rip apart people's lives. But look at you." He stepped closer to his brother. "Go over to that mirror and look at yourself."

Caught off guard, Prince stared tongue-tied as Magnus grabbed him by the hand and pulled him to the mirror.

"Can you see what I see? A stunted juvenile who runs to his mother every time he gets into trouble. An adolescent who uses his mother to help him try to get his brother's wife into bed. A thirty-two-year-old male—and I don't mean man—who lives with his mother and has never had a steady job. Take a good look at yourself. You cheated me out of a brother. Talented beyond belief, but what have you done with it? I pity you."

He didn't wait for Prince's response, and as he reached the front door, he heard his brother say, "What's *his* problem, Mother?" Magnus didn't wait for her reply; he didn't want to know.

Selena closed the door of her office and got to work on Freddie Powell's case. The nine-year-old had run away several times, though his mother swore that, at home, he acted the perfect child. Obedient, well-mannered, helpful, and never negligent of his chores. However, Freddie was a wall that even she, a psychologist, hadn't succeeded in penetrating. He smiled, shook hands, stood when she stood, and behaved properly in every way, proof of home training. But he'd walk past a parked car and toss a brick at the window for no reason and, whenever he got the notion, he'd go hiking—once, as far away as Tulsa, Oklahoma—without leaving a note.

"I see you've got Freddie's file. What's he done now?" Eloise asked, taking a seat beside Selena's desk.

"Walked out of school without permission. Looks to me like he feels caged."

Eloise lifted her right shoulder in a gesture of frustration. "What are we going to do about him?"

"Search me. Say, maybe a weekend at the ranch might do him good. I'll speak to Magnus about it."

Selena parked at the garage door and walked around the side of the house to the garden where she'd glimpsed Tessie cutting flowers for the dinner table. "Tessie, would it burden you to have a young boy visit us one weekend? Just a weekend, and I'd be home to help."

"Wouldn't bother me none, but if I was you, I wouldn't fill the place with kids and dogs that you have to pay attention to. I'd look after Magnus."

Her senses came alive. "Are you trying to tell me something, Tessie?"

Tessie put the flowers in her basket, pulled her tattered straw hat farther down to shield her eyes from the sun and started toward the house.

"Tessie?"

"Look, Selena, you know by now that if you ask me something, I'm gonna tell you just like it is. I watch you with that puppy, and I watch Magnus watching you. Now, you want to bring a kid here so you can shower your attention on him, too. Your husband is dying for the kind of attention you're giving that little old dog." She resumed her march to the back door, and Selena stood rooted in her steps, her mouth agape. Tessie had information that she needed; she followed her into the house.

"In for a penny, in for a pound, Tessie. Tell me the rest."

Tessie looked toward the sky and threw her hands up. "Miss Anna had time for Prince, always coddling, kissing him, and patting him from the time he was born, but I never saw her take that much interest in Magnus. That woman went bonkers over Prince, though with his attitude, only the Lord knows why. Long time back, Magnus said to me you reminded him of Miss Anna. Like I said once before, I don't expect you to put what I tell you to no good use, but this time I sure wish you would. I got to get my supper on."

Selena started upstairs, went back and got the puppy's food. She wasn't stupid. If Magnus liked attention, she planned to give him a steady diet of it, and Rhett Butler could get used to leading a dog's life.

"Let's go in the den," Magnus said to Selena after dinner. "I want to watch that TV show on Lena Horne's life."

She sat in her usual place on the sofa, but he took a seat across form her, rather than beside her as he always did.

For days, she'd toyed with an idea. Maybe this was a good time to bring it up. "Magnus, you remember that baby somebody left on the Center's steps? What do you think of us adopting it?" He might not like the idea, but what if she discovered she couldn't have a child?

He stared into her eyes, and she watched, mesmerized, as his own darkened until they seemed to throw out a narrow beam. He rocked back in his chair, and his body assumed a looseness that said he was up to any task. Answering him would have been a comedian's work. Magnus Cooper's message was clear; if she wanted a baby, he'd give her one.

"Do you want it badly?"

She remembered Tessie's words. He'd give in to her, but not happily, and this was not an issue on which to press him. "If we can find a home for him," she said, "I'll be satisfied."

He got up and sat beside her. "We're trying to cement our relationship, and the presence of a third person would complicate it. That includes Tessie. Maybe especially Tessie. If you're sure you won't be unhappy as a result, let's pass this time." He held her face and gazed into her eyes, and she thanked God for Tessie.

She couldn't have said, for any price, why her fingers went to his jaw and stroked its stubble in a slow caress, or why her gaze caught his sensuous lips and wouldn't move. She swallowed heavily and stared at his mouth, wanting it on her. His strong hand gripped her wrist, and her glance flew to his eyes, eyes that glittered with fierce heat and hunger. Her lips parted, trembling in their anticipation of his fire, and her hand grabbed the front of his shirt. Frustrated, she licked her lips, but his only answer was the wild storm, the hot want in his eyes.

"Magnus!" She raised her lips, but his response was to move her fingers from the front of his shirt and lock them on his erection. She thought her gasp raised the level of his heat, for his eyes darkened and he pressed her hand more firmly to his arousal.

"Yes," he said. "Yes, Selena. This is the way it is with me, and if I hold you and kiss you, how much worse do you think it will get?"

She pulled her hand away. "I'd better go." She'd promised herself that she would avoid such scenes as she'd just started, and she should have stuck with that decision. But what was she supposed to do when she knew he needed her? Hell must be something like this, she told herself.

He shook his head, leaned forward with his forearms on his knees and clasped his hands. "One of these nights you're going to put out the fire you start and, when you do, I may smile at the memory of all your false notices. Right now, though, I couldn't manage a smile if you offered me a gold mine."

She attempted to rise, but his hand on her arm detained her.

"Stay here. I can handle it—you've given me enough practice. Can you get off tomorrow afternoon? It's time I introduced you to some of my business associates. I thought we'd start with some of those in San Antonio. What about it?"

"I'd wondered when you'd get around to that. Twelve-thirty okay?"

He leaned back against the sofa and took her hand. "Fine. You seem to enjoy your work, though it's aeons away from buying and selling on Wall Street. Tell me about it." She described her typical day and included her continuing problem with Freddie, her most troublesome case.

"The kid needs direction," Magnus ventured, surprising her. "Maybe you ought to think of something special that's just for him. Bring him out here one weekend, and I'll teach him how to ride. He might like that." She couldn't tell him she'd thought of it. He wasn't keen on her working at the Center, an easy target for Prince, but he would nonetheless support her in her work. She looked away to prevent him seeing the love that bubbled inside her and that had to be mirrored in her eyes.

"Like it? Freddie will bloom out here. I can imagine the workout his inquisitive mind will give you and Jackson."

"No problem. A man can't get tuned into that business too early."

Her head snapped around, and she stared at him. "What do you mean?"

His hazel eyes glowed, and she could see in them the fiery passion that boiled in him, rearing to break loose. "Do you think I don't want a family?" he asked, his voice gritty with raw emotion. "Do you?"

Her breath quickened, and her pulse accelerated as she tried to calm herself sufficiently to answer him and not reveal so much of herself that he'd think she'd intended to trick him. She couldn't have been more nervous if her foot were poised over quicksand. She wanted to give him children as badly as she wanted to breathe. "I never thought that, though there's a lot about you that I don't know. I'm hoping that as we…as our relationship develops, we'll understand each other's needs."

He threw his head back and let laughter pour out of him, as though releasing a mountain of tension. "Selena, sweetheart, you missed your calling. If you were a trial lawyer and I needed one, baby, I'd go for you any day."

She hadn't meant to be that vague, but if she'd defused that potential bomb without incriminating herself, and letting him find out that she'd married him because she wanted a baby, a little needling was worth it. She looked into his solemn face and smoldering eyes, and cold tremors raced through her. She told him good-night; in another few minutes, nature would have removed their options.

His gaze followed his wife as she tripped up the stairs, her hips swaying rhythmically, enticing him, inviting him to race up there after her. He shook his head, bemused, as he headed toward his quarters. Why should she have been surprised to learn that he wanted children? Was that a signal that she didn't want any? But if that were the case, would she have been so eager to take in that baby? She was almost thirty-one; time she got started. Time *he* got started.

"Lightner backed off," Selena announced to Magnus when he walked into her office the next day. "My lawyer served him a *show cause,* and he turned chicken." She'd thought he'd be delighted and she found his cool reception of her news perplexing.

"Did he rescind the order in writing? Preferably notarized?" he asked her.

"No, but the lawyer says that's coming and, in the meantime, I'm to come to work every day. Actually, I figured that out myself."

"He'll make things as difficult as possible for you, and I'll have to sit on him." He raised both hands, palms out. "I know. I know. You don't want me running interference for you. But, honey, *you're my wife.* You don't have to work. Selena, you don't need this hassle.

She reached for his hand and felt his fingers close around hers. "Magnus, I can't quit because the going's rough. I will never again walk away from a situation because things don't go my way. I intend to change this job to my liking. Lightner isn't half the man that I am woman."

His broad grin enveloped and delighted her. "You bet, sweetheart. Sic 'em!" She had to laugh. Magnus possessed a wicked streak. "Selena, I won't say that your working pleases me—it doesn't. But I stand with you in defending your rights and, if this is what you want, I accept that. We'd better get started."

After lunch at the elegant Texas Ranger on the River Walk, he took her to McClinton and McClinton, livestock brokers. Selena hadn't expected to see the huge pieces of modern art, butter-soft leather seating, Oriental carpets and expensive plants in a San Antonio office. The CEO had called his senior employees to his office for coffee, bourbon or whatever with Magnus and Selena.

Back to the barn, she told herself, as one man blatantly disrobed her with his eyes, ignoring her husband. She would have glared at him, if a younger and obviously less well-placed one had not bowed over her hand at that moment, signaling to her that he'd just been introduced. "I hope I'm on your list of invites for this year's Cooper Ranch barbecue," he fawned, and slipped her his card.

"You aren't by chance the Selena Sutton of Hilliard and Matting, are you?" another asked.

Here it comes, she thought. "I'm no longer a broker," she replied.

The man moved closer. "But you haven't forgotten what made you so hot on Wall Street, have you? Once a stock jockey, always a stock jockey. Right? What do you think of precious metals right now?"

"They're still mined," she was tempted to say, and would have turned away from the man, when she felt Magnus's arm tighten around her.

His crisp tone implied that the man was out of place. "Call her at her office. This is a social visit." Irritation at his proprietary behavior surfaced within her, but she immediately recognized his motive. She had talked with Magnus about opening her own brokerage firm, and he had just given her a push.

She looked at him, her smile luminous. "You're some kind of nice."

After they stopped at the offices of his supplier, he introduced her to his friends at the Carver Community Cultural Center. "I can't remember when I've enjoyed myself so much," she told him as they headed home.

"Don't tell me you enjoyed having that monkey fawn over you. Who the hell gave him permission to kiss your hand?"

Trust Magnus to see the other angle. Giggles spilled out of her. "You're jealous," she accused, when she could get her breath.

"Damn straight, I am. Mosley must have lost his common

sense. Who ever heard of a man ogling a woman when she's standing less than two feet from her husband? I hate to think what he'd have done if you'd been wearing one of your hot dresses rather than that pristine suit. He acted as though he never saw a woman before. Give some men a whiff of liquor and they lose all sense of decency."

"Wall Street in Texas," she murmured to herself.

"What was that? Is that what you had to put up with in your job as a broker?"

"It's what I refused to put up with." And something that she definitely did not miss.

He grimaced. "Men like those ought to move into the nineties. Skirt chasing is out of place in business relations."

"You ought to go on the lecture circuit with that theme," she said. "More people need to hear it."

The following Saturday, Magnus leaned against the door of the tack room, examining the saddle he planned to let Freddie use. Selena hadn't mentioned the boy again, but he intended to raise the matter. He'd had his father to care for him and guide him when his mother demonstrated insufficient interest and support. Maybe Freddie went looking for his father when he ran away. Satisfied the boy could use that saddle, he handed it to Jackson.

"Get it reconditioned and polished. A kid needs softer leather."

"When's he coming?" Jackson asked.

"That's up to Selena, but I expect it'll be after I get back from Sierra Leone."

"You leaving soon?"

"A day or two, but I can't say I'm comfortable with it. I know you'll take care of the place, Jackson, but Prince has already showed his hand."

Jackson snorted. "As long as I'm in charge here, the place is safe from Prince. Any luck finding out who tried to steal those cows?"

"No. And it was so amateurish, it could even have been Prince."

"Or someone trying to implicate him."

Magnus arched an eyebrow. "Now that's a thought." He stepped out of the stable, started toward the house and stopped. Selena strolled toward him, a perfect accompaniment to the quiet and beauty of the setting sun on that early May evening. "Beautiful," he gasped, as his heart hammered in his chest, and desire began its pull on him. He fought it, but it skittered through him, erratic as a summer storm. Her long wide skirt swished as she walked and, in her brown leather boots and a sweater that showed her full breasts to advantage, she was a regal woman. He watched with pride as she neared him, pride that Selena Sutton-Cooper was his wife.

"Hi, cowboy," she greeted him.

"Hi, yourself," he said, taken aback that she'd stopped so close to him, letting her woman's scent tease his nostrils and heighten his desire. She nodded a greeting to Jackson and the other man, barely taking her gaze from his face. Her lips, cheeks and eyes smiled to him, as though she thought him precious. He didn't know what to make of it. He didn't believe she would come on to him, not after their tenuous truce several nights earlier.

"I'd suggest we ride a bit," he said, "but you're wearing a skirt." He took her hand, because he had to touch her someplace.

"A walk would do me good."

He shook his head in wonder; as soon as he thought he understood her, she threw him another curve. "You wouldn't be planning a surprise, would you?" If so, he hoped she wouldn't resurrect the matter of their being parents to a child other than their own.

Selena allowed herself an inward smile, but he must have recognized her secretiveness.

"I'm ready for anything you plan to spring on me. I like a woman who's imaginative, not very predictable, like you. Keeps me on my toes. Feel up to a stroll as far as the lake?"

Don't get overconfident, girl, she told herself. He isn't as easy as he thinks. "Anywhere. As…" She bit her tongue, because she'd almost said as long as she was with him, she didn't care where they went. But that wouldn't win her the prize she coveted. Magnus cared for her, but she knew he'd given himself a thousand reasons not to love, and Anna Cooper was one of them.

"Care to finish that sentence?"

"If you're gunning for flattery, consider yourself flattered," she replied in a voice light with laughter.

"A man can't get too much adulation from his wife. It's like food—loving oils his wheels and keeps his motor tuned."

"Where are we right now?" she asked, daring to change the subject. She didn't want them to get into sexual innuendos and one-upmanship. "I didn't realize a river went through here."

He stopped walking, released her hand and slung his arm around her waist. "That's the narrow end of the lake. We dug it so the cattle and horses could drink there when branch water gets scarce."

"Magnus, look!" A widemouth bass cleared the water by four feet, and another quickly followed.

His arm tightened around her body. "See that? Not even a fish lets his mate fool around. See how fast he took off after her?"

She couldn't help laughing. As they walked along, holding hands, joy suffused her. Every molecule of her body shouted with exhilaration as she took in his towering masculinity, handsome grace and gentle manners. She already loved him, but she risked going head over heels, a barrel tumbling down a hill. He had to love her; she couldn't bear life if he didn't love her.

Magnus tightened his grip on the woman who walked beside him. He wondered if he'd done the right thing in letting her think he'd married her for reasons other than love, that he'd only wanted to protect her, to make amends for his brother's beast-

liness. And when he'd promised her that he wouldn't push her—
after what Prince did to her, he couldn't push her—that he'd wait
until she came to him, he hadn't thought it would take her so
long. More than once, she'd all but succumbed to her passion,
but he didn't want a one-night stand. He needed her to come to
him, tell him she loved him and wanted to be his wife in truth
as well as in law. Then, they could start their family. He knew
how to prevent an unwanted pregnancy, but the best-laid plans
sometimes went awry, and he didn't want a child with her unless
mutual love bound them. The thought that a child of his might
shuttle between divorced parents didn't sit well with him.

Darkness settled around them, and the moon began its climb.
The fireflies flickered at their feet, a mockingbird started its
night song, the scent of roses filled the air, and all he needed to
complete his life, he held in his arms. Some would say he had
everything, but she wasn't truly his. She moved, as though
restless, and her scent wafted to his nostrils, seducing him.

"Chilly?" he asked her, though as warm as it was, he didn't
see how she could be.

She shook her head, released a deep sigh and turned into him.

"Selena. Baby, we've got to stop this. We've got to…" He
lost his war with himself, as he'd known he would, and tipped
up her chin to look into her eyes. Stunned at the want in them,
he capitulated and took her mouth. He ran his tongue over her
glistening lips and, in her eagerness for him, she pressed her
body to his, triggering his swift and complete arousal. He
stepped back.

"Sorry. I know I said I wouldn't let it happen again but,
honey, celibacy is not for the initiated." He leaned forward and
kissed her cheek. "Let's start back." This was happening too
often. With all those starts and stops, going to the brink and
pulling back, if he ever did get her signal to go all the way and
make love, damned if he wouldn't be a three-legged horse in the
Kentucky Derby.

His kiss hadn't been an accident, but he didn't have to know that. She knew that if she went out to the stables, he'd suggest they ride, so she had dressed for walking. If they had gone riding, she wouldn't have been able to set the stage for the intimacy that stole over them, and she had decided that their relationship wasn't moving fast enough. She had to get pregnant, but she refused to make love with a man unless she knew he loved her. The problem was that any trap she set for him proved to be one for herself, and she'd fallen irrevocably in love with him.

They reached the house. She intended for him to know she wanted him, but he wasn't going to find out how much she hurt, so she hid the emotion that welled up in her and quipped, "Mr. Cooper, you do know how to give a gal a great stroll."

"Glad to have been of service, ma'am." He smiled, but she could see that it didn't reach his eyes. He probably knew she was faking, too. Lord, when would they straighten out their lives?

Magnus had similar thoughts, as he wondered about his feelings while watching Selena disappear through the kitchen door. He ought to learn how to forget the dark part of his past, forgive his mother and accept Prince. His common sense told him if he could do that, he'd stop worrying about whether Selena reciprocated his feelings. Shouldn't her desire for him be enough? He'd tell himself it was, and then he'd remember his mother's behavior toward his father. What if the desire cooled before she learned to love him? He didn't want to risk it.

He walked into the kitchen, pulled a chair from the table, straddled it and waited for Tessie's rebuke. It wasn't forthcoming.

Tessie silence Lionel Richie's velvet tones with a flick of the radio switch. "Is there some rule that says you and Selena can't never walk in here together?"

"If so, it's probably part of that rule that says you don't meddle in my personal life, Tess."

"Well, if you don't know what's going on, I do. You're so smart, Magnus. You awed me with your smartness even as a tiny boy, but lately I started to wonder. I just don't see what I want to see with you two. Don't you plan to do nothin' about it?"

"We're working on it." He shuttered his eyes. Hiding his feeling about Selena had become reflexive; he did it so often.

"Saints alive, you had plenty of time. You got more than you bargained for, and I know, 'cause you didn't expect she'd get next to you like she has."

"You're clairvoyant now, I see." Annoyance threatened the peacefulness he'd had when he walked into the kitchen, but from his youth, he'd turned to Tessie for guidance, and she had a right to speak her mind; he didn't move.

"A man can't live around a woman like Selena for long without losing his heart to her." She handed him a glass of tomato juice, which she knew he liked. "And that ain't a bad thing," she went on.

"Wouldn't I have done that before I married her?"

"Most men would have, but you always did sing a different kind of tune. I didn't say nothing, 'cause I knew she was right for you."

"Tess, what would happen if you tried being a little more subtle?"

"People wouldn't understand me, that's what would happen. Besides, if I want somebody to get out of my sight, I tell 'em to do that. No point in saying, 'Will you please excuse me.' They may think I'm the one out of place."

Magnus chuckled. Tessie on a roll was pure symphony. "Not to change the subject, but you wouldn't know why Jackson's acting as though the sky fell on him, would you?"

She threw up her hands and glanced toward heaven. "I don't know a soul by that name. If you're speaking of your on-again, off-again ranch manager, let the sky and anything else that'll drop fall right on him. Means nothing to me."

Magnus let the mirth stream out of him in a gale of laughter, as he unfolded his body from astride the chair. "In that case, you won't give him a hard time when he comes in to dinner, will you?"

Her hands braced her slim hips, and a scowl creased her brow. "I won't even know he's in the house. Grin all you want to," she said, as he started out of the room. "You're gonna get your dose, and you won't be grinning, either. You hear?"

"Whatever you say," he called over his shoulder and headed for his quarters.

Magnus noticed that his private-line answering machine blinked and played the message.

"This is Jeb. We've got problems in Sierra Leone."

He phoned the manager of his Houston office. "What kind of problems, Jeb?"

"That contractor is as slick as crude oil on water. Building supplies, time sheets, you name it—he finds a way to knock down a pile for himself."

"I've been expecting this. I'll tell Madeline to arrange my flight for the day after tomorrow. See you when I get to Houston." Just what he needed. Jeb McCallister, his Houston manager, wouldn't call him unless the situation demanded it. He went into the den and began reviewing his files on Sierra Leone and the Freetown Construction and Supply Company. An hour later, he heard Tessie's ring, signaling two minutes before dinner, and dashed to his room. He showered and dressed in record time and charged headlong into Selena as he rushed toward the dining room.

"Getting a little cheap exercise?" Selena asked as he picked her up from her seat on the floor.

"I'm sorry. Did I hurt you?"

"Doesn't look like it."

"Tessie hates for us to come late to dinner, and I figure if she's worked hard to fix a good meal, I can at least show up when it's ready," Magnus explained.

"If you'd started a little earlier…" She let him imagine the rest.

"Don't be so superior. I got here the same time as you."

She dusted off the back of her dress for emphasis. "Yes, and on your feet no less, which, thanks to you, is more than I can say for myself."

"What's holding you two?" Tessie called out. "There's a man in the dining room waiting for y'all so he can eat."

She felt his strong fingers grasp her arm. "Come on," he whispered. "She's hell-bent on giving Jackson a hard time."

Selena stopped. "Why?"

Magnus shrugged his left shoulder. "Makes no sense to me why she does it, especially since she's crazy about him."

"I had no idea."

"You're gaping," he teased. "Come on."

After an unusually quiet meal during which Jackson barely spoke and Tessie made certain that he noticed her, Magnus put an arm around Selena's shoulder. "Join me for espresso and maybe a cognac?" he asked Selena.

"Love to."

He looked at Jackson. "How about you, friend?"

"No point in spoiling your evening just because mine is shot," Jackson said.

Selena glanced back in time to see Tessie walk over to him and lay a hand on his shoulder. She figured his evening was about to improve.

Selena's wasn't, she soon discovered.

"I'm leaving tomorrow for Houston and, day after tomorrow, I'll fly from there to Sierra Leone on the west coast of Africa. I'll be there three or four days. Want to come with me?"

She didn't want a wedge between them just as their bond had tightened, but she had responsibilities at the Center, and he'd said he accepted that. "Magnus, have you forgotten that I work at the Center, that I'm a paid employee there?" She noticed that Tessie set the espresso on the coffee table, but didn't leave the room.

"I keep telling you that you don't have to work. There are people who need your salary, and you don't."

The bile of irritation foamed in her mouth. "No, I don't need the money, because I'm financially well-off. But I need to honor my commitment, and I need to exercise my mind, just as you do. I also need to rely on your word when you say you understand my need for an intellectual outlet." She knew he was ambivalent about it; he wanted her to do whatever made her happy, but he wanted to protect her from Prince and she suspected that, whether or not he knew it, he might not want to compete with her job for her attention. She wished he wasn't so complex.

"All right. All right. Forget I mentioned it. Tell me one thing. How did you happen to have lunch with Mother and Prince the other day?"

Surprised, she had to cover her reaction. How long had he known, and why had he waited until now to mention it? Was he trying to pick a fight? "I didn't find it unusual that your mother would call and invite her new daughter-in-law to lunch, so I went." And her hope of increasing the warmth that had furled between them during their walk also went.

"Why didn't you tell me about it?"

She sat farther away from him so that she could take in his reactions to her words. "I didn't want to appear to tattle on your mother."

He slapped his thighs as though at his wit's end. "You may as well learn that my dear mother is adept at taking care of herself *and* at fomenting trouble."

He'd told her very little about his mother, so she seized the opportunity. "Doesn't she like you?"

He shrugged. "Says she does."

She hurt for him. "Why wouldn't I have lunch with your mother, if she invited me? There was the chance that she wanted to improve our relationship." She paused, but when he didn't intervene, she continued, "I won't be that naive again."

"I don't believe you want Prince's friendship."

She was glad to hear that. Now, if he'd just behave as though he didn't believe it... "And yet you mention it."

"I cover all bases. I don't like having toothless Carrie Pilgrim grinning at me and telling me the whole town knows you're back at it with Prince, as she phrased it. If a man had said that to me, he'd have found it necessary to dust off the seat of his pants."

"Well, as of now, I'm not accepting any more invitations from Mrs. Anna Cooper. Don't worry about that while you're gone, and stop worrying about my working. I *have* to be busy, Magnus."

"I'm sorry, Tessie," Selena began, and that opening was all Tessie needed.

"Don't mind me. I been expecting this. I could've told—"

"Tessie, *please!*" Magnus said, his tone frighteningly soft.

"Okay. Okay. I'll mind my business, but something's gonna have to give. You can't get blood out of a turnip, Magnus. And, Selena, you ought to realize by now that Magnus could stand out in an open field in a gale-force wind and not move an inch. And that's my sermon for today. Go ahead and fight. When you get tired or miserable enough—whichever comes first—maybe you'll both wake up." She sauntered out of the room.

"Forgive me. You have as much right to the work you like as I do."

Selena wasn't sure she could count on that. He meant it, but something about it galled him. Maybe when she got her business started, he'd relax about it. Knowing she was vulnerable, that was it. He wanted her to accompany him to thwart any move Prince might make. She let her arm slide around his back and rejoiced when he didn't move away.

"I'll be careful, Magnus. I'll go straight to the office and back home. Leave your beeper with Jackson, and don't worry."

"I will." His voice had a far-off, almost hollow sound unlike the southern lilt she loved so much.

"Be careful, Selena. Be careful. Don't let him get you on the road alone. If he knows I'm out of the country, he may try just about anything."

Chapter 6

Magnus looked around his Houston office, leaned back in his chair and buzzed Madeline twice. Instead of responding over their intercom system, she walked into his office. He glanced up at her. "Ask Jeb to come in, please."

She stood there as though waiting for something, her smile in place as usual. "That will be all, Madeline."

She continued to smile. "If there's nothing else I can do for you, sir." He'd told her about the "sir," but though she'd managed after considerable persuasion to use his first name, she insisted on that formality.

"No, that's all. I want to see Jeb." He thought he noticed a flash of displeasure in her eyes, but discounted it. Madeline was not only loyal but self-denying, as well. She gave her all for the company, no matter the personal cost. That didn't earn a lot of points with him, but he valued her nonetheless.

He got up and shook hands with his manager. "Have a seat, Jeb. What have you got for me?"

"I've sent the builder three orders of steel beams, and he tells me he needs more, though he shouldn't have needed the third one. The man's forgotten I sent him a generator, and his payroll is fishy. I've noticed he writes a duplicate order for everything. Doesn't he know we are the people who laid the plans for those buildings, and we know what's needed and what isn't? I suggest we keep your visit to ourselves."

"He's used to loading up on everybody, but he'll straighten out when I tell him how unhappy the government will be if I back out of that deal. I wish I had Malloy out there."

"Think he'd take a short assignment?"

"Nah. He's my silent partner, a happy husband and devoted father who's expecting his first daughter. A cannon couldn't blow him out of Accord. He brought his family to Waverly for my wedding and left the next morning. Couldn't wait to get back home."

"When are you leaving?"

"Ten o'clock tomorrow morning. I hope to be back Tuesday."

"I'll be here if you need me," Jeb said. "Good luck."

He buzzed his secretary. "Madeline, be sure Selena has whatever she wants or needs while I'm away, and would you please hurry and open those charge accounts for her at Neiman Marcus and Saks Fifth Avenue in San Antonio. It shouldn't take so long."

"I'm terribly sorry, sir, but I *have* been terribly busy. It won't happen again."

"I'd be extremely displeased if it did. I'll be back in the States on Tuesday." He hadn't known Madeline to be slow when she had double the work of the past three weeks. He buzzed her again.

"A Magnus Cooper charge account can be opened with one phone call. If you're too busy to do that, Madeline, I'll get you an assistant."

"That won't be necessary, sir. I'll get right to those accounts."

"Good. See you when I get back." He snapped his briefcase

shut, picked up his luggage and left. Minutes before boarding the plane, he phoned Selena.

"I know you probably won't use them, but your charge accounts should be open tomorrow morning, and if you need anything, call Madeline, my secretary. If she can't help you, tell Jackson to take care of it." He knew he stunned her with, "Keep yourself sweet for me," and hung up.

Early the next morning, dripping with sweat after a run with Rhett Butler, Selena dropped into a chair, exhausted. The little rascal could cover a lot of space in a couple of seconds, she'd learned. Now for a hot shower and, before leaving for work, she'd have at least an hour in which to help Tessie with plans for the Cooper Ranch annual Memorial Day barbecue. At least a month was needed to get out invitations, hire caterers and set up a tent. She started to tingle when she thought about Magnus's phone call. With a two- or three-hundred-mile advantage, Magnus had said she should keep herself sweet for him. He'd better not say that when she could get her hands on him; she'd show him what sweet was. If she ever found out what made that man tick, she'd make certain he didn't want to be as much as a yard away from her. Trouble was, Magnus Cooper was a living enigma. "Now who could that be," she grumbled, as she picked up the receiver.

"Hi, baby, I hope you're by yourself and we can talk. Your rich husband is usually making his rounds about now. Right?"

"You must be masochistic," she told Prince. "I don't want anything to do with you, and if you don't stop pestering me, I'll get a court order to stop you. Your hide is as thick as your brain." She hung up.

Tessie dried the suds from her hands and lifted the receiver. "Cooper residence."

"Selena and I got cut off, Tessie. Call her to the phone, will you?"

"You should hold your breath so long, you liar. I know she don't want to talk with you. You won't be satisfied 'til Magnus takes your head off and, if you ask me, that's what you deserve."

"Aw, come on, Tess. Let me speak to her. Sooner or later, I'll get her and your precious Magnus will look about as good to her as a lump of wet coal. When I get a woman, she never wants another man."

Fear streaked down her back. If Prince circulated the lie that he and Selena had been lovers, God help all of them if Magnus believed it. "One of these days, you're gonna hook up with a woman as common as you and just as ruthless," Tessie sputtered. "And I hope I'm around to see you drink your own poison. You want to talk to Selena? Hold on." She pressed the intercom.

"Selena, pick up."

"Tessie, if it's Prince calling, I want you to pick up, too. Pick up first, Tessie."

"Sure, if that's what you want." She listened to Selena's ir-refutable rejection of Prince and her sworn intention to indict him if he continued to harass her and to have the proceedings published in the *Waverly Herald,* Waverly's only paper.

Tessie had had as much as she could stand. "You heard her just like I did, and my head is like an elephant's. I don't forget a thing." She wished Selena hadn't hung up, because she wanted her to hear what she said to Prince. "You could have been as much of a man as Magnus, but you always wanted what wasn't yours. If nobody gave it to you, you took it, and your mama made excuses for you and defended you when she should've put you out on your own. You can't count how many times your mama paid your way out of trouble. If you was mine, I'd 'a blis-tered your behind years ago."

As though he hadn't heard her or Selena, he pleaded, "Tess, will you get off your soap box and put Selena back on the phone?"

"Just hold your breath. Never could tell you a thing. Magnus been getting you out of scrapes since your first day in school, and you pay him back by trying to seduce his wife. 'Course, in your case, treachery and loyalty probably spell the same way. No good's gonna come of you, Prince. You mark my word."

"She was mine first."

"In your head. Like I said, you always did go a little crazy when you wanted something and couldn't get it. Well, you'll soon find out that going after Magnus's wife ain't the same as wrecking his Lincoln or forging his name on his charge accounts. If I was you, Prince, I'd get a ten-year gig in Alaska. I'm hanging up."

"Wait a minute. Who's gonna tell him?"

Tessie held the phone away and stared at it, incredulity masking her face. "You will. One way or another, you will."

"Don't hold your breath."

If only she could knock some sense into him. Tessie shook her head, her spirits dampened by a sense of foreboding. "You go ahead, Prince. If you ain't careful, that stick in your pants gonna be the death of you." She hung up and began her own version of "Amazing Grace."

Selena's loud shriek brought Eloise speeding to her office.

"Girl, what's the matter? I heard you all the way in… Good Lord. *What in the world is that?*"

"Eloise, I… Look at *that!*" She pushed the package toward her friend.

Eloise's eyes seemed to increase their size, and her mouth dropped open. "This looks like a casket. Who'd send you this?"

Selena glanced at the black cardboard box, lined with quilted white satin and empty, except for a few broken white sticks. Fear curdled in her belly. Who could have done such a thing?

"I have no… *Lightner*. Who else? He couldn't get me out of here legally, so he thinks he'll frighten me away. Well, I've got news for that old hypocrite. I'll be here 'til I leave of my own volition."

Eloise cleared her throat. "Well, you're the psychologist, but seems to me Mr. Lightner is too conceited to do anything that underhanded. He's usually nasty where everybody can see it. But you could be right. This is the first time I've known him to eat crow. When you started court proceedings, he knew he didn't have a hope of winning. Still, I sure do hope you're wrong. I'd hate to know my bread and butter depended on somebody who'd do that."

Selena closed her eyes, took a breath and held it for ten counts. "You know, Eloise, I've witnessed some vicious acts, but this one takes the prize for creativity. Could you please shove it back in that bag. I can't bear to look at it again."

"I sure will. You just stop thinking about it." She looked up, and Selena could see the sparkles form in her eyes. "We could save it 'til Halloween," Eloise said, her voice laced with glee, "and send it to Lightner or Miss loose-tongued Cora Moore. It would be a shame to waste this thing."

Selena waved her hand in a gesture of dismissal. "I don't care what you do with it so long as I never have to see it again."

"Okay, okay," Eloise chanted, wrapping her prize with care.

An hour later, Selena remained as Eloise had left her. If not Lightner, who? *And why?* No one else had a motive.

Magnus grabbed his suitcase from the conveyer belt, picked up his briefcase and wove his way through the waiting crowd at Freetown Lungi International Airport. Wet heat slammed into him and, by the time he took the few steps to his waiting car, he had the urge to yank off his jacket and tie. No matter how much time he spent in West Africa, he doubted he'd get accustomed to the unremitting heat that devoured his energy and the dank, musty odors that assaulted his nostrils.

He threw his bag into the backseat and sat beside the driver. The thick mass of trucks, lorries, Mercedes, motorcycles, horse-driven wagons and other assorted conveyances slowed traffic to barely more than a walk. He took in the vestiges of colonialism—poverty, attempts to build modern industry with outmoded, outdated tools and, everywhere, a lack of know-how—that stared him in the face.

He hated their way of doing things. You paid for a service, and then you paid a bribe to get it done. But Houdon, his builder, went beyond that; not satisfied to reap a windfall by falsifying bills and receipts, he took from the workers' wages. Magnus thought of his alternatives and discarded most of them. He couldn't pull out, because the people needed good, affordable housing. But he wouldn't allow Houdon to fleece him, either.

If only he could find another Wade Malloy. He snapped his finger. It was early May, so the Roundtrees' son was two months old, and Melissa ought to be back at work. He'd call MTG Executive Search, and get the man he needed. For the next two days, he interviewed workers, visited the site and examined the builder's work. Pretty good, but not quite good enough.

Deciding he'd done all that he could, he stopped by Barclay's Bank, got a reading on his account and headed for Lungi airport a day early.

Magnus stored his briefcase overhead, settled into his first-class seat, fastened his seat belt, leaned back and closed his eyes. A stewardess placed a pillow under his neck and draped a blanket of precisely the color yellow he detested across his lap. Her fingers accidentally grazed his skin, and when his mind associated that fleeting touch with Selena, he knew he wouldn't sleep.

Selena. She danced through his mind and ravished his thoughts until he began to suspect that he'd rushed through his work in Freetown to get back to her. She had the sweetest smile. In his mind's eye, he could see her lips ease up at the edges just before warm lights lit her eyes. He needed so much more from their marriage than he got, but he had no reason to complain, because she gave him so much more than he'd ever had. She was his. He would swim an ocean for her. And he wouldn't trust himself with the person who interfered with her or who tried to come between them.

* * *

Selena stopped by Eloise's office Monday just before noon. "I have to do some errands at lunchtime, so I may be a little late getting back. Okay?"

Eloise's grin bordered on salacious. "You go right on, girl. I know who's coming back tomorrow, and if I hear you drove to San Antonio and bought something at Victoria's Secret, you won't hear the end of it. I better warn you that my girlfriend works there, and where she's concerned, Victoria doesn't have a single secret. Why, that girl…"

Selena laughed. "If I don't hurry, Eloise, lunchtime will be over." She paused. "Now that you mention it, maybe I will run into San Antonio. I don't have any consultations this afternoon, so I'll take the rest of the day off. See you tomorrow."

She rushed to her doctor's office for her checkup. As soon as she entered the door, she dissolved into a fit of nerves, though she had sworn to accept whatever news she got and be a big girl about it. Still, she walked back and forth in the waiting room, clasping and unclasping her hands as she waited for the doctor.

Finally Dr. Barnes called her into his office. "We're still ahead in this race, Selena." A frown clouded his face. "I'm perplexed as to what you're waiting for."

A rush of blood heated her cheeks, and she looked away from him in embarrassment. There wasn't much you could hide from your doctor. "It's not Magnus's fault that I'm not pregnant," she assured him.

His frown deepened. "Then why? Is there any…any reason…?"

She had to get out of there. "No. There's no problem. I'll be back in three weeks as you suggested." Quickly, she shook hands with him and left.

Eloise had come embarrassingly close to the truth. Magnus had told her to stay sweet for him, and she didn't know what he'd say or do when he got back, so she wanted something nice and very intimate, just in case. She went to Saks Fifth Avenue's lingerie department, selected undergarments, gowns and a negligee. But when she opened her purse, she remembered that she had left her credit cards at home that morning, because she hadn't planned to shop. She apologized and turned to leave.

The salesperson asked whether she'd like to open a Saks account, and Selena remembered that Magnus had opened one for her. She hadn't intended to use it, though she appreciated the gesture.

"I just remembered that my husband opened an account for me. I'm Selena Sutton-Cooper, and my husband is Magnus Cooper." The search took longer than Selena thought necessary, but nonetheless, she didn't anticipate what followed.

"Is there a problem?" she asked the salesperson.

The woman's face had lost its friendliness. "We don't have an account for anyone by that name. May I please see some ID?"

Stunned, Selena shuddered in embarrassment that changed to anger in minutes. "I apologize for taking your time," she told the woman, and left the store. She'd deal with that later. She couldn't think of a better reason why a woman should be independent than the indignity she'd just experienced. When she relied on herself, she didn't meet with such insults. She knew there was a plausible explanation, but right then, she didn't give a snap what it was. At Office Maximum, she ordered a personal computer, color printer and the software she needed for her brokerage business, and left the store singing.

The hood of her Taurus was covered with teenage boys when she reached the car. At first she stopped short and took a deep breath, silencing the alarm that the sight of them triggered. But she needn't have feared.

Russ jumped down and went to meet her, his hand outstretched. "Hey, Selena. How ya doin'? Remember me? Russ?" She greeted him, probably with more warmth than she should have.

"We don't want you to park around here, Selena, 'cause this

is the Alamos's territory, and they can play rough. If you gotta shop around here, park over on Commerce, and we'll look after things. No charge."

"How old are you, Russ?"

His belligerence lasted a few seconds. "I'm seventeen, and I'm in school. Today's Sam Houston day at my school, and we got this special all-day program. I figure I don't have to watch a bunch of kids march around the place carrying flags, so I volunteered for duty out here…looking after things."

She'd thought him about thirteen, but she wouldn't have dared to say so. "Thanks, Russ. Next time, I'll park on Commerce as you suggested."

"Good, 'cause since you don't know those guys, you might find your tires slashed. Say, Selena, where's that cool dude with the short fuse?"

She laughed. "He's my husband, Russ." She could see that the boy was taken aback.

"Well, you coulda done worse," he conceded, grudgingly she thought. "Come on, fellows, we gotta get back to school. See ya 'round, Selena." Intelligence. Leadership ability. Russ had them in abundance, but would those precious traits be channeled away from street life? She hoped so. Well, she thought, at least she hadn't heard rap music on his radio this time.

Selena rushed into the house eager to review her old client roster and sort out the ones she'd contact first. She also wanted to write an ad that she'd put in the *Waverly Herald* and on the region's leading radio stations. She itched to get started; she'd missed the excitement of seeing a stock she'd recommended skyrocket.

"Tessie," she sang, as she dashed down the hall toward Tessie's quarters. "Tessie, just wait 'til I tell you…" Her glance fell on the small package that lay on the hall table. Tentacles of fear scraped her insides. It couldn't be, she decided, gathering her bearings. She knocked on Tessie's door.

"I'm coming. If a person ever got an afternoon nap in this house, the north wind would blow from the south. I declare... What is it, child? You look a little peaked."

Selena looked back at the box and pointed to it. "Where'd that come from?"

"The mailman brought it this morning. Why?"

"Uh...nothing. I just wondered." She walked back to the table, picked up the box and handed it to Tessie. "Somebody played a nasty joke on me once today. You mind opening this? I don't think I'd like another shock."

Tessie looked at her beneath lowered lids. "You'd rather for me to get stung, eh." She opened the box, stared at its contents, closed it and walked back to her room.

"Tessie, wait. What...is it?"

"A casket, honey. No way on earth it could be anything else. Is that what you got earlier?"

Selena nodded. "I want Magnus to come home. I want..." She threw up her hands in disgust. "What am I talking about? He's working. I can take care of myself, or I could, if I knew what caused this."

Tessie rubbed her forearms and shook her head. "If that don't beat all. You got any idea who might not like you?"

Selena had been asking herself that question. "Only old man Lightner. He had to back down when I started court proceedings against him, and I expect he's furious that I caused him to lose face with a lot of people."

Tessie looked into the distance. "I wouldn't 'a thought he was that evil. 'Course, you never know. Come on back here with me, and let's not worry about it. Magnus will figure it out when he gets here tomorrow. You got some mail in the den."

In the den, Selena stared at the document that shook in her trembling fingers. An indictment. She remembered the transaction; how could she forget it? The woman had been told by a friend that Peoples Universal Builders was about to offer shares in a new venture and had nagged her for a prospectus. She eventually sold the woman shares in the company's combined commercial and recreational malls that would be built along superhighways in several Middle Atlantic and South Atlantic states. According to the indictment, the project folded, and the woman had lost several hundred thousand dollars and had sued Selena for having sold her the shares. Just what she needed: another problem. She left the paper on the desk.

Anna Cooper sipped her consommé, pressed her napkin daintily to the corners of her mouth and blessed her luncheon date with a luminous smile. "Mavis, dear, I don't know what to tell you. You know I had hoped that you would be my daughter-in-law, because we have so much in common and you are ideal for Magnus. There wasn't anything I could do—he's always cut his own cloth, so to speak. But he certainly knew how I feel about you. He rushed off and married this woman, and I hadn't even met her. I'm trying to forgive him for that, though you must know how difficult it is."

Always the epitome of good breeding, Anna thought and smiled her approval as Mavis dabbed her napkin at the corners of her own mouth, sat erect and displayed perfect manners. Such a lovely girl, one whom she could have controlled as Magnus's wife.

"I can't understand how he could have done it," Mavis said in a perfectly modulated voice that showed no emotion. "We'd been seeing each other for almost two years. True, he hadn't proposed marriage, but I did everything possible to prompt it."

Not enough, Anna thought with not a little contempt. A sensible woman would have gotten pregnant and settled the matter. But the poor girl hadn't been able to move him beyond the petting stage. "He was always stubborn," Anna said. "If he decides not to bestir himself, you'll have as much success moving Mount Everest as you will getting Magnus to shift half an inch. He is just like his father."

Mavis's eyes grew larger. "That's something. How did you

manage him? I mean, how did you get your husband to do what he didn't want to do?"

Anna gave the woman her staple withering look. "My dear, one didn't manage Jonathan Cooper, one discussed with him and then waited forever until he made up his mind, which, as you've no doubt guessed, he never changed." She knew she was guilty of sentimentality, but she couldn't suppress the dreamy quality that had slipped into her tone. She never discussed her late husband for fear that she might cry, and she couldn't afford that. Crying was the most unladylike thing she could think of; ladies did not beg for sympathy.

"I'm having dessert today," Mavis announced.

A gasp escaped Anna. "My dear, what has come over you? Are you all right?"

Mavis nodded as she studied the dessert menu. "I am indeed. Today, I deserve to treat myself. Nobody gets the better of Mavis Root. *Nobody!*"

Mavis savored the chocolate soufflé with more relish than Anna considered genteel. "Has Tessie sent out the invitations to the barbecue yet?" she asked Anna.

"I haven't received one."

"I don't suppose I'll be invited this year, but I'm dying to see Miss Selena Sutton."

"You haven't seen her?" Anna asked. "Well, I don't suppose there's any reason why you should have, since you live in Kerrville."

Mavis pushed away the remainder of the soufflé. "Is she beautiful?"

A grim expression clouded Anna's features. "If a woman ever was, she is."

"I see. Well…" Mavis shrugged. "A man can get tired of that, too."

Anna stared at her in astonishment. "Not if she's clever. And this one is definitely sharp."

Anna wasn't sure she'd come out the winner in their meeting

as she told Mavis goodbye. She usually enjoyed the young woman's company but, as she walked to her car, guilt settled in her. She hadn't intended to encourage her, only to apologize for Magnus's poor judgment in marrying Selena Sutton. She hoped Mavis didn't plan what was sure to be a futile campaign to get Magnus.

She started her car and eased out of the restaurant's parking lot. Maybe she'd better see less of Mavis. No telling what could happen; a woman spurned could be a vicious enemy and, in her opinion, Mavis was taking this much too calmly.

Magnus stepped off the plane and headed for the nearest phone. "This is Magnus. Everything all right there?" At the sound of Selena's voice, he let himself breathe.

"Magnus? Oh, dear, I… Yes, I'm fine. We all are. Where are you?"

He regretted shocking her, but it didn't hurt his ego to know that hearing his voice could knock her off balance. "I'm at Houston's Intercontinental Airport. Just landed. If I can get a plane out of here, I'll be home tonight. You miss me?" He hadn't meant to ask her that, but he'd done it, so he pressed. "Well, did you?"

"Do mashed potatoes love gravy?"

"What?" He hoped he'd heard right; all the mashed potatoes he'd ever eaten tasted better with gravy. Her light laughter sailed through the wires to him, gay, happy. Sending his heart into a troll and stoking his libido. He hoped her mood didn't change before he got to Waverly.

"You don't think you could stay away from here four days and nobody'd miss you, do you? How'd you get back so early?"

Hedging, was she? Well, she'd get no help from him. "I don't give a hoot about 'nobody.' I'm asking about you."

"Of course I missed you."

That wasn't want he wanted, but he'd have to settle for it. "See you tonight." He went directly from the airport to his office. It wasn't a bad idea to see what the place looked like at seven in the morning. Not a moving thing. He pushed open his office door, threw his bags on the floor beside the leather sofa and whirled around. He'd locked that door before he left. He'd swear to it. He left a message with Jeb's answering service, got a cup of the worst coffee he'd ever tasted and vowed to have that coffee machine taken out. Twenty minutes later he heard Jeb's voice.

"Just got in, Magnus. I'll be over shortly."

Magnus briefed his manager. "Don't send any more supplies over there, not even a nail, until I get a project manager. Houdon is a despot. He knows how to build, but that's all. I want you to go out there twice a month. After I get an engineer on the job, that may not be necessary, but for now, do that. Got it?" He made a note to give Jeb a raise.

Jeb nodded. "You bet."

He dialed Melissa Grant-Roundtree. "Hello, Kelly, is your boss around?"

"Mr. Cooper. It's great to hear from you. Yes, she's right here."

"Hello, Magnus. I don't know who grows faster, Grant or HM, Grant's pony. How's Selena?" They engaged in the requisite small talk for several minutes before Magnus told her what he needed.

"I'll get right on it, Magnus. Why don't you bring Selena to Beaver Ridge for a visit? Adam and I spend our weekends there, and it's charming this time of year."

"I'll speak with her about it. You two would like each other. Yes, it's something I'll look forward to." He said goodbye and hung up.

The lights went on in Madeline's office, and he buzzed her.

"Oh, Magnus, we weren't expecting you until tomorrow afternoon. If we'd known you'd come today, we'd have had flowers in your office."

He smiled his greeting. "Any idea why I found my office

door unlocked?" He thought her momentarily flustered, but that would have been out of character for her. Madeline was, if anything, unflappable.

"Oh, my. I cleaned in here myself personally, because I don't allow anyone in here. I thought I locked the door. Uh… Oh. Is there anything else, sir?"

"Not at the moment." He'd have to pay more careful attention to Madeline. He didn't believe in showing his hand, so he hadn't asked her how long she'd had a key to his office and how she'd gotten it. He'd always called one of the cleaning staff when he wanted his office cleaned, and he sat there while the men worked. He kept it reasonably neat, and he didn't see why she had to clean it, as well. To his knowledge, he alone had a key, and he left his personal papers lying on his desk thinking them safe from prying eyes. He usually had to encourage her to leave his office, but she seemed in a hurry to get back to her desk. She'd been acting quite uncharacteristically lately.

Chapter 7

Tessie drove down Center Street, Waverly's main thorough-fare, on her regular Monday afternoon shopping trip. As she turned into the Longhorn Mall's parking lot, she saw Prince leaning with his back against his car in an animated discussion with a girl of about eighteen; she hoped for his sake that the girl was at least that old. Remembering the odious casket someone had sent Selena, she decided to have a chat with him.

"I need a word with you, Prince." No point in preliminaries with Prince; niceties didn't impress him.

"Hi, Tess. Be with you after a while, doll. I'm busy right now."

He was busy, all right. He hadn't even remembered to turn on the charm. "I can say it right here, if you think that's what you want."

He narrowed his eyes, then flashed a grin. "See you later, baby," he told the girl and turned his back to her.

Tessie watched her walk away, her shoulders drooped in de-jection. "Kinda young, ain't she?"

He shrugged. "What was so urgent you couldn't wait to give me your sanctified opinion on it?"

She shook her finger at him. "I didn't walk over here to tell you about playing with little girls." His dark eyes flashed. His perfectly sculpted face glistened with displeasure. A brilliant ruby dancing on a thunder cloud. Beautiful anger. Brazen. Almost sexual. He let a half smile grace his mouth, and she knew that, for once, he wasn't acting. That was him. Pure Prince. In that second, he sent her the message that, if she'd go with him, he'd take her to bed and wouldn't give it another thought. She'd changed his diapers and given him as much nurturing as he'd accept from the day of his birth, but he had no more feelings for her than for that poor girl on whom he'd just turned his back.

"Prince, do you know anybody who'd hate Selena enough to mail her a nasty present?"

She'd never seen eyebrows shoot up so fast or so high. "Are you suggesting—?"

"I ain't suggesting anything. I'm trying to find out who might 'a done that."

"Well, you have to keep looking. It didn't hurt her, did it?"

Had he really expressed concern? Maybe he could be helped. "No, it didn't hurt her."

"Couldn't be some of those people she plays God with over at the Center, could it?"

She waved him off and hastened to the butcher shop, musing over his words as she went. He had raised a possibility that hadn't occurred to her. She'd mention that to Selena.

I'm not going to welcome him with open arms, Selena told herself, recalling her humiliation about the Saks account. He'd said it would be open Friday. When Rhett Butler ran to the window and began barking, needlelike pinpricks of expectation danced up and down her nerves. She couldn't dress up at four o'clock in the afternoon, yet she had to look *good*. She put on a green silk jumpsuit, pulled it off and put on a pair of jeans and a red turtleneck, cotton-knit sweater.

The front door opened, and she raced for the stairs, stopped and told herself to wait until he made a move. She was gliding down the steps, taking her time, when he looked up at her and grinned.

"You devil. I heard you tear out of that room. Why'd you put on the brakes? I thought I'd get a warmer reception."

"Hi," she said, unable to resist laughing at her foolishness. She could have been in his arms right then but, no, she had to be clever. Magnus picked her up and kissed her on her mouth. Then, he carried her downstairs, set her on her feet and walked with her into the den.

"Anything important take place in my absence?"

She described the two packages and how she'd felt receiving them. He stood at the window and gazed long into the distance, mute. Finally, he faced her. "Anything else?"

"I got a New York State Civil Court summons this morning."

Magnus stared at her. "What about?" She told him.

"I know something about building and the tricks builders can use to attract investors. Do you still have the papers?"

"I have copies."

She hadn't seen his tension until his jaw muscles flexed. "We'll handle that. If you like, Wade can represent you since he's passed the bar, and if he's one-third the lawyer that he is engineer, we're home free. Tomorrow, we can get all this information to him, and let him get started. Is that okay with you?"

"It's a wonderful idea. You don't think I need to go to New York?"

"I'm not sure. Let's see what Wade says." He ran his hand over his hair and smiled ruefully. "If anything else happened, I'm not sure I want to know."

"What about my presents?"

"That won't go unpunished. Trust me, we'll catch whoever did it."

Shock waves plowed through her at the barely leashed furor in his voice and the chill in his eyes. She didn't know this Magnus. The laid-back, almost detached demeanor, the patience and gentleness to which she'd become accustomed were nowhere evident.

He kicked at the carpet with the toe of his left shoe. "If I've got enemies, I don't know it. How about you?"

"The only person I know who's mad at me is Mr. Lightner, and this seems too bizarre for him."

"I don't exclude anybody in this town, except Tessie. I'm driving to San Antonio early tomorrow morning, but I'll leave my beeper with Jackson. Like to go for a ride after I freshen up a bit?"

"It's almost sunset. Wouldn't you rather walk?"

"Whatever you want." His voice had sunk to that low, husky timbre that she loved. Excitement coursed through her, her breath lodged in her throat and her head swam. "Meet me down here in about an hour?" he asked.

She sure would. He was ripe for a move up to the next level, and she had plans for him. If she hadn't been mad with him about that charge account, she'd have kissed him good and hard on those stairs. This time, she wouldn't lure him into a hot session, she'd just give him plenty to look at.

She put on a long, narrow white cotton skirt that buttoned up the front and stopped just above her belly button. She buttoned it halfway down her thigh, put on a red silk knitted blouse that ended beneath her breasts, hugged them tight and had embroidered holes dispersed irregularly throughout. She added a man's long-sleeved white shirt, which she didn't button, but tied beneath her bosom. A pair of white espadrilles encased her feet. She let her hair fall around her shoulders, untamed, put on a pair of large gold hoop earrings, dabbed Opium perfume in strategic places and went to meet fate.

Magnus poured a glass of cranberry juice for himself and stood bending over the refrigerator door looking for a snack.

The time changes from Texas to Freetown to Texas had altered his eating pattern.

"Hi, handsome."

At the sexy softness, the veiled invitation in her voice, he jerked himself away from the refrigerator door and whirled around to face her. He let a sharp whistle express his appreciation for what he saw.

"Want some juice…or something?" he asked in barely audible tones.

Selena cast a skeptical eye his way. Good. He wanted her as off balance as he was.

"I'd like some…some lemonade, please."

He filled a glass for her. She didn't reach for it, but let him walk over to her and put it in her hand. He grinned. He'd never get used to her mercurial ways, and he didn't want to. The unexpected, sensuous dive of her voice. A quick shift from the businesswoman to man's woman, from jeans and sneakers to shimmering sex goddess. Like now, in that getup that was calculated to send him into shock. Thank God he'd learned patience, because she gave him plenty of opportunities to use it.

"Let's walk through the garden," Selena suggested.

She was choreographing the show, and he intended to take his cue from her. "Good idea." His fingers itched to touch her, but he resisted, figuring that if she wanted to hold hands, she knew where to find both of his.

She stopped when they reached the rose trellis and let her gaze sweep over her universe. "This is paradise."

He stepped closer, but put his hands in his pockets. "It's a relief to know you feel this way, because you're not leaving here."

Her pose was worthy of Cicely Tyson or Ruby Dee. "Why would I? This is my home. How about walking over to that little brook?" Following the leader was not a scenario that had ever appealed to him, and he had to check himself when he would have reached for her. Her smile, cool and mysterious, challenged him before she flashed a grin and walked on ahead of him. He stared at her hips, swaying beneath the narrow skirt that outlined their perfect form, and swallowed hard.

"Let's sit." As she said it, she eased up her skirt and sat on the grassy slope.

"It's warm," she told him, struggling out of the white shirt. She pretended not to see his reaction to her revealing blouse, but gloried in his harsh swallow and the fire that blazed in his eyes. As though restless, she turned on her side, bracing herself with her right hand, well aware of the enticing curve of her hip.

"I hope it doesn't get any warmer," she heard him mutter beneath his breath. She moved a little, so that her opened skirt exposed a leg.

"Still warm?" he asked, when she pulled her long hair off her neck.

"Honey, it's hot. You know that," she told him in a tone that implied a possible problem of intelligence. She rolled over on her back, crossed a raised knee, folded her hands beneath her head and closed her eyes. His hot breath teased her face, his wild cologne toyed with her senses and her nipples hardened when she sensed his body, his aura surrounding her. Finally, she opened her eyes and gazed into his. Hot with smoldering desire. Compelling. Magnetic. She couldn't shift her gaze, as he held her mesmerized. Imprisoned both by his passion and her love for him.

"You're as innocent as a lioness dozing after a big meal, but I don't care. I'll have you and on your own terms. Ladle out anything you like. By now, you ought to know that I'm patient. I know that you *are not*." He winked. "One thing, though. I can't promise you full manliness after I'm ninety, so shape up sometime before then, will you?"

She swatted him playfully on the buttocks as he jumped up. Like a striking snake, he pulled her up and into his arms, and before she could open her mouth for his tongue, he rose hard against her. She slid an arm around his neck and fastened her other hand to the back of his head while she pressed her body to him. She forgot about control, forgot her lofty ideal that love had to precede total intimacy. She wanted him inside her. Her left hand went to the button on her skirt, brushing him and, when she undulated against him, he cupped her hips with both hands and lifted her to fit him. But for a cow that began to low a few feet from where they stood, she would have consummated her marriage on the grass beside Runner Brook. When she could corral her thoughts, she reflected that he'd set her on fire, but hadn't uttered one word of love. She looked at Magnus's awe-struck face.

"Where the devil did *you* come from?" he asked the cud-chewing longhorn, then unhooked his phone and gave Jackson the animal's location.

"Sure you weren't in cahoots with that cow?" he asked Selena.

Shaken by thoughts of what she'd risked and *what she'd missed,* Selena no longer wanted to walk. She needed to think about her life. She wanted desperately to conceive, but she wanted her husband to love her. What if she bore him a child, and he fell in love—with someone else? She wanted her child to have a father's love. She picked up a small rock and tossed it into the brook.

"Where's your sauciness, Selena? Thinking about what we almost did and how much you would have enjoyed it? Are you?"

She ignored his taunt and changed the subject. "Wonder what happened to that baby. Eloise doesn't tell anyone where she places a child."

"Do you wish we'd taken it?"

She thought for a moment. "Yes, but I understood your reasoning and agreed with you. By the way, you haven't told me about your trip. Did you find any problems?"

Her experiences in his absence had pushed his own concerns out of his mind. "Problems? If you call a light-fingered despot who's your on-site builder and manager a problem, sure thing. I've engaged Melissa Grant-Roundtree to find an architectural engineer for the job."

"Why don't you fire him?"

He shrugged. "My contract with the government calls for a local builder, and he's their only one. I straightened him out."

"And Houston?"

"Houston's under control. Jeb's a first-rate manager, and I'd wager that not many secretaries would measure up to Madeline. She's a crackerjack."

"Has she worked for you long?"

"Eight years." His answer seemed to relax her. She couldn't be jealous, could she? He wouldn't mind if she was.

The wind shifted to the west, cooling the air, and he watched her slip into the white shirt she'd worn earlier. "Congress ought to pass a law forbidding any woman to wear that blouse." His eyes must have reflected his thoughts as he moved his gaze appreciatively over her breasts. "Believe me, it's worth whatever it cost." He wouldn't be surprised if she read his lascivious thoughts, considering how they thundered in his head, because she tightened the blouse at her waist, and he could see her shiver in response. What a woman! He told himself to cool off.

"Magnus, I forgot to tell you I bought a computer, a printer and software this afternoon. As soon as it's set up and when that judge signs papers acquitting me of wrongdoing in that civil case, I intend to reopen my brokerage business."

"Wonderful. What about your work at the Center?"

"I'm thinking of volunteering a couple of afternoons a week or maybe Saturday mornings."

"Great, but I don't think you should have to wait for a settlement of that case before starting your business. That's in New York. This is Texas. Want to use the office I planned for the secretary I decided I didn't need?"

A smile creased her face. "Super. What's the rent?"

"*Rent?* Woman, you sent me a check for your suite last week. Have you forgotten you're my wife?"

"Of course not, but a deal's a deal. Besides, I'm wife in name only."

Her words roared in his head. "The hell you say! Are you telling me you'll stop paying rent when you share my bed? Quid pro quo? Let me tell you something, lady, I do not, repeat, do not pay for feminine favors. You're my wife no matter where you sleep. Now and fifty years from now, you're the same wife, and I'll thank you not to send me any more checks. Got it? I took great pleasure in sticking a lighted match to that last one."

"Will you calm down, please? We're out here in the open."

"I'm calm. Considering these kooky ideas my wife lays on me, I'm calm as all hell."

"Compared to your usual self, you're raving."

He stopped beneath one of his many pecan trees, leaned his back against it, looped an arm around her shoulder and drew her to him. "Selena, I don't expect a well-educated and successful businesswoman to content herself with knitting and ladies' lunches, though I admit I've always dreamed of a wife and children waiting for me at home in a world of my making. I'm not asking that of you. I don't even want it. But I do want to take care of you. Protect you. Provide for you. Don't deny me that."

Selena eased out of Magnus's arms and faced him. "Why, Magnus? In a marriage like ours, why?" Maybe he'd tell her, finally, what he felt for her. "Why?" she asked him again.

A shadow clouded his eyes. "I need to. I have to."

"All right, I won't send you any more checks. And thanks for the office. It's ideal." Disappointment settled over her.

His fingers grasped hers as they started toward the house. "I don't think I'm self-centered, Selena. My father didn't make a difference between Prince and me, but you see how things are with my mother. As a boy, I dreamed of being special to my wife, of being her world."

She suppressed a gasp. "Didn't your mother love your father?"

He stopped walking, stuck his hands in the back pockets of his jeans and ground the toe of his left boot into the sod. "Maybe. I don't know. I never thought so."

She ached for him as they walked in silence, his fingers pressing hers with such strength that pain streaked up her arm. She didn't tell him, because she understood. And pain was a small price to pay for the joy of knowing at last that he needed her.

He walked with Selena as far as the garden. "We make more progress during these strolls than at any other time. Let's do this regularly." He knew he leered, but a man was allowed certain liberties with his wife. "I'd rather my men didn't see you wearing this getup. Okay? See you at dinner. I've got to speak with Jackson about that stray cow. My livestock don't go to that brook."

She detained him. "After supper, I'd planned to finish my report for *Wall Street World,* but I'm not in the mood to write about African-American women on the Street, since there are a blatantly obvious few of them. Want to go to a movie?"

He let a smile play around his mouth. "Movie, huh? Don't tell me your naughty behavior's clogging up your thinking pipes."

"Movie, yes or no? This'll be on me."

"Now, you wait a…" He glared at the screen door after she ducked inside. The woman could fire up his engine faster than gasoline sent off a Corvette, and he suspected she knew it. But his day would come, and soon.

Selena beamed at the theater marquee, but Magnus frowned. "You want to see *The Hustler?* Come on now, Selena. That's about a pool shark, isn't it?"

"*You* come on," she said, tugging at his sleeve. "What's

wrong with seeing few good games of pool? What a stuffed shirt," she mumbled.

"Selena, that movie is pure fluff."

Her smile broadened. "I know. I don't go to the movies for enlightenment, because I don't want movie moguls distorting social issues for me. Besides, there's nothing like a great game of pool, and I positively love old movies."

He shook his head. "You're a bag of surprises. All right, let's go in." He reached for his wallet.

"I thought we agreed I'd pay. It's only seven dollars. I can afford that."

He didn't smile. "I don't doubt that. Two tickets, please," he said to the ticket agent. "What's so amusing?"

"You. You would've sizzled if I had insisted. And no popcorn," she shot at him when he started to the counter.

"Why not, for Pete's sake? That's one reason why I'm here."

Her head went up in a proud toss. "If you do happen to be ninety when the love bug gets us, I want you to be as tough as you are now. So, don't touch that stuff." She threw the last over her shoulder as she walked toward their seats.

When he didn't catch up with her, she glanced back to see him shaking with laughter.

"We must have been the only people in there who weren't eating popcorn," he groused as they left the theater.

"You didn't need all tha…" He must have followed her gaze, because he stopped short, pulling her close to him as he did so.

"Hello, Prince," Magnus said.

"Well, well. Fancy meeting you at the movies. I didn't know you knew there was such a thing. How could you bear to leave your precious ranch…? Oh yes." He sneered. "The lovely lady dragged you out. When did you get back in town?"

"How did you know I'd left?" She watched as Prince smiled the smile of Satan.

"Didn't you think she'd tell me?"

She held her breath; surely Magnus wouldn't believe him.

"I wouldn't believe a word you say," Magnus told him.

"Of course she did."

She looked into her husband's stony face. "I didn't tell him anything, Magnus."

She hated Prince's victorious grin. "If you didn't tell me," he asked her, "how did I know?" He looked at Magnus. "I spoke with your wife twice while you were away. Don't believe it, ask Tessie."

Magnus glared at his younger brother. "If you weren't my brother, you'd be getting up right now. I've told you to stay away from Selena. This is my last warning. The next time you make a move on her, I'm going to forget we're related." He looked at the girl standing beside Prince. "When you go to jail for this kid you're playing with, I'll allow myself to remember what a loyal and loving brother you've always been, and I'll act accordingly." He took Selena's hand and headed for his Town Car.

He wouldn't like what she had to say, but he needed to hear it. "You're a powerful man, Magnus, and you don't have to tolerate this constant harassment from Prince."

He rested his hand on the door of the car and stared into the distance. "I keep hoping he'll change, that he'll be my brother. Thirty years is a long time to hope and wait, only to give up. Think how you'd feel if you had a sister who showed you practically every human emotion, except sisterly love."

"He hurts you. Can't you cut him loose?"

"He's my brother."

They rode in silence. She wished he'd say something, that he didn't believe she called Prince, that she couldn't be capable of such disloyalty to him. By the time they reached the ranch, the sadness she'd felt for him had given way to annoyance. She hopped out of the car and ran into the house and to her suite without telling him good-night. Seconds later, he knocked on her door.

"Come in, Magnus." He remained at the door, and she could

feel the tension radiating from him, a tautness that hooked into her.

"Was any of what he said true?"

"After the cold shoulder you gave me during the ride home, I don't think I owe you one word."

She'd never seen him so impassive, his eyes so lacking in expressiveness. "Granted that you don't. Nevertheless, I'd appreciate your answering my question."

"If you're capable of believing that I would telephone Prince for any reason, except at your specific command, then we haven't made any progress, and it's unlikely that we will."

"I don't believe you called him, but did you speak with him twice, as he said?"

"He called me, and I told him not to call me again and hung up. He called back, and I had Tessie monitor the conversation. She heard what I said to him."

"You didn't think you had a right to tell me?"

"Why should I deliberately foment dissention between brothers, especially when I know Prince is goading you?"

"All right. We'll leave it for now."

She sensed an unreal quality in his calmness, as though he had distanced himself from the incident, a bystander. Not a participant. An aura of danger clung to him. Ripe. Like thunderheads heralding a storm.

"Still going to San Antonio tomorrow morning?"

He nodded. "I'll try to get back early enough to help you set up your office. If you get another call from him, I want to know it."

"If you tell me to, I'll do it."

He cocked an eyebrow. "I want you to tell me."

"All right."

"See you tomorrow afternoon." She watched him descend the stairs with no spring in his gait. What had begun as sweet and intimate had ended in a debacle. But she wasn't defeated. When Magnus Cooper got home tomorrow, she'd have another surprise for him.

* * *

Magnus completed his business in San Antonio and sped back to the ranch. His thoughts of Selena as she'd been the afternoon before in that red blouse that let him see her brown flesh and most of one areola made driving dangerous. He eased up on the accelerator.

He found Selena at the stables mounting Minerva while Jackson held the reins. Much as he liked the man, seeing him there with her at a moment when he wanted intimacy annoyed him unreasonably. He took the reins from his manager, walked closer and stopped within inches of her.

"Hi." He preferred neatness in women, but the picture she made with her hair disheveled by the wind, her lips glistening in their natural state and a baggy, shapeless sweater hiding her physical attributes kicked his libido into a roaring engine. And when she smiled and extended both hands to him, his engine screamed to rev its motor. The hell with it. Jackson or no Jackson. He pulled her to him, with less gentleness than he'd intended, and found her mouth—soft, sweet and open to him. He couldn't let another man see her effect on him, so he immediately released her. His surprise when he tasted her hot kiss must have been plain on his face, for Jackson regarded him quizzically, grunted, and went about his business.

"What does it take to get you in this kind of mood?" he asked her when they were alone, and he could enjoy the invitation that blazed in the smoldering depths of her eyes. Dark eyes that beckoned him to drown in her.

She laid her head to one side and teased him with a half smile. "You think this isn't my normal self? Dig a little deeper, you'll like what you see."

"Are you flirting with me?"

"Why would I do that?" The smile merged into a wide grin.

He knocked his Stetson back with a flick of his thumb and forefinger and gazed down at her. "You do something to me, Selena. I like you bold, brazen and sassy like this, but when you get ready to pour it on, be sure you're prepared for what ought to follow."

Her lip drooped in a pout. "If you'd prefer I didn't react to you, don't show up here looking like...well, like this."

He frowned and told her in a resigned voice, "Selena, I am trying to keep my word and let you chart our relationship, but lately you've been making that difficult." Plain hell was more like it.

She glared at him with an expression that he recognized as pretense. "I'm doing my part. You're the one who's not doing yours."

He had to laugh at her convoluted sentence.

"How did things go in San Antonio?"

Change the subject, would she? He'd fill her in, but not right then; he didn't want anything to interfere with her mood. "Okay. I'd ride with you, but I have to call my Houston office. See you at dinner." Her stare, warm and compassionate, pierced his heart. Minutes passed, and still she stared.

"Well?" he asked at last, but he was unprepared for her answer. Her arms looped around his neck, and her lips, hot and seeking, seduced him. He burned with desire, but she stepped back, smiled, jumped on Minerva and sent the horse into a gallop, leaving him stunned.

Magnus spoke to Jeb in Houston and spent a few minutes talking with Madeline, finding it strange that she initiated small talk with him. She had always been strictly business and appeared to disdain personal comments. Or did she? He remembered once having told her he liked her pink dress—a departure from her usual drab ones—and he'd returned from lunch to find a vase of pink roses on his desk. The gesture had embarrassed him, but he had thanked her.

After leaving his office, he stopped by Tessie's quarters and knocked on her door. "Hi, Tess. Everything all right here?"

She tightened her apron, a gesture he'd long recognized as

playing for time. "Things 'bout the same as you left 'em. You be home for dinner?"

He nodded and leaned against the doorjamb. "One of these days, you'll say exactly what you mean, and whoever hears you will faint." He softened it with a grin and a pat on her shoulder.

"I been telling you what I mean since you was born. The day you listen, *really listen* to me, *I'll* faint."

He let his arm linger around her shoulder. "If I hadn't listened to you, Tess, I'd probably be less of a man than I am."

"Well, you ain't too old to stop hearing what I say." He noticed that she preened when she smiled at him.

"Magnus, I'd like to finish dinner by seven-thirty tonight. I know that's early for you and Selena, but I'd like to go out."

"Is he somebody I know?" He managed not to laugh when she stuck her hands on her hips.

"Is there somebody you don't know?"

"Well, I haven't met the president," he teased. "You stay out of mischief."

"You go 'way from here. I'm too old for mischief."

Magnus laughed. "But not too old for a one-track mind, I see. Fifty-five is young these days, Tess. Tell the guy to mind his manners, or he'll hear from me." He threw the latter over his shoulder and he headed toward his room.

"Oh, you go on," he heard her say.

After dinner, Selena helped Tessie clear the table, and she and Magnus straightened the kitchen.

"We work well together, don't you think?" Magnus asked Selena. It was more a statement than a question, and he had voiced her thoughts.

"We do, but why shouldn't we?"

Magnus put a bag of leftover curried shrimp into the freezer, closed the door and looked at Selena. "You have the doggoned-est habit of answering my questions with one of your own. It's frustrating. Here's another question for you. If we're a smooth team in the kitchen, don't you think we'd be a symphony at other…er, activities?"

"Search me. I've never played in a symphony, but considering how much I love music, I'd probably learn real fast."

He wrapped the dish towel around the oven's door handle, and she immediately moved it to its place in the pantry. She came out of the little room and started past him. He blocked her way. "You know how to challenge a man, don't you?"

"I'm not selective about being my real self, Magnus. If you're challenged, I expect you'll handle it—you're good at that."

He let it pass. "What's your favorite music?" he asked, moving closer.

She knew he intended to pull them into another passionate exchange, and she didn't consider it wise, but if he wanted her in his arms… She let the thought drift.

"Mozart in the morning and the slow jazz of a sultry alto sax in the evening."

Heat gathered in his darkening eyes. "What about right now?"

"I…I'd better work on my manuscript."

He stood with his legs farther apart, and his hands curved into fists that dangled at his sides. "If you're going, go, because I'm not in the mood to play. If I get my hands on you tonight, we'll be together when we wake up tomorrow morning."

She took her time leaving and, when she reached the door, she looked back at him. "If you'd get your act together, I'd welcome that."

"*My act?* What are you talking about?"

"Didn't it occur to you that I'm not a coy girl playing with a man? I need something that you aren't offering, and I will not ask for it."

His voice, deep, passionate, reached her ears as a seductive lure, but she braced herself against its effect. "If it is within my power to—"

She didn't let him finish it, because he hadn't understood. "It is. And until you give it, I'll wait."

* * *

Minutes later, Tessie jumped out of Magnus's way when he nearly crashed into her as she left her room. "Whatever was it that loosened your dandruff?" she grumbled, as he reached to steady her. "Don't tell me. You and Selena been at it again. Magnus, you'd better take charge of things before they get out of hand. You hear? I know…" The phone rang, and she dashed to answer it.

"You're not backing out on our date, are you?"

She covered the mouthpiece with her hand and whispered to Magnus, *See you in the morning.* "It's not a date," she said to Jackson. "We're only going to a movie."

"What, in your estimation, is a date, Tessie?"

She hugged herself and twirled around the phone cord. "Now don't be getting fresh with me, Jackson. We're going to a movie, and that's all. What you laughing at?"

His chuckles, so warm and nice, just about gave her goose pimples. "I don't remember mentioning doing anything else, but if that's a hint…"

She grabbed her thundering chest. "Now don't you go getting out of line. You hear?"

"Me? I'm as innocent as a lamb. I only want to enjoy your company, Tessie. Any terms you dictate are okay with me."

Heat burned her face, and she patted her hair and smoothed her new dress. "You such a man with words, Jackson. I just about swell up when you talk so nice and soft like that. Remind me of Magnus. I always did like men that's smart and real nice to a woman. You be here on time so we don't miss the opening. You hear?"

"Tess, only a foolish man would waste a minute he could have with you. I'll be there, all right. Bye now."

She hung up. Oh, he was sweet and good. She'd have to remember to send her tithe as thanks to St. Anthony for finding this wonderful man.

Where was that perfume Magnus gave her for her birthday?

Maybe she'd better ask Selena for a little lipstick. Better not. Jackson would know she had primped for him. She wished Selena and Magnus would solve their problem, whatever that was. She longed to see him happy like she was right then, but Prince wouldn't stop until he separated them. She wondered if Selena had told Magnus about Prince's calls. Well, Prince had better watch it. It took a lot for Magnus to go into a rage, but when he did, you wanted to be somewhere else. She found the perfume and dabbed it behind her ears, at her temple and beside her nose. If St. Anthony had done his work real good, maybe Jackson would kiss her.

He held her hand throughout the movie.

She wanted to give him every chance to declare his interest one way or the other, so she invited him to have coffee and some of her lemon meringue pie.

"I had a wonderful evening," she told him as she walked with him to the kitchen door.

"In that case, maybe we could do it again," he said, in a matter-of-fact manner.

She lowered her gaze and folded her hands behind her. "You sing a real good song on the phone, Jackson, but when we get together, you forget all about it."

He stepped closer. "And you are very encouraging on the phone, miss, but soon as I show up, you act like you're out with the girls."

Her hands went to her hips. "I want you to know that I ain't never wore this dress out with no girls."

A wide grin transformed his face. "You wore this especially for me, did you? It sure is pretty, Tessie, and you are, too."

She hadn't figured him for a slow man, and she had a mind to ask him what was taking him so long. Well, he could go fly a kite; if he didn't have guts enough to take a kiss, she wasn't going to offer it. For two cents, she'd shake him.

"You know I have to get up early," she said, not bothering to hide her disappointment. "So, good night."

He didn't move. "Don't I rate a kiss?"

Her heart nearly burst through the skin of her chest, but she held his gaze. "If you're man enough to take it, you can have it."

"That mouth's going to get you in trouble. Come here." She would have moved if any part of her body had obeyed her brain.

His smile sent her senses into a tailspin. "Come here, honey."

Tremors raced through her, splintering her nerves when his mouth came down on hers. Her arms found their way around his strong neck, and he squeezed her to him until she trembled against him, sapped of will and drained of energy.

"I don't want you kissing anybody else, Tessie. Do you understand?"

His face didn't bear a hint of a smile, and shivers raced through her at the seriousness of his tone and manner.

"Well…I…"

"Do you understand?"

She cocked her head to one side and smiled at him. "I sure will think about that, Jackson. I sure will."

Jackson grinned. "Think hard while you're at it." His kiss was of such brevity that she wasn't sure she'd felt it. He left, and she closed the door. *He'd kissed her.* She leaned against the refrigerator and sobbed.

Chapter 8

Selena removed the remaining personal items from her desk.
She had enjoyed counseling at the community center, but she
could barely contain her enthusiasm for returning to the work she
loved.

"If you need me," Selena assured Eloise, "give me a ring, and
if it's an urgent case, I'll come after work. The stock market
closes at two-thirty in New York, three-thirty here, so I could
probably get to the Center by four."

The way Eloise spread her arms, you'd have thought she was
embracing all of mankind. "I guess you're excited about
opening your own brokerage business. I sure would be. I wish
you luck, girl. I've got some exciting news, myself. Bertil
Swenson, that Swede who moved into the rooms you had at the
inn—you've seen him—well, he's taken a real shine to me. He
doesn't care if I'm short and plump. He says Swedish men like
a little flesh on a woman. Honey, nobody ever made me feel so
good about myself as that man does."

Selena's eyebrows arched. "Well, now, I guess you'll stop grousing about the way you look, because Bertil Swenson could just about have his pick. I thought women in this town would fall over backward when he showed up. Great if you like 'em blond."

Eloise gaped at Selena. "You mean you don't? I thought you New York girls were more used to…well, you know…continental people."

Selena laughed. "Honey, my clock won't tick unless tall, dark and handsome winds it up."

It was Eloise's turn to laugh. "Get outta here, girl. It's been so long since my clock had a chance to make any noise that it started ticking before this guy got to the winding stem. Besides, he's—" She paused when the phone rang.

"Excuse me." Selena answered her phone. "We'll talk some more later," she told Eloise and turned her attention to Magnus.

"Would you have time to pick up a gift for a client? You'd probably have to get it in San Antonio."

"Sure. What would you like?"

"A silver card case for a man with initials LNN. Okay?"

She wouldn't get angry. "I don't think I have enough cash," she said evenly.

"Use a charge. Either Saks or Neiman Marcus ought to have something interesting."

She leaned back in the chair, started counting, and when she reached six, blurted out, "So I can be humiliated again?"

"I'm not sure I understand." Her words tumbled out, and the hurt she'd stored for over a week poured out with them.

"Are you telling me that account hadn't been opened Thursday afternoon after I left for Freetown?" he asked, his voice cold and every syllable of his words articulated to perfection.

"Right. You can imagine that I didn't try to shop at the other store."

He waited so long to comment that she asked him, "Did you open the accounts yourself?"

His reply, crisp and pregnant with suppressed anger, fell on her ears like damp cement. "No, I definitely did not. Thanks for wanting to help, but I'll get it in Houston. I've decided to take the noon flight over there. Be back as early as I can. See you then." He hung up. She stared at the receiver. What in heaven's name had come over Magnus Cooper?

Magnus hung up and called Saks. No, Mrs. Cooper's account had not been opened on that Thursday, but the following Tuesday afternoon for an amount not to exceed one thousand monthly. He managed to remain pleasant and courteous.

"My wife's last name is Sutton-Cooper, and there's to be no dollar limit on her account. Whose idea was that, anyway?"

The clerk replied, "We give gentlemen options when they open accounts for ladies, and…"

"That's enough. I'm sorry, it isn't your fault," he added after roaring at her. "Please mail the card to my wife." His anger had not subsided when Jeb called.

"Magnus, I think you ought to consider changing the lock on your office door. I haven't been able to determine why you found it unlocked, and I discovered it open when I made an unscheduled check last night." Magnus thanked him and made a note to visit a locksmith when he got to Houston. He walked out to the garden, where Tessie collected vegetables for dinner.

"Tess, I have to fly to Houston, but I should be back by eight this evening. Save me some dinner." He stared. *Tessie wearing makeup?* A new hairstyle? In over thirty years, he hadn't seen her hair out of its tight knot.

"You like him, do you?"

"Who?"

Magnus laughed aloud. "Tell him I said go easy on you— you're a babe in the woods compared to him."

She ducked her head and replied in a voice so soft as to startle him, "You always teasing and talking foolishness."

Magnus put an arm around her shoulder. "This time, I'm

serious. Take care." He'd embarrassed her, and he hadn't intended to, but he wanted her to know that even so respectable a man as Jackson could be a source of tears and unhappiness.

Magnus entered the eleven-story, redbrick building marked Cooper Enterprises, Inc., got the elevator to the executive floor and walked into Madeline's office without knocking. If he had misled her, he would correct whatever impression she had of him. For the eight years she'd known him, she had seen a gracious, appreciative and even-tempered man. But he'd have her know that was because she had been the ideal secretary. She'd better have a good excuse.

"Magnus!" she exclaimed, quickly hanging up the phone.

"If that was a business call, Cooper Enterprises may be accused of rudeness," he told her without the preliminary of a greeting.

"Oh, well, I…" She patted her hair and stood. "May I help you with something?"

He hated obsequiousness and, though he thought Madeline guilty of it at the moment, he'd give her the benefit of the doubt. No point in letting his anger obscure his judgment.

"Yes, you may help me, Madeline." He walked into his office, which he noted was not locked and, as expected, she followed. "When did you open those charge accounts for my wife?" Satisfied that her explanations and apologies amounted to baseless excuses, he told her, "When I tell you to do something for my wife, do it immediately. If anything like this happens again, I'll get a private secretary and relieve you of all but company business. Is that clear?"

Her distress sent the blood rushing to her face, and deep red discolored her light complexion. "Yes, sir, I just thought—"

He cut her off. "And my wife's last name is Sutton-Cooper. I could forgive you for forgetting to open the account, but not for putting a ceiling on the amount of *my* money that *my* wife may spend. You did not forget, Madeline. Whatever your reason for behaving this way, don't let it happen again if you want to work for me. Got it?" He ignored her tears.

"Yes, sir." Her lips quivered, he didn't know whether from anger, shame or distress but, no matter, she deserved a reprimand.

She hadn't shown reluctance in the past to take care of his personal affairs, and he had assumed she didn't mind. He suspected she had difficulty telling him no, so he'd be more considerate in the future; he didn't want to lose so priceless a secretary, one whom he knew was loyal beyond measure.

He used his private phone to telephone a locksmith with whom he'd been associated on several building projects and whom he trusted. Within the hour, he had a new lock on his office door, one that responded to three different combinations in a computerized system that recorded the date and time of opening and closing the door. He gave one combination to Madeline, one to Jeb and kept the other for himself, and he didn't tell either of them about the computer system.

Looking through the mail on his desk, he picked up one envelope, marked personal, and addressed to him and Selena, and opened Wade Malloy's letter. The woman's suit against Selena claimed that Selena had used undue pressure in selling her the junk bonds, a tactic that the firm's CEO swore none of its brokers used. Wade wanted a trial to determine how the woman learned about the bonds before the public offering. "She's not forthcoming about it," he wrote, "and I plan to focus on this as the weakness in her case. I suspect she traded on inside information, which is illegal. I'll keep you posted." He put the letter in his briefcase, tested the combination lock on his door and locked it.

That business finished, he stopped by Saks Fifth Avenue, bought the silver card case and headed for the airport. He'd be in Waverly by seven-thirty.

Madeline held back the tears for as long as she could but, as she stood at her window and watched Magnus jump into a taxi, moisture streamed down her cheeks. She knew she had slipped a few notches in his estimation, and he would no longer see her as the perfect secretary, his right hand and indispensable support. Wringing her hands, she trudged back to her desk nearly stumbling on the thick, rose-colored broadloom carpet. She went into her private bathroom and washed her face. She had always eaten her lunch, and often her supper, in the privacy of his office, sitting in *his* chair at *his* desk. Peace and contentment had filled her during those times and, in her mind, she'd been close to him. Now, he complained about his unlocked office door, and it wouldn't be the same. She shouldn't have forgotten to lock it but, after all she'd done for him he ought not to have given her a tongue-lashing.

If only things had remained as they were. She'd given eight years to Cooper Enterprises, eight years of service to Magnus, and now he threatened to replace her. He had spoken to her in harsh, cold tones, his voice devoid of its usual warmth and his face lacking the charm that made you want to do for him whatever he asked. Fury rose like bile inside her until she could taste her anger. Let him cast her aside: he wouldn't find another one who'd give up her life for him as she had.

"Cooper Enterprises," she mumbled automatically, answering the phone. "May I help you?"

"You sure can, doll. This is Edwin Cooper, your boss's brother. Is he there?"

"Why no, he just left. I'll be glad to give him a message." She wondered at the long pause.

"What do you say I come over and introduce myself, write him a note. That way you and I can get acquainted, and the next time I call you won't be so distant and businesslike. I like to know who I'm dealing with."

She couldn't make another mistake with Magnus. He hadn't talked about his brother, but… "I didn't know Mr. Cooper had a brother."

"I've been living in the northeast. Just moved back to Texas.

If you see me, you'll know I'm his brother, so why don't I come over now? I'm a couple of blocks away."

"Well…all right. I'll tell the receptionist in the lobby to let you come up."

Madeline nearly fell from her chair when Prince walked in, saw her and stopped in his tracks as thought struck by lightning. His whistle, long and sharp, split the air.

"No wonder he's never mentioned you—he's keeping you for himself. A real woman. And to think I almost didn't call here. I'm Edwin Cooper, but call me Prince. Everybody does."

She watched as a grin spread over his face, stars seemed to fly from his large, long-lashed gray-brown eyes and he strolled toward her, hypnotizing her with every step. He didn't stop until he'd reached her, leaned over and kissed her lips.

"I may never recover from this, love, so tell me who you are," he drawled in honeyed tones. She stared at him, tongue-tied. The most generous person wouldn't call her beautiful, though she was presentable with her high coloring and lovely straight hair, but no man who looked like Prince Cooper had ever glanced at her a second time. At least six feet tall with an athlete's body, and *that face*. She had thought Magnus a handsome man, but this man was an example of God's perfection in humans.

"My name is Madeline," she managed at last and wished he wouldn't stand so close.

"Ah. Madeline. It's a lovely name, but there must be more."

"Price. Madeline Price."

"Doesn't that brother of mine shell out for office coffee? I could use a cup," he said, dropping into the chair beside her desk and making himself comfortable. She went into the hall pantry, got a cup of coffee for him, and when she returned, stopped in the doorway at the sight of him sitting behind her desk.

He grinned. "Just wanted to see what it's like to sit behind a desk at Cooper Enterprises. I've been in Madison Avenue offices where the boss wasn't as well fixed as you are." His face creased into a luminous smile. "Thanks." He sipped the coffee. "Guess he likes you, huh? His office must be out of sight."

She thanked God for the presence of mind not to bite that one. "Mr. Cooper's office befits his station. Now, I think you'd better give me back my desk."

He jumped up, grasped her elbow lightly, and helped her sit down. "The more I see of you, Madeline, the more I want to see. You live around here?"

She nodded.

He put the cup on the desk as though in haste. "Wait a minute. You're not married, are you? Tell me you're not."

"I'm not married." She watched, perplexed, as he expelled a deep breath telling her of his relief.

He sprang up suddenly. "Thanks for the coffee. Mind if I call you sometime? The thought of not seeing you again unsettles me and, since you're not married, I'm putting in my word. Wait. You did say there was nothing between you and Magnus, didn't you? I wouldn't want to…to foul up anything."

"Mr. Cooper is a married man, as you must know, and I am not involved with him. I hope that answers your question." She didn't know what the man's motive was—she hoped he was like Magnus, but you never could tell, and she didn't want Magnus mad with her again.

"It sure does, honey." Before she could register his notice, he'd stepped closer and kissed her on the mouth again. "Bye. I'll let myself out." He left. A tornado. A real twister. But what a gorgeous one. Men didn't fall all over her, but he had seemed transfixed from the moment he looked at her. Her mother had always said there was no explaining chemistry. She'd see. He was one good-looking man. Four-thirty. She might as well close up and go home. First Magnus and then his brother. She'd had about as much as she could handle in one day. When she left the building an hour later, she thought she saw Prince cross the street and get into his car. Where had he been for the past hour? In the Cooper building?

* * *

Several days later, Selena sat on the floor of her new office sorting through memorabilia from her days on Wall Street. She picked up the little black porcelain doll that one of the partners at Hilliard and Matting, her old Wall Street firm, had given her at the first office Christmas party she'd attended and pitched it into the wastebasket. Magnus, who had been hooking up her color printer, retrieved it.

"Why would you throw this away? It's one of your nicest dolls."

That wasn't smart, she told herself. "It was a Christmas present from a colleague who subsequently proved to be a snake. I don't want it."

"A man?" She nodded.

The phone rang, and Magnus reached across the desk and picked up the receiver. "Yes, Wade. She's right here." He placed the phone in Selena's hand.

"Hello, Wade," Selena said. They exchanged pleasantries for a few moments. "What do you mean, she can document her claim?"

"Did you send her an unsolicited announcement that the bonds would be offered and that smart investors could get a good deal if they bought before December third?"

She released her breath. "Certainly not. And if anyone claims that, it's a lie, and I'll countersue."

"Right on," Wade responded, obviously relieved. "That's what I thought. I'll find out who printed that paper. I'm also planning to interview the owner of the company whose shares you bought for her, because I suspect he may give me a good lead. Regards to Magnus. Be talking with you." Selena relayed Wade's side of the conversation to Magnus.

"Do you think we need a secretary here?" he asked her after the phone interrupted them for the fifth time.

"I don't, but you men seem to need office wives."

He leaned against her desk, folded his arms and crossed his knee. "Is that so?"

She eased herself off the floor to a kneeling position where she'd be at less of a disadvantage. "Would you please shove that box over here?" she asked him, pointing to a large and very heavy one. He regarded her steadily, and it occurred to her that he might outwit her.

"That one over there," she repeated, pointing to the same box. He let a grin wind slowly over his face before releasing a gale of laughter. She picked the moment as a safe one, sprang to her feet and started for the door, throwing herself against it to hasten her getaway. But the hard object with which she connected was Magnus Cooper.

Mischief danced in his hazel eyes as he looked down at her. "I'll have pity on you for now, but I aim to collect, babe."

She tossed her head. "You don't say."

He was no longer amused. Tension suddenly seemed to coil in him, heat radiated from his body and his nostrils flared. She quickly swallowed her retort. "May I pass?" she asked him, knowing her request was a futile one.

"Put your arms around me, Selena." His voice rang dark, hot and hoarse in her ears. "Selena. Selena, hold me," he rasped.

"We're in my office," she stalled.

His arms tightened around her, his hand caressed the back of her head, and as he gazed into her face, his eyes seemed to search her and to judge her. "Sweet. Ah, Selena, what keeps you from me?"

If only she could tell him how she longed for just three words, that she would open her soul to him if he only loved her. She couldn't stifle the groan of pain that welled up in her. She needed him. Her arms went around him, pulling him to her until her shoulders ached and her bosom heaved against him.

"You do care, don't you?" he asked in barely audible words.

"I care."

His mouth settled on her lips. Seeking. Demanding. Draining her of energy and will. She held him, stroked his shoulders and tried to keep her wits, because if she gave in to her feelings, she'd lower the price. And what she wanted from him was love. He kissed her eyes, her face and, unable to hold back longer, she parted her lips for what she knew he wanted to give her. His tongue plunged into her mouth, dancing furiously and claiming her until he shuddered violently against her. She buried her face in his shoulder and would have taken him to her suite if Tessie hadn't knocked.

"What is it, Tessie?" he asked, his voice strained.

"Selena just got a little package, and you told me to let you know whenever she gets one that doesn't have a return address. Sorry to interrupt anything."

"Thanks." Cold shivers streaked down her back as Magnus released her and, without another word, followed Tessie to the house.

"Do you want me to open it?" he asked Selena when he returned with an eight-inch-square package.

"If you don't mind."

She searched his face for a clue as to the nature of its contents, but his impassive visage told her nothing. "Awful, huh?" she asked him.

The muscles of his jaw flexed rapidly. "Not worth a glance. I'll get rid of it."

"What was in it?" Tessie asked him when he went into the kitchen, got a plastic bag and wrapped the package in it.

"Badly decayed plants with an odd odor."

"Good Lord, you're not saving it, are you?"

"I may need the fingerprints. Never can tell." He found Selena staring into space, as would a catatonic.

"Magnus, did you have a girlfriend who'd want to make me miserable?"

"I've never made a promise to any woman but you. I haven't led a woman other than you to think marriage to me was a remote possibility."

"I despise cowards," she spat out contemptuously. "Whoever dislikes me or is dissatisfied with me should face me, accuse me and allow me to defend myself." She felt his arms around her. Comforting. Soothing.

"We'll get to the bottom of this. Don't doubt it, Selena. It will not go unpunished."

Tessie looked at her hands, shrugged and picked up the phone. "He ain't here, Miss Anna, but I'll tell him you called."

"I suppose Selena's with him."

"Selena's in her office. You wanna talk to her?"

"I don't have anything to say to her. Where is Magnus?"

Tessie clutched the phone between her shoulder and the side of her head and tried to clean the flour from her hands. "He ain't in a habit of telling me his whereabouts."

"And if you knew, you wouldn't tell me. We both know that."

"No, ma'am," Tessie said in her sweetest voice. "I sure wouldn't, unless he told me to, but I'll let him know you asked for him."

"Have you sent out the invitations for the barbecue? I didn't get one and neither did Mavis. We *are* on the list, aren't we?"

One day, she was going to tell Anna Cooper a thing or two. She sliced the air above her head in a gesture of impatience. Thirty-seven years of the woman was cross enough for anybody. "Miss Anna, I ain't in charge of this house. I'm the housekeeper, and I don't issue invitations to your son's social affairs. Now if there ain't nothing else, I got my hands full of biscuit dough." She waited until she heard the dial tone, hung up and checked the invitation list for the annual barbecue. A smile creased her face; Mavis Root's name was not there. She put the biscuits in the oven, filled a tall glass with iced tea and went out to the offices.

"Thought you'd like a cool drink," she said, as she handed the glass to Selena.

"Thanks, Tessie. Well, what do you think of my office?"

Tessie glanced around at the framed reproductions of paintings by Doris Price, Elizabeth Catlett, John Biggers and Wadsworth Jarrell that brightened the sand-colored walls, and at the colorful copies of *American Visions* magazines spread out on the table. A large carpet of Native American motif covered the center of the floor, and tubs of large cactus plants scattered among the walnut wood furnishings added to the ambience.

"It looks just like you," Tessie announced, "and that's saying a whole lot. What time is Magnus coming back from Houston?"

"Around seven. I can serve the dinner if you want to go somewhere."

"No need for that. The men finished setting up the tent and the barbecue pits. I'll call the caterer tomorrow to finalize the arrangements, so please check the list again."

"Magnus and I checked it last night. Add a guest for Eloise, please. I can't remember his name."

"Miss Eloise got a man? Do tell! Well, I sure will do that. I didn't notice any of the Houston people on the list. Last year, he invited some of them."

"I don't have the answer to that. But he'll plan something for them, I'm sure. He's very fond of his Houston staff."

At the moment, however, Magnus was not pleased with at least one of them. Why the devil had Prince lolled around his office for half a day, and why had Madeline allowed it? She stepped into his office almost as soon as he'd buzzed her.

"Yes, sir." Had Madeline always stood with her hands clasped in front of her? He didn't think so, and he wished she wouldn't do that. He did not want subservience from his employees, only loyalty, competence and efficiency.

"Madeline, how is it that my brother spent half a day roaming around this building day before yesterday?"

"Your brother is so nice, Magnus. Such a gentleman. He made a hit with all of us."

He covered his impatience. "Prince uses his charm for a purpose, Madeline, and he's never been known to waste it. Any one of his numerous victims will attest to that."

"Oh, Magnus, I'm sure you misunderstood him. He did say there'd always been friendly antagonism between you two, but that it didn't amount to more than normal sibling rivalry. He told me how he admires you and wants the best for you. You're very lucky to have a brother like him."

What the devil was Prince up to? He'd bamboozled Madeline, of all people. "You still talking about the Prince I've known for the last thirty-two years? Watch it, Madeline."

He gazed in fascination as her demeanor changed to that of a demure young girl when she lowered her head and looked at him from beneath her lashes.

"I was only going on what I saw of him, and he couldn't have been more of a gentleman. Of course, I can imagine a man that good-looking would get on other men's nerves."

That comment took some chutzpah that he wouldn't have associated with Madeline. He leaned back in his chair and drummed his fingers on his desk. "He's to be allowed in this building only when I'm here. No other time. And that's final. Got it?"

"Yes, sir."

Thinking their conversation over, he lifted the receiver and began to dial his home, glanced up and saw her expression of icy disdain. A deep red tinged her face when he looked back quickly, revealing his astonishment at her rapid change.

"Thanks, Madeline. That will be all." He replaced the receiver without having dialed and mused about her odd behavior. She'd been his right hand for years, and he'd taken her for granted. If that annoyed her, he wouldn't blame her. He made a note to give her an extra bonus at Christmas.

He called Selena and told her he'd be home around seven or seven-thirty, locked his office and headed for the airport.

Ten minutes after she heard the executive elevator close, Madeline lifted the receiver of the black phone on her desk. She'd ordered one, because phones were supposed to be black.

"Cooper Enterprises. May I help you?"

"You sure can, baby," Prince said. "I just saw him leave the building. I'll be right over."

"No. You can't. You'll get me fired. He said you're barred from the building unless he's here."

"He's just jealous. Doesn't want me around you."

"You want me to believe that, along with all his other virtues, Magnus Cooper is the world's greatest actor?" she asked him, flabbergasted at what he'd suggested.

"Wouldn't surprise me. If I can't go in there, you come out here to me. I'm at Renaldo's down the street. I'll wait for you."

On her feet now and clutching the phone with both hands, she thought briefly that she was about to be disloyal to Magnus and quickly dismissed the idea. But her thoughts raced over the past eight years. How far had she gotten? When he looked at her, he saw an office machine, but Prince saw a woman. She'd been office furniture long enough.

"Are you trying to start something with me?" she asked Prince.

"Couldn't you see? You shot a hole in my middle the moment I laid eyes on you. Why do you think I hung around there so long? Certainly not because I've suddenly taken an interest in Cooper Enterprises."

"I'm a good seven or eight years older than you."

"Just the way I like 'em—old enough to know what it means to have a real good man."

This could be the mistake of her life, but she needed somebody's arms around her. If she couldn't have the man she wanted, she'd take what she could get. And what she could get wasn't bad.

"You sing a sweet tune," she told Prince, "but I wonder if there's anything else to you. See you later." She hung up, walked to the window and gazed down at the almost empty street. Her nerve endings crawled like busy ants beneath her skin while she made up her mind. She went back to her desk, opened the bottom drawer and took out the old copy of the *Waverly Herald* that had the story on Prince and Selena. She wondered if it told the truth as to why Selena had been found thumbing a ride into Waverly and what had prompted Magnus to marry his brother's leavings. Maybe she'd been pregnant, and Prince had run out on her.

She had given the best years of her life to Magnus, taking care of his office and his business as though they were her own and protecting him in every way she could. But he still didn't know whether she bought her lingerie at Victoria's Secret or wore Jockey shorts. She hadn't asked for much out of life, but what she'd wanted had always been beyond reach. She dispatched the e-mail, locked the computer, turned off the lights, took the executive elevator to the first floor, locked it and left the building. Prince had a smooth tongue, as obvious as sunshine, but a woman could break into a sweat from looking at him. She crossed Durham Street, headed for Renaldo's and prayed that none of her co-workers would be there.

Selena and Magnus had been sharing adjoining offices for several days, when she tapped on his office door. "Feel like a short break?"

He looked up. "What's on your mind?"

"Freddie. Eloise said he ran away again and, when they found him, he said he was on his way to Washington to speak with the president about his problem."

She watched a half smile play around her husband's lips. "And what's his problem?"

"He says the country needs schools where adults can learn about children's problems. Nobody understands him."

Magnus got up and walked over to her. "When do you want him to spend a weekend with us?"

"Well, I hadn't gotten around to—"

"No, but you were going to. I'll be here next weekend. How's that?"

She itched to hug him, but she knew that if she did, she'd start a fire. No matter what she asked, he wanted to give it to her. If only he wanted to give her all of himself. "That will be wonderful."

"There's a catch, Selena. The boy will be visiting me. He has his mother, Eloise and you, and he apparently needs more. Let's see if I can help. How about a date tonight?"

"Doing what?"

He grinned and stepped closer. "We can drive into San Antonio. Tessie can have the evening off, and you and I can have some fun."

She could think of some fun they could have right there on the ranch, but she'd do it his way. "Seven?" She wanted to dress up and go dancing. She had plans for him. If he wasn't tuned in to his own feelings, she'd wake him up and, before she finished with him, he'd scream "uncle" more than once.

"Meet you in the den at seven," she told him, glancing up and down his long frame and then fixing her gaze on his mouth. "And how about wearing a hankie to match that tie I like."

He blinked. "You want me to dress?"

"Well…" The word dangled. "Think of the newspaper headlines if you don't."

He caressed her shoulders, squeezed them and backed off. "You are one fresh woman. Okay. Seven o'clock."

He's possessive, she thought. Maybe she liked that; she wasn't quite sure.

Selena took her time dressing for their date. Feeling reckless, she slipped into a miniskirted, red silk sleeveless dress—a skimpy thing that looked more like an undergarment than a dress and which, a couple of decades back, would have been considered scandalous, put on black patent shoes, threw a lightweight black silk stole across her arm and left her room.

Magnus poured a tonic for himself and a glass of white wine for Selena and reached into the bar cabinet for some napkins just as the scent of her softly seductive perfume reached his nostrils. He turned abruptly, nearly spilling her wine. Her smile, cool and inviting, curdled his insides. If she intended to show him what he had, who she was and what she offered, she could stop right there. He knew.

"All this for me?" he asked.

"Who else?"

He drank in her bewitching smile, the joy she seemed to exude in being a woman. "You could have dressed for yourself," he replied, although he hoped she'd done it for him.

She tossed her head, sending her long hair swirling around her shoulders, and let her eyes provoke him with an age-old invitation. "If I please you, I automatically please myself."

He'd never known a woman to have so many sides. If anybody had told him he'd married a siren, he'd have disputed it, but the Selena Sutton facing him was a seductress. "Wait right here," he said. It took him ten minutes to change his shirt and put on a red tie and handkerchief that matched her dress. "Let's go." Her smile of appreciation heightened his pleasure in being with her.

"You're taking the Town Car?"

"I'm out with my best girl. What else would I drive?"

Ten minutes after they gave the waiter their orders, he looked away from Selena to see Prince walking toward their table.

"Mind if my date and I join you?" Prince asked, gesturing toward a young woman who sat alone at a nearby table.

Magnus observed the direction of Prince's gaze with disgust. "What are you doing here?"

Prince winked at Selena. "Tell him. This is my favorite restaurant." He glanced at Magnus. "Didn't she tell you?"

"You know that I've never been in a restaurant with you, Prince. This is the first time I've seen you in one."

He gave the appearance of one who had just suffered a great injustice. "Selena, I have never met a woman so good at pretense. You can't make him or anyone else believe that I'm nothing to you," Prince said before walking back to his table.

Magnus made a pyramid of his ten fingers and let a few minutes of silence precede his words. "Next time, just tell him to go to hell. He doesn't understand your ladylike behavior." She had to sense his displeasure, but he couldn't pretend.

"That isn't my style, but if it were, I'd hardly resort to it with you sitting here."

He knew the evening's magic was lost the minute Prince saw them. "Don't hold back on my account. As far as I'm concerned, you can say anything you want to, whenever and wherever you like and to whomever you please."

"Magnus, could we forget about Prince? I was so happy."

"Happy?" He gazed at her for a long time. Searching. Somewhere in that woman was all he'd ever longed for, everything he needed. Why couldn't they get together? "Let's finish this and go."

From the lobby, he walked into the men's room, because he hated waiting in front of the ladies' room for his date.

Prince walked in right behind him. "Why don't you wake up?" Prince sneered. "She's mine, and she'll always be, because I know her inside and out."

"I don't believe you," Magnus said. "You're a pathological liar, and if you persist with this one, I promise you will regret it." He spun around and left the room, but all he wanted for the remainder of the evening was to get back to Cooper Ranch. He had sworn never to get involved with a woman who'd had a relationship with Prince. Maybe Prince was lying, but what difference did that make? The man wouldn't leave Selena alone. Selena stepped out of the ladies' room, and her reaction to his changed mood and attitude was mirrored on her face; her smile died when she looked at him.

"Let's go home."

She nodded. So much for their romantic evening.

Chapter 9

"Southwestern Securities, Selena Sutton-Cooper speaking."

"Hey, girl. How's it going?"

"Well, I could use a secretary, but Magnus handles this ranch without one, and he's challenged me to do the same. Other than that, I'm excited to be back in the brokerage business. What's on your mind at eight-thirty in the morning?"

Eloise cleared her throat. "Well, it's something my sister said. She lives in Houston, you know, and last night on the phone, she said Prince is driving the Cooper Enterprises car around town. I didn't know Prince worked for Magnus."

"Are you sure?"

"Girl, it's not possible for my sister to mistake anybody for Prince. She'd recognize him a block away. She should—she spent enough time in perpetual arousal, mooning over him."

"Maybe he hitched a ride with one of the drivers."

"Oh, yeah? Well, from what she said, he must have gotten rid of the driver. You take care, girl."

Selena hung up. Magnus wouldn't like that news. She heard him enter the office around nine, after having completed his morning rounds, and went in to speak with him.

Goose pimples covered her arms when he quickly placed a small parcel in a bag and shoved it under his desk. From that glimpse she knew that her anonymous bedeviler had sent her another "gift."

Realizing that she'd seen it, he explained, "Don't worry, Selena, we'll get to the bottom of this. My suggestion is that you not open any package or letter unless you know the sender's name and address."

Selena nodded in compliance. "Thanks. I won't." She told him what Eloise had said about Prince. "Did you give him permission to drive your business vehicles?"

He bounded out of his chair. "Absolutely not!" He paced a few steps, turned and stopped in front of her. "Selena, something peculiar is going on in Houston. I have always found my employees to be loyal and trustworthy, but if Prince is driving my cars, one of them has fallen on the job."

"Or maybe Prince has hoodwinked someone. I'd be careful, if I were you."

His grim smile brought an ache deep inside her. He didn't want antagonism between himself and his brother, but Prince provoked him at every turn.

"You're right," he said. "Prince can charm an alligator out of its hide."

The phone rang, and Magnus lifted the receiver. "Cooper speaking." Selena watched his face ashen. "You're lying," he said. "I don't believe a word of it." He stared at the phone, and she realized that the caller had hung up.

"Who was that?"

"Nothing important," he replied, but from his suddenly rigid stance and the icy, almost unfriendly air he projected, she knew that whatever he'd heard had irritated him. And he hadn't told the truth when he'd said he didn't believe it.

"I'd better get back to work," she said. But she couldn't; her mind was in Magnus's office. That caller had in some way implicated her.

Exasperated, she pushed open the door to Magnus's office. "If that phone call was about me, why can't you tell me?"

He spun his chair around and faced her, his face a sea of bottled-up rage, and she knew she'd just provided him with the opportunity to vent his irritation.

"If I have something to tell you, Selena, I won't bite my tongue. You'll know it."

"All right, if you want to pretend."

In a flash, he was out of the chair, imprisoning her arms to her sides. "Look at me, Selena. Oh, *Selena!*" His arms went around her, pulling her to him with such force that shudders raced through her. She knew that frustration and rage, not love, possessed him, but in spite of that, an unearthly sensation heated her blood, and she couldn't hide her heart's response to him. His mouth settled on hers, but she tasted anger and pushed at his chest.

He released her at once. "I'm sorry. I don't know what came over me. It's just…just so damned frustrating. It's right here in my hands, everything I've ever wanted." He held out his right palm to her, spread his fingers and continued. "And it flits right through my fingers—like air."

Her eyes must have reflected the hollow hopelessness that she felt, for he enclosed her in a gentle embrace and whispered, "We'll work this out, Selena. We've got to. I've never been so frustrated in my life." She didn't ask him why. She knew. It was Prince who had called him. She told herself that she wouldn't worry about it; he'd know the truth.

Magnus didn't want to judge Madeline on the basis of hearsay, especially since he'd had occasion to reprimand her a few days earlier. And questioning her about Prince's use of the cars was tantamount to saying he thought her capable of violating company policy. He saw no alternative, however, since all car keys remained in her safe when they weren't in use.

He dialed his Houston office. "Good morning, Madeline." She responded in her usually pleasant voice which, for once, he found off-putting. Same tone of voice no matter what he said to her, he realized with a flash of insight. Hell. He'd give it to her straight.

"Can you think of any reason why my brother would be driving one of the company cars? And especially after I told you that he wasn't to be allowed in the building unless I was there."

"Oh, dear. I'm so sorry, Magnus. Someone obviously mistook him for one of the drivers or messengers. It could only have been a mistake. I have never given car keys to anyone who wasn't a uniformed employee of Cooper Enterprises. I'll look into this immediately. I've invested a lot of myself in our company, Magnus, and I do whatever I can to promote it. I hope you believe that, sir."

He did believe it, but he had to know how Prince got that car. "All right, Madeline. Let me speak with Jeb."

"Are you sure of this, Magnus?" Jeb asked him. "I don't keep the keys, but I can check the log. I'll get back to you as soon as I do that." Magnus hung up. He furrowed his brow and rubbed the back of his neck, but he couldn't place any woman in his employ who might be susceptible to Prince. Only two were under forty, and one of those was pregnant. The other one was a chief engineer who wouldn't brook nonsense from Prince or anybody else. He'd have to wait for Jeb's report.

After Magnus's call, Madeline replaced the phone in its cradle, wondering whether she'd regret it if she cast her lot with Prince. She hadn't given him permission to use that car; she could only surmise that the keys, with the miniature license plate attached, had been on her desk where the previous driver had put them, and that Prince had walked off with them. She telephoned him at the number he'd given her.

"This is Madeline. How'd you get that car? You're going to make me lose my job, because Magnus is furious. I want those keys."

"Not to worry, babe. The keys were on your desk, and I figured my brother wouldn't mind if I borrowed them for a couple of days."

"Come on, Prince. He doesn't even want you in the building."

"That's because he's jealous. He knows I can get any woman I want, and he wants you for himself."

Madeline snorted. "Humph. You keep saying that, but the truth is you're a handsome phoney with a line as long as from here to New York."

"Now hold on, baby, you don't mean that. I've been straight with you, and you know it. I told you up front that you slammed into me like a hurricane the moment I laid eyes on you. That's not something a man can control. If it happens, it happens."

"I am not a beauty queen, Prince."

"Icebergs don't attract me."

"I'm hanging up."

"You won't get rid of me so easily. When I want a woman, I get her. Don't think I'm pining after Selena. Magnus got her away from me, but now that I've seen you, I don't want her. But Magnus isn't going to have her."

Madeline tried to steady her trembling hand. "You mean you're going to break them up?"

"Bet on it." She could hear wickedness and satisfaction in his voice. Satan personified, she thought. But, if he could... Maybe she still had a chance with Magnus. Working herself to shreds for the company hadn't brought him to her, but if he lost Selena, maybe he'd turn to her.

Prince's voice interrupted her musings. "Stick with me, baby, and we'll settle the score for both of us."

Her antennae shot up. "What do you mean by that? What are you planning to do to him?" Stridency colored her every word.

"I told you. I intend to break them up. I know you've got the itch for him. I just can't figure out why. Play along with me, and you'll wash him out of your system and get a good man, to boot."

"You don't know any such thing. If that were the case, would I be talking to you right now? Magnus can't hold a candle to you, and you know it, so what's all this talk about evening up things for me?" She knew he'd believe any compliment she paid him, and it hadn't taken her long to understand that his life's goals were to outsmart Magnus and to prove his sexual superiority. Maybe he knew what he was talking about. She could do worse than lose herself in a man who looked like Prince. A lot worse.

She could almost see his tantalizing smile when he said, "You want some sugar? I've got an endless supply, babe. Like I said, you hang out with me, and I'll keep you well preserved. Meet me for the weekend, and I guarantee you'll be walking on air for the rest of the month."

"You sure talk big, Prince. I'd better not find out that that's all there is to you. Where do you want us to meet? How about San Antonio, since this town is full of Magnus's buddies."

"So's San Antone," he said. They settled on Bastrop, midway between Houston and Waverly, though he complained that the place offered little apart from antique cars, turn-of-the-century people and the Colorado River.

Madeline and Prince ate dinner at a small restaurant near the edge of town and, though he joked and talked about himself and Magnus with little of the animosity he'd expressed earlier, she couldn't banish her uneasiness. His volatile personality disturbed her, but her hatred and envy that she felt for Selena and her desire for Magnus allowed her to dismiss it. He opened the door with his key.

"Who lives here, Prince?"

"A buddy. Fellow I gig with. He's in New Orleans at the Jazz Festival."

Anything to postpone the moment of truth, because she

knew he wouldn't let her back out without a nasty fight. "Why didn't you go?"

He shrugged. "Playing in tents for a lot of hicks isn't my style. I'm a concert man. Come here, baby."

She closed her eyes, suffered his primitive lovemaking, and pretended to enjoy it, but his self-involvement was so intense that he was unaware of her true feelings and reactions.

His swagger matched his self-satisfied smile. "I bet you never got to heaven that fast or stayed there that long."

"How'd you guess?"

"I know, baby. I always know."

They drove back to Houston in her car, and when she stopped near the Civic Center to let him out, he suddenly began a diatribe against Magnus, swearing that he would ruin his brother. Appalled, she told him goodbye and drove off, aware that he hadn't let her know where he stayed, hadn't given her the keys to the Cooper Enterprises car, and that he represented a threat to Magnus.

"I owe you one for that lousy toss in the hay, Prince," she said aloud. If he used her, she'd use him. He'd get rid of Selena, but she'd thwart any move he made against Magnus. And he was so sure she was enamored of him that he'd tell her everything he planned.

Selena put two glasses, a large Thermos of iced tea and some peanut butter cookies on a tray and knocked on Magnus's office door.

"If you're tall, willowy, the color of my arm and gorgeous from head to foot, come in."

Selena couldn't help laughing. "Is that somebody I know?"

He went to meet her. "Ah. I see you've forgiven me for my morning madness," he said, referring to his reaction to the phone call.

She handed him the tray. "Not so fast. I came to let you grovel."

His eyebrows shot up. "Now, or later?"

She didn't intend to dwell on that morning's incident. His smile told her that he'd come to terms with whatever had unsettled him, and that was enough. "I'll let you know when I'm ready to see you crawl."

He flashed a grin. "Give me a couple of months' notice so I can get it right. I wouldn't want to disappoint you." He teased, but she knew that fawning was not in his character.

He stretched out his long legs, poured tea for each of them and bit into a cookie. "I see you've been talking to Tessie. I could eat a ton of these. Sometimes she swears she ruined them but, to me, they taste the same as usual. I love these things."

In response to a knock, he got up and opened his door.

"Come in, Jackson. Sorry I can't offer you a cookie, but I want these. Go ask Tessie, if you want some."

"I will. Afternoon, Selena. Right now, I have to look after Lacey. She's going to calve any minute, and she's not doing so well."

Selena looked at Magnus for reassurance. "I thought longhorns didn't need help giving birth."

"Usually, they don't," Magnus replied, "but it's Lacey's first time." He drained his glass.

"Is she in the barn?"

Jackson nodded.

"Let's go."

Selena looked from one to the other. "Shouldn't you call the vet?"

Magnus took his Stetson from its home on a hook over his desk. "Jackson's as good as they come."

Selena walked out with them into the scalding heat, and Magnus draped an arm lightly across her shoulders and told her, "You might not want to see this."

"Who wouldn't? Of course I do. I wouldn't miss it."

"All right. But if it gets too unpleasant for you, you might be sorry you came along."

She gave him a withering look. "Never."

Selena watched the heifer closely as the cow moaned and thrashed before becoming still, her breaths deep and long. Jackson cooled her with damp cloths and examined her at short intervals.

"How much longer?" Selena asked them.

"Any minute," Jackson told her, and the animal's renewed moaning verified his judgment. Selena sat down in the hay beside the cow and began soothing her sweat-soaked head and neck with a cool, damp cloth. Lacey opened her eyes and looked at Selena.

"I think she likes it," Magnus said, an expression of awe shining on his face.

"She does," Jackson agreed. "Keep it up, Selena." He examined her again. "Let's get to work, Magnus. This is a breech." Selena stroked, cooed and crooned to Lacey until her arms and shoulders ached from hours of sitting in an awkward position. But each time Magnus suggested that she go to the house, she refused. Nearly three hours after they began the delivery, Lacey had a calf. Magnus assured her that the cow would be fine.

"What's on your mind?" Magnus asked, after she'd stared into space for a minute or two.

"Being a female can be hazardous to your health," she joshed. She had no intention of letting him know that the experience had shaken her. It had humbled her, too, because Lacey had immediately gotten to her feet and looked for her calf. She walked over to Magnus, reached up and kissed him. His startled look told her that he'd expected any reaction but that one, and she realized that her husband wanted a family. He stood there, mute, gazing down at her, shook his head as though disbelieving what he'd seen, then he took her hand and started to the house.

Selena had the sense that experiencing Lacey's confinement had changed her irrevocably.

"You're very quiet, Selena," Magnus observed at dinner that evening.

"It's been quite a day," Selena said and realized that she'd hugged herself. And then she knew. At last, she was no longer an interloper, a displaced New Yorker. She was one of them.

"Yes," she said, and she could feel the smile that claimed her face, "it's been *some* day."

As though reading her thoughts, Tessie said, "I see you got to be a ranch wife." She passed the thick medallions of filet mignon with potato puffs and gravy.

"Feels good, too," Selena said. "Next, I'll have to learn to cook."

"That wouldn't hurt one bit, either," Jackson said. "Come to think of it, this steak would hit the spot if it had a few buttermilk biscuits under it."

Tessie stood, balanced the platter in her right hand and braced her hip with her left one. "You don't see Magnus complaining about my cooking. Seems to me you oughta be tickled pink."

Jackson looked at Magnus for support. "She sure is sassy."

The sound of deep-throated merriment flowed out of Magnus. "You two carry on like you've been married for years," he told them.

Selena thought Tessie's blush would have suited a girl of fourteen. "Magnus, you suggesting I went and hocked my head?"

"You weren't talking like that last night," Jackson put in.

Selena went to Tessie's defense, stifling her amusement as she said, "Don't lean on her too hard, Jackson. We gals are delicate when it comes to this man-woman business."

Magnus stopped eating and focused his gaze on Selena. "You sure manage to hide it."

"We do not go around screaming about how tough things are for us," Selena retorted. "You didn't hear Lacey yelling about that pain this afternoon, did you?"

Selena glanced at Magnus and quickly took a second look. He stared at her as though seeing her for the first time, and as if he were unwilling to believe what he heard and saw. She glimpsed Tessie as she put a small package on the sideboard, but didn't allow it to register, for she'd locked her gaze, her thoughts and her emotions on her husband. Joy suffused her when he reached beneath the tablecloth and clutched her fingers. His lips moved, but only he knew what they said.

How had he been so fortunate? At best, he'd hoped for companionship in his marriage to Selena, along with the satisfaction of keeping her safe from his unscrupulous brother. One by one, she had demolished his arguments against a love marriage with her. After the tender care she'd given Lacey, he couldn't deny her nurturing instinct. Nor could he ever again associate her with his mother, for Anna Cooper wouldn't have ventured near that barn and she wouldn't have touched that cow. If only he could get Prince's charges out of his head.

"Come walk out to the road with me," he said. The moon, full and bright in the cool May evening, lit their way as they strolled along the gravel path to the gate that marked the entrance to Cooper Ranch. His senses whirled when he felt her fingers entwine with his own. He squeezed gently and tugged her closer to his side. A cloud covered the moon, and a rising wind rustled through the tree leaves.

"Chilly?" he asked her when she rubbed her bare arms.

"A little," she said, facing him. He removed his jacket and placed it around her shoulders and, as if she'd been waiting for the chance, her arms slid up his chest. She stood on tiptoe to grasp the back of his head, and rivulets of heat cascaded through every molecule in his body when her parted lips touched his. She molded her body to his own, and tongues of fire rioted throughout his big frame and settled in his groin. Her mouth opened to him and he leaped forward in full readiness, reaching for the home he'd wanted since the first minute his eyes beheld her. He welcomed the sweet heaven and cursed the hell of it as he plunged his tongue into her waiting mouth. She inched closer, holding him tighter, and he wanted to scream when her soft hips moved frantically against him. Begging, pleading for more. He lifted her, found her nipple through the thin cotton dress and suckled her until she trembled against him. Dazed, he looked around for a bed, and his gaze fell on his home in the distance and the lights that shone from its many windows.

"Good Lord, Selena." He set her on her feet and sought to regain his self-control. How was it, that with her and no one else, he could let himself go, could sense a wildness surging in him, fighting for release? He wanted to know that man, to feel what he knew that man would feel when he finally sank deep into her. Though residuals of doubt remained, he was ready to give in, to declare his feelings, take her to his bed and teach her to love him. But his subconscious mind wouldn't let go of the old misgivings.

"Selena, I have to know. For once and for all, has Prince ever meant anything to you? Have you ever encouraged him? He swears the two of you were lovers. Tell me he lied, and I'll believe you."

Selena flung herself away from him, turned and glared. Pain seared her heart. Damn his timing. She had intended to take him to her suite, to tell him what she felt and to ask him if he loved her, if he thought he could love her.

"What a low opinion you have of me," she spat out. "You actually believe I'd bed first your brother and then you, or maybe take on the two of you as suits my fancy? Rhett Butler's got better sense." She turned, avoided his outstretched hand and walked rapidly back up the gravel path.

I am not going to let this defeat me, she told herself, sitting on the edge of her bed and dialing her godmother.

"You're not going about this right, honey," Irene told Selena after hearing of her troubles with Magnus. "If he and his brother have been competing for thirty-two years, I wouldn't think

Magnus would want to spend the next thirty or forty living like that. It's up to you to put a stop to it. And don't worry about making things worse between them. From where I sit, things can't get any worse. You either solve this, or get out."

"I'm not getting out. I love him, and I want him. Period."

"I'm glad to hear it. So straighten it out."

"I can, and I will."

Selena prepared for bed, her godmother's words echoing in her head. She had played for the highest stakes. Until he told her he loved her, she wouldn't be his lover. But something held him back, as well, and it was her move.

Magnus waited for Selena to join him for breakfast, and he let his eyes mirror his feelings when she strolled in, her smile brilliant and warm as though their previous evening together hadn't ended in a tiff. She removed the package that Tessie had left on the sideboard the evening before and read the return address: A. Lucus, Waverly Public Library. She tried to remember whether she had a book on order from the library in San Antonio as she frequently did. Magnus poured her coffee while she opened the package. Immediately, black ants swarmed all over her, covering the white tablecloth. She jumped up, knocking over her chair. Quickly, Magnus ripped her dress from her and called Tessie to rid the table of the ants. He raced upstairs with her and stood her under the shower, washing the ants from her body.

"I'm hiring a detective today," he fumed, as he wiped her tears with the tips of his fingers.

"It'll be all right, sweetheart. I swear it."

He swallowed his breath as his eyes beheld for the first time his wife's full, firm breasts and her luscious body adorned by the scantiest bra and bikini panties.

Disgusted with himself for wanting to take her right then and there, he reached up, pulled her bathrobe from the hook on the door, wrapped her in it and left. Shaken by the turn of his thoughts and the force of his desire, he went into his den, closed the door and covered his face in his hands. Something had to give. And soon.

It didn't surprise him that his call to the library yielded the information that no one named Lucus worked there. Four incidents. Why would anyone want to harm Selena? He retrieved the box, but could see nothing distinctive on it.

He answered Selena's knock. "Come in." He looked up at her, prim and innocent in a T-shirt and slacks. But appearance didn't help now that he knew what was hidden beneath. When she didn't seem upset, he asked her, "Honey, think again. Who could hate you so much? Those ants could have stung you seriously."

"I haven't come up with one suspect. It amazes me."

"Me, too. I promised to meet my mother for lunch, but I hate to leave you right now. Will you be all right?"

Her smile, serene as ever, reassured him. "I'll be fine, but you don't know how glad I am that you were here."

"From now on, don't open a box, not even if you think you know the sender. Names and addresses can be faked. I'm going to have the fingerprints taken from all of these boxes. It's time we got help with this. I'll see you later."

He walked into the inn dreading the encounter. "Hello, Mother. You're looking well as usual," he said and kissed her on the cheek. He winced when she immediately launched an attack on Selena.

"You don't know her," he replied.

"I know enough. I'll never understand how you could marry this…this person, when you could have had Mavis. That wonderful girl is crushed. It pains me to think of it. Mavis would have given you beautiful children."

"Children, eh? Now, that's a surprise. She told me she didn't want any, but I suppose she thought it best to surprise me later on with her motherly instinct." He spoke very deliberately. "No man could want or deserve a more beautiful woman than Selena."

"How can you speak that way?" Anna whined. "Mavis has beauty as well as social status. How can you give her up?"

Magnus's eyes blinked rapidly of their own accord. "Is my straitlaced mother suggesting that I, a married man, have an affair?"

"How *could* you?" She laid back her shoulders. "People get divorced, you know. Every day, they do it."

He rested his knife and fork and gave up the idea of eating. "Forget it. Instead of stabbing your daughter-in-law in the back, you should be getting to know her. She's a wonderful woman, and you might as well accept her, because if I have my say, she'll be with me forever."

"Never. She was Prince's girl, and you took her. She's...she's detestable."

His bottom lip dropped, but only for a second. "I have an appointment, Mother. Please excuse me." He left the inn.

Almost immediately after Magnus left the house, Eloise called Selena for help in dealing with Freddie Powell. Selena drove to the Center at once, but whatever had caused Freddie's distress righted itself when she arrived. He had missed her and let her know that he was tired of having people drift through his life.

"Want to spend a weekend with my husband and me? He said he'd teach you to ride."

Freddie's eyes rounded. "A horse?"

She nodded.

"All *right!*" He promised to settle down and she rushed back to her car, only to find Prince sitting on its hood.

"Your injunction against my phone calls doesn't prohibit me from seeing you in a public place," he said and, for the first time, she detected a near-surface rage in him.

"Hang around, if you want to. Magnus is at the inn having

lunch with your mother. I'll just walk over there and tell him you're here."

He grinned. "Your bigshot husband wouldn't start a fight here in the middle of town. He wouldn't ruin his image."

"Pray that you're right," she said. She got in the car, turned on the motor and leaned out the window. "Maybe I'll run into a tree or a post at about ninety miles an hour and get rid of you for good."

He jumped off the hood, and she backed out of the parking lot and headed for the ranch.

Magnus drove up to the house as she got out of her car. "I ran into Prince in town. Did you see him?" She explained how she happened to be there and related her encounter with Prince.

He exploded. "He isn't going to leave you alone until I smash him to pieces." His tightly balled fists hung at his sides, and his stance was that of a predator. "He'll stay away from you... If I can't protect my wife from—"

"And that's why you married me. To protect me. Which makes the marriage a flop, since Prince ignores your orders." She whirled away from him and raced into the house.

Magnus opened his mouth to reply, but couldn't force out the words. Speechless, he shook his head in bewilderment at the bitterness in her voice, unable to imagine its source.

Jackson hastened his recovery with a report of an eight-foot hole in the fence they'd mended the previous month. If that wasn't enough, a check of his computerized records showed orders for concrete and for steel beams that neither he nor his foreman at the North Hackberry building site in San Antonio had requisitioned.

"Something's rotten in Denmark," he muttered to himself. He telephoned Madeline who, after some hesitation, explained that the problem had to be with the files.

"I'll check at once and straighten them out, sir."

He couldn't finger the problem, and he might have to transfer his confidential records to his personal computer, separating them from the central files. In twelve years, he hadn't had one problem with his records, but, of late, there seemed to be no end to them. He wasn't foolish enough to believe that his once perfect computer system had become unreliable without human help, and he'd find the culprit.

Magnus walked out of his office into the blazing four-thirty afternoon heat, went back inside and asked Selena, "How about a swim in the lake? It's murder out there."

"I'd love it," she said. "Give me twenty minutes."

"We'll take the horses." She nodded and raced into the house.

She rides like a belle of Sherwood Forest, he thought with pride. "I think Minerva's fallen for Cougar. Look how close she is to him."

"Humph. I was thinking that he's sidling up to her," she said. "Just like a man to take the position that he's the one with the drawing power."

"Not this man. If you want me to, I'll get a skywriter and have it blazing across all of Texas that Magnus Cooper is drunk with desire for Selena Sutton-Cooper. I'll even list the reasons why, from your regal beauty to your…great assets. Me? Think I'm a lure? Perish the thought, woman."

"Shows how much *you* know," she muttered under her breath. "Talking about hot bait!"

"What was that? I heard that." He knew he preened, and he didn't care if she saw it. "You really think I'm a… What did you call it?"

"You know what I said. At least you're modest enough not to repeat it."

They reached the lake, and he jumped from the big stallion.

"Aren't you going to help me down?" He walked around to her and lifted his arms. To his amazement, she slithered down his body like a snake, stayed close longer than necessary, moved about six inches away and began pulling off her clothes. He began to breathe again when he saw that she wore a bathing suit. Tiny scraps of cloth, to be sure, but at least he'd be spared the madness he knew he'd have experienced if she hadn't had that bit of protection. When he removed his jeans and shirt, her gaze swept him from his toes to the top of his head, then drifted slowly back down and paused on his swim bikini. Magnus had to laugh. She'd turned the heat on with those little pieces of red spandex, but his choice of swimwear wasn't exactly modest.

She walked up to him, raised her hands as though to slide them over him and stepped away without yielding to the temptation. "Why did you bother to put on anything?" she asked him.

His eyes promised her heat and passion as he looked her over, letting his gaze rest where it seemed to please him most. "You can talk?" he asked in return.

She let a smile drift over her face. "Not bad, I tell you. In fact, I'd say, neat."

He sauntered closer. "Like what you see?"

She grinned and tossed her head. "Well, I'm sure there's worse out there."

He grasped her arm with the tips of his fingers. "You can have it, if you want it. Every bit of it."

Her heart skidded into her belly. "What do you mean?"

"I mean I'm yours for the taking." His answer disappointed her, even as it gave her hope.

"See that you don't welch on that offer," she threw at him over her shoulder as she raced for the lake.

He caught her seconds after she dived in the water, and she yanked the straps from her bathing bra, knowing that he'd pull her swollen nipple into his mouth. She let her hands learn his naked body but, as badly as she wanted to hold him in her hand, she couldn't get the nerve to do it. But she would. Oh, she would. His busy mouth tormented her other breast and she wrapped her legs around him. His breath came in short gasps, and his fingers moved to her bikini. She broke away, swimming as fast as she could. Senseless though she was from his loving, she had the presence of mind to call a halt; she didn't want her marriage consummated in the cold water of Missionary Lake.

Magnus caught her, lifted her and carried her out of the lake. He eased her to her feet and glared at her, and she sensed anger such as he hadn't directed at her.

"Don't ever do that again, Selena. Don't promise what you're not prepared to give."

"How do you know I wasn't?" It wasn't a fair question, and she knew he had a right to his anger. "I know you're human," she said, her voice soft and sad. "I am, too, Magnus."

"I know, sweetheart, and I'm beginning to think we should settle this one way or the other."

She didn't answer, for, to her mind, it could only be settled by their mutual acknowledgment of love. That sound. Her head snapped around as the horses whinnied.

"What's the matter with them?" she asked, moving closer to the man she loved.

Magnus looked at the suddenly darkened sky and quickly cut the horses loose. He grabbed her hand and ran for the nearest ditch, glad that he kept them free of weeds and debris. He settled her on her back and lay on top of her.

"What is it, Magnus? What's the matter?"

He put his arms under her back to protect her as much as possible from the rough ground. "Looks like a cyclone."

She shifted as if to get up. "But the horses. *What about the horses?*"

He recalled her love of animals and her readiness to defend any vulnerable creature. "Shh," he whispered in a soft, soothing voice, wanting to reassure her. "It's all right. The horses know how to get out of the way."

"Are you sure? I'd hate for…" Her voice drifted off, and he knew that his entire body had telegraphed to her what he felt right then, holding her in his arms, and looking down in her face for the first time. Her heat singed him, and he saw desire reflected in her eyes. A want that he didn't doubt matched his own.

"I won't make love to you in a muddy ditch, but you better believe I never wanted anything so badly in my life." The sound of trees breaking and of objects being hurled about was all around them, and he knew from her body's trembling that she feared for them. He tightened his grip on her.

"We're safe here, honey. Don't be afraid." She relaxed, and he risked brushing her lips with his own.

After minutes during which they didn't hear a sound, he said, "We can go now. The storm is over." He stood and gave her his hand. Her trembling hadn't stopped, and he wanted to hold her, but he suspected that he finally knew the limit of his self-control.

"We need another swim to wash off this dirt. How about a short one?" She nodded. The horses walked back to the tree to which he'd tethered them.

"You think that cyclone was an omen?" Selena asked him.

"An omen? As far as I'm concerned, there's no such thing. Just rotten timing. You and I have these little spats, misunderstandings and hot sessions because we don't discuss our root problem. I was mad enough back there to tell you everything."

She paused and treaded water, gripped with anticipation. "Everything? Why not now?"

"I'm not that angry anymore, and it would have been unwise. We need to clear this mound of debris out of our lives. Left to ourselves, we stand a chance of making a real life together, but we're damned from every direction."

He started to swim back to shore, but she stopped him. "Do you want us to make a life together?"

"I'm a logical man, Selena. If I've wanted something for nearly thirty-seven years, I won't settle for less. It's not the way I run my life. I know what I need, and I go after it. I see the peace I've always wanted, but it flirts with me just beyond my reach."

She didn't ask what he meant, because she thought she knew. She looked at him when they reached the banks of the lake. "Until I knew you, I had no idea that a person could make such a fine distinction between want and need. Our root problem, as you called it, is right there. Think about it."

His love was worth fighting for. And fight, she would.

Chapter 10

One morning, two weeks after opening her business, Selena skipped into Magnus's office waving a sheet of paper. She was back in the big-time, she told him, feeling as though she could dance the boogaloo.

"I just got an order from one of the biggest pension funds in the country. Parsons Fidelity used to be one of my best clients. Last week, I sent them a letter saying I was back in business, and would you just look at this transaction."

Magnus whistled. "You're on your way, sweetheart. Go check your e-mail. You might find something else interesting."

She rushed back to her office, gazed at her computer screen and refused to believe her eyes. An order for two thousand shares of Wade Tool & Electronics from Magnus Cooper. She dashed toward his office, brought herself to a sudden halt and put on her best professional manners.

"WT&E is selling for a dollar twenty-nine right now, Mr. Cooper. I'll place your order immediately. May I help you with anything else?"

Magnus swung around in his swivel chair, his brow furrowed. He threw his head back and let go with uproarious laughter. "I almost didn't recognize you. With your professional persona, you could sell ice to Eskimos. Honey, I'm impressed. Send me a bill."

Magnus concentrated on the report of the investigator he'd hired to find out who sent Selena those "presents." The woman had checked both their acquaintances and come up with a blank. He balled up the report, reconsidered, flattened it out and filed it. She'd suggested he get the fingerprints of all their close friends and associates. Easier said than done. He could just see himself taking his mother's fingerprints. He answered the phone.

"Cooper."

"My name's Freddie, sir, and Miss Selena says you're going to teach me how to ride. Only she doesn't work here anymore, and I don't know when I'm supposed to go see you."

Magnus didn't show his surprise. "Do you have your mother's permission, Freddie?"

The boy didn't hesitate. "She's tickled to death. I can come out any weekend. When?"

Aggressive little rascal, Magnus decided. "Give me your address, and I'll pick you up this Friday afternoon around four." He alerted Selena that they'd have Freddie for the weekend and got back to work.

Tessie walked into Magnus's office without knocking, her face the picture of distress.

"What's the matter, Tess? What's upset you?"

"Miss Anna strolled in here a second ago and started looking around the house. When she headed upstairs, I thought I'd better come tell you. I ain't never…" Her last words were lost to his ears. He dashed into the house and up the stairs just as his mother entered Selena's suite and closed the door. He walked in.

"Oooo. Oh, my. You frightened me." She sat on the nearest chair and clutched her chest.

"Your heart is perfectly sound, Mother. I suspect it's your mind that needs some repair. I'll walk down the stairs with you. I'm sure you didn't know that this is my wife's private room."

"I thought it might be the guest room. Where *is* your bride, Magnus?"

She wanted to unsettle him, as if her mere presence hadn't already done that, but he refused her bait. "My wife is in her…" He glanced down the stairs. "There she is. You wanted to see her?" Her eyes rounded, her lower lip dropped and she grasped the banister for support. So she hadn't expected Selena to be at home, he mused, and probably thought he'd be out on the range.

"Mother was just asking for you, Selena."

"Hello," Selena said, and he was sure he didn't imagine the lack of warmth in her greeting. "Have a seat in the den. I'll get us some iced tea."

Anna Cooper started for the living room, but Magnus stopped her. "My wife invited you to join her in the den." He'd never guessed that his mother was an iron-hard battle-ax.

"Oh, yes. Of course."

He went to the kitchen to reassure Selena. "This is her first time here since last year's barbecue. I didn't know she intended to visit us."

Selena's fingers gave his arm a gentle caress. "Don't worry. I can take care of myself."

Maybe she could, but he didn't know who'd been sending her those nasty "presents," and one of his suspects was sitting in his den. He'd stay close by.

After a few minutes, their rising voices reached his ears, and he walked into the hallway. He wouldn't allow his mother to intimidate his wife.

"That's absurd," he heard Selena say, and he could tell that she'd risen and started to walk out of the room.

"Oh, no, it isn't," Anna rejoined. "You're having an affair with Prince. He told me, and he told his brother."

"It's a lie, and I can prove it. Don't you know Prince for what he is, Mrs. Cooper? You have one wonderful son here, and you're trying to destroy his marriage. You can believe what you like."

"And I will. You were Prince's woman, and you hooked up with Magnus because you knew he was rich."

He could see Selena's fight with herself and wondered how she managed to be civil to a person who had the gall to face her with such an accusation. His admiration for his wife soared when she said, "I'd appreciate it, Mrs. Cooper, if you'd leave."

Magnus rushed to the kitchen and sat down. He'd deal with his mother when he had her alone, and he'd do a thorough job of it. But if Selena knew he'd overheard that conversation, it would only cause her distress, and his mother had most surely given her enough of that. He'd deal with Prince, too.

Prince gave Magnus the opportunity sooner than he'd expected. He'd just backed his Town Car out of his garage, when he spied Prince's car in his rearview mirror. He glanced at Selena, who stood at the driver's window telling him goodbye.

"Excuse me, Selena." He got out of the car and waited.

"Well. Well. Caught you just in time," Prince said jovially, not taking his eyes from Selena. "Going somewhere far, I hope."

"What do you want, Prince?"

Prince flashed one of his famous grins, looked at Selena and winked. "I thought I'd hit you for a couple 'a thousand. I need to get my instrument out of hock."

"Not for your guitar or anything else will I give you one dime. Go to work. I started keeping records of my loans to you, loans that you've never repaid and, in the last four years, you've taken one hundred and twenty-four thousand dollars from me, either as bail or in bad loans. I've finished."

Prince looked at Selena. "Baby, you tell him to let me have a couple 'a thousand." Magnus narrowed his eyes as Prince started toward Selena, seemingly forgetting that her husband, his brother, was within three feet of them.

"Come on, baby, get him to fork it over." He reached toward her, and Magnus swung him around.

"I'm going to savor this," he told Prince. "I've been aching for this inside and out for years."

He watched the smile float over Prince's face. Plastic. Superficial, like the man. "Hell, if she can't get you to fork over a few thousand bucks, what's she good for?"

Blood roared in his head; pounding rocks jarred his belly; his heart thundered in his chest; and he thought he'd suffocate. Sweat streamed down his face, nearly blinding him.

"Magnus, no."

He didn't hear her or anything but the thunderous roar inside his head. He reached for Prince's collar, jerked his brother to him and slammed his left fist into his face. Prince stumbled backward, but Magnus rushed to him and picked him up.

"That one was for me. This is for Selena." He lunged forward with a powerful thrust that brought blood to Prince's nose and mouth, knocking him to the ground. "Get up. Act like a man for a change. You're always bragging about your manhood. Where is it? Get up, and stop cowering down there like a sniveling puppy."

Prince covered his face with his hands, and Selena turned away and walked into the house. Magnus looked down at him.

"What a sorry mess. Get in your car and go. That was nothing compared to what you'll get if you ever speak to my wife again. And you be sure you tell Mother you lied on Selena. If you don't, I'll thrash you to within an inch of your life."

Pain seared his heart as he watched Prince pull himself up, drag himself to his car and drive off. He hadn't lost control; he'd nailed him because he'd wanted to, longed to, and because Prince deserved it. He went in the house to wash his hands, and Selena met him with a towel and a basin of water. She put an arm around his waist, walked him into the kitchen and examined his swollen knuckle.

"I'm sorry, Magnus. I hate that it had to come to this, but I knew he'd go as far as you let him. I just didn't want it to happen because of me." She put his left hand in the cold water.

He heard the tears in her voice and studied her face. "If I think about it logically, I know it didn't concern you at all. He merely carried his normal behavior and attitude to the extreme. Wanting what isn't his, especially if it's mine. I didn't get any pleasure out of it, just unbelievable physical release. I think I'll stay home and go to San Antonio tomorrow."

Selena strolled out to the barn around five-thirty that evening when she knew Magnus would be there. She'd made up her mind to put an end to the gossip and to what she suspected were his own misgivings about her. That meant events wouldn't proceed as she'd planned, but some things were more important.

"Hi, cowboy. How about a date tonight?"

He frowned and rubbed the back of his neck, his face shrouded in bewilderment.

"Uh...sure. When and where?"

She twirled the long-handled little black purse in which she carried the house keys. "Front door, seven o'clock. Dress up."

He raised an eyebrow and knocked his Stetson to the back of his head with his thumb and forefinger. "You sound kind of sassy, lady."

Selena didn't feel sassy. Indeed, her overwhelming emotion right then was fear, pure trepidation and anxiety that she might not be able to carry out her plan. Displaying an impudence she didn't feel, she wrinkled her nose and eyed him through lowered lashes. "No guessing, cowboy. I'll see you at seven."

He tipped his Stetson and bowed from the waist. "Yes, ma'am."

She thought she saw him run his tongue over his top lip just before she swung around and headed for the house. Good. Let him anticipate it. Tonight, she promised herself, I'm dressing for success. She went to her closet and examined her red sequined minishift with spaghetti straps. Great. She filled the tub for a perfumed bubble bath, got in and began her crusade.

"Think your ego will let me treat you to dinner?" she asked him when they met at the front door.

"Why not? It's your show, sweetheart." She'd noticed that since their encounter with that tornado, he frequently called her "sweetheart." Well, she'd take all the progress that came her way.

"Where to?"

"The Gray Dove."

He glanced quickly at her as he eased the big car into the driveway. "In San Antone?"

"If there's a restaurant in Waverly good enough for my date with you tonight, I haven't seen it."

"Whew! Whatever you say."

She appreciated that he didn't rush to the men's room or look the other way while she paid the check, but she didn't express her thoughts. Magnus was comfortable with who he was, and she doubted that his ego could be easily rattled.

"Thanks for the elegant dinner," he told her as they left the table. "That was your part of the evening—this is mine."

"Whatever you say," she mimicked.

"Aren't you going to ask where we're going?"

She half smiled. "In my New York days, I wouldn't have taken two steps without asking, but I figure you're harmless."

His warm gaze probed into her. "That's news to me." He placed a finger at her elbow. "I'd have thought that your experience here didn't justify confidence in Texas men."

She didn't look at him. Time enough later to succumb to his lure; right now she needed her wits. "On the contrary. A Volkswagon Beetle can't compare in power and beauty to a Lincoln Town Car. And you'll admit that, although the lovely little fireflies give off light at dusk, in a full moon, you can't even see them. I've met many men, some real fine brothers and some of questionable virtue, but you're a new experience."

Magnus paused in the act of opening the door to the restaurant's vestibule and let himself enjoy her warm, seductive smile. "You're flirting with me again."

She strolled through the door, brushing him as she passed him. "Any law against that down here in Texas?"

"We're fairly permissive, though there are a few well-publicized exceptions," he said and nodded toward the bar. "Drink?"

She shook her head. "Which are?"

"You don't get in the way of a man's gun, and you don't get between him and his woman."

She shrugged. "Macho to the core. That all?"

He grinned, as happiness overtook him. "That's what matters right now," he said, taking the stole she handed him and draping it around her shoulders. Her perfume teased his nostrils, and his belly knotted when he looked down at her deep cleavage. "Look at me."

She faced him, and he swallowed hard. "A man can kiss his wife anyplace and anytime she lets him, right?"

With a half smile, she observed him through long lashes, and heat seared his face. He looked at her slightly parted lips and her wicked invitation, a flaming seductress who stood inches from his hungry body. Pictures of her in her red nothing of a swimsuit, and the way she'd looked when he had her almost nude in the shower washing black ants off her flashed through his mind. If she lived up to her notices, he didn't think he'd survive the experience.

"You don't want a kiss here," she said, moistening her lips. "Not with all the citizens gaping."

Damn the citizens. He had to get a grip on himself. "You pick one heck of a place to tease me."

She closed the three inches of space that had separated them, and her fingers danced from his navel to his spine. "Feels good here."

"Selena!"

She let her hand soothe his cheek. "Don't worry. You're safe with me."

He drew back and stared at her. What in the name of kings was she up to?

Selena laid her head on his chest. "I guess I go a little wacky when I wear red."

He took her arm and led her to the street. "That so? Remind me to hang all of your red dresses in my closet."

"Dresses aren't the only things I wear that are red."

"Tell me about it. I've seen some of the stuff."

"You didn't like it?"

"*Like* wasn't the word. How do mice feel about cheese?" He parked near the Hyatt Regency. "Ever been in The Landing?" She hadn't, and he had the pleasure of seeing her steps change to a rhythmic sashay as they entered to the music of Jim Cullman's Jazz Band. He claimed a table and laid her stole across a chair.

"You know how to dance to this New Orleans jazz?" he asked, wanting to provoke her into showing him her best.

"Watch me," she returned.

This was what he'd needed in his life, he understood now, a woman who was his intellectual equal, who'd wolf down a good meal without consideration for the extra pound she gained, who was feminine to the core, kept him guessing, and who, when she wanted to, could raise his temperature to boiling point with a look or a touch.

If she wanted a challenge, he was up to it. The band swung into a number that he guessed was from the thirties or forties.

"What's the name of that?" she asked, stepping into him with the smoothness and precision of a Pete Sampras service ace or a George Foreman knockout punch. He was damned if he'd move back and let her know her little move had knocked him off balance.

"I don't know what it's called, but if I had to pick a name for it, I'd call it 'Selena in Her Element.'"

"What?"

To his immense satisfaction, she missed a step. But she quickly moved back as close as decency would allow, squeezed his hand and said, "I'm only following your lead." She paused—for effect, he thought—and added, "Though I'm not sure that's wise right now."

He pulled her closer. "Wisdom doesn't have one thing to do with what you're thinking and doing. I've told you before, you're going to have to live up to your notices. So, watch it."

She danced away, never losing the beat, and treated him to a withering look. "I suppose you practice what you preach."

Hot energy shot through him, pummeled his belly and threatened to settle in his groin. He sent both of his hands to her waist, pulled her as close as he could and locked her in his arms. Desire rioted inside him. "Keep this up," he threatened, "and before you get back to the ranch, you'll know something you didn't know when you left."

He thought he'd swallowed his tongue when she moved away, looked up at him and asked, "You planning to let me drive us back in the Town Car? I've never been behind the wheel of one of those cars. I'd love it."

He couldn't help laughing. "Selena, honey, you're a fresh downpour after a long, hot draught. I don't know what I ever did without you."

She let her hips roll with the slow moan of the tenor saxophone, and air swished out of him. She wasn't innocent of her effect on him, and he intended to get some of his own. He stopped dancing, walked them to the table and grabbed her stole.

Her wide eyes projected a questioning look. "Can't we... I'm not ready to leave. I'm just getting started."

"You're wrong there. You aren't getting started, you're well into it, and you have been most of the day. You've been having fun, and now, I'd say it's my turn." He assisted her into the car, walked around and got in the driver's seat. He'd thought she'd be annoyed, so he stared in amazement, disbelieving, when he looked over and saw her face in full bloom, a smile dancing on her lips. He grinned. The witch.

She prayed that his mood wouldn't change before they got home, because she couldn't think of a way to keep the heat up without risking an accident. Not to be outdone, she asked him, "It's your turn to do what?"

He eased the big car onto Route 35 and headed for the ranch. "Show you who you've been playing with," he said, matter-of-factly. "I like to have fun, too, Selena."

"I haven't noticed you doing much playing lately."

"I don't waste my energy," he told her.

"And you're planning on conserving it for...you know."

"Sissy. You haven't got the guts to say it," he taunted.

"Have, too."

He laughed, drat him. "You're not dragging me into that. Show your cards. For months now, you've been *telling me* what a great hand you've got. I want some proof."

Selena hugged herself and rubbed the goose pimples that popped up on her arms. "What kind did you have in mind?"

He took his gaze from the highway long enough to glance at her, and she could see that his light banter belied very intense feelings. "Just think of it as your just rewards, lady." He turned off the main road and onto the long dirt lane that led to the ranch. "I'll even give you a choice." He stopped at the front door.

"What kind of choice?"

He slung his right arm over the back of the seat, faced her and tipped up her chin with his finger. "Your place or mine?" With that, he got out, walked around and opened her door. Her heart thundered in her chest, and her wobbly legs barely held her as she walked with him to the front door. But as they entered the foyer, a chill hovered over her; he hadn't touched her since he helped her out of the car. She squared her shoulders, looked up at him and gave him her brightest smile, a stunt that belied the sinking feeling in her heart.

He didn't keep her guessing as to his intentions. His arm encircled her waist, and frissons of heat shot through her as he stepped close. "Thank you for the elegant dinner and the provocative dance." Heat flew out of his hazel gaze, and she trembled in anticipation when his hand tightened on her waist and he lowered his head.

"Kiss me." Her arms went to his shoulders, and her fingers squeezed him to her. "Kiss me," he repeated, his drawl overlaid with urgency. She gave him her parted lips, and nothing he'd ever said or done had prepared her for the hunger of his mouth. His lips sapped her will, moving wildly, possessively over hers, while his tongue fired her with its rapid strokes, demanding her submission. Wanting to take in all of him, she clutched his head and his tortured groan filled the air when she began a rhythmic sucking on his tongue. His quivering lips signaled his mounting passion. Heated to a frenzy, she brought his hand to her aching breast, and her breath gushed out of her when his thumb and forefinger rolled her distended nipple. A flush of warmth settled in her love nest, and the sensation of his erection rubbing against her sent the fire of desire roaring through her, blistering her veins. She trembled uncontrollably as hot arrows of need coiled around her nerve ends. When he grabbed her hips and pressed himself to her, she undulated against him helplessly, and he moaned her name.

"I need you, Selena. I'm on fire for you. Take me. Take me in." She grasped his hand and led him up the stairs. He would finally be hers. Not the way she had hoped, not with love bursting both their hearts, but she would lay to rest any misgivings he had about herself and Prince. Maybe one day he'd love her.

He stood at her door, pulled her close, and let her feel his need of her. "If I go in there, you move to my bed. Is that clear?"

"It's what I want, Magnus." He picked her up, walked in with her and kicked the door closed. Within seconds, his hands found the zipper in back of the little red sequined dress.

"After tonight, you'll forget your suspicions about Prince and me. Then maybe we can get on with our... What is it? What's the matter?" He'd backed away from her, and his lips curled into a snarl.

"So this is what you've been aiming at all afternoon and evening. Did it pain you when I knocked my brother down and gave him what he deserved? Did it?"

Her heart seemed to stop, and she had to gasp for breath. Fueled by her desperation for a healing between them, she pulled the words out of herself. "What? How could you think such a thing?"

"That's what this seduction is all about, isn't it? Well, sweetheart, I'm not bought that cheaply. Good night, Selena."

His words were sharp darts into her chest, and she reached toward him with both arms outstretched. "Magnus. Magnus!"

He shook his head. "I'm sorry. You'll never believe how much."

Over and over she relived the evening as she tossed and turned in bed. Every few minutes, she glanced at the clock on her night table, longing for daylight, as the night crawled on. At three-thirty, unable to tolerate it longer, she decided to get a sleeping aid, threw a dusty rose negligee over her matching camisole and tiptoed downstairs without her shoes. Instead of going to the kitchen for a warm milk as she'd planned, she decided instead on a glass of liqueur, stepped into the darkened den and clicked on the light.

"Oh!" Magnus stood at the window gazing out at the moonlit night, dressed as when he'd left her.

He whirled around. *"Selena!* What are you doing down here?" His head swam. Had he wanted her so badly that he'd conjured up her image? He took a step toward her and stopped when she backed against the door. Her negligee hung open, and less than an inch of lace shielded her love nest from his eyes. Desire slammed into him, but he refused to let it distract him; he wanted more than her body.

"Why are you here?"

"I couldn't sleep."

"And you thought I could?"

She stood straighter. The scent of lilac swirled around him, bruising his olfactory sense. Her hair fell in sensuous disarray, and he could see most of her beautiful breasts. She's a fighter, he recalled, as she took a few steps toward him. "You did me an injustice. Yes, I set out to get you, but I made no secret of that. I wanted to show you that Prince is of no importance to me, that no matter what he says or does, it's you I care for. I thought that if we…if we gave ourselves to each other, your mind would be at rest."

"You care for me?"

"Magnus, I love you. Do you think I would have married you if I didn't? I can hire a bodyguard to protect me, and so can you."

Rivulets of heat cascaded through his frame. Tremors racked him, shaking him, and he didn't care if she knew it. "*You love me?* You're telling me that you love me?" He stood immobilized, and she closed the distance between them.

"Yes, I love you, and I have for months."

He lifted her from the floor and clasped her to him. "Oh, Selena. Selena. My wife." Her woman's scent furled up to his nostrils, her warm, turgid nipples grazed his chest and shudders claimed him as she opened her mouth for his tongue.

"Darling, let me show you how I feel," she said, and her soft voice washed over him, soothing, calling him home.

All he'd wanted from that day twelve months earlier, when he first saw her, was her love. Nothing could turn him back now. She pressed the base of his neck, deepening his kiss. He had to know her, every centimeter of her, and he greedily took the honey from her mouth until she began to feast on his tongue. He nearly exploded from the sucking motion, and gripped her naked hips to his body when he rose to full readiness. She grasped his buttocks and moved against him. Giving. Promising. When she climbed his body, he knew she was out of control.

How many times had he dreamed of her helpless before his on-slaught of loving? He lifted her, pulled the peignoir and camisole strap from her shoulder, took her hard nipple into his mouth and suckled her until she cried out.

"Magnus, take me to bed."

But he continued his ministrations to her breasts, squeezing and sucking until she fitted her body to him, wrapped her legs around him and fumbled for his zipper. An unearthly sensation heated his blood. If he didn't stop it, the whole thing would be over before he began. He carried her to his bedroom, removed her peignoir and laid her on his bed.

He had to fight for self-control when he looked down at her in his bed, beautiful, waiting for him. Standing within her reach, he stripped off his shirt and tie, pulled his belt through the loops and threw it on a chair. When he reached for his zipper, she fitted her hand to the waistband of his pants, and stopped him.

"Let me." She released his zipper, and he sprang into her hands. She stared at him, seemingly fascinated. When he realized that she wouldn't venture further, he joined her in bed.

"May I take this off?" She nodded. He leaned over her and, when she raised her arms to cradle him, he thought he'd never regain his breath.

"You're so beautiful, Selena. So lovely. Ah, honey, hold me."

He felt her arms tight about him, before she stroked his back. He had to strain to understand her soft murmuring and, when he heard the words, "with all my heart," he cradled her head, brushed her lips with his own and kissed her eyes, cheeks, ears and the hollow of her neck. She moved slightly to aid his comfort, and he kissed her throat.

"Do you like that?" he asked her.

"Yes. Oh, yes."

"And this?" His hands skimmed over her breast, and he bent his mouth to her flat belly, kissing. Dipping his teasing tongue into her navel. She squirmed, and he could hardly wait to show her how precious she was to him. He let his fingers skim over the insides of her thighs until, in her eagerness for more, she wantonly spread her legs.

"Ooo!" she yelled, when he lifted her, spread her velvet folds, inhaled her woman's scent and loved her while she twisted and thrashed beneath his rapacious kisses.

"Don't fight me, baby. Give yourself to me. I want all of you."

He worked his way up, kissing and nipping until she became a sapling helpless in the storm.

"Magnus, please do something. I can't stand it. I'm going to explode. It's awful." He found her love petals again, and his talented fingers played their tune, possessing her, claiming her for his own, until love's hot potion spilled out of her. He leaned over her and nuzzled her cheek until she opened her eyes and gazed at him.

"May I?" he asked. She nodded and lifted her body to him. *"Magnus!"*

Her outcry stunned him. "Sweetheart, what is it? What's the matter?"

"Could you…could you go a little slow?"

"Wait a minute. You aren't intact, are you? My God!" He saw the tears streaming down her face. "Honey, is this your first time? Why didn't you tell me? I'll stop if it hurts." He attempted to move away from her, but she gripped him with her knees and held his buttocks.

"Please. I know it won't be fun for you, but I want to make love with you. I want to be your wife. I don't care how much it hurts."

He was a big man, and she was over thirty. He'd spare her as much as he could. Gently, he probed until she seemed to lose patience, flung her body upward, and the barrier gave way.

He kissed her tears as he sank into her sweet heaven, girded himself in willpower and waited for her to recover. "Are you all right, sweetheart? Have I hurt you badly? I wish—"

"Shh," she shushed him. "I've never been so happy in my life."

"Are you sure?"

"Of course I'm sure." She frowned. "What happens now?"

He laughed. He couldn't help it. "You in a hurry?"

"I want to know what's going to happen."

"Relax, sweetheart, and do whatever you want to with me. I'm yours." He kissed her, and spirals of almost unbearable tension crept over him when she eagerly returned his caress. He bent to her nipple, suckling and teasing, and put his hand between them, stroking and rubbing her little nub of passion until she began to thrash from side to side. Slowly, he began to move. With one hand supporting her hips and the other around her shoulder, he increased the pace. She caught his rhythm, held on to his buttocks and moved with him.

"Do you feel it?" he asked her. "Talk to me, honey. Tell me what you feel."

"Full. I'm… I want to burst… I don't know, Magnus. I never felt anything like… Oooooo."

He accelerated his strong thrusts, buoyed by sounds from her lips that were music to his ears. She cried aloud as her throbbing sensations began to grip him, draining him, and her wild body squeezed and pulsated around him until he gave up his essence and splintered in her arms.

The haze cleared away, but her sense of not belonging to herself, of not knowing herself heightened. She wanted to sit up in bed and get her bearings, but she still held him in her body.

"Magnus…"

"Don't leave me. I'm not sure I could handle that. Stay here."

"I'm not going to leave you. I can't seem to find myself."

He reached for the light on his night table, turned it on and searched her face. "Are you telling me you're sorry?"

"Oh, no. I wouldn't exchange what you gave me for anything."

"Then what do you mean, you can't find yourself?"

A sigh escaped her. "Have you ever felt as though you didn't know who you were? Am I supposed to feel like this?"

"I've certainly never felt like this before, as though I could throw a bull, or lick an entire brigade."

She blinked. Had he grown inside her? "I've never felt as though I'm part of someone else. It's strange."

The tenderness of his smile tore at her. "Will you live with me as my wife and lover?"

"Yes."

He separated them and pulled her close to his side. "We could have saved ourselves a lot of pain if you had told me that you were a virgin."

She sat up and leaned over him. "Magnus, I'm not going to get angry, because this is the second happiest day of my life. You as much as said that now that I've given you proof, you believe me. I don't exactly like that."

"I didn't mean that." He slid his arm beneath her waist and urged her closer. "Is it possible that I'm your first love?"

"You are. I've had suitors, but I never fell in love, and it has never occurred to me to make love with a man I didn't love. I went to work on Wall Street when I was twenty-three, and I put my private life on hold in order to succeed. I had to—the competition was fierce."

He mused over that for a second, but didn't pursue it. "What was your happiest day?"

"The day we married. Don't avoid the issue. I know it's settled. That's what I intended. If you can mange to shut your mother up, I'd appreciate it. Otherwise, I'll have to ask my gynecologist to send her an affidavit."

He sat bolt upright. "Don't you dare. You don't have to prove anything to her." He eased back down and put his arms around her. "You could be pregnant, you know. I forgot about contraception and, in my entire life, this is the first time." He stared into her eyes. "Would you believe this is the first time I've even been naked, I mean unprotected, with a woman? Yes, you could be pregnant."

She'd thought about it, but only to thank God that he hadn't mentioned it. "Who knows, we may be lucky," she said, certain that he'd question her enigmatic reply. But he let it slide, and she soon learned that his mind was elsewhere.

"How could he have done it? How could he have lied like that? There's no hope for him. How could he swear to me that you'd been in his bed?"

"Magnus. Don't let him come between us now when I...when we're together like this."

He hovered above her. "How did you tolerate it? I believed you, but there were times when he behaved as though he owned you and, I confess, he shook my faith more than once. Then, I'd remember his passionate need to own everything that was mine. If only I could help him."

He fell over on his back and stared at the ceiling, and she knew that he was once more beyond her reach. The long arm of Prince was never far away.

She watched, wanting to comfort him, as he locked his hands behind his head and spoke as though to himself. "After all these years of witnessing his cruelty and insensitivity, his disregard for the truth, how could I have let him sway me even a little? I never considered myself gullible. I should have silenced him the first time he threw that lie at me. I just can't figure out why I didn't."

Feeling his pain as though it were her own, she lifted her arms and urged him to her. "You love your brother, Magnus. It's clear to me now that, in spite of all he's done, you hope for his salvation, that he'll someday be the brother you long for in him."

He let her soothe and coddle him, and she urged him down to her and held him. "He won't stop trying to separate us, Magnus, and if you let him shake your belief in me, remember that I no longer have the means to prove he's wrong."

"And you don't need proof."

His chest hairs tormented her nipples. He brushed them with his palm and gazed down at her. "What's this? Do I detect an interest in these little buds?"

She turned her head aside. "I don't know what you're talking about."

"Yes, you do," he growled, and covered one with his open

mouth. She jerked forward, and he asked her, "What's the matter? Did I pull too hard?"

"I'm not used to it. I didn't know they'd make me feel this way."

He looked up and grinned. "Baby, have I got a lot to teach you."

"Starting when?"

He stopped and glared at her. "*Continuing* right now."

Each nerve in her body stood on end as he kissed every part of her that he could reach. Her breasts tingled as his tongue sent the fire of desire shooting through her. Realizing that she'd been trying to control her emotions, she let go, and spirals of unbearable tension shot through her.

"Magnus…"

"It's all right, honey. Scream if you want to. Do anything. Just give yourself to me like I'm giving myself to you." His fingers found her petals of fiery passion, unfolded them and began their love dance. He ignored her entreaties to make them one and, with his mouth, his fingers and the movement of his body against hers told her who she was.

"Magnus, honey, you can't do this to me. I'm going out of my mind."

"I know. You're not supposed to think. Just feel. Feel what I'm doing to you. You want me to use something?"

The urgency in his voice fueled her excitement. "All I want is you inside me."

He settled in place and stilled her body with his hands. "We have to be careful, sweetheart. You're still a novice. I don't want to make you sore."

She didn't care. He was there and he was hers. She took him in her hand, raised her body and guided him home. Already at the point of explosion, her groan of passion soon echoed throughout the room.

Oh, the wonder. The sweet hell. The freedom. "*Magnus!* My love. I love you so," she screamed, and gloried in the power of his release as he shouted his triumph.

Minutes later, still shielded within her, he locked her in his arms. "You're all I want. All I'll ever want."

Some kind of draft cooled her flesh and dampened her joy; she was all he wanted but he hadn't said he loved her.

"Well, saints be praised," Tessie announced the next morning, when Selena walked into the breakfast room wearing a robe and her hair hanging around her shoulders.

"Morning, Tessie."

"Well. Well. Looks like some changes been made. I see you managed to come in here this morning looking like a wife instead of a visitor."

"Try not to say everything you think, Tessie. It's really not much of a stretch to mind your own business."

"Honey, you and Magnus *are* my business. I took care—"

"Yes. I know. You changed his diapers. Fine. He doesn't wear them anymore."

Tessie's laugh floated through the room. "All right. I'll mind my business, but you sure look good to me this morning. Yes, sirree. There've been some changes made. No wonder Magnus come through here whistling his head off."

She put pancakes, country sausages and coffee in front of Selena and sat down. "Jackson didn't want to leave me last night, but I made him go."

Selena wasn't sure she wanted a personal conversation with Tessie right then, not when cherished memories of the night before still crowded her mind. "Why'd you do that?" she asked Tessie.

Tessie folded her arms and, with uncharacteristic reticence, replied. "I don't want to be his convenience, Selena. He means too much to me."

Selena reached out and took her hand. "He's an honorable man, Tessie. I'm sure of it."

"We'll see. In all my life, I never come this close to having what I always dreamed of. A man of my own. I don't want to drive him away."

She sniffed, and Selena caressed her gently. Better not let it get too heavy. "Tessie, you've nothing to worry about," she told her, only partly in jest. "Magnus will make mincemeat out of any man who mistreats you."

Tessie jumped up and wiped her eyes with her apron. "That he will, and I aim to remind Jackson of that fact."

Selena cut her laugh short when her glance fell on the sideboard. "What's that?" She pointed to the box.

"Magnus found it at the front door this morning. He said you shouldn't touch it. Something in it shakes like little marbles. He's going to take it to the police."

Selena got up, her appetite gone and her joy abated. Magnus's workers at the ranch liked her and were friendly toward her. He hadn't introduced her to his Houston staff. An oversight, maybe, but perhaps not. She made up her mind to talk with every one of them.

Chapter 11

Still floating in euphoria in spite of the mysterious box's arrival, Selena began her working day as usual. Tessie brought the morning's mail. A letter from Wade Malloy contained good news: he'd found a woman who could support her case.

This was strange. She'd made handwriting analysis a hobby while in college, and her use of it to read character had made her a favorite at parties. She observed the envelope carefully; whoever addressed it had been trying to change their natural handwriting, to hide their identity. Her hands shook as she opened it.

"You think you're the shine of Magnus Cooper's face, Miss Priss. Well, you'd better watch where you walk. And if you're smart, you'll go back where you came from."

That was all, but it was enough. A thinly veiled threat. She put the letter back in its envelope. It was postmarked San Marco. Not that it mattered, because someone had taken a long ride before posting that letter.

She hadn't gone to his adjoining office that morning, because she dreaded facing him after her wild abandonment the night before. Reluctantly, she knocked on his office door. What would he think? How would he act? Blood heated her face when she thought of the way in which she'd responded to him, of the wanton things she'd said and done. The urge to turn around and run hit her with force, but he opened the door, and she had to face him. He made it easy for her, as she should have known he would.

He swept her into his arms and hugged her. "I'd begun to wonder if you were having second thoughts about us. I've been sitting here waiting for your usual morning greeting, but I didn't even get a piece of paper under the door."

When she frowned, he explained. "You did that once when you were a little sore with me, remember? Got a kiss for your hungry husband?"

She grinned. "Didn't you have any breakfast?"

His laughter wrapped around her like his warm, loving arms. "Yeah. Twice. But I could use another one of those meals right now." He nodded toward the leather sofa in his office. "What do you say?"

Uncontrollable giggles poured out of her. "You're crazy."

He winked. "That's debatable, but I serve a first-class meal."

She doubled up with laughter. "You're telling me!" When she could calm herself, she said, "I'll take you up on that another time." The words of that letter troubled her, and she couldn't fully join in his carefree mood. She took a deep breath and plunged in.

"Things are different, now, Magnus. Don't you think I should meet your Houston employees?"

"When can you go? If we fly, we can wait 'til the stock market closes in New York, since we're an hour behind them, and take a two o'clock flight. Tomorrow okay?" She nodded, but now that she'd set it in motion, a sense of unease pervaded her.

* * *

The Cooper Building wasn't what she'd expected. It stood eleven stories high, with a modern redbrick facade and a black and white marbled floor and several marbled columns adorned its three-storied lobby. White stone planters held tall live plants, and a carpeted seating area with leather chairs and a glass coffee table provided comfort for visitors.

"I thought of rounding up everybody and introducing you to them in the conference room, but if I did that, they'd wonder if I'd gotten haughty just because I had a wife." He laughed. "I'm very informal."

"Unless the occasion calls for your 'tweeds,' right?"

His grin brought goose pimples to her arms. Where did this man get such powerful charisma? "This is my office suite." He opened the door, and her gaze fell on Madeline Price.

As though to support her, his arm encircled her shoulders. "Selena, this is Madeline, my right hand. Madeline, my wife, Selena Sutton-Cooper." Madeline sat with her hands folded in her lap and, when she didn't stand, Selena walked to the desk and extended her hand, forcing Madeline to rise.

"I'm glad to meet you, Madeline," she said. "Few men have the advantage of three right hands." She looked the woman directly in the eye and satisfied herself that she didn't imagine the hostility that seeped out of her. Madeline rose, glanced first at Magnus and then extended her hand. Selena was certain that she'd never had a weaker handshake.

"I don't know what I'd do without Madeline. She practically runs the shop," Magnus said.

Her light-colored skin betrayed her, and she reddened with her pleasure at his compliment. "I only do my job, sir." She glanced at him before lowering her eyes in humility. The true office wife, Selena decided, not a little puzzled as to why her devotion to her job should make her antagonistic toward her boss's wife. No warmth emanated from the woman, and she hadn't bothered to pretend friendship. Well, it was mutual.

Selena moved around to the side of Madeline's desk. "I'm sure you're exceptionally competent, or Magnus wouldn't be able to run this establishment from our home in Waverly." It never hurt to let a person know you appreciated her.

Madeline smiled without looking at either of them. "Thank you. I do my best for Magnus." Her voice softened and dropped a few decibels, unmistakably more feminine. Selena took that in, letting her gaze sweep the desk until she saw the large square letters that were Madeline's handwriting. So much for that guess. *Madeline Price had not written that threatening letter.*

She found Jeb McCallister more to her liking. Strong men had always attracted her, and strength emanated from Jeb. "I'm glad to meet you, Selena. Ever since Magnus got married, he's been telling me I oughta jump in. I'm thinking about it. I don't know, though." He looked at Magnus, then winked at her. "He's a tough bird, but he's the best boss if you're careful not to ruffle his feathers. If he took the plunge, it must be the thing to do." His gaze returned to Magnus. "Man, I'm real glad for you. You hit the jackpot."

Selena looked at her husband, whose obvious pride in her made her heart kick over. They made the rounds, stopping at each desk and each worker's station. His employees liked and respected him, and she couldn't identify one whom she thought would have sent her an unpleasant "gift" or letter.

Magnus took Selena's hand as they stepped off the plane. His happiness almost frightened him. Selena had made him feel like a giant the night before and again that morning, loving him, giving herself without reservation. She'd opened her body and her soul to him, and when he'd needed to lose himself in her, she had clasped him to her fiercely and told him to love her any way he had to. She loved him, and she had never loved anyone else. He had wanted to tell her what he felt, but he'd bottled up his feelings so long that he didn't know how. But he would. He needed desperately to share himself with her. He wanted her to know everything about him, and he'd tried that morning to say she'd renewed his life, but it hadn't come out right. He'd just said he'd known all the time that she was the right woman for him, and it had sounded so weak, so hollow compared to what was inside him. He found her looking up at him and smiled. How had he been so fortunate?

"How long has Madeline worked for you?"

Seems she'd asked him that before. "Eight years. Why?"

"Just curious. Can you think of a reason why she would be hostile toward me?"

His eyebrows shot up. "Madeline? Hostile? Honey, you're mistaken. Madeline is the most passive person I know. She's shy. You've completely misunderstood her."

"What do you mean, Magnus? Are you suggesting that I would mislead you about one of your employees if I had even the smallest doubt? I am, after all, a psychologist, and I think I understand something so simple as direct hostility. A child can recognize that."

"I know, honey, but Madeline's puzzling to me sometimes, and I've worked with her for years. I'm sure you've made an honest judgment, but I'm just as sure that you're wrong."

He wondered why she didn't persist in the argument until he recalled that she didn't nag, but said what she thought and left it at that. Still, he sensed a slight chill about her. He shrugged. She was wrong, and it was his duty to give her his opinion.

"When are you moving your things down to my room?" he asked her after supper that evening. "I've been waiting for you to ask me about closet space."

She leaned against the banister and took a deep breath. If they were going to have an honest relationship, a marriage of true intimacy where they could be themselves and have the other accept it, she'd better start right then by being true to herself.

"We're not ready for that, Magnus."

"We're not rea... *What did you say?*"

His hand rubbed the back of his neck, and it didn't surprise her when he began to pace the floor. "Let me have that again?"

"I said we're not—"

He winced as though hearing the words brought pain. He didn't let her finish it. "I know what you said. What I want to know is why?"

She stiffened her back and looked him in the eye. "I want to be your wife in every sense, to have a normal, loving marriage with you, but we can't have that if you don't take my feelings and my opinions seriously. If I tell you something that's important to me, I expect you to at least give it serious thought, not pooh-pooh it as the frivolous idea of a child."

He stared at her. "What on earth are you talking about?"

"I told you that Madeline Price was hostile to me and she was."

He shook his head, and she could see that he was perplexed. "And I told you that you misunderstood her. She's a very shy person. I have no intention of dressing her down about something she's not guilty of, Selena. I'd be crazy to do that. Madeline is the perfect employee."

Selena pushed back her anger, but she had less success dealing with the hurt. "Yes, of course," she said in barely audible tones. "I didn't ask you to dress her down or even to mention this to her. I only wanted you to listen to me. Really listen. But don't let me interfere with your right hand. Good night, Magnus."

"Selena, for heaven's sake. Are you going to throw away what we found over a little thing like this?"

She turned to look back at him, pain searing her insides. "What makes you think it's little? I can't throw away what I don't have. I haven't asked you to split your loyalty, because I assumed that loyalty to your staff and to me were not comparable. I love you, Magnus, but I also loved you all those weeks when I told you good-night at the bottom of the stairs and went to my quarters. The difference is that now I know what

I'm leaving behind when I walk away from you." If he had any idea how badly she wanted to stay with him, he's make it right. He'd fix it. But he gazed at her, saying nothing and showing nothing except his disappointment.

"Good night, Magnus."

"Good night, my darling wife."

I should have kept my counsel, she told herself, and waited until he knew he loved me, loved me enough to tell me loud and clear. She didn't look back again, but she knew he hadn't moved.

She sat on the edge of her bed and held her face in her hands. Raw pain ate at her, devouring her. Only last night, he'd told her that she was his and that he'd never let her go, but ten hours later, he'd done just that. Not in reality, it was true, but he'd left her to float in a sea of uncertainty. In his arms, he had shaken her, churned her, remade her, showered her with tenderness and sweet loving. And he had mastered her body, tuning and playing it as though it were a lyre of his own making. In the end, she had exploded in a torrent of joy and ecstasy, no longer her own self, but a part of him. She got up and began preparing for the bed that she now dreaded. She didn't know much about love, but she knew she had to teach her husband its meaning.

What the devil had come over her? What had he done that upset her so? He couldn't believe his defense of poor Madeline had caused her to renege on her promise to live with him as his wife and lover. He turned, walked into the den, poured himself a shot of tequila and tossed it to the back of his throat, relishing the strong burning sensation. He lifted the bottle to pour another drink, gazed at it for a second and set it down. The liquid burned the lining of his stomach, and he downed a glass of club soda to cool it. He'd had a taste of her, and he didn't want to be without her. He didn't think he could stand it. A harsh groan tore out of him. He needed her. She'd said he hadn't listened to her, that he'd brushed aside her words as nonsense. Well, if he found out that he was wrong, he'd tell her. What else could he do? He got in bed, kicked off the cover, rolled over on his belly and started counting sheep.

As she often did when her spirit drooped, Selena took the playful puppy to her office. "If you're going to stay in here, Rhett, you have to be quiet, and you can't disturb my papers." A knock on the door got her attention.

Magnus opened the door and leaned part of himself inside. "What if I ask Jackson to pick Freddie up this afternoon?" He moved back a few steps to discourage Rhett Butler, who had taken up the habit of gnawing on Magnus's shoes. "This dog is getting pretty big, and his teeth are sharp, too."

"He's just a big baby," she said in the dog's defense. "Rhett, you stop eating my husband's shoes."

"That's right, *dog*. I'm her husband. But you can crawl up in her lap, lick her face and play all over her. I'd say you're one smart bastard. Wanna change places?"

Selena whirled around in her chair, got up and faced him. "Rhett Butler would never take sides with anybody against me. No matter what I do or say, he'll defend me. If you don't believe it, make a move."

"All right. All right, I shouldn't have said that. What about Freddie?"

"Fine. I'd planned to run over to San Antonio today for some software, but I should be back by five."

"I'd offer to go with you, but Jeb's leaving for Sierra Leone tonight, and I ought to be around in case he has any questions or problems. Be careful. I don't expect any more trouble out of Prince, but he's been known to surprise me. I'll call Freddie back and tell him we're expecting him."

Selena finished her shopping and headed for Commerce Street where she'd parked her car, as Russ had advised. She turned the corner and stopped. Prince leaned against the driver's door of her Taurus. Recovering quickly from the shock of seeing him, she turned and started back to the store to phone Magnus, but a low whistle got her attention. Russ and three of his friends crouched behind a parked van.

"Hey, Selena," Russ called out. "Over here."

Her heartbeat slowed, and the needles that had attacked her nervous system disappeared. She rushed to the young boy. "Russ, you don't know how glad I am to see you."

"I know," he preened. "That guy leaning against your car ain't the cool dude with the short fuse. You want us to take him out?"

"I'd appreciate it if you see that I get in my car and drive off without any trouble from him. But please don't start a fight. That's all."

"Leave it to us, Selena. Who is this parasite, anyway?"

"He's my... He's a nuisance that I don't seem able to shake."

Russ drew himself up to his full height, which had its limits. "A good-looking woman has to be careful. I hope this brother never runs into the, er...your husband. Let's go, fellas."

To his credit, she thought, Prince stood his ground when she approached with the four boys. "Don't tell me you're into child molestation," Prince said.

"Watch it, pal," Russ commanded. "Me and the boys here don't allow nobody to mess with Selena. You get out of line, and we'll make sure you get back in. Real quick."

"You ever see Jackie Chan in the movies?" one of them asked Prince. "No? Too bad. We've been studying his technique."

"Get in the car, Selena," Russ said, and the boys huddled around her. "Move it, buddy." Selena stared at Russ's menacing face. He meant business, and she hoped Prince realized it. "Get in, Selena, and give me your husband's phone number. I'll let him know you're on your way home. Meanwhile, this parasite ain't leaving here, 'til you're so far away he can't catch you." She opened her pocketbook, found a pencil and wrote the number on a piece of the bag that held her purchases. The boy reached around a startled Prince and opened the door for her.

"Wilson County courts don't have jurisdiction in San Antonio," Prince told her, "but I didn't lay a hand on you, so you can't tell your husband I did. And there's no law that says a man can't look."

Her head swiveled around at the sound of Russ's nasty laugh. "Who said you didn't touch her? Me and the boys mighta seen you do that, so you'd better be careful. Go on, Selena."

She waved the boys goodbye. She didn't want to encourage their behavior. They hadn't broken the law, but they might have and, any way you measured it, gangs contributed to delinquency. But she had to give thanks for them. If Prince had followed her and waited for her, it hadn't been because he was anxious to give her the time of day. She'd promised Magnus she'd tell him if his brother bothered her, but she didn't want to widen the rift between them. She plugged in her tape of *Purlie Victorious* and had settled back to enjoy it, when her glance skimmed the bag that held her shopping. She noticed the place where she'd torn off a piece to write her number for Russ. So much for that. By the time she got home, Magnus Cooper would be in a rage.

Consequently, it did not surprise her when the big Lincoln Town Car whizzed past her at law-breaking speed just before she turned off Route 35 into the lane that led to the ranch's gate. She pulled over and waited in case he'd glimpsed her as he flew by. The sound of splitting tires warned her that he'd swung back and headed up the asphalt lane. She got out and waited.

He pulled up behind her Taurus, jumped out and had her in his arms before he said a word. "What happened? Did he touch you? Are you all right?"

As far as she was concerned, the incident with Prince was history. Forgotten. She nestled where she most wanted to be. Tight in her husband's arms. "I'm fine."

"What did he do? Talk to me."

She told him as much as she thought he could take in, given the heightened state of his nerves. "Didn't Russ tell you what happened?"

"Russ? Yeah. How old is that kid? He said he had Prince up a tree and planned to keep him there until he figured you'd gotten home. He really helped you out, did he?"

"I'll say. I'm not sure what the outcome would have been if he and his friends hadn't been looking after my car."

Magnus loosened his grip on her. "I'm going to have to horsewhip that man. And the sooner, the better."

"I hope we can find a better solution. I'll drive ahead of you. That ought to keep you well within the speed limit."

He opened the car door for her. "What do you say we invite Russ and his friends out here one Saturday or Sunday?"

"Oh, I'd love that. By the way, do you know what they call you?"

He rested his hand on the door of her car and raised an eyebrow. "I'm not sure I want to know, but you'll tell me anyway."

"The cool dude with the short fuse."

"What? The cool…" Laughter rumbled in his chest and poured out of him, taking his anger, frustration and anxiety with it. "Looks as though I made a jackpot impression on that bunch. Not bad. Not bad at all." He grinned, closed the door and spoke to her at the window. "Cool dude, eh?" He shook his head as though in wonder. "Well, let's go. Freddie may have walked off by now." Selena looked in her rearview mirror and watched him walk back to his car. He'd been so concerned for her that his emotional state had been dangerous to his health, but he couldn't tell her that he loved her. She had to conclude that he didn't, that he was a man who'd protect anyone in his care. He'd wanted to see that no harm came to her. That, and nothing more.

"Did Jeb get away?" Jackson asked Magnus, who was busy hitching up a young mare for Freddie.

"He's leaving around ten, but it's bad timing. Something's amiss in the plant, and he can't figure out the source."

"Like what?" Selena, who walked up just in time to hear the

exchange, asked Magnus. She greeted Freddie and turned back to Magnus. "What's wrong at the plant?"

"You know we don't manufacture anything, but I warehouse a lot of what we need for my building projects here in the States. The system gives me better control at lower cost. But for the last couple of weeks, it hasn't been running smoothly. Orders are misplaced and not filled, bills are marked paid when I haven't written the checks. Anything that can go wrong does, and I can't spot the cause. Madeline says the computer is to blame, that one incorrect entry sends the wrong message to the entire system."

Selena had to control her temper. *Madeline says.* Words from a saint's mouth were not to be questioned. "I'd ask her why the computer didn't do those silly little things earlier." She ignored the storm warnings in the hazel eyes that glared at her. "Of course, you could control your disbursements from here." She feigned a humble sigh for his benefit and was pleased that it didn't escape him. "Even though I know practically nothing about computing compared to you," she went on, rubbing it in, "I can control my own records. But then again, I don't have Madeline." If the woman ran the shop, as he'd said, she knew where the problem lay. She hadn't previously been suspicious of Madeline's loyalty to Magnus, but who knew how much of an actress the woman was, or why she'd turn on him? She eyed her husband. If looks could singe, she'd have blisters.

Magnus tightened the strap under the mare's belly and gave Freddie his first lesson in mounting a horse, a pleasure he'd someday know with his own son. They passed the brook, rounded a grove of pecan trees and dismounted. "All these yours?" Freddie asked.

Magnus looked down at the excited, happy boy and thought of the joy he'd know if he had a son, if Selena gave him a son, or a daughter. He didn't care which; he wanted a family.

"I'm the only rancher in this part of Texas who raises longhorns." He frowned as Freddie stood motionless, looking at him. Disbelieving. "Why do you doubt me?"

"I didn't say I did," Freddie hedged, "but I saw a man with some early one morning when I was running away from home. Were they his, or yours?"

Magnus grabbed the boy by his shoulders. "Wait a second. When was that?"

Freddie stared up at the big man. "Maybe three weeks ago. The last time I ran away. Why?"

Tension coiled in him, but he controlled his excitement. "Tell me exactly what you saw, Freddie, and where you saw it."

Magnus patted Freddie's shoulder. "Those were my cows, Freddie. Someone cut the wire over there and stole them."

"Will you get 'em back?"

Magnus told him that the cows had come back home, but that the fences had been cut again. "You've helped me more than you know, son. You're worth your weight in gold."

A wide grin settled over the child's face. "Gee. I am? And I can come see you some more?"

Magnus hoisted him up on the mare's back. "You betcha."

Magnus knocked on his wife's door after dinner. He hadn't knocked hard, but his knuckles hurt and, when she opened the door and peered at him as though expecting a stranger, his discomfort amounted to pain. Why the devil did he have to announce himself? He tried to relax, to throw off the weight that wanted to drag him down and drain him of his spirit. Didn't she know how much he loved her and needed her?

"Come in."

"You didn't eat much dinner."

"Have a seat, Magnus. I wasn't hungry."

He didn't take the proffered chair. "Are you sick?"

She shook her head. "Medically, no."

"Then how?"

"If I thought you were prepared to hear what I have to say,

I'd tell you, but you're not. When you came to me in the hospital, I thought you were the gentlest man I'd ever met. And you are gentle. I believed you understood my pain and my unhappiness. You're a wonderful man, but you're imperfect in ways that obstruct our relationship. I know I'm not all I could be to you, and I'm so far from perfect that it's laughable to think of perfection in relation to me. But I'm willing to bend your way, if you'll help me. Before we have this conversation, I want you to think back over your adult life and count the times you decided you were wrong. Do that, and then we'll talk."

He wanted to make things right between them. He'd come to her hoping to clear away the debris that had thrown them off track, but she'd upped the ante, and she hadn't bothered to sugarcoat it. He switched gears.

"I wanted to tell you that Freddie saw the fellow who made off with my longhorns. He'd sneaked out of his house and was running away. Jackson's gone into Waverly to get more information on the man. Just thought you'd want to know." He moved toward the door, aching want churning in him and eating at him with every step he took. If she'd only say something. Encourage him. Well, hell. He'd done without plenty of times.

"Would…would you mind helping me with this?"

He stopped, but didn't turn around, because he didn't want to look at her, didn't want her to see the naked want that he knew blazed in his eyes.

"I… Of course not. What do you want me to do?"

"This… I think my hair is caught in the zipper of my dress."

He faced her, but he didn't move closer. His need already raged close to the boiling point, and he'd as soon she didn't know how much control she had over him. "Can't you do it? I mean…oh, hell, Selena." If she didn't want him close to her, she wouldn't have asked him; she'd have gone downstairs to Tessie. He walked over to her and looked down in her face. Oh, Lord, he loved her.

"Turn around."

He got the hair out of the zipper in a second and looked at his hand suspended over the gadget that would make that dress pool around her feet and bare her to his starved senses. He inhaled for his life, but the clean scent of her hair caught his nostrils. He wouldn't let any woman, not even this one, poleax him like this. He had to leave there, but she didn't move, and not a word came from her. She stood mute and motionless with her back to him. His nose got a whiff of her woman's scent, and he ground his teeth. He raised his closed eyes to heaven and, in that air-conditioned room, sweat streamed down the side of his face. He looked down at her womanly hips—so close to his throbbing need—and almost turned her to face him. He let the perspiration drip into his eyes as his shaking hands found their way to her shoulders and rested there. Why didn't she say something? *Anything*.

His body quivered from head to toe, when he realized that her hand lay on top of his own, and desire roared through him. He turned her around to face him, and the dark brown eyes that lifted to his were pools of hot woman's need. He made no attempt to stifle the groan that tore out of him when she lifted her lips for his kiss. He crushed her to him and massaged her mouth with his eager lips, pouring out his longing for her. She trembled against him, and he gingerly touched the back of her neck, letting his fingers move slowly to her zipper. He knew he couldn't bear it if she rejected him, but he also doubted that she'd forgiven him. She moved closer, pushed her tongue between his lips and twisted her body against him.

"Sweetheart, I want to take this thing off you. I…I want to make love with you. *Selena!*" Her hand was on the most vulnerable part of him. Stroking. Caressing. Squeezing. The dress pooled around her feet, and he pulled her bra over her head, picked her up and ran with her to her bed.

Selena tore at his clothes, pulling his T-shirt over his head and yanking off his belt. He stripped off his jeans and shorts in one sweep and, in seconds knelt above her. They attacked each other without finesse, driven by bald need, and she didn't care that no word of love came from him. His kisses fired her from her head to her belly, but when he would have gone farther, she attempted to shield herself.

He raised his head, his eyes glazed with passion. "Don't deny me this. I want all of you. I have to have every bit of you."

She would have refused him nothing and, when she let him have his way, she thought he tore open her soul and claimed it as his own. When, at last, he forced her to explode, sending her into ecstatic oblivion, she couldn't help screaming her love for him.

He moved up to her and buried his face in the curve of her neck. "I've never needed anyone or anything so much as I need you."

She let her hands skim over his arms and back, kissed his eyes, his cheeks and his lips. Her hand brushed one of his pectorals, and he moved against her with the force of one who'd been torched. She took him in her hand and ran her fingers along his hard length.

"Ah, Selena. Selena. What you do to me." She brought him to her, and he filled her with his masculine power and loved her, teasing and tantalizing, until she begged for relief.

But he let her know that it was he who charted their course and that he wouldn't rest until he'd given her all he had and bound her so closely to himself that she wouldn't be able to think of a life without him.

"You're mine. Mine. Do you understand?" When she didn't answer, he thrust deeper, carrying her to the brink, then bringing her back with slow, gentle movements.

He meant to tantalize her to distraction. "Do you love me? Do you?" Her tremors began, but he kept completion just beyond her reach.

"Magnus, please."

"Just tell me you love me, honey. That's all I want. It's all I'll ever want."

"You know I love you. I'll always love you," she whispered. "I only ask the same of you." He wrapped an arm beneath her hips, and drove for her satisfaction.

She cried out when the blessed relief thundered through her. He unraveled in her arms, and she wasn't sure, but she thought his tears dampened her breast.

After a few minutes, he raised his head and looked in her eyes. "Are things all right between us? I want things to be the way they were yesterday morning. You were mine. The world was mine," he said with a shake of his head. "And then…" He rested his weight on his left elbow and spread the fingers of his right hand. "Right through my fingers. Tell me what the real problem is."

Selena saw that they'd headed back to that impasse, but she didn't think she had a choice other than to tell the truth. "If you're prepared to hear me out, I'll talk."

"I'm listening."

"I know that," she warned, "but will you hear what I say?"

He bolted upright. "What kind of question is… Sorry, I'll try to understand," he said, though his restless shifting and air of impatience didn't give her much hope. Magnus Cooper was accustomed to being in charge and, at the moment, it was not he who called the shots.

"You're having difficulties at your office, and you don't know who's behind it. It's a recent problem. Every employee should be suspect until you know who's guilty. But not all of them are, because you've exonerated Madeline. Yet, she has the key to every lock in that building."

It didn't surprise her that he swung away from her and let his feet hit the floor, and her heart constricted in her chest when she looked over and saw him reaching for his pants.

"So now you're accusing Madeline of undermining my business. Pick another horse, honey, because that one's not in the race. First, she's hostile to you. Now, the poor girl's out to ruin me. And you want me to chew her out or maybe get rid of her."

Fully dressed, he walked to the door and leaned against it. "The easiest way to put this is that I'm disappointed. You and I could roam the heavens at will, Selena, but this attitude won't get us off the ground. I came up here to ask you to come downstairs and live with me, but you're right. We're not ready for that. Sleep well."

She sat up in bed and stopped him. "Magnus, I think I can handle this rejection, if you'll promise to tell me when you find out that you've made a mistake. I can even be reasonably happy while I wait."

His posture lost some of its boldness, she noticed, and he shifted from his right foot to his left. Her words had found their mark and, for the moment, she couldn't ask for more. "Well?"

"If you'd enjoy seeing me eat crow—"

"I won't enjoy it. I'll know you're putting order in that place and that you're not being misled."

"Whatever. Good night." He left then. But she'd shaken him, and no matter how certain he'd been, from now on, he'd be careful of everyone there, including his precious Madeline. She hid her face in her pillow when she thought of the things he'd just done to her and of her wild response. And to think, it was she who had started it. She'd known that if she got him that close, he wouldn't leave without making love to her. Tessie would have unzipped her dress; she'd done it countless times. That was the last time she'd resort to tricks; such double-dealing could backfire. She got up and took a shower. The water streamed over her body, arousing her, but if she went to him, he'd never find his way out of his protective cocoon. And he'd never be as close to her as a deep love would propel him. His heart would remain forever safe from damage, protected from the vulnerability that a confession of love invited.

He had begged for her confession but, when she'd asked for the same, he hadn't said a word. Could he have so driving a need for her love if he didn't feel it himself? She didn't think so, but she'd trained herself to deal with fact. Intuition had its place, but not when your life was in jeopardy, and Magnus held her life, her future in his hands.

Magnus leaned against the doorjamb of the side porch adjacent to his bedroom wondering how much credence he should give to Selena's accusations of Madeline. He didn't like the implications, but he wouldn't stick his head in the sand. He walked to the edge of the porch and peered around the tall hedge. No one. Only the shadow of another shrub.

He went back in his room, pulled off his shoes, took his socks out of his pants pockets and threw them across the room into a chair. He hadn't missed. His glance fell on the phone beside his bed, and he considered calling Prince. His brother had pestered Selena with the threat that his presence represented, but he hadn't touched her. As much of a trial as Prince and their mother represented to him, he didn't want to hurt either of them. Nothing would please him more than to know that Prince had become a mature man and that, at last, he had the brother he'd always wanted. He meant to have a talk with Russ the next time he drove to San Antonio. The boy had good potential, but only if someone polished it. And soon.

What was he going to do about Selena? What could he do? They both believed they were being true to themselves, which, for all he cared, amounted to nothing more than the abuse of time that they could have together.

Chapter 12

Magnus greeted Madeline warmly, as usual, when he arrived unexpectedly at his office on Friday morning. He hadn't accepted Selena's view of Madeline, but he didn't think himself infallible and, moreover, Selena had a gut instinct about people. He'd keep his ears and eyes open.

"I've been concerned about the way some of these orders are duplicated, and some bills are marked paid, when I know I haven't paid them. Do you think we need this system updated?" He'd been careful to walk around to the front of her desk and face her rather than stand in his door and talk to her as he usually did. Her face held surprise, but was there also fear? He wasn't certain.

"Changing the whole system would cost a lot of money, sir. The computer does act up once in a while but, most of the time, it's just fine. I wouldn't bother."

Since when had Madeline become content to accept short-comings from a human being, not to speak of a computer? He decided to press a little. "But whenever we have a problem with the records, you find that the computer was unreliable." He forced a smile. "But if you say it's all right..." He let the sentence trail off, deliberately looked away for a second, and turned swiftly back in time to see a hard mask on her face.

He made himself smile again. "Being able to count on you, Madeline, means everything to me, since I can't be both here and at the ranch." He looked closely at her when he said it, and her deep blush perplexed him. He couldn't know whether the compliment had embarrassed her or she thought she'd been caught out.

She fidgeted and wrung her hands. "Thank you, sir. Your approval means everything to me." She said it so convincingly that he shamed himself for having doubted her. Still, he couldn't help noticing that, in the last four or five weeks, he'd gotten stock answers to every complaint; the mainframe was down, she hadn't had a chance to do it, she'd been busy, and so on. This from Madeline, who had never given him excuses, because her efficiency had made that unnecessary. He wasn't certain, so for the time being, he'd give her the benefit of the doubt, but he wouldn't gainsay Selena's views on the matter, either. He'd go back on a weekend, and he'd do it soon, because he wouldn't be expected back immediately.

"I want to go to Seattle next weekend to see my godmother, Magnus. I'd love for you to go with me. It's time you and Reenie got acquainted." She didn't know what kind of response to expect.

He surprised her. "And I want to meet her, but I've planned to be in Houston."

"For the entire weekend?"

"Right. You're welcome to join me, though I can't promise we'd see much of each other. I've got a ton of work facing me."

What had brought this on? she wondered. He'd spent three nights away from home since she'd moved there, and that had involved his trip to Africa. But Magnus ordered his life carefully, and he did not make abrupt changes. So why did he have to spend a weekend in Houston, when businesses were closed?

"Sounds like the perfect time for me to scoot off to Seattle," she said smoothly, as though that was nothing out of the ordinary. She got up from the table and took her dishes into the kitchen. *A ton of work?* Or a refuge? "I'd better get busy," she called out. "The Dow Jones dropped by over eighty points yesterday, and I'll have a bunch of nervous clients."

"I'll bet." She held the cup suspended in the air. Who would have thought the events of the previous evening had so effectively stripped them of their ability to communicate?

She opened her computer, looked at the previous day's closing stock quotations and made a list of those among her clients who had sustained big losses. She answered the phone, hoping that Magnus wanted a conversation. No such luck.

"Hey, girl. Guess what?" Eloise asked, her voice full of mystery.

"You'll tell me," Selena replied.

"Whoever left the baby at the clinic left us an unsigned note. If we put that baby up for adoption, she'll sue." The phone almost slipped from Selena's hand, and she thanked Providence that she hadn't insisted she and Magnus adopt that baby. "We're going to send the note for fingerprints to see if they match that of a mother who gave birth anywhere near here around the time that baby was born. This may be the clue we've been looking for. Child, I'm so excited."

"How do you know he was born in a hospital?"

"That kid had regulation hospital clothing."

Selena's alert button switched on. "You mean welfare. I remember the clothing was yellow with little white dots. If you send all the information you have to the county welfare office, they should be able to tell you whose child it is, or to narrow the search down to two or three women. Let me know if I can help." Selena was about to hang up when she remembered. "How's Bert? You two still an item?"

Eloise's gush flew through the wire. "Couldn't you figure it out? I thought you'd know that if I didn't have time to make a call, it was because that man is keeping me busy. Girl, I never... Child, he is something. I don't even eat Butterfingers."

"You're kidding. Why not?"

The joy in her friend's voice was unmistakable. "I don't think about 'em, and when I do see some, it doesn't occur to me to eat five or six of them. My daddy said that in itself is proof Bert's a miracle worker."

"Your daddy met him, and didn't object?"

"Daddy said Bert wasn't responsible for what these folks down here in Texas did. Besides, my honey plays a mean game of chess. You'll get to talk with him at the barbecue. Gotta go."

Magnus held Selena to his body while they waited for her flight to Seattle, and he wasn't sure that her kiss hadn't drained him of his soul. He didn't like the idea of her being so far from him. And he knew his attitude didn't make sense, but that big hole was reopening inside him, reminding him of those years of aloneness, of his life before she loved him.

"I'll be waiting for you at this same gate when your plane lands at four-thirty Sunday afternoon. You'll be on it. Right?" He told himself to get it together. He'd left *her*, hadn't he? But then, he hadn't had that sense of abandonment when he'd gone to Africa, because he knew she'd be there when he got back.

"I can't shake this feeling that you don't want to be with me," he said. "Correct me, if I'm wrong." He took in her composure, that way she had of standing or walking as though the whole world was hers, and she didn't have a care.

"I don't remember having tired of your company, not even when you vexed me," she finally said, looking him straight in the eye.

"Okay. Let me put it this way. Are you going because you

want to see your godmother or because you want some breath-ing space?"

"Magnus, if you don't want me to go, say so, and I won't. But I haven't seen Reenie in months, and I don't want her to get the impression that, now that I have you, I don't need her. When I lost my parents, she took me in and raised me at a time when she could hardly support herself. You'll never be second to anyone, Magnus."

She hadn't answered his question, at least not directly, and he had to be satisfied with that. "Planning to miss me?"

Selena laughed. "What's gotten into you?" She stepped closer, reached up and rubbed his lips with her own. The fire of desire roared through him. Every time she got aggressive with him, she stirred a fever in his loins. "You know who's captain of this ship, don't you?" she murmured. Her hand went to the back of his head and increased the pressure of his kiss and, when her parted lips invited him to deepen it, he gave her his tongue and had the pleasure of feeling her tremble in his arms.

He heard the words, "Flight one-o-one to Seattle now boarding," and she moved out of his embrace.

He whispered to her. "We have to straighten things out when you get back. I can't live with you like this."

"Me, neither. While I'm gone, figure out what you feel and let me know."

Figure out what... He knew what he felt. He'd have to think about that one. He put her flight bag on her shoulder and watched her stroll toward the plane, ever the self-possessed lady, his heart.

"He's taking good care of you. I can see that," Irene said, as they entered her redbrick, Cape Cod–style house. "Roe ought to be home any time now." They settled easily into their mother-daughter relationship, and Selena wondered at her good fortune in having Irene in her life.

"Are you happy?" Irene asked.

"I will be."

Her godmother's anxious look was one she'd seen many times. Irene was unacquainted with pretense, and her face usually mirrored whatever she felt. "*Will be?* You aren't now?"

"For now, I'm contented. Magnus and I have a few small bridges to cross, and I have decided to stop waiting for him to take those steps by himself and to help him do it."

"Well, if I can help, honey…"

Selena laid a hand on her godmother's arm. "You're the first to know, Reenie. I'm pregnant."

"Thanks be," Irene shouted, but her joy seemed to cool with the speed of sound. "What do you mean I'm the first to know? You haven't told Magnus?"

"I know that sounds bad, Reenie, but not to worry, a lot of women tell their mothers before they let their husbands know. I just hope he'll be as thrilled as I am."

"You never talked about having children?"

"Ours hasn't been the normal marriage, Reenie. You know that."

"But it's…all right with you two? You know what I mean?"

"Magnus is wonderful. He just can't make himself tell me he loves me."

Irene reached across the bed and grasped Selena's hand. "And does he love you?"

"I think so."

Irene's expression was one of impatience. "Then worm it out of him. If a man loves you, you're the boss. Get him on the blind side, honey, and tell him what you need. Once he hears himself say it and realizes that it didn't kill him, he'll find it easier the next time. Work on him." She stood and extended her hand. "Come on downstairs. I think I heard Roe come in." Roosevelt had planned a big weekend for them, and Selena looked forward to it. But she hadn't counted on her worrisome reaction to Magnus's plea that he needed her with him. If only he'd realize why and tell her. Much as she loved Irene and Roosevelt, she could barely contain her eagerness for Sunday afternoon when she'd head for Waverly and the man she loved.

Magnus couldn't remember the last time he'd been the sole person in the Cooper Building. Just the way he wanted it. He strode off the elevator, pushed at Madeline's door and, for a minute, he thought she might be there, for her door was unlocked, and so was her computer. He went into his office, checked his computer and discovered a problem that hadn't existed the day before.

Discouraged, he phoned Selena. "How's the weather out there?"

"Magnus? You called just in time. We were leaving to go sightseeing. Where are you?"

What he wouldn't give to hug her. "I'm in Houston. Just wanted to touch base with you. Be sure you got there safely. You miss me?"

"You don't need confirmation of that. Think back a ways. Remember those times we heard the angels sing, and then ask yourself whether I'd miss you."

He felt a tightening in his gut. "You talk like that when we've got a thousand miles between us. Make sure you're on that plane, baby."

"And you be certain you're there to meet it, cowboy."

Yeah, she missed him. She only called him cowboy when she was hot and frisky. "I'll be there. You have a good time, and give my best to Irene and Roosevelt." He hung up. His libido was giving him hell.

He had to call Madeline, and he dreaded it. "This is Magnus," he said, skipping preliminaries. "I walked in a while ago and found both your office and your computer unlocked." He didn't like what he heard. Her sputters and labored attempts to speak weren't the reaction of an innocent person.

"I don't know how that could be, Magnus," she finally managed, "unless somebody is trying to frame me."

"And that person would have access to your keys and to your computer code? How is that?" He spoke in as gentle a tone as he could manage, because he didn't want her to know he'd begun to suspect her.

"I don't know, sir. I've always treated my colleagues fairly. If one of them doesn't like me, I don't know why. I'll make sure that door is locked, sir, and thank you for telling me. I'll let you know what I find when I get to the office on Monday. Anything else, sir?"

He told her goodbye and hung up. With Jeb in Africa, Madeline had responsibility for the entire building, the computers, vehicles, everything. He rubbed the back of his neck, deep in thought. He hadn't imagined that Madeline attempted to rush him off the line; she'd all but terminated the conversation. Perhaps she had company. *But in the morning?* He took off his jacket and settled down to work.

Magnus's guess had been right. Madeline poured another cup of coffee for Prince, sat across the table from him in her tiny kitchen and took a sip from her own cup.

"Did you go in my office last night?"

As far as she was concerned, his grin missed its mark; he'd repeatedly failed to deliver the hot lovemaking he promised, so his charm didn't curl her toes. Fortunately, she hadn't been tempted to love him, but the reason wasn't with either of them, but with Magnus Cooper, and she shouldn't have let Prince lure her into disloyalty to Magnus.

"You know I wouldn't do a thing like that and risk your job," Prince soothed.

But she didn't know it; in fact she doubted him, but she had learned that his grin often camouflaged a cruel nature, so she kept her doubt to herself. She'd get those locks changed, if she had to do it at her own expense.

"You never gave me back those keys. Why are you keeping them? That was Magnus on the phone, and he just found my office and my computer unlocked."

He stretched out his legs and locked his hands behind his head. "I'll get 'em in a minute. Right now I want you to act like a real woman and stop snapping at me. Just because you know you've got me wound around your little finger, doesn't mean you can be so sure of me, baby." He reached for her and, when she pretended not to see him, he went into the hallway, came back with the keys and handed them to her.

"Did you have duplicates made?"

He winked, grinned and narrowed his eyes seductively. "Now, you know that wouldn't be decent. Come over here." He sat down and patted his right thigh, but she didn't move.

Worried that her chicanery may have been for naught, she asked him, "Are you making any headway with Selena? You ought to be in Waverly. When Magnus called a minute ago, he was here in Houston. Didn't she tell you she could see you while he was out of town?"

He shifted in his chair and looked everywhere but at her. He's uncomfortable, she realized.

"I told you I didn't want anybody but you. She's tried, but she's wasting my time."

"I know, Prince, but you said you'd break them up." She had to keep the anxiety out of her voice, because Prince was as clever as he was unscrupulous, and if he knew he had an advantage, he'd wring it dry.

"You still got the hots for rich boy? I thought I cooled you off."

She forced a smile. "How could you think that? I just want to see her get what she deserves."

He lifted his chin, narrowed his eyes and stood, as though to reinforce his estimation of himself. "And she will, baby. Trust me, she'll get what's coming to her." She winced when he locked his thumbs in his belt and ordered, "Come here. I've had enough of this talk."

Her heartbeat accelerated, and she thought she could count the goose bump as they popped out on her arms. Animals headed for slaughter yelled and screamed in anticipation of their fate; she had to take her medicine quietly. She dropped her arms to her sides and let him have his way.

Madeline lingered over her shower after Prince left. If she scrubbed away her skin, she might still not feel clean. She mused over her conversation with Magnus. He had questioned her, but he hadn't seemed angry, and he hadn't reprimanded her. She wondered if he was really crazy about Selena and whether Prince could split up their marriage. Images, ideas and plans swirled in her brain. She'd bet anything that Selena told Magnus his secretary had snubbed her, but it was clear Magnus hadn't believed it.

She'd find a locksmith who could change all the locks. Prince didn't care if he made her lose her job, but she didn't have to watch him do it. He had some kind of fixation on Selena, but that didn't mean Selena spent her time scheming to meet Prince.

Selena hugged her godmother a second time, ashamed of her eagerness to get on the plane, and guilt washed over her when Irene asked her to come back soon.

"Love him with all your soul, honey, but don't let him take you for granted," Irene counseled.

"Don't worry, we'll get it together," she assured the woman who had been her rock.

Selena scrutinized the crowd, and her face glowed with a brilliant smile as her gaze settled on him. He could barely wait to get to her, but he wouldn't let himself run. She wasn't any of the things he'd once thought. No. She was a man's dream. But she had a price. Oh, she wouldn't demand constant devotion, because she needed room in which to be herself, and she'd grant him the same. But if he opened himself and allowed her to see everything in him, his soul, would she use it against him as he'd witnessed in Anna Cooper's treatment of his father? He tossed the idea aside and let himself revel in the pleasure of having her with him again. She dropped her bag on the floor as she reached him, and opened her arms.

"Hi, woman."

She pinched his cheek and snuggled up to him. "Hi, cowboy. What wonderful eyes you have."

He knew his happiness showed. "All the better to see you with, my dear," he replied, entering into her lightheartedness. "Ready to go home?"

She nuzzled his neck. Maybe a couple of days' separation was what they'd needed. "I *am* home," she said, and he sensed a difference in her. She was driving for something, and he sure hoped he was her goal. He made up his mind not to push her, but to figure out what she wanted of him and give it to her.

Monday afternoon, Magnus peeped into Selena's office. "Honey, do you mind calling Madeline and asking her to e-mail her log to me? I can't pick it up on my computer. Jackson wants me to go with him to check on a mare that's having a hard labor, and I have to hurry. Okay?" She told him she would, and dialed Madeline's number.

"Hello, Madeline, this is Selena Sutton-Cooper. My husband would like you to e-mail him your log."

"He can retrieve it on his computer and print it out there," she said without so much as a greeting.

Selena let her annoyance show. "I know what he can and can't do, Miss Price. I'm telling you what he said."

"Well, if he'd call me and tell me which log he wants…"

"And I wouldn't be so transparent if I were you," Selena shot back. "Be a smart girl and get that log over here." She hung up. The temerity of that woman.

Selena answered her phone on its first ring. "Southwest Securities. Selena Sutton-Cooper speaking. How may I help you?"

"Hey, Selena. This is Russ. Your friend in San Antonio. Remember?"

"Of course I remember you, Russ. What a surprise."

"Well, I wanted you to know I just saw that cat who was leaning against your car that day. This worm was buzzing a teenager, and I'm one of the guys in my school who's supposed to watch out for that. He saw me and the boys and took off, but I'm sworn to report that stuff."

"Wow!" Should she lie, and why should she? "Russ, I told you he was a nuisance, a guy who pesters me. I'll find out what I can about him, and call you. Give me your number." He did. "Russ, tell me about yourself. You're not a gang member, are you?"

"Who, me?" His shock floated to her through the wires. "How'd you get it so wrong, Selena? I'm an honor student. Me and my boys got sick of some of the things we see, so we started protecting people who need us. We got into a little trouble about that, and our school gave us an assignment—looking after kids and keeping old men away from girls."

She wasn't certain. "What were you doing on my husband's car that time? He said you liked to harass him."

"You mean the cool dude?" He laughed. "The guy's got no sense of humor. We love big, expensive cares. We used to look around 'til we found it, and when we realized we could give him a fit, we laid into him."

"But you were belligerent."

"Sure. That guy's big, and anybody could look at him and tell he was ready to fight. We don't hurt people who don't hurt us."

"But you're not hostile anymore, I hope."

"Nah. We'll even protect him. You gonna call me, Selena?" She said she would. Russ disliked Prince, and he wouldn't rest until he identified him.

She went in the house, changed clothes and headed for the barn. In spite of the short distance, the intense heat and humidity had sapped her energy and wilted her clothing by the time she reached Magnus and Jackson, both of whom had tired, haggard faces.

"Go back, Selena. This is no place for you," Magnus said, advancing toward her as though to stop her.

"What's the matter? What's wrong?" She looked from one man to the other, but Jackson put his hands in the back pockets of his jeans and looked down at his feet.

"We're not sure she can make it. She's tired and the heat's too much for her," Magnus said.

"But maybe if I talk to her and calm her, she'll pull through."

She started past him, but he braced a hand on each of her shoulders. "You're not going in there. She's thrashing, and she could hurt you. We can't even get near her. Besides, I don't want you to see that—"

"But you can't just stand here and wait for the inevitable. She needs help." Selena tore past Magnus and headed for the stall. He was right behind her, but not fast enough.

A scream tore out of her throat. He grabbed her up in his arms and sprinted out of the barn.

She tore at his clothes. "Shoot her. Don't let her suffer like that. Jackson, do something." She didn't try to control the heaving sobs that racked her nor the tremors that rioted through her flesh.

"It's all right, honey. Jackson is taking care of it."

She pushed him away. "It isn't all right. She's torn and bleeding, and she's suffering so." Her sobs began again. "She's…she's…only trying to…to have her baby. Why does it have to…to be th…this way?"

Jackson hunkered down to where Magnus sat on the ground with Selena cradled in his arms. "She finally gave birth, but it's doubtful that either of them will make it. She caught a virus last week, Selena, and we thought we could save her and her colt, but she was too weak to help with her delivery. That's why you saw what you did. I've done everything for her that can be done. We just have to wait."

Without a word, Selena eased out of Magnus's arms and walked back to the house. She needed to talk with her god-mother or Tessie, but Tessie didn't know she was pregnant. A woman would share what she was feeling. She wasn't scared, but she couldn't understand how nature could be so cruel, when that was the only way mammals had of being born.

"What's wrong, Selena?" Tessie asked when Selena entered the house through the kitchen door.

"Jackson will tell you. I want to forget it as soon as possible." She rushed up to her rooms and closed the door. Magnus had been right, she shouldn't have gone in that stall, and she doubted she would ever forget it. Her hand went to her belly, and she whispered to the little fetus, soothing it as Irene had advised. "You be a sweet little darling, and don't rough me up. You understand?"

She pulled the damp T-shirt over her head, tossed it in the bathroom hamper and reached for her belt. "Yes," she said, knowing that it was Magnus who knocked.

"Are you all right, sweetheart? I want to come in. Don't lock me out of your life when I know you need me."

"Come on in. I'll be out there in a minute." But he didn't stop walking until he was in her bedroom. Embarrassed at her state of near undress, she folded her arms across her bosom, but he ignored her gesture of modesty.

"I know you're upset. You have to be. But don't shut me out. Let me hold you."

She dashed into his arms. "It was so awful. Is she... Did she...?" She couldn't ask the obvious.

He folded her close. "Honey, females are the same no matter the species. The colt got to his feet and wanted to nurse, and that tired mare stood and accommodated him. It was enough to bring tears to a man's eyes."

His arms tightened around her. "Jackson says she has a

chance. She let him take care of her, and he made her comfortable, so try to forget about it."

"She's not in pain?" Selena asked, knowing he read disbelief in her face.

"We gave her a painkiller. By the way, did you come out there to tell me something?"

"Uh…yes. Let's see. Oh, yes. I gave Madeline your message, and Russ called me."

"He did? For what?"

She related what Russ had told her. "And don't make an issue out of my not squealing on Prince. I figured it wasn't my duty to send my brother-in-law to jail. If you want to tell Russ that Prince is his man, go ahead. I think he deserves it, but I won't report him."

Magnus ran his hand over his hair and shrugged first one shoulder and then the other one. He remembered having seen Prince with a girl who looked underage when he and Selena were leaving the movie house. "This is a tough one to call. I'll speak to Prince and find out how deeply involved he is with the girl. If he's gone too far, I won't cover for him."

"He should know better."

Magnus ground his teeth. He'd planned to surprise Selena, but this wouldn't wait. "He does know better. I'll see if I can get hold of him. Tessie's making enchiladas for supper, so come prepared to stuff yourself." He thought he saw her wince. "What's the matter? I thought you loved Tessie's patties."

"I do, but the thought of them or anything else to eat turns my stomach."

"That scene was too much for you. Why not rest 'til dinnertime? I could get you some mint tea. How's that?"

"Thanks, but I think I'll take your advice and rest. See you later." He loved that way she had of teasing him with a quick peck on the cheek. She was a drug, and the smallest taste of her set him off. He wanted more; he could take care of that business about Prince later.

"Sure you wouldn't like some company?" She must have seen the hot want in his eyes, because she swallowed heavily, and her own eyes glazed over with the signs of passion. He let his hands go to her bare nipples. Hard and hungry. He knew he shouldn't press her in her emotional state, but he thought only of the evidence beneath his fingers that said he could have what he wanted. He lifted her above him, fastened his mouth on her breast and suckled her. The trembling of her flesh against his body sent the blood arrow-straight to his loins, exciting him. She wrapped her legs around him and tightened them, but he sensed that her desire was not at its peak and released her. He should have been more forceful, should have stood his ground and kept her away from that mare, but he didn't relish compelling his wife to do anything.

"I think you'd better rest. We'll get back to that." He went downstairs and called his brother.

"I'm glad I found you home," he told Prince.

"To what may I attribute this recognition, brother? How'd you get down off your throne long enough to contact a mortal?"

Magnus was determined to have a civil conversation with Prince, so he refused to lash back. He told him about Russ's inquiry.

"That girl is nineteen at least."

But when Magnus probed, he learned that Prince had never asked the girl her age. "You could be in trouble, Prince. That kid has a commission from his school to report any such incident that he sees, and he won't make an exception with you."

"What are you planning to tell him?"

"I'll tell him you said you'd leave her alone, but if he catches you again, I'll give him any information he wants right down to your social security number. Got it?"

"Uh...yeah. Thanks."

Magnus stared at the phone after he'd hung up. The day would come when neither money nor Anna Cooper's social status would keep Prince out of jail, and he didn't look forward to his mother's tears. He telephoned Russ.

He went to the dining room prepared to enjoy his fill of Tessie's specialty only to learn that Selena didn't want dinner, saying she was too upset to eat, and he was hard-pressed to enter into the camaraderie that flowed between Tessie and Jackson.

"Tessie, these are proof positive that you can cook," Jackson remarked.

"I don't care for that kind of backhanded compliment," she said with a frown on her face and a hand on her hip. "You've had other proof that I can cook."

"That doesn't count at the table," Jackson said, as he savored another enchilada.

Magnus's head snapped around. Jackson wasn't given to innuendoes, but that had certainly sounded like one. He scrutinized Tessie, who hadn't responded to the remark. No doubt about it, their relationship had tightened; Tessie was more sure of herself with Jackson. He left the table and called over his shoulder, "Let me know what you two want for a wedding present. Anything up to a hundred thousand, Tess." He got out of the way, before she could answer him.

Selena sat on the edge of her bed, hoping that Magnus wouldn't want to see her and that Tessie wouldn't bring her any food. She expected morning sickness, but everything she ate made her sick. She got up, checked her calendar and decided to see her doctor before her scheduled appointment. She had to find a good time to tell Magnus, too, but not now when he'd see it as the reason for her strong reaction of the mare's confinement. She didn't think she could stand up straight and, when Tessie knocked, she had a wave of panic.

"Brought you some mint tea, child. These men can take it, but I don't go near that stable when those heifers and mares are down." To Selena's surprise, Tessie set the tray down with barely a glance her way. She couldn't help laughing; the reason for Tessie's preoccupation wasn't discretion, but a date with Jackson. She yelled her thanks after Tessie's departing figure.

The next morning, Magnus poked his head in the door of Selena's living room. "I'll be in Houston today, but I'll see you at dinner. How do you feel this morning?" His relief at her gaily sung "I'm fine" was palpable. He loped back downstairs and waited for Jackson.

"Let Selena know immediately any progress the mare and colt make. She's reacted to this more strongly than I would have thought. I'll be back here around five."

He walked into his office building, greeting employees as he went. Madeline wore pink again. Why? he wondered.

"Morning, Madeline." He paused. "I must say that pink dress brightens up the office."

She stood at once. "Thank you, sir. Good morning. We weren't expecting you today, but we're happy to see you."

He'd almost said thanks, before wondering why he should, and swallowing the word. "I'd like to see Jeb, please."

"Certainly, sir."

He went in his office and opened his computer. So far, all was in order. He glanced up as a whiff of sweet perfume settled in his nostrils. He hated sweet-smelling lotions and perfumes. "Yes, Madeline. What is it?" Strange. He hadn't noticed it when he walked through her office.

"I don't know where Jeb is right now, sir, but I expect he's called a meeting. He's started having meetings with the whole staff—except me, of course. I have to tend the phones." She patted her hair and reddened. "Would you care for coffee…or something?"

Magnus stared. Nearly dumbfounded. A man of his age and experience knew when he was getting a come-on. *But from*

Madeline? "What kind of something?" he asked, phrasing the words carefully.

Damned if she didn't bat her lashes. "Whatever you need, sir."

He leaned back in his chair, smiled and kept his voice gentle. "And you think I need something, Madeline?"

"Everyone does, sir. It's human nature." She took a step toward him, but he wiped the smile from his face and stood. His lower jaw dropped, and he knew without being told that the vein in his forehead stood out like a pulsing cord. He ground his teeth and did his best to control his tongue. Without taking his eyes off her, he threw the paperweight up in the air and caught it, put it back on his desk and sat down. If that didn't beat all!

"My wife takes care of my needs, Madeline, and she does a damned fine job of it," he managed to say between clenched teeth. "Send Jeb in here."

What in hell had she been thinking about? He wasn't sure he wanted to work with Madeline any longer, though he didn't think her foolishness constituted grounds for dismissal. Or did it? The grin that spread over his face dissolved into pure merriment. Sexual harassment. He could fire her for that, and then sue her. He glanced out of the window at the sunshine, the swaying bougainvillea that had climbed up to his office window, and began to whistle. It would serve her right.

A look at his watch told him he'd barely make that plane if he dropped in on the computer specialist he hoped to hire. On second thought, he'd pay the fellow to come out to the ranch. Half the time he forgot he was a wealthy man and that he could buy any service he needed. He laughed at himself, as he locked his briefcase, grabbed his Stetson and started to dash out.

"That wouldn't do," he said aloud to himself. "Loose strings can hang you."

He stopped at Madeline's desk. "I don't know what that encounter we had this morning was all about, and I expect you don't, either. See you when I get back."

Her reply was slow coming. "You're right. Goodbye, sir."

He took his seat on the plane, ordered coffee and opened his briefcase, but work held no appeal. A thought frolicked on the fringes of his conscious mind, and he couldn't bring it to the fore. Yet he knew it had importance for him, for his life.

To his surprise, Jackson waited for him at the airport in San Antonio. "I'm glad to see you. How's Selena?"

"Doing fine, far as I can see. She's been working all day. She's been out to the stable three times to see the colt and its mother, and she nearly had a fit when she went the last time and didn't see 'em in the stall. I took her out in the pasture where they were, and it sure did cheer her up."

"That's a load off my shoulders. I don't know how she would have taken it if we'd lost that horse."

Jackson cleared his throat. "It's none of my business, Magnus, but don't you think her reaction was extreme?"

Magnus took the front passenger's seat, threw his briefcase in the back and closed the door. "I know it was, but I'll deal with that after this crisis has passed."

Selena had closed the office, so he dashed upstairs to greet her, and stopped midway up the stairs. She'd insisted that Madeline had been hostile and discourteous to her, and he hadn't believed it. But it made sense after Madeline's brazen, if ineffectual, attempt at involvement with him. Jealousy had prompted Madeline's hostility to Selena. He owed his wife an apology.

"Hi, woman." He planted a hard kiss on her upturned mouth.

"Hi, yourself. How did everything go in Houston?"

He tugged her to him and immediately felt a stirring in his loins. "Well enough. No big problems, honey. The details will have to wait until I get a shower. A couple of steps from the car, and I'm wilted."

* * *

Madeline wanted to evaporate, to disappear, but she couldn't make herself move. She sat with her hands folded in her lap long after Magnus left the office. Fuming. She'd made the biggest blunder of her life, and he had been nasty. Her precious Magnus had scorned her. She'd show him how it felt to lose face with a person who meant something to you. After all she'd suffered in order to get him. And that was another thing; she wouldn't have done anything so stupid if Prince hadn't sworn that Magnus wanted her. Prince's information about Magnus and her was like his boasts about his hot prowess as a lover, and he scored zero on both counts. She got up and started pacing. Scheming. Prince was using her, and she'd use him. She'd pay Magnus Cooper well for having turned his nose up at her.

Chapter 13

"Magnus, look at this. It's the same handwriting that was on that other letter I got." She placed the five-and-dime stationery with its schizophrenic scrawl on his desk in front of him.

Magnus looked up at her with narrowed eyes. "What other letter? You didn't tell me you got a…" He gestured toward the letter. "When did that happen?"

Selena had forgotten that she'd decided not to tell him and, in spite of her determination to brazen it out, she knew her voice had a subdued quality. "A couple of weeks ago."

"This is ridiculous." He almost yelled it. What the devil *is* this? he asked himself, remembering Madeline's bizarre behavior.

He bounded out of his chair and looked down at his wife. "Do you believe I made promises to a woman and didn't keep them?"

She shook her head. "Do I think you'd mortgage your life to anybody that crude? Of course I don't."

"Do you suppose Madeline is the devil in this?"

She knew from his reaction that her face had mirrored her surprise at his question. "She didn't write these letters. I saw her writing on her desk, and it's a large, blocked scrawl that can't be changed to this tiny script, though I suppose you can see that someone attempted to alter their handwriting."

"Yes. But I doubt anybody can change fingerprints. I'll get the prints of everybody who could be a suspect."

"When?"

"Don't looked so skeptical, honey. The barbecue is the perfect opportunity." He looked down at the note and read: "Well, Miss Priss, you're still flying high. But don't get used to it. A lot of us were here before you arrived, and Magnus Cooper didn't spend all his nights alone. Pretty soon, you'll be history.

"In your dreams," Magnus muttered. She could see that the letter both perplexed and angered him, but she hadn't left Wall Street to become a victim of stress and fear. Her marriage to Magnus would last for as long as the two of them wanted it, and she was doggoned if she would worry about anybody's cowardly behavior.

Selena reached up and kissed her husband quickly on his lips, turned and started back to her office.

"Come back here, woman," he growled. "Your teasing little kisses do more damage than some of your onslaughts."

She grinned and waved at him. "Sorry, Mr. Cooper, but I have to send this report off to *Wall Street World.* Corporate Wall Street will not be pleased at what I've found, though. Executive women, black and white, are in short supply, not only on the Street, but in money management as a whole. The rise in computers brought an increase in the number of jocks, as they call the stockbrokers, but the number of women didn't rise proportionately. And as you can imagine, Latin women trailed behind African-American women, and even farther behind white women. I put a footnote thanking you for the use of your computer for my research."

"Thanks. And you owe me something," he grumbled. "You and your hot little nibbles. Better yet, *I owe you one.*"

"Darling," she cooed, "I'm not worried in the least. You're a master at...collecting." She ducked out of the door and laughed aloud when she realized that she'd licked her lips.

Magnus mentally listed the possible culprits who might hound Selena. The "gifts" could be the work of either a man or a woman, but those letters came from a jealous female. Suddenly, his insight sharpened, and little tremors of excitement raced through him. Not necessarily; that might only be what the culprit hoped Magnus and Selena would believe. The letter could also have come from a member of either sex. Its author could be anyone.

Memorial Day arrived and, with it, the famous Cooper barbecue party. Selena ambled through the big tent making certain that the caterer did his job. She almost failed to recognize Tessie, because she had never seen her with her hair combed down and dressed in stunning yellow linen pants and a matching short-sleeved jacket. She stared until Tessie laughed aloud.

"Honey, you wait 'til you see me in my 'tweeds.' I already kissed fifty goodbye, but there's plenty fire in the old girl."

Selena grinned. "I'm sorry, Tessie, but you'll admit this is some transformation."

"Tessie doesn't have to wear that black uniform and those old shoes," Jackson said. "Magnus told her to stop putting on that silly stuff like she was a servant." He preened. "But she's pretty no matter what she puts on."

"I wear it 'cause it makes the house look proper," Tessie said. "I told that caterer if any of his men came here wearing anything but white shirts and pants, they wasn't getting one cent."

"What a crowd!" Selena observed.

"Give it another hour, and there'll be twice as many people here. At least two hundred and fifty," Tessie told her, then asked, "Where's Magnus?"

"Right here. Selena, I want to introduce you to some of these people."

Selena let her glance roam over him. His beige silk shirt set off his dark good looks, seeming to match the color of his hazel eyes. Tall, big and muscular. The use to which he could so capably put his big frame filled her thoughts and must have shown in her face, because his eyes suddenly blazed with desire. I've got to tell him about the baby, she reminded herself, and realized why she feared doing so. Tessie had warned her not to adopt a baby and to pay less attention to Rhett Butler, lest Magnus feel deprived of her affection. But surely he would want his own child.

Magnus let himself enjoy his good fortune in having Selena as his wife. He'd always thought her skin lovely, but her brown face seemed to have taken on a soft glow, almost as though she had rouged it, and he knew she hadn't.

"Take my arm, sweetheart. I know it's old-fashioned, but I want all the people to know whose woman you are." He was so close to being happy. That would come; he knew it now.

"Magnus, there you are at last. I've been looking all over for you." The tall African-American woman wore a pale green, sleeveless cotton jumpsuit, large silver hoops in her ears and half an arm of silver bracelets. He attempted without success to sidestep her embrace, but she managed to give him a full kiss on the mouth. His ears welcomed Selena's gasp with all the joy with which golfers embrace a sudden thunderstorm.

He stepped back, wiped his mouth with his shirtsleeve and didn't hide the sneer that formed on his trembling lips. How dare she! "Selena, this is Mavis Root. Mavis, this is my wife, and she's probably wondering, as I am, how you got the temerity to kiss me." He let his gaze flicker from one woman to the other. Selena's cool facade didn't fool him; Mavis's brazen gesture had both surprised and angered her.

"Oooo. I had no idea," Mavis said, her face enveloped in the sweetest of smiles.

"Of course you didn't," Magnus countered. "What woman other than my wife would be walking so intimately with me at my home among my friends?"

"Well, you always were a fox," Mavis said. Selena turned sharply and waved, ignoring Mavis.

"Hey, girl. Over here," Eloise called, waving Selena to her table.

Selena's smile and her arrow-straight dart at Mavis restored his equilibrium. "Do the best you can to stomach it, darling. Remember when you had to take castor oil as a kid, you always got something sweet afterward to get rid of that taste. Come on over and meet Eloise's friend." She sauntered off without having said a word to Mavis. He watched her hips tease onlookers with their rhythmic sway and had to get a deep breath. He glanced back at Mavis and found her gaze locked on him, her whole demeanor advertising her annoyance. She hated being bested, and Selena had just done a royal job of it.

Mavis stepped closer, and he backed off, and nearly toppled the table behind him. "I don't remember sending you an invitation, Mavis, but if I'd bothered to remember your tactics, I'd have expected you nonetheless."

Her pretense at hurt wasn't a bad job of acting. "Don't be mean, Magnus. Of course I came, Everybody's here, and I couldn't afford not to be seen. Besides, you aren't seriously planning to stay married to her, are you?"

"Until the day I die, lady, and maybe longer. Whatever and whoever gave you the notion that I don't love my wife? That kind of ignorance can get you into serious trouble. Since you're here, stroll around and meet people." He walked toward Eloise's table. Up to then, he hadn't suspected Mavis of tormenting Selena, because she had the gall to be open with her tricks. But she'd just added herself to his list. He let his gaze sweep over Bertil Swensen. The poor guy's besotted with Eloise, he told himself, so he might as well ask Selena what to give them for a wedding present. He waved at them and headed for Tessie's table.

Tessie examined her well-manicured fingernails, leaned back in her chair and glanced around the tent. This was one day in the year when she took time to appreciate what Magnus had become, to glory in the fruit of his hard work and personal sacrifices. "I want us to wait for Selena's godmother and her husband. Jackson sent one of the hands into San Antonio to get them. And Miss Anna ain't here yet."

Magnus shook his head. "Don't wait for mother—she has to make an entrance."

Tessie nodded in understanding, and ordered a round of drinks. The sounds of musical instruments being tuned filled the tent, and waiters rolled serving trolleys among the tables. Some bore whole roast pigs, others barbecued spareribs and whole roasted Cornish hens. Those preferring hot dogs or hamburgers could order them. Buttermilk biscuits, jalapeño corn bread, tacos, Texas potato salad, baked beans and coleslaw were available in abundance. Tables laden with raw vegetables, fresh fruits and cheeses rolled along the aisles.

"You planned a great menu, Tess," Magnus told her, and she detected an unfamiliar tightness in his voice. "Whenever you want to retire, Tessie, just tell me. You can keep your little apartment, or I'll build you any kind of house you want. You've been in my life so long, I wouldn't want you to go far. Nobody could want a better mother, Tess." He patted her shoulder, got up and left, but the weight of his emotion lingered.

When tears pooled in her eyes, she felt Jackson's arm gentle around her shoulder. "No finer man ever walked this earth."

"Don't I know it. Uh-oh." Anna was walking their way, and Tessie wished she hadn't put her table near the entrance. To her amazement and gratitude, however, Magnus's mother only nodded as she passed and kept walking. If that woman had encouraged Mavis to be there to harass Selena, she'd tell her a few things, so help her God.

"Now simmer down, Tessie," Jackson told her. "The woman hasn't done anything, yet. Wait 'til she does before you go into a tizzy." He squeezed her shoulder, and she didn't give a hoot about Anna Cooper, though she didn't want their party spoiled.

She needn't have worried about Anna's manners with Selena, because Selena had already laid out their rules of engagement.

Selena stood. "Hello, Mrs. Cooper. You know Eloise." She introduced Bert as her friend's significant other and got a raised eyebrow from Anna. It amused Selena that Magnus seemed to appear from nowhere as though he had to act as a buffer between them.

"You didn't by chance ask Mavis to join you here, did you, Mother?"

Anna stepped back and looked down her nose. "Of course not. I didn't know she'd planned to be here." She looked around, scanning the growing crowd. "You've outdone yourself this time, Magnus. It's a lovely party. I just hope those men are going to play chamber music."

Magnus grinned, exuding such pleasure that one would have thought he'd been given a trophy. "Well, it'll be a kind of chamber music, that is, if you consider that chamber music groups are, in a sense, small orchestras. This small orchestra plays real funky New Orleans jazz. It's great stuff. You'll love it."

"You enjoy shocking me," she chided, "and you should shame yourself for not having invited your brother. He was too proud to come without an invitation."

"I'll just bet." Magnus snorted, waved to bandleader Sooky Matthews and the Dixieland jazz filled the air. "Not so bad, now, is it, Mother?" His smile cradled a wink as well as his hope for some evidence that she could bend toward him. Just once. But Anna Cooper tossed her head and walked on to the table where Mavis sat alone.

"It's all right, love." Selena, who had risen to stand beside him, tugged at his arm, and he knew that his smiles had not covered his sadness.

"I'm okay, Selena."

At dusk, he watched the crowd thin, shook hands until his arms ached and walked back to the house, arm-in-arm with Selena. As usual, his employees had brought their families and close friends. He'd counted six three-generation families and one of four generations and, as he'd watched them, he'd longed for his own children while Tessie still had her energy and drive; every child needed a grandparent. It occurred to him briefly that Anna would be his children's grandmother. Well, if she accepted the role, he'd rejoice, but she'd have to change her attitude toward his wife.

"Feel like a stroll over to Running Brook? I could use a little quiet. How about you?"

Selena squeezed his fingers. "Now that it's cooled off, I'd enjoy it."

He sat on the grass near the edge of the brook, taking her with him. "We've never had a honeymoon, and our relationship could stand one. I had planned to surprise you with tickets and reservations, until I remembered that you run a business and have to plan your leave. What about it?"

"I have to give my clients at least two weeks' notice, or get someone to cover for me, but I'm for it, Magnus."

"Roll over here in my arms. I ought to pay you back for some of your sexy needling, but if I do, I'll just be giving myself a hard time. What's the matter?" he asked when her hand went to her chest. "Are you having chest pains?"

"Heartburn," she said. "Too much barbecue."

"Yeah. I've noticed you doing that a lot lately. Maybe you ought to see a doctor, Monday."

"If it doesn't go away, I will."

He wrapped her to him. He'd pay for it with a sleepless night, but he didn't care; he was after a bigger prize, one that he would have for a lifetime. Selena's hand wound itself around his neck, and he fell over on his back, bringing her supine on top of him. Shivers darted up his spine the minute her parted lips invited his tongue. She pressed his mouth with her soft kiss and, when he decided to test her need of him and withheld his kiss, her other hand found his most vulnerable spot. He thought he'd die for want of her as she caressed him mercilessly. Hot need burned his insides and settled in his throbbing groin, and he had to give in or cry out with the sweet and embarrassing torture of unscheduled release. He relented and gave her his tongue and, with both arms cradling his head, she feasted on it. If he'd set out to punish her, to remind her what it was like to be teased, he'd failed. The hot arrows of desire pummeled his starving body and, when he rocked against her, she dropped kisses all over his face. You belong to me, she seemed to be showing him, and he couldn't deny it. But could a man love a woman clear into his soul and still belong to himself?

He moved her to his side and sat up. "The last time we almost lost it down here by this brook, a cow broke it up. I wouldn't like us to entertain one of the hands out here."

Her smile soothed every raw nerve in him and calmed his restless libido. "You're the one who starts it."

"Yeah, but how far would it get if you didn't cooperate?" He stood, dusted the back of his pants, helped her up and started back to the house. "I'm a simple man, Selena. I don't want much, but what I want, I want badly." His hand swept around to encompass what he saw. "I can get along without all of this." He stopped walking and grasped both her shoulders. "But I don't plan to get along without those few things that I do want, Selena, and that includes you."

They walked along in silence and when they neared the house, Selena turned to him. "Let's go up to my room for a few minutes. I want us to talk."

Magnus stuck his hands in the pockets of his slacks and gazed down at her, trying to figure out her mood. "This sounds serious."

She nodded. "It is."

Her foot touched the first step when she glanced at the hall table and saw the Saturday-morning mail. She walked over and shuffled through the letters.

"What's that?" Magnus wanted to know. Her face must have revealed her sense of trepidation, for he hurried to her. "Is that another…"

"Yep. It's another love letter." She dropped it on the table, unopened, turned and took his hand. "Come on. I'm not letting that spoil my mood."

She closed the door. Now that the time had come, would he be angry because she'd known for over two weeks and hadn't told him? Would he hate the idea of competing with his child for her affection, or had he stopped seeing his mother's traits in her?

He seemed to have closed himself up, as though expecting unwelcome news and, indeed, that could be what he got. Getting no help from him, not even a smile, she decided to deal first with the matter of the half dozen nasty little gifts she'd received.

"Magnus," she began, aware of the unsteadiness of her voice, "all of your workers here at the ranch seem to like me, and I'm satisfied that none them would deliberately harm me. I'm not that certain about your folks in the Cooper Building and other places, so I want to go to Houston Monday, if possible, and talk with them. I'll find a pretext for doing it, but I'm certain that ten minutes with each one is all I'll need."

She thought his face brightened. What, she wondered, had he expected? "All right, I'll ask Jackson to drive you. Can you leave at two?"

"I thought I'd fly."

"Then I'll ask Jackson to fly with you. If you suspect anyone there, I don't want you to go alone. I know my protectiveness doesn't sit well with you, but humor me."

"All right. Jackson it is." He didn't have to know that she'd agreed because of the dizzy spells caused by her pregnancy.

His gaze had focused on her hands, and she realized she'd been wringing them. "Now, give me the real reason for this…this conference. If you're so nervous about telling me, maybe I ought to be nervous, too."

"It…it's not anything I ever had to say before."

Seemingly chastened, he took the few steps that separated them and put his arms around her. "Just tell me, honey."

She looked up into his beloved face, the image that she hoped she'd see whenever she looked at her child. "Magnus, I'm…I'm carrying our child."

"That's fine. That… *What? What* did you say?"

"I said, I'm—"

"I know what you said. I asked you what did you say?"

She'd never seen him excited. "Honey, you're shaking me."

"Oh, sweetheart, I'm sorry. I didn't mean… What did… Did you say you're…"

She hugged him as tightly as she could. "I'm pregnant, Magnus."

He walked over to her chaise lounge and sat down. "This is nothing to joke about, Selena. There isn't anything on this earth that I want more than a family. Our children. Are you sure?"

Her heart slowed to its normal rate. "I'm sure. Are you happy, Magnus? You don't mind? I mean, we've never discussed having a family, and I was scared to death to tell you."

"Mind?" He bounded off the chaise lounge, pulled her into his arms and swung her around. "I've never been so happy in my life. If you only knew how badly I want children with you, Selena. Oh, sweetheart, we'll get our life on track, Selena, and I promise you'll never be sorry you married me."

She had to say it now. They had to talk about it. "Magnus, don't fear that I'll neglect you in favor of our children or that I'll give one of them more love than I give the other. I have more love in me than I know how to handle, Magnus, and I've had all these years to nurture it while I waited for you and my children."

He picked her up and sat on the edge of a chair with her nestled in his lap. "Tessie told you?"

Selena nodded. "She gave me a strong hint, and I figured out the rest."

He buried his face in her bosom, and held her to him, and she couldn't doubt that he was sharing for the first time a pain that he had not even revealed to Tessie. "I know you're aching for a child of your own, Selena. I've seen it on your face as you watched children, babies. And I wanted to give them to you, wanted to see you hold my children and love them. The softness you display toward any person or animal in need is all part of your motherly instinct, and that's one of the traits that makes you so different from my mother. Yes, I've thought that you were like her is some ways, but as I got to know and understand you, I realized that you two are sunshine and rain. She knows how to spoil a child, but not how to love one."

He needed holding, and she held him as close as she could. If only he meant it, and if he could open himself and let her love him the way she knew she could, she would be all he wanted and needed. But she wasn't as sure as he was that Anna Cooper didn't hover between them. She doubted he could ever forget or stop suffering from rejection by his mother.

He raised his head and, for the first time, she saw the heart of him. Vulnerable. Hopeful. Joy filled his hazel eyes. She could see beyond their mesmerizing beauty and, from them, his strength, his masculinity, and his passion reached out and clutched at her. She'd meant to share a sweet kiss with him, but when she touched his lips, fire flared in her, and she wanted him as she never had before.

He stared at her as though stunned by her sudden, fierce arousal. "Don't tell me to go down those stairs, because I won't unless I take you with me. We're a family." He pressed his strong hand lightly on her belly. "I'm here. Right here inside you. I'm your man, and I'm putting an end to this foolishness."

But correcting their relationship wasn't what loomed before Selena as most important, much as she wanted that. She straddled his lap, wrapped her arms around his shoulders and opened her lips over his. "You leave here at your own risk," she whispered. His hazel eyes darkened, and she watched him swallow.

"You tease and play, Selena, but if I took you right now the way I want to, you'd never forget it."

Her legs tightened around him, and her hips rocked. "I want

you to love me like you never loved any woman. You hear me? I can't stand not knowing that you're mine. Take whatever you want, whatever you need, but, Magnus, let me know that you're mine, that you belong to me. I need to know it."

He picked her up and strode with her into her bedroom, threw back the bed covers and laid her there before him. He sat down to undress her, but she stripped off her own clothes.

"Come here," she said. She unbuttoned his shirt and pulled it from him.

Needing the heat of her body, he lay beside her, and she peeled off his pants and shorts. He sat up and leaned over her. "You spend tonight and all future nights in my room with me, or we don't go any further. I want you badly enough to eat nails, but I won't compromise on this. I belong to you, but we belong to each other. Do you understand that?"

He'd do anything for her. Why didn't she know that? He held his breath and waited, and nearly capitulated when her smile invited him to her. "Baby, give us a chance."

"I'll move tomorrow," she said and he fell into her open arms.

Selena stared at the ceiling conscious of every breath Magnus took. He hadn't said he loved her, and his lovemaking had held such desperation. What did he need that she hadn't given him? Something had driven him. Surely, he no longer thought of her in relation to Prince.

"You didn't go to the doctor this past week, Selena. How long have you known?"

She wouldn't lie. "Three weeks."

"And you couldn't tell me earlier?"

She reached down for his hand and laid it on her belly. "I was scared, Magnus. You didn't want us to adopt or to be foster parents, and I…I didn't know how you'd feel."

"What about you? Do you want this baby, Selena?"

She sprang up in the bed and knelt beside him. "What kind

of question is that? I married you without knowing your real reason for proposing, and I did it because I wanted a baby."

"What did you say?"

Words poured out of her, tumbling over each other in the relief that honesty with him brought her. "I wanted a baby. I loved you, but that wasn't reason enough to marry you when I hardly knew you. If I didn't hurry and get pregnant, I might never have been able to conceive."

She didn't know what he intended to do when he sat up, and she breathed again when his arm slid around her. "Calm down, and let me have all of it. Every bit."

"After you asked me to marry you, I said I'd think about it. I wanted to, but I didn't think it was wise. Then the doctor told me I had a problem that could make it impossible for me to have children, that I'd better hurry. So, I considered that you were the only man I'd ever known whom I'd want to father my child, and I said yes, I'd marry you." She fell back on the bed, exhausted from her outpouring.

His silence roared as loudly as a howling winter storm. And she waited, her only solace the warmth of his hand holding hers.

After a long time, he spoke. "Is your health problem a serious one?"

She explained what her doctor had told her. "It may never be worse than it is now or I may not be able to have any more. We don't know. I could have five, or one. Are you mad with me?"

He squeezed her hand. "How could I be? You're giving me what I've wanted most—a family." He turned on his left side and held her to him. "I want you to postpone that trip to Houston for a while. That can come later. If anyone is trying to separate us, we both know they won't succeed, no matter what they do. We need some time alone. I can rent a comfortable house on Copano Bay near the Gulf of Mexico in an area where there are few tourists. We won't be disturbed. Or, we can take a suite in a hotel right on the Gulf. Whatever you like. Will you come with me?"

"I still have to find a broker to relieve me, and when he or she goes on vacation, I have to return the favor."

"But will you do that?" he persisted. "Will you take two weeks and come with me?"

She told him she would, that he couldn't want their marriage normalized any more than she did. "Copano Bay sounds good to me."

"Good. When is our baby due, Selena?"

"March sixth."

"I can hardly take it in. I've waited so long for this news that I almost can't let myself believe it. I feel as if I could straddle an ocean."

His arms cradled her with such tenderness that she felt his caring in every pore of her body. "What are we going to name him?"

She swatted him playfully. "I'll have you know, mister, that this 'him' will be a girl."

They discussed the names of the three children they hoped to have and everything that concerned them until Selena fell asleep deciding whether Morehouse or Harvard would be best for her son. When Benjamin Mays was president of Morehouse, he'd said that if parents sent him a boy, he'd send them back a man. And the country had had a plethora of outstanding Morehouse men, including Martin Luther King, Jr., to prove his argument. She clutched her son's Morehouse College degree as she drifted in dreams.

Had a freight train rolled over him? He lay beside his wife, the woman who carried his child. Numb. She'd been afraid to tell him that, in a few months, he'd be a father. Unsure of his reaction. And he had so little intimate knowledge of his wife that he hadn't recognized the changes in her. As he reflected on it, the signs of her pregnancy had been as clear as a harvest moon. Her heartburns, refusal of meals, sleepiness at all hours, the sensitiveness of her nipples to his slightest touch and her rapid-fire arousals. He'd thought that, in the past few weeks, they'd grown close, had developed a oneness unrelated to their desire. But he had to admit that they didn't know each other deep down.

He hadn't been honest with her about his reasons for asking her to marry him. She hadn't given a reason for accepting, but she'd had one that she should have shared with him. He tossed it around in his mind. When they said their vows, a wise person wouldn't have given their marriage a chance, but they loved each other, and they'd made a child; it had to work. He'd make it work. He eased out of bed, dressed and went to his office.

He opened his e-mail. Wade Malloy had news for them. He wanted permission to countersue in the case against Selena, because he couldn't shake the complainant's story, though he had proof that she'd lied in her affidavit. He put a copy on Selena's desk and opened the letter from Melissa Grant-Round-tree. She had the perfect person to manage his building project in Sierra Leone. He e-mailed back that he'd interview the man at his Houston office. He then reserved a house on Copano Bay for two weeks hence, and he had to put one more thing right. Irene and her husband had missed their plane and hadn't made it to the barbecue, so he'd ask Selena if she'd go with him to Seattle the following weekend. It was time he met Irene Perkins, who was as much mother to Selena as Tessie was to him.

Magnus knew he'd done the right thing, when Selena walked with him toward the receiving area in Seattle/Tacoma International Airport, scanned the crowd and ran toward a woman who rushed to meet her with outstretched arms.

"Reenie, this is Magnus."

The woman stood as she was, looking at him, then she smiled and opened her arms. "I didn't pray for as much," she said. "You'll do just fine, Magnus. Thank you for coming to me."

He'd never been so thoroughly scrutinized, and in only a split second. The woman was confident of her judgment. He liked what he saw. "I though it was time I put my house in order, Irene.

Getting to know you as the woman who nurtured my wife is part of that. I'm glad to meet you."

Selena hadn't prepared him for Roosevelt, Irene's husband, who got in from work a few minutes before dinnertime. "I know you Texans love the best of everything," Roe said, "so I brought you a couple 'a sides of the best smoked North Atlantic Salmon that you can find. Treat my girl right, Magnus. She's the apple of my wife's eye."

He hadn't expected to enjoy a calm, relaxed weekend, but he did. He'd forgotten the pleasure of being with people who liked him for himself and insisted on being themselves with him. Roosevelt liked beer with his smoked salmon, and if Magnus wanted wine with his, he was welcome to it. He liked his in-laws and, for the first time in his memory, he wasn't of a mind to rush back to the ranch. And why should he? He'd left it in hands that were as dependable as his own.

Tessie awakened and sat up in bed. She was alone in the house, not too happy about that, and ill at ease, thanks to Rhett Butler's persistent barking. Warily, she dressed, took the dog and dashed over to Jackson's house just as he stepped out on his porch.

"I was on my way over to you," Jackson told her.

She wouldn't dare tell him how much better she felt now that he was with her. "Jackson, why do you think he's so upset?"

"He's a good watchdog, and somebody's out here somewhere who doesn't belong here. You go back in the house."

He couldn't be serious. "You're not going out there alone and get yourself killed, Jackson, so you might as well not argue. I'm going with you." She needn't have worried. Given his head, Rhett Butler snagged the culprit and wouldn't release him until Jackson and Tessie reached the would-be thief. With the aid of a Colt forty-five, Jackson detained the man until the sheriff arrived. They watched the two men leave, and Jackson smiled at Tessie and walked over near where she leaned against the kitchen wall.

"That little dog's worth something."

"Sure is," she gulped, and eased away from Jackson.

He reached toward her. "Yeah. The little rascal's smart. Haughty, too, like he walks on four legs just for the hell of it."

His masculine heat swirled around her, scattering her senses. "Don't you come sidling up to me. I'm so mad I could spit. You was going out there by yourself, not knowing how many men was out there. You coulda gotten yourself killed. Mister big man who ain't scared of nothing. You coulda been dead. Not that I'd care."

"I don't believe you, woman. Come here to me."

"I'm not moving out of my tracks," she told him, all the while praying that he'd ignore what she said.

His smile, gentle but filled with promise, addled her, and she didn't know whether she walked or ran, only that he had her in his arms, loving her. Frissons of heat shot through her like wildfire, when his tongue drove into her eager mouth, seeking, conquering, laying a claim.

"Kiss me back, honey," she heard him say. "I love you, Tessie. You hear me? I love you, and I need you. Take me. Baby, take me and love me." Her jellied legs wobbled, and he lifted her. "Do you want me, sweetheart? Tell me. *Tell me.*"

Hot arrows of desire ricocheted through her body and settled in her feminine core. "Jackson, honey, I... Oh, Lord, I think I'll die if you don't make love to me."

He closed her room door and turned the lock. "Are you sure, Tessie, because there'll be no turning back. I love you, and I'm not looking further for any other woman. Do you love me?"

She had to force herself not to give him a clever answer. "Yes. I love you." When he'd undressed her and laid her in her bed, she was glad she'd told him. "I've loved you a long time, Jackson. A long time." He didn't answer, and she held out her arms in welcome as his full masculine energy pulsated before her.

"You won't be sorry?" he asked, giving her a last chance to back out.

"I just want you to get started, Jackson," she moaned, crossing and uncrossing her legs. She looked up into his face as he knelt above her, his flesh on her flesh, and the rekindled fire of desire blazed within her. The answering expression in his eyes sent her heart into a gallop, and she raised her body to meet him.

"Oh, God," she screamed, as he made them one and minutes later rode her into ecstasy.

Tessie snuggled as close to Jackson as she could get. His arm held her tightly, and she thought he trembled. She kissed the wet, salty flesh of his biceps, and trailed her lips down to his fingertips. Besotted. In her fifty-five years, she'd never had what he'd given her, never once been so completely lost in a man that she hadn't belonged to herself. And she'd never loved. If he didn't feel for her what she felt for him, she didn't think she could stand it. Her fingers roamed over him, idly caressing his belly, stroking his chest.

"Put you mind at ease, Tessie. I'm not going anywhere, and neither are you. I waited a long time for you, honey. It's been years since my wife died and long before that, I must have been looking for you."

She sat up and gazed down at him, even bigger lying there beside her than he usually seemed. "I don't want no mind reader 'round me, Jackson. This occult, or whatever you call it, business gives me the willies."

She could curl up and sleep in nothing but his laughter. So warm and comforting. And he laughed out loud. "So I was right. After what just happened to us, you were lying right here beside me making up your mind to be miserable. Now, Tessie, when we get married, you're going to trust me. You're stuck with me for as long as both of us are breathing. So you—"

"*We're getting married?* Is that what you said?" Was that hoarse, high-pitched whisper coming out of her mouth?

"If you'll have me."

She collapsed on him. "Lord, have mercy. If I'll…" She sat

up abruptly. "You'll have to behave yourself, Jackson. You hear?"

His body shook as laughter rumbled out of him. "Baby, you are without an equal. I wouldn't take anything for you. Not anything on this earth. You love me?"

She couldn't hold back the grin, though she didn't want him to know how eager she was. Giggles wormed their way out of her and she whispered, "I sure do, Jackson. You just wait 'til you see how much."

"When?"

"Soon as I get me my finery."

He rolled her over and gave her a taste of her future with him.

Chapter 14

Nobody was going to sneak into his computer system, destroy his records and get away with it. Magnus checked the personnel records of every one of his Houston employees. None had the training or experience that would enable him or her to reconfigure his computer system even after he'd installed safeguards.

He phoned Madeline. "I want that mainframe computer locked at all times, and only you are to have the key. If anyone requests it, stay with them until they give it back to you. Someone is tampering with this system, and I'll put an end to it if I have to fire every person in the Cooper Building."

Her loud gasp might have reflected her fear of losing her job, but he wasn't sure. Startled was more like it. Someone knew how to get her keys.

He wondered why her normally docile manner annoyed him. "Yes, sir. You know we'll do everything possible to prevent any problems for you. We'll stay on it, sir."

"See that you do, Madeline. I'm depending on you. Jeb's been in Sierra Leone and, when he's away, it's your responsibility to maintain our safeguards and keep that place running smoothly."

"Thank you for your confidence, sir. If there's nothing else, sir…"

Magnus hung up, leaned back in his chair and put his feet on his desk. He remembered that Prince had gotten a company car, driven it around Houston, and maybe other places, and that neither Madeline nor anyone else at that office knew how he'd gotten the keys or the car. Sweat beaded on his forehead and shivers crawled all over him. It couldn't be. His brother could assemble a desktop computer and was an expert programmer. And he was the only person around Waverly or Houston who was both capable of maneuvering his way into that building and sufficiently savvy with computers to do that kind of damage. He'd majored in computer science before dropping out of college at the end of his third year.

He called Horner, the Cooper Building receptionist, and told him, "Phone me at once if my brother enters that building, and check the camera every morning. If it records a picture of him, let me know at once."

He had his consultant change the system, called Jeb, and told him why. "What does your brother look like, Magnus?"

"Pretty much like me, though he has darker eyes and is about an inch shorter."

"Okay, I'll keep an eye out for him."

That ought to do it, he decided, walked in the kitchen and told Tessie, "I have to go into town to the sheriff's office. I don't know what to do about that poor Joe whom you and Jackson caught trying to steal my cows. I've left a note on Selena's desk, telling her where I'll be."

"You can make restitution by mending my fence," Magnus told the man after refusing to press charges, "but if it happens again, I'll see you in jail." He left the sheriff's office and took the Town Car for a quick tune-up in preparation for their trip.

* * *

"I thought we'd fly," Selena told her husband when he packed their things in the trunk of his Town Car. "That's a long drive."

"You'd rather fly? All right with me—what mama wants, mama gets." How could a man's smile make her feel as though he'd wrapped her in a warm blanket? He propped his foot against the garage doorstop and used his cellular phone to call the airport.

"We can get a one-ten flight to Arkansas and rent a car at the airport. We'll be there around four-thirty. That better?" he asked Selena.

"You'd change all your plans just like that?" She snapped her fingers.

"Why not? Selena, we're going on our honeymoon. It's my pleasure to please my bride." He grinned and knocked his Stetson back with his thumb and forefinger. "Boy, that sounds strange. We really didn't do this right, you know?" He shook his head, as though bemused. "Selena, we've got to fix this thing. No more half-marriage."

"That was never my plan," she informed him. "I wanted the whole nine yards from the start."

Their situation did indeed perplex him, she saw, as he shook his head slowly, grinned up at the boiling sun and remarked, "You know, in all my years as a rancher, I have never seen a horse back into a stable nor a cow go tail-first into a barn the way we backed into this marriage. Until a week ago, when you moved into my room, I wouldn't have believed what you slept in. Those rose-colored things don't cover any part of you but your naval. And who ever heard of anybody laughing out loud in their sleep. First time you did that, I started to call the doctor. Nearly scared the hair off of my head."

Selena looked at Magnus with new insight. Her husband was happy and knew it, but he was also aware that a vital ingredient was lacking in their relationship. He didn't know what it was, but he intended to find out.

"It hasn't surprised me that you take ninety percent of our

king-size bed," she shot back, "That you kick off the covers leaving your bedmate to freeze in that air-conditioned room and, heaven forbid, that you snore—'scuse me, you call the cows while sleeping, but to wake up singing? I couldn't believe it."

He moved closer. "If we were normal people, sweetheart, we'd have this discussion inside away from this heat."

She sat with him at the kitchen table drinking orange juice and eating pecans. If Anna Cooper understood what she'd done to her sons, would she beg their forgiveness? Magnus and Prince were as different as men could be, but each carried wounds inflicted by their mother. One exacted revenge by refusing to grow up and by sucking life from everyone foolish enough to allow it. The other folded himself up, healed those who came to him needing it, and refused to let anyone heal him.

"You're so beautiful, Selena. Are you happy?"

"I'm happy, Magnus."

"Because you're pregnant? Is that the reason?"

She reached for his hand. "You're not to think about that anymore. I'm happy because I'm carrying your baby, yes. But if I didn't have you, Magnus, I wouldn't feel this joy."

He inclined his head, as though stripping each word of its meaning. Thoughtful. "When we get back there, all this doubt should be behind us." In two short weeks? What a miracle that would be, she mused.

Selena walked out to the pier at the end of the property they'd rented. Less than a block away, Mission River could be heard emptying itself into the Gulf of Mexico. Great blooming water lilies spread their leaves on the tiny inlet that led to the lake, and not a breath of air jostled the leaves of the tall, moss-draped trees that looked down at her. She'd expected a cabin, but great glass panels served as windows in large airy rooms, woven Aztec rugs covered the floors, and attractive, modern furniture assured their comfort.

She turned to go back into the house and bumped into him.

"How about a quick ride down to the Gulf? Takes about twenty-five minutes. I want to show you a sight that you can't see from anywhere but there. Come on."

"Like what?"

He tweaked her nose. "It can't be described, either."

Half an hour later, she stood with him at what seemed like the edge of the world. The sun inched toward the water, seagulls circled overhead and the sky showed off the colors of the sunset. She'd never felt so close to him as she did then. Even if he couldn't say he loved her or, if he didn't, she wanted a life with him.

"What is it, love?" He whispered it, as though to preserve the silence around them. "Why are you crying, Selena?" His arm tightened around her. "Talk to me." His big hand stroked her back, and she snuggled against him.

"I don't know. I guess it's so heavenly that I couldn't bear it. Seeing all this with you, I realized what's important to me."

"And?"

"You. Not the way I want you to be or think you ought to be, but like you are. You're here for me when I need you. That's what's important. I didn't understand that before, but now I do."

"You want something from me that you don't get?"

She had to look at him then, to know what his question meant to him. "I imagine I do, but I know that you and I want the same for us. Everything else will fall in place." She smiled, turned and watched the sun disappear. She'd realized that, but she had also understood at last, that what was missing between them was complete trust. When he felt that, he'd withhold nothing from her.

She loved their idyllic days, walking the beach on the Gulf of Mexico—where she collected Lightning Whelk seashells—boating or swimming in the lake. Learning about each other. Mornings, she sometimes awakened alone to find a bunch of bluebonnets beside her pillow or a vase of late spring prairie verbena on the night table beside her. But he would soon rejoin her. And at night, music filled the house. They read poems to each other, told stories of their childhood, their comings of age and the events that had shaped them as adults. They sated themselves with loving. Magnus cooked breakfast each morning, took her to lunch at a nearby café and had their dinner sent from the caterer who plied his wares to the local tenants.

"I hate to leave," she told him the evening before their scheduled departure. "These days have been so wonderful. I wish it could be this way forever."

"What about the nights?"

She knew she blushed. "Nights? What nights? I'm serious, Magnus."

He shrugged. "I am, too. This can last, Selena, provided we don't let other people get in the way." He walked over and scrutinized her as she bent to fold her clothing. "You aren't getting any bigger. Shouldn't you be… Well, your belly's hard, but that's all. How come?"

"I'm just two months. In a few more, I probably won't be able to tie my shoes."

"I'll tie them for you."

She turned into him, wrapped her arms around him and hugged him. His stroking fingers sent the fires of passion roaring through her. After the way he'd rocketed her to ecstasy, embroiling her in wave after wave of mind-blowing passion only hours earlier, how could she want him so badly, so soon?

"Th…thanks, but right now, I…" She wouldn't tell him. She was doggoned if she would. She moved her breast against him, rubbing from side to side, aggravating her desire with the friction.

Drat him; he stepped back from her. "Whoa. What's this, sweetheart? Can't you tell me you want me? I'd have thought that, if we had accomplished nothing else the past two weeks, we'd learned to communicate our need for each other. Tell me straight out. Do you want me, Selena?" She nodded. "Words, baby. I need to hear them just like you do."

Before she could speak, his mouth found hers, and he treated her already sensitive left breast to the rhythmic teasing of his fingers. She squirmed and opened her mouth wider for more of his tongue, but he didn't accommodate her. Spirals of unbearable tension whipped through her, and her hips moved against him.

"Magnus."

"Yes, honey, what is it?"

"Please, I…"

"Please, what?"

Her knees buckled when his talented fingers found her feminine core, began their wicked dance and sent a gush of love liquid streaming from her.

"Love me," she moaned. "Oh, Magnus, take me to bed." He lifted her into his arms and took her to the place where the world was theirs alone. If he hadn't joined them at once, she would have done it herself. Oh, the sweet torture of it; the hell of it; the heaven of it. She thought she would die. His groan of passion echoed through the room, and then she burst open and flew with him to the stars.

"You all right?" he asked her some minutes later.

"If I had whiskers, I'd be purring."

"Purr anyway. A guy likes to know his woman is sated." A laugh laced his speech. "If you aren't, though, I'm in trouble. Sweetheart, you burn up my energy the way my Town Car drinks gasoline."

She snuggled closer to him, questioning whether she'd been sane those weeks when she could have slept with him and didn't. "If you don't go light on the accelerator," she teased, "you have to expect heavy energy consumption." *Light on the accelerator.* She sucked her teeth. "Honey, you don't even know what that means."

He swatted her playfully on her bottom. "Am I getting a complaint?"

She kissed his neck. "If you thought you were, you wouldn't ask, so stop fishing for compliments."

"I believe in stopping trouble before it starts. A train won't run on a torn-up track."

She climbed on top of him, and closed his mouth with the palm of her right hand. "Shh. If every guy in this country kept his track as orderly as yours, this place would be a field day for women."

He wrapped both arms around her, and a grin spread over his face. "Just checking, babe." Heaven. Pure heaven. If they could find out who was trying to terrorize her, she'd get their marriage in order. She'd start with that Houston office first thing Monday morning.

"Those little anonymous gifts didn't come from anyone working at the ranch," Selena told Jackson, as they walked through the lobby of the Cooper Building.

"What about some of those old biddies in Waverly? You don't think any of them could be behind it?"

She pressed the elevator button. "Not a chance. Too sophisticated and too symbolic. My bet is here."

"Hello, Madeline," Selena said. "You know Mr. Griffith, I presume."

"I can't say that I do, though I've heard Mr. Cooper speak of him." She stood. "How can I help you?"

"My husband thinks I ought to learn how this office operates." Did she imagine that Madeline winced? "We're going to look around, see what everyone here does and how it's done."

Madeline's pursed lips gave her a steely demeanor. What a battle-ax, Selena thought. "We're very busy, especially at this time of the month but, of course, we'll help however we can."

Selena had to laugh. *I wish you wouldn't bother me,* floated, unspoken, between them. "We wouldn't want to interrupt your work," she told Madeline. She lifted the phone and asked the operator for Jeb. Knowing that she'd deprived the woman of an opportunity to claim martyrdom gave her a feeling of triumph.

"Jeb, this is Selena. I'm here in Magnus's office with Jackson

Griffith, our ranch manager. We want to meet the staff. All of them." His jovial reply was what she had expected.

"Great. Be right there."

She smiled at Madeline. "See you later on." But Madeline's barely contained hostility as the three left Magnus's office did not escape Selena. The woman did not like her.

Later that day, her mission accomplished, Selena sat with Jackson on their flight back to San Antonio, making notes. Workers absent from their station had informed her that they had Madeline's permission to take short breaks at regular intervals. Some had her consent to work from noon to eight, while others extolled the company's policy of awarding leave in exchange for such services as running errands outside the building. When she'd asked Jeb about the strange system of rewards, he knew nothing of it.

After dinner at home with Magnus, Tessie and Jackson, she followed Magnus into the den and told him what she'd found.

"That doesn't make sense. Why would she do that? If you caught them fooling around on the job, you wouldn't expect them to admit it, would you? Madeline may be many things, but nobody can tell me she's disloyal. What would she gain by passing out favors to my employees in violation of company policy?"

She bristled with anger, but she marshaled all her willpower to avoid showing it, because she had an ace to play. "Then, what do you think of this?" she asked, handing him a roll of red-and-gray checkered corrugated paper, the same paper in which each of her little gifts of terror had been wrapped.

He lunged forward. "Where'd you get that? Let me see it."

She handed it to him, but the moment held none of the sweet triumph she'd felt when she first saw it. "I took it from Madeline Price's desk."

Her heart ached for him as he gazed at the evidence, shaking his head mutely, not wanting to believe it.

"Madeline's desk?"

"Yes. And Jackson will verify it. By now, she's probably missed it, but she doesn't know that I took it."

Magnus rubbed the back of his neck, walked from one end of the den to the other. He shook his head in wonder. He would never have associated the recent problems in his once well-ordered business with his trusted secretary. But it all came together, proof of disloyalty that had been staring him in the face: Madeline's apparent loss of control over the day-to-day workings of the office, and her feeble excuses about computer malfunctioning; the occasions of late that he'd seen hostility in her, when she'd dropped her guard; her behavior when he'd asked her to open charge accounts for Selena; the damage to the computer system that couldn't have been carried out without the use of her keys; Selena's charges that Madeline had shown her hostility.

It was clear to him now that Madeline had made her brazen advance to him because she knew Selena had told him about her attitude and reasoned that if he had believed her, he would have reprimanded her.

"Why would she do it?" he asked at last. "She has always been loyal, efficient, even self-sacrificing."

"Yes," Selena said, "but that was before you married me. Madeline wanted you for herself and, as long as she knew you weren't seriously involved with a woman and she had no competition, she was content to feast on your praise and admiration of her work."

"But I haven't given her reason to believe—"

"You didn't have to," Selena said. "What will you do?"

"I have to find out what else is going on. Then, I'll act. I don't plan to show my hand 'til I have the right cards." He shook his head in dismay. "This doesn't make sense. Madeline has a very high salary, and she can't duplicate it, unless I give her a reference."

Magnus propped his foot on the rung of a chair. "At least everything is clear between us."

Her silence slowed down his heartbeat. Puzzled, he closed the short distance between them. "Everything *is* straight with us...right? I just couldn't believe Madeline would be rude to my wife, but she's a better actress than I'd have thought. Just shows I don't know everything. Why're you so quiet?" He tugged her gently to him, primed for her affection and loving, but she didn't touch him.

He released her and stepped back. "What is this?"

"Now, you believe me. Twice I told you how she behaved toward me, but your faith in her was so great that you didn't even give serious thought to the charge. You practically dismissed it with a wave of your hand. Now that I've given you proof of her meanness, you are able to believe me. No thanks." She backed away. "Can you imagine my humiliation when your response to my complaint was that you trusted her implicitly? Marriages are built on faith, Magnus. Good night."

He stared in stunned realization that the mileage they'd gained from their idyllic two weeks had just been wiped out.

Selena trudged up the stairs that seemed higher than ever. She entered the suite and dropped into the nearest chair. Why, she wondered, did a man capable of such deep feeling shy away from trust? He'd had an impersonal faith in his secretary, because she didn't touch him emotionally. But if he trusted his wife, he'd have no control over his heart. Well, he had to learn, and she would teach him. She shook her fist. Anna Cooper had a lot for which to atone.

The sound of a bucket or some other metal hitting a tree sent her running to the window. Clouds had eclipsed the moon, a young sapling snapped, larger trees swayed and debris swirled in the wind. The garage door banged open, and rain pelted the window with such force she thought the panes would crack. She heard Rhett Butler's ominous howl and knew that she was experiencing a wild Texas storm. She raced down the stairs to bring the dog inside, stumbled as she reached the bottom and fell face forward.

* * *

"What on…" Voices faded in the distance as she drifted back to the world of strong arms, rough white sheets and the smell of alcohol and disinfectant.

"What happened?" she asked Magnus, who perched beside her hospital bed holding her hand.

"You fell."

"Did I… Have I still got…?"

He squeezed her hand and smiled. "You still have our baby, and there's no danger to it. I thought those benign tumors might cause a problem, but the doctor said you're fine. I want a family, but not at your expense."

She sat up. "Magnus, right now, the tumors aren't our problem, and they may never be."

"What is?"

She took a deep breath and let it out. *"Maybe we both are."* He let it pass.

"Where're you sleeping?" he asked her when they got home near daybreak the next morning.

"With you, because I promised to try to make our marriage what we both know it can be, but I want more from you, Magnus. I want much more than you seem willing to give."

She'd hinted at it before. He rubbed the back of his neck. "If I only knew what you want."

He didn't know which disturbed him most, her sadness or her words. "What good will it do if I tell you? When it comes from you, deep down, spontaneously, we'll both know it."

Ice balls rioted in his belly when she went into the bathroom, changed into a long gown and crawled into bed. He hadn't known that she owned anything like it. She'd sleep in his bed, the gown said, but not with him.

He walked around to her side of the bed, brushed a kiss on her lips and walked outside. When he'd seen her lying at the bottom of the stairs with her eyes closed, icy-cold thorns had pricked his heart. He knew now what it meant to be scared, to come face-to-face with the end of his dreams. He let his gaze roam over his vast holdings, virtually untouched by the storm that could have indirectly cost her life and that of their unborn child. All that he saw would have been as nothing if her fall had resulted in tragedy. He gave silent thanks and went back into the house.

The next morning, he called Madeline and asked her how successful she'd been in guarding the keys to the mainframe computer, though his reason for calling had been to know whether she knew he suspected her.

"I hope you've been keeping a record of the requests?"

"Yes, sir, and I've also stayed right there and watched them sign off and lock up, though I don't understand what they type in there."

He assured her that nothing more was required of her. "I'll be over there in a few days. Meanwhile, place that order for tubing, and tell Jeb to ring me."

"Yes, sir. We're looking forward to seeing you."

"I'll bet you are," he said aloud, after hanging up.

Madeline slammed down the phone and called Prince. She had already placed the order for the tubing. She wished to heaven she'd never seen him. How had he gotten to that computer? She sat upright, perspiration pouring down her face. She'd heard that computer hackers could tamper with a machine although they were a thousand miles away from it. And Prince knew their codes.

"What've you been up to now?"

"What kind of way is that to talk to your man, honey? Maybe I ought to come over there, put you in the sack and straighten you out."

She rolled her eyes. If he got her in the sack, he wouldn't know what to do with her. "I'm in the office, Prince. And you'd better be careful. Magnus knows somebody is tampering with the system, and he said he'd catch the culprit if he had to fire everybody who works here."

"Don't try to lay it on me. I gave you your keys. Check elsewhere, baby."

Madeline sucked her teeth. "By now, I don't believe a word you say. You were going to break them up, but she's still Mrs. Sutton-Cooper."

"You expect me to make it easy for you to move over to him? That's a laugh."

For a little, she could hate him. "Don't forget that you've committed some crimes in this, Prince."

"It's me and you, baby. You're in this deep right along with me, and you can trust me on this one. When I finish, the great Magnus Cooper will be as poor as I am. Well, poorer. If I want to, I can pull in five hundred bucks a night gigging with my guitar, but he won't have a single cow left."

"You're out to break him. That's all you ever wanted. You're obsessed with Selena, but you can't have her, and you know it, so you're going to ruin him."

She could imagine the sneer on his face when he said, "No more than you're obsessed with rich boy. You want him as badly as I want Selena, but you'll never get him. Never. He doesn't know you're alive."

She slammed down the phone. Humiliated. Anguished, as wave after wave of shudders violated her body. She held her head up; no point in crying. She'd been a fool to believe him. She looked at the keys on her desk and noticed, for the first time, that her office door key didn't have the pink nail polish with which she'd marked it. *Replicas.* He'd lied about that, too.

"Vengeance will be mine," she spat out.

Happy to be back at work after her near catastrophe, Selena called Eloise.

"Hey, girl. Bert wants us to get married, but the devout

reverend who's always shouting that everybody's equal in the sight of God doesn't practice what he preaches. Said he has qualms about officiating at an interracial wedding. You know, girl, right out loud I said, 'Screw it, Rev, 'cause I don't need you in order to get married.' And he started 'now, Eloise-ing' me. Can you beat that?"

"Now you know that no one group has a monopoly on bigotry. We're just as good at it as anybody, and it didn't take us half as long to learn it."

"Tell me 'bout it, girl. Would you and Magnus go to San Antonio with us and stand up with us?"

She welcomed her friend's happy news, but tiny pangs of sorrow pricked her heart when she remembered her joy as she anticipated life with Magnus. "Of course I'll be your matron of honor, Eloise. I almost take that as my right, and I'm sure Magnus will stand with Bert. I'll speak with him."

"Thanks, girl. You're a piece of gold. Look, the baby's mother wants her child back. I don't know if we can do that."

"I'll be there tomorrow afternoon, and we'll review the whole thing. Okay?"

Eloise agreed, and Selena turned her attention to the suit that Wade Malloy had filed on her behalf. She didn't want monetary compensation; she wanted her unscathed reputation restored. She knocked on Magnus's office door.

"Come in." He had turned his chair around so that it faced the door, and his back was to his desk.

Selena took in his expressionless face and the dullness in his eyes—lackluster, where sparkling lights, so attractive to her, had once lived.

"Hi."

"Hi. I wouldn't have thought you'd be working this morning."

"I'm fine, Magnus." Such banalities; how she hated them. It was as though they didn't know each other, hadn't been swept away in each other's arms. She told him that Wade had entered the countersuit on her behalf, and that Eloise and Bert wanted them as witnesses to their marriage.

He sat forward, and the lights returned to his eyes. "Great, on both counts. Is this a formal wedding?"

"Full dress." It pleased her that he seemed to welcome his role in her friend's wedding.

He swaggered over to her, a new spring in his steps. "Mind if I...examine this little gem?"

Did he need an excuse to touch her, and did he feel as if he had to ask? What on earth was happening to them? She prayed that the chasm wouldn't widen before he came to terms with himself. Before he found in himself what she knew he searched for. She took the hand that had given her unbearable pleasure and placed it on her belly.

"It's not one bit bigger," he complained. "When do you start growing?"

This is love, she wanted to tell him. Even if you don't know it, she wanted to scream, we're deeply in love with each other.

But those were words for that time, she knew. So she said, "We're both tall, and I'll probably get so big, you'll wonder when I'll stop growing. You don't have to rush it, love, this is one contract that gets fulfilled whether you like it or not. Thought of a name yet?"

He walked back to his desk and sat down. "No. Every time I realize I'm going to be the father of my own child, I practically black out. Name? I just want our baby strong and healthy. Any name you want." He mused over it a bit. "Magnus, Jr., would be just fine."

"Don't you believe it, pal. I'm not shackling my kid with somebody else's name."

His eyes rounded, his bottom lip dropped and he stared at her as though she'd just strolled in from outer space. "Oh. You sure?"

"Do squirrels eat nuts?"

His mercurial grin made her heart flutter. "Well, I guess you're sure."

She hated to introduce an impersonal note, but she wanted his views on Wade's plan.

"I think it's a great idea," he said with genuine enthusiasm. "If the woman doesn't have proof, she'll have to retract." He locked his hands behind his head and leaned back in his chair. "Planning to go for the jugular?"

Selena shook her head. "I just want my name cleared. I don't need her money."

"Maybe not, but it would teach her a lesson. She who gouges gets gouged."

Deciding to use every opportunity to weave herself into the very fabric of his being, she moved closer, stroked his arm and was rewarded with the signals of his awareness, when his hazel eyes darkened, he spread his legs and, with his hands in his pants pockets, rocked his chair back on its hind legs, unconsciously asserting his masculinity.

"I want her apology on the second page of the *New York Times* and page one of the *Wall Street Journal.*"

He shrugged elaborately. "Something tells me she'd rather give you money than do that. When is Eloise's wedding?"

"She didn't tell me. Typical."

"Let me know. I may need to rearrange my time, but I wouldn't miss being there." He answered the phone, thrilled her with a suggestive wink and she went back to her office.

"What did you say?" Magnus bounded out of his chair, walked around the desk with the phone cradled between his neck and shoulder, rubbing his left index finger and thumb. "Are you sure you know him when you see him?"

"I know you have a brother," Jeb told Magnus. "Except for his dark eyes, this man looked like you. At first I thought it *was* you."

Magnus paced from one end of his big desk to the other. "You're telling me something's going on between Madeline and my brother?"

"You got it, man. There isn't a chance I'm wrong. A woman can't say those things to a man, unless she's intimate with him."

"What things?"

"Believe me, you don't want to know."

Magnus swore. "You're talking about Madeline Price?"

He heard Jeb's deep sigh. "I don't like ratting, Magnus, but considering the problems we've been having at the business and what she was mad about, I figured you ought to know."

Magnus loosened his collar and took a deep breath, hoping he wouldn't have grounds to prosecute Madeline. "Were they in the Cooper Building?"

"They were coming out of Captain Benny's Oyster Bar at about eleven-thirty last night."

Magnus released a sharp whistle. "That ought to be about a block from where Madeline lives."

"'Round the corner, according to company records."

"I take it they didn't see you."

"Nah. I saw them just in time."

"Thanks, Jeb. If you see him in that building, put him out."

"What about Madeline?"

"I'm not ready to deal with her. I'll give her a little more rope, and she'll hang herself and Prince, as well."

He hung up. That was the clue he'd needed, but he had no proof that Prince had tampered with his system, nor, for that matter, that Madeline was, in any way, responsible. He shook his head, bemused. If Prince was her man, why had she let *him* know in plain English that she'd go to bed with him? Wasn't one man enough? And since when had Prince begun to spend time with older women? He'd never seen his brother with a girl over twenty-two. The more he thought about it, the more per-plexing the whole thing seemed.

He walked over to the window and looked out at Tessie's garden. He never tired of feasting his eyes on the lovely flowers and beautiful vegetables. As he stood there, Jackson stepped over the low fence, walked up to Tessie and pulled her into his arms. She moved to him with lips parted and arms open, joy itself adorning her face. He and Selena should be like that—sure of each other. He went back to his desk and made plans to go to Houston the next day. This time, he wouldn't alert anybody, not even Jeb.

Chapter 15

Selena waved at Cora Moore, the local gossip queen, as she strode purposefully up the Center's steps. As it usually did on Saturdays, the Center hummed with activity. In the projection room, *Star Wars* held a group of teenagers spellbound. Across the hall, several boys and girls loudly expressed their disgust that a few influential people wanted them trained in broken English.

"I'm going to Morehouse College," one boy said, "and if you gotta wear a jacket and tie just to register in those hallowed halls, you can bet your sweet butt you'd better speak English."

"I hear you," another chimed in. "Suppose they'd trained Thurgood Marshall to speak that stuff. President Johnson wouldn't even have considered putting him on the Supreme Court."

"Yeah, man. What the hell is ebonics, anyway? It's not written, so how can you be educated in it?" another asked.

A girl's cynical laughter rang out. "It's a form of sabotage," she quipped. "Since too many of us are making a liar out of the evening news, somebody wants to teach us how to be uneducated losers. My daddy said we're not going on any more vacations, because he has to use the money to send us kids to private schools. It's the pits."

Selena walked on to her office, her steps lighter. No one need worry about that group, but she was less certain of the future of the boy who leaned against her door, waiting for her.

"Hi'ya doing, Miss Selena? Miss Eloise told me to come see you. I need a place to stay." She opened the door, gave him a seat and got busy. Another child slipping between the cracks. She completed his referral, wished him good luck and went over to see Eloise, whose door was always open when she was alone.

Selena walked in. "You'd better give me a good reason for lousing up my Saturday."

"Hey, girl. Wait'll you hear this. The illustrious Mr. Lightner has ordered me in the name of the board to sign these adoption papers. I'm doing no such thing. Where's Magnus? Maybe he can knock some sense into that old goat."

Selena had to laugh. Eloise didn't need advice; she needed approval. "Lock them up in your drawer, and wait 'til the board meets. You and Magnus shouldn't have a problem trashing Lightner's plan. When are you getting married?"

Eloise seemed to hold her breath. "Is Magnus coming? Bert is so anxious about that. Oh, Selena, I love him so much. If anything happens to—"

Selena hugged her. "Magnus will be there, and stop worrying, because nothing will happen. I'm going over to the inn to get some lunch. Want to come along?"

Eloise shook her head. "Thanks, but I've got to finish this before Bert gets here. We're going shopping in San Antonio for our rings. Just think," she marveled, "dumpy little me is going to be Mrs. Bertil Swensen. How do you like them apples, baby?"

Selena grinned. "You go, girl."

Less than three yards from their table, Selena saw them: Anna Cooper and Mavis Root. She had no choice but to walk over and speak, because Anna had seen her and was dabbing at the corners of her mouth with her napkin. Waiting.

"Hello, Mrs. Cooper," Selena said and managed a cheerful smile.

Anna Cooper replaced her napkin in her lap and looked Selena up and down as though deciding whether the woman before her was worth a reply. "Good afternoon, Selena. I don't suppose you've had the privilege of meeting Mavis Root."

Selena hadn't realized that the two were friends, and the knowledge did not endear Anna Cooper to her. "Miss Root and I have met, Mrs. Cooper," she said, her tone frosty. What did her mother-in-law hope to gain by a friendship with her married son's ex-girl, one who denied the validity of his marriage?

"Enjoy your lunch," Selena told them, in an attempt to be civil, and walked on. She couldn't help being grateful that the table reserved for her nestled beside a huge plant on the other side of the dining room. She finished her lunch as quickly as she could, paid and walked outside but, to her chagrin, the two women stood on the sidewalk facing the restaurant door.

"I hope you've given up working at that foolish Center with those people, Selena. Someone has to deal with those types, but it needn't be you."

Before Selena could reply, Mavis needled, "That's a job for Miss Goody Two-shoes, and you don't seem the type. Miss Priss is more your style."

"I beg your pardon," Selena said. "I can't see that what I do is any of your affair. Now, if you'll ex…" Her jaw dropped and she stared at Mavis. "Say that again. What did you call me?"

"This is ridiculous," Anna said, obviously uneasy with the conversation.

Selena stepped closer to Mavis and summoned all her power of self-control. "You said, 'Miss Priss,' and that's what you called me in those poison pen letters you wrote me."

She had the pleasure of watching the woman blanch. "You're crazy. I have no idea what you're talking about."

"Oh, but you do," Selena said, allowing a cold smile to surface. "You sent me those nasty letters, and you made a play for my husband right in my face, though that didn't bother me, since he made it clear that you're a nuisance."

Mavis pursed her lips. "You're talking nonsense, and you'd better stop it before I—"

Selena smiled. "Before you what?"

"What are you two talking about?" Anna wanted to know. "What's this about poison pen letters?"

Selena took pleasure in describing the letters to her mother-in-law. "Not very ladylike, huh?"

Anna Cooper turned to Mavis, her face stricken with disbelief and impatience. "This isn't true."

Selena knew her smile was evil, but the scene gave her soul wings. She didn't care. "It's true, ask Magnus. He has the letters and the fingerprints from them." Never mind that he hadn't identified the owner of the fingerprints; Mavis's suddenly sallow complexion was all the further proof Selena needed.

Anna Cooper glared at Mavis, her nose tilted upward. "Shame on you, Mavis. I would have thought that anything so common as writing nasty anonymous letters was beneath you." She frowned and turned away. "That's so tacky."

Selena watched her impervious mother-in-law pull on her white crocheted gloves and pat her broad-brimmed hat. "How could you do such a low-class and unladylike thing? I don't know when I've had anything get by me like this." She sighed. "And to think I wanted you to marry my son." She avoided looking at Mavis and let her gaze linger on Selena's face.

"Good day, Selena," Anna said and walked away, her head high and shoulders straight. Selena could see the woman was shaken by the knowledge that she'd bet on the wrong horse. She'd have less trouble with Anna now. Selena smiled at Mavis, not bothering to hide the feeling of triumph that she knew her eyes mirrored, and left the woman standing there. Defeated.

Back at the Center, she reached for the phone to call

Magnus, but remembered that he'd gone to Houston for the
day. No point in calling him there. First Madeline and now,
Mavis Root. She'd thought the little boxes of horror were
from Anna and the letters from Lightner. She tried to imagine
her husband's reaction to the news.

Magnus, too, had a puzzling bit of chicanery on his hands.
Whoever had tampered with the system had done a clean job,
or hadn't done it from within the building. If one of his employees was the culprit, he or she had kept that precious computer
expertise a secret. He couldn't find any evidence of complicity
on Madeline's part. As for her involvement with Prince, she
wouldn't be the first woman to fall for him and get caught in
his net. He'd bet Prince had begun plying his mischief as soon
as he'd planted himself in Madeline's way. The answer was
there somewhere, but he had to be certain of his ground.

He wasn't ready to confront Madeline about her attempts to
terrorize his wife. He intended to fire her, but not until he found
the culprit who tampered with his record-keeping system,
because she had the clues. Chances were good that she either
bore responsibility for it or was a party to it. She was part of the
solution and, until he got that, she'd stay, but not a second
longer.

Selena had changed from her office attire into a short red caftan
and sat in the den sipping iced mint tea and waiting for Magnus
to get back from Houston. She liked to wear red when sitting in
that huge room, because it contrasted so sharply with the soft tan
of the decor. She answered the phone reluctantly, hoping that it
wasn't Magnus prolonging the time before she'd see him.

"Cooper Ranch," she heard herself say. "Good evening. Hi,
Russ. What's up?" she asked the boy after he identified himself.

"Nothing good, Selena. I hate to spring this on you, since this
parasite is your brother-in-law, but I have to do my thing. I'm
turning him in, Selena, just like I told you I would. The other

time, he had an excuse—he hadn't asked the girl her age. Even if she lied, he oughta not play it so close to the line. She's seventeen. He'll be arrested, Selena, and he'd better pray he ain't done nothing but look at her."

She let out a deep breath. It would pain Magnus but he'd keep his word and let Prince go to jail. "I'd be the last to suggest that you not honor your responsibility, Russ. Do what you have to do."

"Yeah, but won't that get you in trouble with uh...Mr. Cooper?"

She laughed. Russ would never see Magnus as anything but a thorn in his side. "I doubt it. Magnus doesn't approve of Prince's friendships with young girls."

"Humph. Friendship? He'd better hope that's all it is."

"Thanks, Russ. I'll ask Magnus to call you."

"Chickens coming home to roost," Magnus said, when she told him.

"And what does that tell me?" she asked.

"Eventually your sins catch up with you, and you have to pay for your mistakes. He may not be guilty this time, but he's been to blame so often, that he won't have anybody's sympathy."

She leaned back in the big wing chair, crossed her legs, got comfortable and prepared herself for a long argument. "Are you going to bail him out?"

He didn't speak for a long time, but walked from one end of the room to the other. Finally, he stopped in front of her. "If I do, how many other girls will there be? He has to learn to be responsible, and he won't if I don't help him." Her eyebrows shot up, and she leaned forward, anticipating the worst.

"He's my brother, Selena. In spite of everything he's done, I can't forget that we came from the same womb, had the same father. He won't believe I care about him, and neither will my mother. But for his own good, I'm cutting him loose."

"They'll say you did it because of me."

He shrugged. "Tough. I know better."

"What about your mother? She'll run under him, won't she?"

He shoved his hands in his pants pockets and kicked at the carpet. "If she ever sees Prince behind bars, she'll probably have a stroke." He answered the phone. "What? Not for that, I won't." He hung up, and when he looked at her, she knew he'd just crossed a bridge, and a precarious one at that.

"What is it, Magnus? What's happened?"

"That was the bailiff. Russ meant what he said. My brother is going to spend his first night in jail, unless my dear mother springs him, because I will not. He should have had better sense than to walk down the street locking arms with a teenager."

Selena pushed her mint tea aside. She'd better tell him. "Your mother just had one shock this afternoon. I hope she has the strength to withstand this one."

"What are you talking about?"

She told him about her encounter with Mavis and Anna earlier that day and her certainty that Mavis had written the anonymous letters.

His eyes hardened, and he ground his teeth. "Mother's tough. But *Mavis!* Damn. I always figured she faked her graceful manners and genteel behavior, because she'd occasionally slip up and show her real self. Turns out she's evil. That surprises me."

They both ignored the ringing telephone. "It's Malloy up there in New York," Tessie said through the intercom.

"Thanks, Tess." Magnus took the phone. "How's it going, buddy?"

"Good news and plenty of it. Dina Regine Malloy made her appearance at seven o'clock this morning. We named her for Nadine and my dad. My wife is fine, Christopher's in orbit and I, my friend, am beat. I feel as if I had that kid all by myself. And don't laugh. Your day will come."

"Yeah." He couldn't help showing his pride. What a sensation! "Sooner than you think, too."

He could almost feel Wade's pleasure at that remark. "I take it Selena's expecting. Way to go, man. Nothing like it. Let me speak to her." His shirt seemed to tighten across his chest as he watched her, face animated and eyes sparkling while she talked. Did she grow more beautiful by the hour?

"Thank, Wade. This is wonderful. All's well that ends well, and I got the best end of the stick. Love to Nadine, Christopher and Dina."

She hung up and spun around to face him. "We won, honey. We won. The woman's retracting her story, apologizing and having it inserted in every New York newspaper no farther back than page three, plus, she agreed to give money to two soup kitchens. First case of this type he ever took, and he won big. He's real proud."

"He shouldn't be surprised. Wade Malloy will succeed at whatever he does. The man is thorough and clever."

"Did Melissa Grant-Roundtree ever find a manager for your project in Sierra Leone?"

He poured two fingers of bourbon for himself, took a sip and sat opposite her on a footstool. "Yes, she did. Don't you remember my telling you about him? He got to Freetown a few days before Jeb left there to come home. So far, he's what I wanted." He looked at her leg, an endless beauty swinging from her beneath her red caftan. How could she be as contented as she seemed with things between them so uncertain? But if she had a care, it didn't show. He gazed at the rhythmic movement of that leg. Reminded him of a purring cat swinging its tail. If he didn't get out of there, he'd do something dumb.

"Feel like a stroll? It's not quite dusk."

For an answer, she stood and held out her hand. He rather regretted that; he enjoyed looking at that leg.

They got as far as the stables, and Magnus stopped. Tessie and Jackson sat against the wooden rail, arm in arm, absorbed in each other. Selena nudged Magnus in the side with her elbow, hoping he'd take a hint and leave them alone. She'd wasted her energy.

"Jackson, don't you think it's time you had a talk with me about Tessie? If she were my sister, you'd already have done that. But this woman is more like my mother, man, so..."

Selena noticed that Tessie lowered her head in embarrassment. They'd progressed further than she'd thought. "Ignore him, Jackson," Selena said.

Jackson cocked his head to one side. "Seems to me that's exactly what I was doing."

Magnus ran his hand over his hair. His mood had been jocular, but there was no doubt that he'd meant what he'd said. "I'd rather you didn't ignore me. Tessie's important to me."

Jackson glared at his boss. "If you want to know, ask her." He pointed to Tessie. "I don't answer to any man about my private affairs, Magnus. That's something I just don't do."

Magnus glared right back. "I don't mean to lean on you, Jackson, but Tessie's carried away with you, and I don't want to see—"

"Now you just wait a minute, Magnus," Tessie broke in, jumping up and putting her hands on her hips. "I ain't never been carried away with no man, and I don't want no man to get that impression."

Jackson stood and put an arm around her. "You are so carried away with me, and you stop denying it. You're nuts about me."

"Now you listen here, Jackson. Don't you get too sure of yourself, 'cause I haven't walked down that aisle with you yet."

Selena couldn't believe her ears, and it was as much as she could manage to keep her mouth closed.

The man smiled and hugged Tessie. "But you're going to, and everybody present knows that." He stepped behind her, wrapped both arms around her waist and rocked her. "So stop being difficult, and tell Magnus what's going on." He kissed her cheek, and Selena smothered a laugh. Tessie melted.

She turned and faced her future husband, but spoke to Magnus. "I went and agreed to marry him, Magnus, and it looks like he's gonna hold me to it."

Selena didn't think she needed to hold back that laugh, indeed she couldn't have. It poured out of her, and when she saw that Magnus had doubled up with merriment, she let her laughter flow.

When their hilarity had subsided, Magnus grabbed Jackson in a solid bear hug. Then he turned to Tessie. "You need to be brought under control. You're the feistiest woman I ever saw in my life." He bent and kissed her. "Jackson, you're going to have your hands full."

Jackson half laughed. "Sure am. And I'm going to enjoy every second of it."

Selena shielded her gaze, because she didn't want them to see the envy that she knew was reflected in her eyes.

Magnus took his wife's hand and started back to the house. "It's too late to walk down Running Brook. This time of year, those adders crawl up on the bank, and I'd as soon not run into one of them."

She grabbed his arm. "You mean snakes?"

He wished he hadn't mentioned that. "You're scared of them?"

She was practically walking on top of him. "Pray that I don't see one, at least not until after this child is born."

He let his gaze sweep their moon-lit world with its twinkling stars, swaying trees and blessed silence. He thought of the contentment, the serenity he'd seen in Tessie as she stood with Jackson's arms around her and mentioned it to Selena.

"She's in heaven," he said.

Selena stopped and turned to face him. "That's because he's left nothing to her imagination. She knows he loves her."

He frowned as he gazed down at her. Perplexed. "Of course she knows it. Anybody can see he loves her."

Exasperated. Annoyed. A gamut of perplexing emotions raged within her, and she didn't want to walk another step with him. Still, she sensed that he was not solely responsible for this undeveloped side of himself and that if she stayed her course, she would win. Magnus Cooper would one day recognize within himself the ultimate feeling. But he'd better hurry; her child would not be born to a half-married couple.

* * *

"I may have to spend a few days in Houston," Magnus told Selena several mornings later when she walked into his office. "Jeb called me a minute ago. Madeline was in her office at six o'clock this morning and, three hours later, her desk was clean and her office looked as if no one worked there. I have to see what's going on."

"Madeline Price still works for you, in spite of what you know?"

He gave her his reasons for keeping the woman and added, "Her days with me are numbered."

She left his office without his knowing why she'd come. Selena could be mysterious. "Yes, mother," he said, when he answered the phone. "You promised your buddy, Judge Lang, the sky and Prince doesn't have to serve time for his sins. One of these days he will, though." He listened to her reprimand and her defense of his brother. "Five years' probation for consorting with an underaged girl? That's all he got? But that's something. If he doesn't stay clean, he'll have to give up five years of his life."

He called the airport and made arrangements to take the one o'clock flight to Houston. Not even Jeb expected him. At five o'clock the next morning, he sat at his desk, but Madeline arrived at eight-thirty as usual.

He wondered at her loud gasp when he opened her door. On a hunch, he walked over to her desk, leaned over it and stared into her face. "Why did you give my brother the keys to my files?"

She nearly jumped out of her chair. "How did…" She lowered her voice. "You must be mistaken, sir. I only saw your brother that one time he came here."

"You're lying, Madeline. Clean out your desk. I don't need your keys, because every lock and every code will be changed the minute you're out of this building."

Fear, stark and wild, shimmered in her eyes. "But, sir, this is my job. I… You just can't…" Her voice tapered off, and he almost pitied her.

"I'm waiting for you to go." She dumped the contents of her drawers into a shopping bag, took her umbrella from a hook beside the door and walked out without meeting his gaze. He called an agency for a temporary secretary, hired a locksmith and told Jeb what he'd done. Then he called Melissa, asked her to get him an office manager and got the next plane home.

"And all this because I listened to you," Madeline railed at Prince. "You talk to him. I need my job."

"You're joking." He sneered. "It's not my fault that you believed me when I told you rich boy had the hots for you. You wanted him so bad, you'd have done anything to get him. I knew you went to bed with me hoping you could convince me to get rid of Selena for you. Well, he's onto you now, so you're no use to me. You should have been smarter. Next time, baby, cover your tracks."

She stood, her body trembling uncontrollably. She calmed her chattering teeth, picked up her small overnight case and walked to the door of their motel room. "As sure as the sun rises, buster, you will pay for this." He owed her plenty, and she would collect. She didn't care if she ruined what reputation she had left and never got another job; Prince Cooper would pay.

She telephoned Magnus and told him in minute detail what she had done and why. "Your brother is a charmer, and I believed what he said. I just got in deeper and deeper. He's not a nice person, and I guess you'll say I'm not, either, but he owes me and I aim to collect."

Magnus swung his chair around from his desk, spread his legs and grasped his kneecaps with his damp hands. He contemplated what Madeline had told him, and wondered at their daring and their evil minds. He called his brother.

Prince showed no remorse. "You win some, you lose some,"

he said. "But you ought to shore up your system, brother—wouldn't take much to put you out of business."

"You're not ashamed, Prince?"

Prince's laughter flowed through the wires. "Every time I'd think about you and Selena, I'd be cleansed of any guilt that might've snuck in. Not on your life, brother."

"It's just occurred to me, Prince, that you're obsessed with jealousy. Why? You've got so much that I've never had. Talent. You studied guitar less than two years, but you can hold your own with Chet Atkins, George Benson and their ilk any day. You've got stunning looks, and Mother would gladly give her life for you. Fact is, she's obsessed with you. You wind people around your fingers if you want to, but never with good intent. You could use all this to make a good life, Prince, but you're no further ahead than when you were twenty years old."

Prince sneered. "Why do you care?"

Magnus realized then that he did it to cover his shame. Good seed wasted on stony ground, Magnus mused. "Because you're my brother, and my father loved you."

"You're wasting your breath trying to lay a guilt trip on me, man. Later."

Magnus rested his hip against his desk and stared at the phone, the dial tone paining his ear.

"What are you doing, child?" Tessie asked Selena.

"Moving my red dresses out of here and back to that suite upstairs."

"But I thought you and Magnus had got things straightened out."

Selena didn't pause, but laid several dresses across her arm and started upstairs. "Death's about the only thing that can't be reversed, Tessie," she threw over her shoulder, and kept walking.

"But—"

"Sorry, Tessie. I'm in a hurry." She finished transferring her clothes from the room she'd shared with her husband back to the suite that she'd come to dislike, got in her Taurus and drove to the Center. Two full weeks after he knew Madeline was the one who'd sent her those nasty, and sometimes frightening, packages, Magnus hadn't fired the woman. She was doggoned if she'd sleep with a man who valued his faithless, conniving secretary more than her.

Her session with Freddie completed, she locked her desk and turned to leave.

"Miss Selena, Miss Eloise said you're the person for us to talk to." A man of about forty-five or fifty and a girl around nineteen stood in the door.

"Have a seat," she said, warding off an eerie sense of fore-boding. "How may I help you?"

"Well," the man began with some reluctance, "my daughter here wants her baby back, and I aim to see that she gets it. But that fellah who deserted her is going to have to pay."

Selena took their names and addresses, noting that they lived in Kerrville. "The Center doesn't service people who live outside the county."

"But my baby's here," the young woman said. After she ex-plained, Selena realized that the baby of which they spoke was the one she had wanted to adopt. Magnus had been right, she thought. She told them that the child was listed as having been abandoned, but the girl protested that she hadn't left it alone, but had sat in front of the building in a rented car until Eloise took the child in. Asked if she could identify the father, the girl hesi-tated.

"If you don't tell her, I will," the father said, his voice dripping with venom.

The girl faltered several times, before she said, "Prince Cooper."

Unprofessional though it was, Selena made no effort to stifle the gasp that exploded from her. "This is a serious charge," she managed. "Are you certain?"

The girl glanced at her father and lowered her head, embarrassed. "There's never been anyone but him, Miss Selena. Nobody."

Selena believed her. After questioning the girl further and making extensive notes, she told them, "The child is in foster care, but you'll get it back, and I'll see that Mr. Cooper honors his parental responsibility."

They left, seemingly less burdened than when she'd first seen them. She packed her briefcase, called goodbye to Eloise and drove home dreading what she must tell her husband.

"Mother wants you to call her," Magnus said, after greeting her. She observed the man who stood before her, not loose and relaxed with his usual calming demeanor, but strung tight as a bow. The sight of him—agitated and impassioned as was his wont when he wanted to get inside her— sent the blood rushing to her feminine center, and she struggled not to send him the signal of her own desire, his cue that she needed him.

"What's the matter, Magnus?"

He took a step closer to her and stopped. "Nothing of yours is in our room. Not one thing. You said we'd live together as man and wife, but first you put that blasted nightgown between us and went to sleep on your left side. Now, you've moved your clothes. And you ask *me* what's the matter?"

If he hadn't mentioned it, she'd never have known that he hurt; hiding his basic feelings had become so ingrained a habit that he did it reflexively. "That matter cannot be discussed in this foyer. Madeline Price continues to work for you weeks after you knew it was she who had terrorized me. You always said you wanted to protect me, to shield me. I didn't need that, Magnus, but I have to believe that you wouldn't knowingly sip tea, as it were, with my enemies."

"Madeline no longer works for me. Please call my mother." He turned and walked into the den.

He's in pain, she acknowledged to herself, as she forced

her fingers to dial the number. "You wanted to speak with me, Mrs. Cooper?"

Did she imagine Anna's stammer? "The… When I was last at Cooper Ranch, we had a misunderstanding." What an underestimation, Selena thought. "Well, I need to see Magnus," Anna went on, "and…I want to go out there and see my son. I hope you don't mind."

Selena wanted to laugh. The woman had never heard of the word *humility,* or, for that matter, *apology.* "Of course you may visit us, Mrs. Cooper, so long as you don't bring Prince."

"Thank you. I'll be right out."

Selena changed into an attractive short-sleeved pantsuit, let her hair down and walked slowly back down the steps. Magnus had fired Madeline Price. When, she wondered, and what had prompted it? She'd just decided to ask him when the doorbell rang.

"He's in the den, Miss Anna," she heard Tessie say.

Magnus greeted his mother with a kiss on the cheek. "This is a surprise," he told her. "Anything wrong?" He refused to respond to her pointed look at Selena, the subtle suggestion that she'd rather be alone with him. Catching the gesture, Selena rose.

"Stay where you are, Selena. There are far too many secrets in this family. What is it, Mother?"

Anna pursed her lips, "Well, if you insist. Some woman, Madeline something or other, has disgraced the Cooper name. It's all over the *Waverly Herald.* She's accusing Prince of having seduced her and then defrauded her of her life's savings. I tell you, these women are always after him and, when he ignores them, they want to cause a lot of trouble. Magnus, you have to do something. She's asking for thousands of dollars, and what's worse, she says you're a witness to her involvement with Prince."

Magnus appraised his mother. Elegant. Beautifully turned out, as usual, with her perfect salt-and-pepper coiffeur that was a pretty frame for her toasty complexion. Still a beauty. He didn't want to see her stripped of her dignity, but it was time she faced the truth; they both had to deal with it.

"If that's all she said, she only publicized half of it." He shrugged, and watched as his mother gasped and clutched her chest. He ignored it; that was her idea of hysterics. Aware that he was also informing his wife about it for the first time, he explained what he knew of Prince's involvement with Madeline, the reasons for it and their tampering with his business.

Selena's rounded eyes and quick intake of breath did not measure up to Anna's dropped jaw and startled expression.

"I refuse to believe this," Anna said, though in a noticeably subdued voice.

From what seemed like a considerable distance, he heard Selena mutter, "Wait'll she finds out she's a grandmother."

He jumped up, strode over to his wife and grabbed her shoulders. "What was that I heard?"

Selena told them both about the baby, and that she had believed the girl's story. Anna denied the possibility, stood and prepared to leave.

"Why don't we ask him if he knows the girl," Magnus said. "For once, Mother, let your thirty-two-year-old son fight his own battle. And don't forget, he's on a five-year probation for consorting with a young girl." She sat down heavily, as though defeated.

Magnus looked at the two women before him—one's worried face filled with a concern that he knew was for him, and the other stone-faced and imprisoned by her obsession with her younger son. It was time for honesty, and he meant to have it in full, right then.

He looked his mother in the eye. "Do you wonder that you are the grandmother of a child born out of wedlock?"

She sprang forward. "Not a word of it's true. Not a—"

"This isn't the time for denial, Mother. A DNA test will settle it. I don't know what kind of girl she is, but I can imagine she's suffered. You didn't give your sons a great example of what to look for in a woman, though I'm not excusing my brother. But the fact is, I have avoided women who reminded me of you." He knew his voice was laced with bitterness, but that was a part of honesty.

Anna's eyes widened. "I never thought you were cruel."

When Selena stood to leave, Magnus raised his hand. "You're my wife, and if you want to know who I am, I suggest you stay." She sat down.

He looked at Anna. "Did you think about me at all? From the day Prince was born, you were obsessed with him. You ignored me, and you ignored Daddy."

She shook her head fiercely. "You apologize this minute for that remark. I didn't ignore your father."

He paid no attention to her protest. "Every time I saw him touch you, try to caress you or kiss you, you pushed him away. You can't deny it."

His mother jumped up, stood over him and spoke in a high, trembling voice. "I was crazy about your father. You were watching with a child's eye."

He shrugged. "At eighteen, I wasn't a child."

She went back to her seat and seemed to fold, like a punctured balloon. "When I first met your father, I wondered why he wouldn't ask me out, wouldn't approach me. I was going crazy wanting him to notice me, and I finally had to approach him. He said I was so perfect, he was sure I wouldn't waste time with him, that he admired me so much. He always told me how beautiful, how flawless I was. So I never let him see me the least bit unkempt. Every day of our marriage, I got up first, dressed and put on my makeup, so I'd look pretty for him. I'd wake him up with a kiss and a cup of coffee." She seemed caught up in the memory, as though alive once more in her dream.

Unconvinced, Magnus pressed. "You expect me to believe

that? If he so much as put his hand on your hair, you'd jump away, telling him he'd mess up your perfect hairstyle. And if he tried to hug you, you swore he'd crush your perfectly pressed dress. Yeah. He was crazy about you, but it stopped there." He looked up to see Selena shift uncomfortably in the big wing chair.

"Don't you understand?" Anna urged. "I wanted to look perfect for him. I *had* to. *That's all I had to offer him.* I wasn't smart, and I didn't have a profession. I'd never, ever worked and had no idea how to hold down a job. Beautiful women are everywhere. I had to be special."

He stared at her, shoving aside the niggling feeling that he might have judged her too harshly. "To me, you were cruel and unfeeling."

She was a fighter, he realized. "Not where it counted, I wasn't. Your father was a man and then some, and I was woman enough for him. Talk what you know."

He saw the pain in her, but he couldn't turn back. The heaviness in his heart demanded freedom and, for it, she was the catalyst.

"As far back as I can remember, I was afraid to crawl up in your lap, because your precious dress would be crushed. But it didn't seem to wrinkle when Prince wanted to climb up on you." He glanced at his wife and saw the water cascading down her cheeks. But he couldn't stop. "I used to wonder how you could make such a difference between us and live with yourself. Now, I don't care."

Anna dabbed at her nostril with her lace-edged handkerchief, ever the impervious dowager. "It's something that I've come to regret. I wanted a large family. I thought that if I gave your father a lot of children, he'd always love me. But after you were born, I was told I couldn't have any more. When I learned I was pregnant with Prince, I had to decide, for health reasons, whether I should try and keep him. I took a chance, but I was sick the whole nine months, and he weighed less than four pounds at birth. It wasn't that I didn't want to pay attention to you. He needed me. By the time you were seven and he was two, you rejected me. You only wanted Jonathan and Tessie."

"I needed Tessie."

"I know that now, but I resented her then, and I resent her today."

"Forget about me, Mother. Can't you step back now and let Prince be a man? If not for his sake, then for your grandchild."

She held her hand up, palms up. "That's enough. You have no basis—"

"Selena believes the girl's story, and that's good enough for me. For years, Prince has been slow dancing with self-destruction, and we abetted it by getting him out of every scrape he got into. Let's give him a chance." He telephoned his brother.

"Can you come over here, Prince?"

"I'm not sure I could stand the sanctity of your hallowed home, brother."

Magnus clutched the phone, and told himself not to respond in kind. "Unless you want to be tried as a swindler or, failing that, as an irresponsible parent, or maybe both, get your...yourself over here. Now!"

Prince didn't deny having had an intimate relationship with the girl nor the possibility that he might have fathered her child. "I wanted her to go with me on my gigs," he explained, "but she wanted to go to college, so I split."

Magnus walked from one end of the den to the other. "What are you planning to do about this?" He held his breath and waited.

"Why is everybody staring at me like I'm some kind of ogre?" Prince asked, himself the picture of innocence. "Where's the baby?"

"Miss Ellis is his foster mother. Why do you want to know?" Selena asked him.

"If it's my kid, I want it. I'm not going to let that dumb biddy raise my kid. Wait a minute. He's a boy?" He poured his charm into a broad grin. "Well, I'll be damned. No indeed, that silly woman isn't keeping my child."

Selena gaped at him. "You mean Miss Ellis? Everybody knows her. She must have taught half the people in this town who're between ages six and twenty-five. She—"

He walked up and down the room, slapping his fist in his palms as Magnus often did. "So what? She's a stupid woman. Where's Lindsey?"

Selena couldn't believe what she was seeing and hearing. And it didn't escape her that for the first time since she'd known him, Prince failed to make a pass at her or to recognize her womanhood. "She's with her father, and I can promise you, he's mad as the devil." Selena glanced at Magnus, who gaped at Prince.

Prince shrugged. "I can handle her old man."

Anna, however, seemed unable to tolerate more. "Have you lost your mind, son? Just think what everybody will say. And you don't even know whether it's yours."

Prince whirled around. "If Lindsey says that kid is mine, it's mine. She's a decent, respectable girl." He paused as though recalling a pleasant experience. "She's real nice, and if I had known she was pregnant, I'd have married her."

"But, darling, you can't just—"

"Mother, would you let me run my life for a change? I'm damned sick and tired…" He looked at his watch. "I gotta go."

Magnus stopped him. "What about Madeline?"

"Humph. Another dumb broad. She hasn't got a leg to stand on. I never took anything from that building that she didn't give me with her own hands, including more than one set of keys."

Selena watched them and knew that they'd never be friends, because Prince was unrepentant, and Magnus would always resent being deprived of a loving brother.

"Why'd you do it?"

Prince's shoulders shot upward in a quick motion. "She wanted you, brother, badly enough to…to fool around with me in the hope that I'd take Selena away from you, and she'd have a chance. As for me... It's an old story with you and me. I've gotta be going. Give you a lift, Mother?" She shook her head. He flashed a smile. "See you."

"Prince!" Magnus's voice rang out.

Half in the door and half out of it, Prince turned to stare at his older brother. "Yeah?"

Seeing Prince's sneer, Magnus pleaded with him. "You shouldn't take that child unless you intend to settle down, work steady and support him. Don't do it so you can boast about your manhood, Prince. Do it because you want to give him every opportunity that our father gave you."

The sneer dissolved into defensiveness. "Give me a break, will ya? I never had a reason to pull a nine to five. Besides, I can make five hundred bucks a night, every day of the year, just for showing up, and a hell of a lot more if I want to. I'll take care of my son. You look after your wife. See you."

The door closed behind him, and Magnus couldn't decide what to make of it. His brother still lacked morals, but he wanted his son enough to work at a steady job. He wished him well, though he wondered if Prince would be able to change. He walked back into the den.

Anna Cooper stood and looked straight at her elder son, pulling on her white crocheted gloves as she appraised him. "Is it too late?"

Afraid that he'd deal mercilessly with her, Selena quickly intervened. "It's never too late, Mrs. Cooper. Just give it a little time." Magnus looked at his mother and shrugged his shoulders.

She regarded her daughter-in-law. "Forgive me for misjudging you." Without waiting for a reply, she lifted her chin and walked toward the door. "I wish Prince was your equal," she said to Magnus. "I've wished it for years."

Alone with her husband, Selena hoped he'd share his feelings with her. Only a heartless person could have experienced that scene without having been altered in some way.

He ran his hand along his left cheek and to the back of his neck. "It's too much. Too much from both of them. I…" He began to pace. "I've never felt so uprooted. It's as if I've never known either of them. Oh, Prince is still callous and unprincipled, probably always will be, but he actually behaved like a man. And my mother. She didn't say she was sorry, but what she did say amounted to more of an apology than I've known her to utter." He looked at his watch. "We have a couple of hours before dinner. Want to go for a car ride?"

"A what?"

"We'll take the Town Car. I need some air. I feel empty or—"

"Let's walk down to Running Brook instead."

Suddenly, she wanted to tell him to take her into their bedroom. For the first time, she understood him, knew at last why he didn't confess love for her. He'd thought, perhaps subconsciously, that if a woman knew you loved her, she withheld herself. And he'd once thought she reminded him of his mother. It was she who, from the beginning, had orchestrated their relationship. He had let her pull the strings, so to speak, and from what she'd just seen of him, he was capable of moving to center stage and sweeping away all that he saw. If he did, she doubted he'd consider her wishes. It would be too late.

"Are you in cahoots with any of my cows?" he asked in a reference to her affinity for the banks of Running Brook.

She laughed at his attempted joviality. "Are you serious? They let me down." Suddenly alert, she realized that he meant to gloss over the unpleasantness she'd just witnessed. If they didn't talk about it, come to terms with his living, never-ceasing pain, they could forget about their marriage. She took his hand and turned toward his bedroom, but he didn't move.

"Where do you want me to go, Selena?"

No point in being subtle or indirect, she knew. "I want us to go into our room, close the door and talk to each other."

"Why? Have you found something else wrong with me?"

She squeezed his hand and forced herself to smile. "Can't you see that this is our first real chance to get rid of whatever it is that's hampering our relationship?" She had his attention. "I relived your hell with you, and I'll never get over it. I didn't know that part of you, but I do now, and because of that, I understand better the rest of you. Come with me."

He closed the door and stood with his back to it. "Before you go any further, explain to me why your red dresses aren't in my closet."

"I thought I told you…"

"You said something about Madeline still working for me, but I'm closer to forty than thirty years old, Selena, and I know your reason is more deeply rooted than that. What about—"

This was it, no more waiting for the impossible. It had to be cut-and-dried. "Let's sit down. We aren't going to work this out in a few minutes."

He didn't move, and she wondered if the tiger in him was about to spring. "What about the nights you got in that bed over there, said good-night and went to sleep, or pretended to. What about that, Selena? Does pregnancy make a woman frigid?"

Much as she longed for a resolution, she refused to be the bargaining chip. She looked him in the eye. "Quite the contrary—it's been all I could do not to climb all over you."

The first spark of arousal flickered in his hazel eyes, but she knew he could control his libido as easily as he mastered his horse. Go for it, she told herself. "I decided I wouldn't spend the rest of my life wondering whether you loved me…" His Adam's apple bobbed rapidly, his nostrils flared and she thought his eyes might have doubled their size, but she wouldn't back down now. "That's right, Magnus. Even when your passion hurls you into the stratosphere, you manage not to tell me what you feel. So I decided that when you want me badly enough, you'll put your cards on the table—right beside mine." There. She should have said it long ago, but she hadn't known what she'd learned during Magnus's exchange with his mother. She put her trembling hands behind her. And waited.

"So that's it. All these weeks of on-again, off-again, when I did everything I could to show you what you meant to me."

She grasped his hand and relished a small victory when he didn't withdraw. "But as long as you didn't say it," she dared tell him, "to your mind, you weren't vulnerable. You hadn't sworn love, so if you didn't get love, you hadn't lost anything, least of all your pride."

She softened her voice, praying that she wouldn't hurt him. "Magnus, most of your life, you've been obsessed with the fact that Anna loves Prince more than you, so you haven't let yourself see what happened here today. Because you finally told her off, you no longer care. You said you felt empty, and that you needed fresh air. If you still need it, why not walk out to Running Brook alone and take stock of things?"

He reeled beneath the punch of her candid assessment, knowing that he'd protected himself, just as she'd said. He rested his head against the back of the chair and closed his eyes. "I didn't get a kick out of her saying I'm a better man than Prince, though I used to imagine my joy at hearing those words. If he's less of a man, she molded him.

"And right now, I don't give a hang about any of that. You've hinted more than once that I don't give you what you need. I'm tired of things the way they are, Selena. What do you need?"

She stepped closer and sat on his thigh. "I want you to be free with me. Sure of me. Open up to me, Magnus." She curled into him, and her tremors reverberated through him. "I have no complaints of you as a man or a lover."

"But as a husband?"

"Oh, darling, if only you could trust me enough to let yourself fly free with me, I'd be so happy."

He could see the hurt in her. Hurt, where all he'd wanted from the minute he first saw her was happiness. "Subconsciously, I made you pay for mother's treatment of me, but I didn't realize I was doing that. I hope you'll forgive me."

She lifted her head, and he gazed into her luminous eyes. Eyes that adored him, proclaimed him without equal among men.

"You're everything to me, Selena, and you have been since the first minute I laid eyes on you." He drew in a long breath and struggled against his deeply ingrained sense of self-protection. "Never believe a man who says he wants to marry you in order to protect you."

Her jaw dropped, and she gripped his arm. "I don't follow."

"I know you don't. My carefully guarded secret, Selena, is that I fell in love with you right in front of the taxi that brought you to the Waverly Inn."

She slid off his thigh. "This is precisely the reason why I never told you what I needed. Those words mean everything to me coming from your lips, so don't say that if it isn't true."

"What words?"

She sat back down on his thigh, this time somewhat farther up, and her arms snaked around his neck. "All I want in this world is for you to love me. If I knew that…I'd…"

When the moisture from her eyes streamed down his fingers to the back of his hand, he gathered her to him. "Selena, baby. There's nothing to cry about. Please. We're going to make it all right, honey."

"I'm not crying. I never cry." She turned her face into his chest and sobbed. He carried her to the bed, laid her down and stood over her, marveling that so beautiful and talented a woman could love him. He stood there, fighting desire as sweat soaked his shirt. He ripped off the tie he'd worn since morning and loosened his shirt collar. His damp hands slid up and down the sides of his trousers, rubbing, itching for her flesh. She licked her top lip, and he knew he'd explode any second. His scalp tingled, and his eyeballs burned in their sockets. Three weeks since he'd known the sweet hell of release within her. He had to get out of there.

But as he took a last look at her, her arms opened to him, and he fell to his knees, gathered her to him and rocked her. "Sweetheart, don't let anything stand between us. I'm not a perfect man, but I'm yours and you're mine. My whole life. Everything." Her fingers stroked and comforted and soothed him. He lifted his head. "I've never loved anyone, really loved them, but you, my father and Tessie. No one else would let me love them. I wanted to love my brother, but he just won't allow it."

"What did you say to me? Did you say you love me?"

His chest tightened, and he stared deeply into her eyes. "Yes." A long breath escaped him. "From the first minute I saw you. I love you more than I love my life, and I can't understand how you didn't know it."

Selena urged him closer, hated the air that separated them. He'd said it. At least, he'd been able to take the risk. "I thought you did, and that's what kept me going, but I doubted it as often as I believed it. Thinking is one thing, but knowing is something else. Could you…could you come up here where I am?" she whispered. "Oh, Magnus, why—"

He interrupted, "Why couldn't I tell you before now?"

Suddenly, she knew herself as never before, and she told him. "It wasn't that you didn't tell me you loved me, but you shut me out by deliberately refusing to say it. I knew you loved me, but I felt that you didn't want to." His eyes shone with the love he'd confessed, glistened as though reflecting the sun.

"I missed you so, Magnus. All those nights when I lay beside you, suffering for want of your arms tight around me, holding me still for the power of your loving…"

"You're whetting my appetite."

She looked at him through lowered lashes, hoping to send him a message. "I doubt that's necessary. Your appetite stays whetted."

"Yeah," he said, tearing off his shirt, "and it's been overwhetted for almost a month."

She tugged off the slacks she'd put on for her mother-in-law. "I'm kinda starved myself."

He dropped his trousers and stepped out of them. Her eyes glazed with delight at the sight of his proud manhood, pulsating with eagerness, and she fell back on the bed and raised her arms.

"Selena. Oh, sweetheart. Love me."

She took his tongue deep into her mouth, and he twirled, fired her and possessed her. She knew her whimpers always excited him, and let herself go. His educated fingers streaked along her spine and inside her thighs until hot marbles seemed to somersault inside her and arrows aimed themselves unerringly at her feminine core. Heat coiled within her and she felt herself pumping and squeezing as though grasping for him.

"Magnus, I need you."

He lowered his head. "In a minute, honey." But his lips fastened around her nipple, and her body bucked beneath him. She spread her legs and invited him to join her, but he charted his own course. His long fingers skimmed her flesh, barely touching, and jolts of electricity whistled through her veins. Her pleas went for naught, and she cried out. "Magnus, darling, I can't stand this."

His mouth moved to her other breast, and his fingers began their wicked frolic at the seat of her passion. Her keening cry ended in his mouth and, in frustration, she found him and guided him to their pleasure. But he would go no further.

"We're together for the rest of our lives. Yes or no?"

She opened her eyes, then, and smiled. "Forever." He joined them, and carried her swiftly to a shattering climax.

He'd taken her to paradise, fully satiated, every time he'd loved her, she thought as she lay there trying to reclaim herself, but this time, the heat in her wanted more. She shifted, and realized that she, too, had been remiss, that he hadn't scaled the heights with her. She slid down, and teased his pectorals with the tip of her tongue, until he dragged her up. Then he began to move.

"You're mine, darling," she told him, "and I'm yours. Give yourself to me. I need you. All of you." Her breathing raced with her movements. You want his honesty, she told herself, give him the same. "I'm not satisfied," she said, her voice rising. "I'm still hungry, because you won't let go."

He'd never heard those words before, not from any woman. "I want you to be complete," he said, driving for it with all his power.

"Then love me," she screamed.

"I do. *I do.* Oh, I do love you. I love you." He rocked powerfully, hurtling her into ecstasy, and collapsed in her arms, his emotions shredded by his powerful release.

Minutes later, he fell to his back, pulled her gently to his side and kissed her forehead. "Don't ever doubt that I love you, sweetheart."

"I'm getting to be a crybaby," she said, wiping her eyes with the sheet. He let his feet hit the floor, grabbing his trousers as he did so.

"Magnus, where are you going?"

"Upstairs to get those confounded red dresses."

Book #2 in the Three Mrs. Fosters miniseries...

THE PERFECT MAN

National bestselling author

CARLA FREDD

Renee Foster's genius IQ intimidates most men—
but not Chris Foster, her late husband's brother.
Chris seems the perfect man for Renee, except he refuses
to settle down...and Renee won't settle for less..

"Fire and Ice is a provocative romance that snaps, crackles and
sizzles into an explosive, unforgettable reading experience."
—*Romantic Times BOOKreviews*

Coming the first week of June wherever books are sold.

KIMANI™
ROMANCE

The second title in the Stallion Brothers miniseries...

TAME A WILD STALLION

Favorite author

DEBORAH FLETCHER MELLO

Motorcycle-driving mogul Mark Stallion falls fast and hard
for gorgeous mechanic Michelle "Mitch" Coleman. But
Mitch isn't interested in a pretty, rich boy who plays with
women's hearts...despite the heat generated between them.

"Mello's intriguing story starts strong
and flows to a satisfying end."
—*Romantic Times BOOKreviews* on *Love in the Lineup*

Coming the first week of June wherever books are sold.

KIMANI™
ROMANCE

www.kimanipress.com   KPDFM0690608

Wrong DRESS, Right GUY

Award-winning author

SHIRLEY HAILSTOCK

Cinnamon Scott can't resist trying on the gorgeous wedding dress mistakenly sent to her. When MacKenzie Grier arrives to retrieve his sister's missing gown, he's floored by this angelic vision...and his own longings. With sparks like these flying, can the altar be far off?

"Shirley Hailstock again displays her tremendous storytelling ability with *My Lover, My Friend.*"
—*Romantic Times BOOKreviews*

Coming the first week of June wherever books are sold.

KIMANI™
ROMANCE

Destined
to
MEET

Acclaimed author
devon vaughn archer

When homebody Courtney Hudson busts loose for one
night, she winds up in bed with sexy Lloyd Vance, an
Alaskan cop escaping a troubled past. Then tragedy strikes
and they're caught in a twist of fate that threatens
to destroy their burgeoning love.

"[Christmas Heat] has wonderful,
well-written characters and a story that flows."
—*Romantic Times BOOKreviews*

Coming the first week of June wherever books are sold.

KIMANI™
ROMANCE

www.kimanipress.com   KPDVA0710608

NATIONAL BESTSELLING AUTHOR

ROCHELLE ALERS

invites you to meet the Whitfields of New York....

Tessa, Faith and Simone Whitfield know all about coordinating
other people's weddings, and not so much about arranging
their own love lives. But in the space of one unforgettable year,
all three will meet intriguing men who just might bring them their
very own happily ever after....

Long Time Coming

June 2008

The Sweetest Temptation

July 2008

Taken by Storm

August 2008

ARABESQUE®

www.kimanipress.com

KPALERSTRIL08

Meet the Whitfield sisters—

experts at coordinating other people's weddings,
but not so great at arranging their own love lives.

NATIONAL BESTSELLING AUTHOR

ROCHELLE ALERS

Long Time Coming

Book #1 of The Whitfield Brides trilogy

When assistant D.A. Micah Sanborn and Tessa Whitfield wind up
stranded together all night in a citywide blackout, they discover a
passion most people only fantasize about. But their romance hits a
snag when Micah is unable to say those three little words.

***Coming the first week of June
wherever books are sold.***

ARABESQUE®

www.kimanipress.com

KPRA0520608

Her dreams of love came true...twice.

ESSENCE BESTSELLING AUTHOR

DONNA
HILL

Charade

Betrayed by Miles Bennett, the first man she'd let into her heart, Tyler Ellington flees to Savannah where she falls for photographer Sterling Grey. Sterling is everything Miles is not...humorous, compassionate, honest. But when she returns to New York, Tyler is yet again swayed by Miles's apologies and passion. Now torn between two men, she must decide which love is the real thing.

"A lighthearted comedy, rich in flavor and unpredictable in story, *Divas, Inc.* proves how limitless this author's talent is."
—*Romantic Times BOOKreviews*

*Coming the first week of May
wherever books are sold.*

ARABESQUE®

www.kimanipress.com   KPDHI010508